The old woman seized Sara's wrist. Her bony grip was unexpectedly strong. "I know when people are lying, Sara. It's one of my gifts."

"You're hurting my wrist."

"You're fragile, Sara Klein. Where is Mark?"

"Please, let go of my wrist. I don't know where my husband is—"

"Think before you answer, Sara."

"What is there to think about? I don't know where he is. I don't know how many times I have to tell you."

"Think, Sara Klein. Think." The woman's sharp nails dug into Sara's flesh. Sara tried to pull herself away, but the old woman was tenacious. Sara looked onto her face, the thick layers of makeup, the determined brightness of the eyes, the scarlet slash of the mouth. You couldn't win a contest with this woman, she thought. The eyes suggested a lifetime of doing battle and emerging victorious from all kinds of conflict.

# T.C. BLACK

# THE TRADER'S WIFE

AVON BOOKS NEW YORK

This is a work of fiction. Names, characters, places, and incidents either are the product of the author's imagination or are used fictitiously. Any resemblance to actual events, locales, organizations, or persons, living or dead, is entirely coincidental and beyond the intent of either the author or the publisher.

AVON BOOKS, INC.
1350 Avenue of the Americas
New York, New York 10019

Copyright © 1998 by T. C. Black
Published by arrangement with the author
Visit our website at http://www.AvonBooks.com
Library of Congress Catalog Card Number: 97-94762
ISBN: 0-380-79444-6

First Avon Books Printing: June 1998

AVON TRADEMARK REG. U.S. PAT. OFF. AND IN OTHER COUNTRIES, MARCA REGISTRADA, HECHO EN U.S.A.

Printed in the U.S.A.

WCD  10  9  8  7  6  5  4  3  2  1

**THEY** came at first light to the house overlooking Long Island Sound. Sara, asleep in the upstairs bedroom, woke abruptly when she heard pounding on the front door. She rose, drew a robe around her, took the .22 caliber Walther from the drawer of the bedside table—*always keep the gun handy*, Mark had said more than once, *you never know when you might need it*—and stepped quietly to the window.

She saw two unfamiliar cars parked in the driveway. More hammering, upraised voices. She walked out of the bedroom, held her breath. From the top of the staircase she could see figures on the porch. Four, five, she couldn't be sure. She moved halfway down the stairs with the Walther level in her hand. *If you're going to use the gun, just point it and don't think twice.* She didn't like the feel of the weapon in her fingers, the intimacy of flesh and steel.

She heard her name being called. "Mrs. Klein?"

A moment of small relief. *Burglars don't generally call out your name*, she thought. *They don't usually come in groups at daybreak and bang on your front door either. No, they come in darkness and stealth.*

"Federal officers, Mrs. Klein. Open the door."

*Federal officers?* She stopped when she reached the foot of the staircase. Her heartbeat was irregular. "Show me some ID," she called. Her voice was hoarse and dry.

A badge was pressed against the glass pane on the door. Sara moved a few steps until she could make out the emblem. She had an impression of the man holding the badge, thick white hair seen dimly through the glass.

"What do you want?" she asked.

"Open the door, Mrs. Klein."

"Tell me what you want."

"We've got a search warrant. Either you open the door, or we come in the hard way."

"A warrant for what?"

"Just open the door, Mrs. Klein."

She thought: *This is an incoherent dream, a chaos of the mind.*

"Mrs. Klein. One last time. The door."

She hesitated, stared at the badge again, then slid the bolt. The brass chain brushed her knuckles a second. The man with the white hair, parted neatly to the right of his head, was still flashing the badge as he entered the house. "Thomas McClennan. Federal Bureau of Investigation. You won't need the gun."

The photograph on the badge matched McClennan's face. Somebody else, one of McClennan's associates, shoved a couple of sheets of paper into her hand.

"The warrant," McClennan said. He reached out and took the gun from her limp fingers.

"I'm not following this—"

"You *are* Sara Klein, right?"

She nodded.

"And you *are* married to Mark Klein?"

"Yes."

"And this is 3242 Midsummer Avenue?"

"Yes."

McClennan gazed at her, and there was something unsettlingly paternal in the look for a moment, as if he were concerned for her welfare. His associates, four men in dark suits and ties, fanned out past her.

"What are they doing?" she asked.

"Following orders, Mrs. Klein."

She turned. She watched the men entering the downstairs rooms. "What orders? I don't understand. I don't understand any of this."

McClennan said, "Read the warrant."

She stared at the papers, but the words drifted away from her, didn't make sense. Her attention was drawn to the sounds of the intruders, doors being opened, closets, somebody sneezing. "You better have a damn good explanation for this," she said.

"I think it's your husband who needs to do the explaining," McClennan said.

"My husband?"

She turned from McClennan. She watched one of the agents, a man with a large brown mole on his cheek, go inside the room Mark used as an office. He said, "Bingo. The fox's den."

"For Christ's sake, that's my husband's private office," Sara said to McClennan.

She walked quickly to the door of Mark's room. Two agents were forcibly opening locked filing cabinets. Another had switched on Mark's computer, which glowed in the poor light. The fourth was removing papers from the drawers of the desk. A lamp was suddenly turned on, illuminating the room. A stark space, walls devoid of pictures. She touched the side of her head where she felt a short flicker of pain. Deep in her stomach there was nausea more wrenching than the usual morning sickness.

She turned to McClennan and struggled to keep her voice normal. "Why in God's name are you doing this?"

"Searching for evidence," McClennan said.

"Evidence? Evidence of what?"

McClennan's blue eyes were unexpectedly kind. He didn't answer her question.

She said, "I'll call a lawyer."

"Go ahead," McClennan said.

She ran a hand over her face, surprised by the cold of her own palm. A lawyer. The name of Mark's attorney had gone from her memory. She could see his plump red face and smell the pungent aftershave that hung around him like a cloud, she remembered his dense eyebrows and the turquoise rings on his fingers, but the name had vanished. "No, I'll do better than that. I'll call Mark," she said. She heard herself rattle on, breathless sentences. "This is some kind of big-time blunder on your part. You people are always making mistakes, I keep reading about the way you barge into people's homes—"

"Call your husband," McClennan said. "If you can."

The agent behind the computer said, "I'll copy everything onto floppies, okay?"

Somebody else said, "Take the whole computer, Jack. Forget the backups."

Sara went to the desk. She pushed her way past the men grabbing files from the cabinets and reached the telephone. She was conscious of McClennan watching her, his expression one of—what?—pity, sympathy? She held the receiver to her ear and turned her back on McClennan's gaze.

*Mark. Where is he?* She'd written it down somewhere, and now she couldn't remember where she'd scribbled the information. She shut her eyes and thought: Concentrate. Let it come flooding back to you. She had the weird feeling her brain had slipped a gear, and all the stuff she should have been able to remember instantly had become scrambled. *Where is he?*

She watched one of the agents unplug the computer from the wall, and the black power cord slithered across the surface of the desk. For the first time since she'd been wakened, the sense of having been invaded was strong inside her. She wanted to hit out at these men, to erase the look from McClennan's face. All this activity was unreal, dreadful. Even the dawnlight, fibers of pink slanting through the slats of the blind, seemed to originate from a sun she'd never seen before.

*Mark's hotel.* She couldn't remember. She held the receiver against the side of her face and watched the agent roll up the power cord. He did this with an air of finality she found alarming. She had an urge to grab his hands and stop him. Five men carrying badges of authority come into your home at dawn and flash legal papers and before you know what's going on they're removing your property. They're robbing you. She listened to the persistent dial tone, the way it whined inside her skull.

"Go ahead," McClennan said. "Maybe you'll get lucky."

Lucky. What was that supposed to mean? She frowned at him, as if she were trying to focus all her shapeless rage in his direction, but his benign expression frustrated her, and the meticulous way he parted his white hair annoyed her.

She turned away from him and thought: *the Kimberley Hotel. That's it. The Kimberley in Hong Kong.* She punched the buttons for Directory Assistance and asked for the number of the hotel because she still couldn't bring to mind where she'd left the paper on which she'd scribbled the name of his hotel. She had a feeling of dislocation. The sickness rose from her stomach to her throat, and she was dizzy. She imagined the baby floating in the amniotic sac, unaware and safe. She clutched the side of the desk and steadied herself. The international operator was giving her a number. She found a pencil, wrote it down. The lead snapped as she was writing. Hong Kong seemed an impossible distance away, the other side of the moon. *Why isn't Mark here? Why isn't he here to confront these intruders?* She pressed the buttons, waited.

"The Kimberley Hotel." The voice was friendly and singsong.

"I want to speak to Mark Klein," Sara said. She caught McClennan's eye. He was watching her in a somber way.

"Mark Klein?"

"Yes. Hurry. Please."

There was a period of silence. The voice came back on the line. "We have no guest of that name registered here, madam."

"You're mistaken," Sara said.

"No mistake, madam. There's no Mark Klein."

No Mark Klein. The phrase might have been a terse epitaph. "Has he checked out?" she asked.

"There's no record he ever checked *in*, madam. Perhaps you have the wrong hotel?"

"Look. Check the name again. Please."

"I'm very sorry, madam. There is nobody of that name registered here. I assure you."

She slammed the receiver down. The Kimberley. That's the name Mark had given her. She was certain of it. She looked through the blind. The sun on the rise had layered the sky with shades of tangerine.

"It's simple. I just remembered incorrectly, that's all," she said to McClennan.

"I don't think there's anything faulty with your memory," McClennan said quietly. "Mark's gone."

"Gone?"

McClennan crossed the room and touched her shoulder in a fashion that might have been avuncular. She moved away from his touch. She didn't need his sympathy. She didn't want to be touched. This whole outrage had some simple explanation—this invasion, the warrant, the absence of Mark from the hotel, all this was grounded in errors and misjudgments and flaws of memory. It had to be.

"Gone where?" she asked.

McClennan said, "That's what we'd like to know."

"Look, he phoned me from Hong Kong—"

"How do you know he was calling from Hong Kong?"

"Because he said so."

"Because he said so." McClennan stared briefly into the sun. "The plain fact is, Sara, he could be anywhere. Anywhere in the world."

"Mark's not in the habit of lying to me," she said.

"He told you the Kimberley, right? But we already checked, and we got the same response you did."

"How did *you* know to check the Kimberley?" she asked.

McClennan didn't answer.

"The goddam phone," she said. "You've tapped the line, haven't you? You've been bugging our phone."

She rattled the sheets of paper in her hand. Intruders, eaves-droppers, people listening in on private conversations. She had a sense of spiraling downward into panic. She stared at the papers. The print was small and blurry; she needed her reading glasses. She'd have to go upstairs to fetch them, but a paralysis had gripped her, and she couldn't move. The effort of climbing stairs struck her as too demanding. Draining. She watched the agents go about their business, as if she were seeing them through a sheet of clouded plastic. Her gaze drifted to the telephone, no longer a harmless instrument of communication, but something else: a treacherous device. She stood very still, hands by her sides, lips slightly parted.

"What is he supposed to have done?" she asked. "What the hell are you accusing him of?"

McClennan folded his arms and leaned against the jamb of the door. "You don't look very good, Mrs. Klein. You want a glass of water?"

Water. Sure, she wanted water. But she'd get it herself. She didn't need McClennan's help. The air in Mark's office was unbreathable. She took a few steps forward, then her legs yielded, and the dizziness became acute, upsetting her percep-tions. She lost her balance and would have fallen if Mc-Clennan hadn't acted quickly to catch her.

"Careful," he said.

She drew back from the agent and, with an attitude of certainty she didn't feel, walked in the direction of the kitchen, where she ran cold water over her wrists. Then she filled a glass, but the notion of drinking anything sickened her.

McClennan appeared in the kitchen doorway. "If he contacts you, you inform me at once," he said. "You ought to be clear about that."

She dried her fingers in a paper towel. She gazed through the window at the rear of the house, where a small area of trimmed lawn yielded to a tangled clump of trees and shrubbery. She saw the tree Mark had planted a year after their marriage, a silver birch, spindly as yet. He spent a lot of time on that tree, watering it with special solutions, tending it with a curious devotion, as if its growth were a symbol of the strength of their marriage. Once or twice, he'd even referred to it as the Marriage Tree.

McClennan said, "I have questions I need to ask you."

She said nothing. She studied the young tree.

"Are you listening to me?"

She turned, looked at him fiercely. "I'm not answering any questions until I talk to a lawyer."

"Smart move." McClennan was silent for a time. "When's the baby due?"

When's the baby due? Like this was a social call. Like this was an ordinary morning and life was totally normal and Mark was at the Kimberley in Hong Kong and God was still in his heaven.

"I told you," she said. "I'm not answering any questions. Not about Mark. Not about myself. Nothing."

McClennan lingered a few seconds in the doorway. "I'll be in touch," he said, then he was gone.

Sara crumpled a paper towel in her fist and dropped it in the wastebasket and listened as the lid closed with a sharp metallic sound. She stood in the center of the kitchen and felt the gleaming surfaces and the white walls squeezing in on her and imagined for a moment she was a discarded item crushed inside a trash compactor.

**2**

SHE went upstairs and sat on the bed and concentrated on reading the warrant. She tried to tune out the noise of the agents coming and going. She had the feeling she should have stayed downstairs and made an effort to watch them, to monitor them in some way—but what would that have accomplished? She couldn't stop them. They were carrying out Mark's belongings, stuffing them inside the trunks of their cars.

She twisted her wedding ring round and round and pondered the contents of the papers. They authorized the federal agents to remove all documents pertaining to "financial transactions" from the home of Mark Klein. *Financial transactions*: the phrase was so vague it could have covered anything associated with money. But why? What was the reason for the search, what grounds? The warrant was remarkably uninformative. She saw that it had been signed by somebody called Judge Cecilia Askew.

She scanned the words *You are therefore commanded in the daytime to make a search of 3242 Midsummer Avenue* . . . In the daytime, she thought. Dawn. They'd timed it just right. She flicked the pages and saw the following: *canceled checks, telephone bills, keys to safe deposit boxes, airplane tickets, notebooks, diaries, ledgers, escrow papers, legal documents, vehicle registration titles, deposit slips, passports, savings account passbooks, computer hardware and software, floppy disks, hard drives, keyboards, monitor screens, printers, documents containing lists of names and/or telephone numbers, copies of any and all income tax returns* . . . It was a license to remove just about everything from Mark's office. It was a kind of rape. A brutal penetration, and you could do nothing about it because you didn't have the power to resist.

When the cars eventually drove away, she took off her reading glasses and walked to the window. The waters of the Sound glimmered in sunlight, broken gold, brassy flecks. She dressed and went downstairs. She closed the door of Mark's office—that violated space—and wandered the rooms of the house, aware of the kind of silence she associated with vaulted churches.

She thought: *Do something. Just do something. Find the paper on which you scribbled the name of Mark's hotel. A memory check.* Start with that. She searched drawers, explored the trash can under the sink, found nothing. She went back upstairs and rummaged around in the bedroom, looked inside the pages of books and magazines. But she couldn't find the paper. Now she wasn't sure if it had been a sheet of paper at all. She might have written on the back of an envelope or in the margin of a newspaper. It was something she'd done absentmindedly and quickly.

Irritated by her own carelessness, she went back down to the kitchen and took her address book from a drawer and flicked the pages. She remembered now that Mark's lawyer was named George Borbokis. She called his office. She got an answering machine. It was only 8:00 A.M., the office probably didn't open until nine. Without saying anything, she hung up. The telephone was blighted; she didn't want to speak into it anyway. How long had the line been tapped? There would be recorded conversations between herself and Mark, intimacies shared. Husband to wife, phrases spoken in the private language of marriage.

She sat for a time without moving. Her thoughts were disjointed. The whole process of thinking in logical steps had become derailed. She still had the feeling she was caught up in a web of error, a madness of bureaucracy. She was still convinced, on the level of the heart, that Mark was at the Kimberley, and the clerk who'd answered the phone had made a mistake.

She walked back and forth through the downstairs rooms. Familiar objects—black-lacquered piano in the lounge, the Japanese prints Mark collected, the array of peacock feathers flowering out of cylindrical containers—had become tainted with strangeness. She couldn't stay indoors. The house had begun to feel like an elaborate wooden box in which she was trapped.

She put on a coat because a wind was starting to blow across the Sound and rain clouds were drifting from the Connecticut shoreline. She folded the warrant and stuck it in a pocket, then hesitated when she reached the front door. What if Mark phoned in her absence? She flicked the answering machine on, went outside, got in her car, and decided to drive in the direction of Port Jefferson, where her father lived.

*Running to Daddy*, she thought. *Daddy always knows. Running home.* She watched the house diminish in the rearview mirror.

In Port Jefferson she parked the car outside her father's home. She noticed that leaves were already beginning to fall, the process of decay. The year was sliding down toward winter. Halfway up the drive she stopped and looked at the house, a large ornate structure built at the turn of the century for a retired ship's captain. It was shabby, shingles missing from the roof, brown paint flaking from the deep porch, a chimney cracked. She'd grown up here. All her childhood memories were tethered to this place. The giant oak rising from the front lawn, the relics of an old swing hanging from branches, the window of her bedroom upstairs . . . What was she supposed to tell her father? He'd always been somehow neutral when it came to Mark. She'd never been sure if he altogether approved of her husband.

She saw him appear on the porch. He wore his usual shapeless brown cord pants and a grey sweater. He'd given up the tiny vanity of combing his few remaining strands of hair across his scalp.

''Stranger,'' he said, and smiled.

She climbed onto the porch, embraced him. He kissed her brow the way he'd always done. ''It's been weeks,'' he said.

''I know.''

He patted her stomach. ''How's junior?''

''Junior's fine.''

He put his arm around her shoulder and they went inside the house. In the living room she sat down.

He said, ''It can't be much longer.''

"About another three months," she said.

"You keeping okay?"

"Sure." She was nervous all at once. She looked round the room—photographs of herself as a kid, of her dead mother smiling in defiance of the leukemia that ultimately killed her. The room was huge and gloomy, weighted with memories.

Her father was watching her. "I always know when something's troubling you."

Sara said nothing.

"You want to talk about it? Or do you mean to maintain this silence?"

She folded her hands in her lap. She thought about the warrant in her coat pocket. She should have gone to the city to see George Borbokis. She shouldn't have come here. Her father was a retired math professor; he knew nothing about the law. Besides, why burden him with problems that weren't his? She looked at his expectant expression. He was a man of infinite patience. He spoke and acted slowly, weighed all the angles before he did anything. His life had been utterly uncontroversial. Twenty-two years of tenure at Stony Brook, then retirement, which he spent listening to his beloved classical music and reading the biographies of dead statesmen.

"It's Mark," she said. No, it wasn't about Mark. It was about a system that had malfunctioned.

"What about Mark?"

Sara took the warrant out of her pocket—and as she did so felt depth charges of delayed shock detonating through her. She closed her eyes and cried briefly, and her father went down on his knees in front of her and clasped her hands. The papers slid to the floor.

"I hate to see you cry," he said. "Let me get you something to drink."

She shook her head and wiped the sleeve of her coat against her eyes. She looked at her father through her tears—the benevolent concern, the way her own hurt resonated in his expression.

"Look at the papers," she said.

Her father picked up the sheets from the floor and read them in silence for a time. When he'd finished, he asked, "Do you believe Mark has done anything wrong?"

She shook her head firmly. "Not in a hundred years."

"You think this is all bullshit."

"Of course it is. It has to be."

The old man got to his feet and frowned. "Where is Mark?"

She didn't want to get into the intricacies of this question, didn't want to mention the business about the hotel. In a vague way she said that he was traveling in the Orient on business.

"But you don't know exactly where?"

"Not exactly," she answered. "But he'll call. He always calls every other day when he's on a business trip." She steered away from the subject of Mark's whereabouts. "I got the warrant first thing this morning. The agents came, and they took stuff from Mark's office. Papers, files. They even took his computer. It's a mistake, Dad. One enormous screwup."

John Stone said, "Listen, you want me to put you in touch with Stan Jacobs? He's been my lawyer for years. This kind of thing might be out of his league, though."

"It might be better if I spoke to Mark's attorney," she said.

"Maybe." The old man scanned the warrant again.

Sara said, "The FBI wants to question me, Dad. Christ, what am I supposed to say?"

"That's going to depend on the questions, Sara."

"I mean, I live a pretty ordinary life. I've never broken a law, unless you count some speeding offenses. I've never knowingly harmed anyone. And the FBI wants to *question* me." The baby moved inside her just then, a quiet shudder in her womb. A restless new life forming, waiting to emerge—into what? The thought of the baby depressed her suddenly. She imagined a small beating heart, improbably tiny hands.

Her father stood with his back to the fireplace. On the wall behind his head was a framed photograph of Sara on her wedding day. She looked at it absently, noticing the optimism of her own smile, the bright blue-eyed intensity of Mark's expression. Four years had passed since the wedding. Good years.

Her father said, "Have you made an appointment with Mark's attorney?"

"Not yet."

"Do it now. Don't waste time."

She got up, went to the phone. She checked the directory for Borbokis's number—Borbokis, Slaney and Reichmann was the firm's name. When she got through she introduced herself and asked for Borbokis. A secretary informed her that he was in a meeting.

"I need to see him as soon as possible. When's the first available time?"

"Let me see . . . Two-thirty this afternoon, Mrs. Klein. He has a window for half an hour."

"Two-thirty. I'll be there." *A window*, she thought. She hoped it would be the kind you could see through. She hung up. She contemplated the idea of calling the hotel in Hong Kong again. Maybe she'd get a different clerk this time, somebody competent, who could confirm that Mark Klein was in fact a resident. But she couldn't go through the whole rigmarole in front of her father.

Her father asked, "You want me to drive you in?"

"I'll take the train. It's easier."

"I could keep you company. I wouldn't mind that."

"I think I'd like to be on my own, Dad."

Her father nodded. He looked spent, whittled down by the years. He was moving, she realized, toward frailty. She hugged him hard in silence for a time.

"Don't worry about me," she said.

"Impossible, Sara. You always worry about your kids. It doesn't matter how old they are. You always worry. It's the condition of parenthood. You'll find that out."

She touched the back of his hand. "I'll let you know what the attorney says."

He appeared not to have heard her. He drifted briefly into some private zone of his own, then smiled in a sad way. "The country's gone to hell, Sara. The Feds can come inside somebody's home and take what they like, and they don't even have to specify the reasons. What the hell does *financial transactions* mean? For Christ's sake, what kind of system are we living under? The FBI is supposed to stand for law and order, and yet it behaves with blatant disregard for basic privacy. Sometimes I don't know the difference between criminals and law-enforcement agencies."

He followed her onto the porch. A wind was scattering fallen leaves. The big oak tree crackled, the old swing creaked.

"You sure you don't want me to come with you?" he asked.

She said she was sure.

*    *    *

From the window of the passenger car she watched the landscape. Countryside gave way to urban density, a clutter of houses, apartment buildings. The rocking motion of the train lulled her for a time. She looked at the other passengers—an African-American woman with two fretful kids, a short bearded man studying a horse-racing sheet with a look of concentration, a few teenage girls sniggering at something in a sex magazine. The diversity of lives on the Long Island Railroad.

She was aware of somebody settling into the seat next to her. He was a well-dressed young man with black hair. Her attention was drawn to his manicured nails. She caught his eye, and he smiled nicely. She'd noticed that total strangers sometimes smiled at her these days, as if pregnancy brought out a basic human sympathy.

She turned her face back to the window. The city, as it loomed up, created a screen of pollution against the sun. Before she'd quit her job because of her pregnancy, the city had always energized her. Only two months ago she'd worked here, and now it seemed an uninviting, artificial place, where people scurried in demented pursuit of their ambitions.

The young man touched her arm and she looked at him. He was handsome in a perfect way, like a model in a magazine. The features were a little too symmetrical. He leaned toward her, and said, "Nice old guy."

"Sorry?"

"Your father, I mean. Nice old guy. He'll make a terrific grandfather. He's the type."

"Who are you?" she asked.

"I have different names," he said.

"You're one of McClennan's people," she said. "You're following me."

"Keeping an eye on our interests, that's all," he said.

She felt blood rocketing to her head. "You tell McClennan, you tell him I find this an outrageous intrusion on my privacy, and completely unacceptable."

"Unacceptable?" The young man laughed quietly. "That's strong stuff, Sara. I'm quivering."

"Tell him to fuck off and get out of my life."

"Oh boy. Language."

She got up from her seat and slipped past the young man, who was still smiling at her. She moved down the aisle until she reached the end of the car. She locked herself inside the toilet. The floor was slimy; wadded balls of sodden tissue lay around. She clutched the edge of the sink and saw her reflection in the broken mirror. She ran her fingers angrily through her short dark hair. Her small face, which Mark had once described as elfin, appeared drawn and anemic. A blur of features—large brown myopic eyes, high cheekbones, the easygoing mouth that could only belong to someone of a basically happy disposition, an intelligent friendly face, but the whole architecture of it seemed to have collapsed.

Followed. Tracked. Like a criminal. She felt sick, a lurching motion in her stomach. She leaned over the toilet bowl and retched. A few sticky strands of saliva came up, nothing more. She found herself staring down into an oval of discolored water shimmering against dirty grey porcelain. Weakened, aware of a great pressure behind her eyes, she leaned against the wall and listened to the changing rhythm of the train slowing toward its destination.

**3**

SHE had time to kill before her appointment with Borbokis, so she decided to walk down to Wall Street. After the train ride she needed air, she needed to get her blood circulating. The city was vast and intimidating, and she felt tiny, as if she were perceiving herself from a helicopter hovering far overhead. She paused every so often to gaze in shop windows. Occasionally she glanced back at the crowded sidewalks for a sight of the young man from the train, but if he was still following her he was well concealed.

*Nice old guy*, he'd said. Why had he mentioned her father? Maybe he'd said it just to prove he could track her around undetected. It was a menacing consideration: wherever she went, she was being watched.

She was still thinking about the young man when she reached Wall Street. Two blocks away was the building where, on the third floor, Mark's firm was located. She'd worked with the same company for six years as PA to old Sol Rosenthal. Mark had joined the firm a year after her. A classic office romance, the rush of love, the giddy heart. She remembered how they'd tried to keep it quiet in the beginning because relationships between company personnel weren't officially encouraged—but you couldn't keep a thing like that secret, the conspiratorial encounters at the watercooler, the lunches, the way he was always finding excuses for visiting her office and lingering there. People inevitably noticed, even old Sol— who was perfectly amiable when they decided to announce their marriage.

"I hate the idea of losing you, Sara," Rosenthal had said. "You're a tough act for anybody to follow."

She'd told him she had no intention of quitting.

"You say that now. But it's going to happen. I've seen it before. Marriage. Kids. Career and everything else outta the window."

*A tough act to follow*, she thought. *I was good at what I did. Damn good. Efficient, reliable, resourceful.* Rosenthal had once called her his left arm. Ancient history. The life and times of a former self. What had become of that person? When she reached the entrance to the building, Tony Vandervelt, wrapped in a fashionably long black wool coat, was coming out. He spotted her instantly.

"Hey, so you can't stay away from your old haunts," he said. "Drawn back to the armpit of capitalism, huh?"

"How are you, Tony?"

"Cruising along," he said. "How about you?"

"Turning into a blimp."

"Crap. You look terrific. What brings you down to this madhouse?"

"I have an appointment nearby," she said.

He rubbed his hands together briskly. "Rosenthal got himself a new assistant, but she's not up to scratch. So he's bad-tempered most of the time. Can't find this file. Can't find that. Moan moan."

She looked into Vandervelt's face. It was one of sharp angles; nose too prominent, cheekbones protrusive. She'd known Tony for six years. They'd dined together a few times before Mark had arrived on the scene. She was about to mention the search warrant, but what good would it do to unload herself on Tony?

He looked at his watch. "Gotta dash. Next time you're in the neighborhood, give me a call and we'll do lunch or something." He brushed his lips lightly on her cheek. His breath was cold.

"Tony . . ."

He was already moving away. "Yeah?"

She didn't respond. She'd had an impulse to ask him if he knew the name of Mark's hotel in Hong Kong, but she stifled it. *You wouldn't happen to know where Mark's staying, would you*? How would that have sounded? He'd have come back with something too close to the bone: *Can't keep track of your own husband, huh?* She raised a hand in a gesture of good-bye and watched him step away and vanish along the crowded sidewalk. She found herself gazing at the entrance to the building. Something in Tony's manner—she couldn't quite pin it down. Less than his normal effusive self?

He'd terminated the meeting abruptly, and he hadn't asked after Mark—which was perhaps a little unusual. But he'd obviously been in a hurry and didn't have time for small talk. Still, she had an unfocused feeling of discomfort.

She entered a cross street where the wind coming from the river was chilly. She drew up the collar of her coat and walked to the building where Borbokis had his office. On the sidewalk a man in an orange hard hat and protective goggles was drilling a slab of concrete, his body vibrating to the drill. The noise penetrated her. She wondered whether the baby heard. Whether the grinding sound infiltrated her womb.

She entered the building, rode the elevator to the tenth floor. She took the warrant from her pocket and looked at it, seeing Mark's name in bold type. She was beset by a sense of loneliness, a darkening in her head. It was as if the papers in her hand were the only connection she had to her husband—a couple of flimsy, accusatory sheets. She thought: *If he's lied to me, it would be like a nail hammered into my flesh, a crucifixion.* But the marriage had been founded on mutual trust; Mark had always talked about the importance of honesty. *You can't have a marriage under any other conditions*, he'd said. *It doesn't work that way. It only functions if you're open with each other. Nothing hidden.*

She stepped out of the elevator. The offices of Borbokis, Slaney and Reichmann were furnished in a style suggestive of an Edwardian gentleman's club; dark wood panels, upholstered leather chairs, hunting and fishing prints. All this was designed to make the client feel he'd entered a genteel world, a place of honor and old-fashioned dignity where handshakes had the authenticity of notarized contracts. The receptionist was a middle-aged woman in a dark brown suit that almost camouflaged her against the walls.

"I have an appointment," Sara said.

"You are . . . ?"

"Sara Klein."

"Of course. To see Mr. Borbokis." The woman picked up a telephone and announced Sara's arrival, then said, "Go down the corridor. Second door on the left."

Sara entered a large chocolate-colored room. George Borbokis was rising to greet her. His turquoise and silver rings flashed. The smell of his aftershave was strong and sharp, like a hundred lemons freshly pulverized. He wore a pin-striped double-breasted suit tailored to disguise his stomach. He shook her hand, and said, "It's been a while, Sara."

"Two years, I guess."

"The will, I remember."

"The will. Right." She recalled Mark's insistence on making a will and how she'd objected to it because she felt too young to think of wills and death. But Mark had argued that it was a sensible precaution, nothing more—like the Walther in the bedside drawer.

Mark was the planner, the one who looked after the finances; he completed income-tax forms and paid car insurance, the mortgage, the utility bills, balanced the checkbooks. Mark the arranger, the family comptroller. If anyone had asked her about the balance in the joint checking account or how much was in savings, she couldn't have answered.

"Take a seat," Borbokis said.

She sat down, stretched her legs.

"Impending motherhood, I see. My congratulations. I didn't know. Then again, I don't see much of Mark."

Sara had a momentary fascination with the attorney's eyebrows and how they fused in a tangled bush over the bridge of his nose.

"How is Mark?" the lawyer asked.

"I don't know. I don't know how to answer that." *Nothing hidden*, she thought. Then how come she was in a position where she couldn't answer the attorney's simple question? How come she couldn't just say *Mark's fine*?

She slid the warrant across Borbokis's desk.

He picked up the sheets and read them without any change of expression. He had a poker player's face. He gave the impression of a man who knows a thousand secrets, somebody who'd encountered every kind of human folly and was immune to astonishment.

She said, "FBI agents came to our home this morning. They took things from Mark's office."

"This warrant gives them the legal right," Borbokis said. "Mark wasn't present when the warrant was served?"

"He's away."

"Where?"

She said, "Hong Kong."

"Have you contacted him?"

"I haven't been able to."

"So he doesn't know about this."

She shook her head. She was hesitant. "He gave me the name of a hotel. I called. They say they've never heard of him."

Borbokis was quiet a second. "He misled you. Is that what you're telling me?"

"I don't know what I'm telling you." She heard a note of despair in her voice when she said, "I don't know anything, it seems."

"You could have called the wrong hotel, of course," Borbokis said.

"I think I must have."

"You don't sound certain."

"Because I'm not."

Borbokis paused a moment. "You remember the name of the agent in charge?"

"Thomas McClennan."

Borbokis noted this on a yellow legal pad with a fountain pen. He asked, "Don't you work at the same place as your husband?"

"I quit a few months ago."

"On maternity leave?"

"No, I quit the job entirely. I don't want to raise a child and work a job at the same time. At least not for a few years."

"Rosenthal Brothers . . . that's the name of the firm, right?"

"Yes." She felt suddenly impatient. Why did she have to answer these inconsequential questions? "McClennan wants to interview me. I don't really know what he thinks I can tell him."

"You're Mark's wife. McClennan imagines you might have useful information."

"Like what?"

Borbokis smoothed the warrant with his fingertips. "It depends what he's looking for, Sara. The search warrant doesn't have to *specify* the nature of a suspected criminal act. The Feds work on the basis of 'probable cause.' They present an affidavit to a judge in order to obtain the warrant. Since this warrant is restricted to a search for documents relating to 'financial transactions,' it doesn't take a genius to figure out that they think Mark has been involved in some kind of fiscal irregularity."

"Such as?" she asked.

"Oh, it could be any number of things. Mismanagement of funds. Fraudulent dealings in stocks and shares. Illegal transactions."

"Illegal transactions? Mark?"

"You asked me for examples, Sara. I'm only giving you a few."

Sara was about to dismiss all this, but Borbokis kept talking. "Understand how a guy like McClennan works. He's probably thinking that you know something."

"That's preposterous."

"Preposterous to you. Not to McClennan."

"You're saying—"

"I'm saying that in his eyes you might be just as guilty as Mark—"

"Terrific. Except I don't see where it says that Mark is *guilty* of *anything*, never mind *my* supposed guilt. Don't we have some kind of system in this country that says you're innocent until you're proven guilty? Or is that horseshit?"

"No, it's not horseshit. I'm only trying to explain the way McClennan functions. He's in the business of suspicion. Obviously this warrant indicates that he's thinking of making a case against Mark. And since you're Mark's wife . . ."

"I don't like where this is going," she said.

"Plus there's the fact you worked in the same company—"

"What has that got to do with anything?"

Borbokis tapped his fountain pen on the legal pad, as if he were weary of explaining the obvious to clients. "Okay. For the sake of argument, let's say Mark *has* been involved in quote unquote *fiscal irregularity*. And let's say, again for the sake of argument, that whatever he's done has involved the company in some detrimental way . . . Do you see what I'm getting at?''

''Yes, I see.''

Borbokis massaged his eyelids. ''McClennan sniffs complicity.''

Her throat was parched. ''Can I trouble you for a glass of water?''

''No trouble.'' Borbokis buzzed his secretary. A slender young blond woman came into the room with a tall glass of iced water, then left again at once. Sara sipped the liquid. The smell of chlorine was strong. She was curiously sensitive to smells and sounds these days, as if the biological changes of pregnancy had enhanced her senses. She couldn't drink the water. She held the chilled glass between her hands and thought of the word ''complicity'' until it had been stripped of any meaning.

She said, ''He was practically standing next to me when I tried to phone Mark. He *knows* I couldn't reach my husband. He heard me try, George. For Christ's sake, if he's thinking complicity, how can he explain the fact that I couldn't get in touch with Mark? That's a goddam weird kind of complicity when one partner can't contact the other, wouldn't you say?''

''He might think you were playacting.''

''*Playacting,*'' she said.

''Sure. In his reality, you know where Mark is. You go through the sham of calling a hotel where you know he won't be found. Then you pretend you're baffled.''

''That's shit,'' she said. ''What kind of planet does McClennan inhabit?''

''Think of a murky green pond, you'd be close,'' Borbokis said.

She said, ''Our phone line's tapped.''

''Did McClennan tell you that?''

''He didn't deny it.''

Borbokis wrote something on his pad again. What was he scribbling? She had the odd feeling he was going through the motions of work, jotting things down because clients expected it. He could be writing meaningless hieroglyphics for all she knew.

She said, ''If they have tapes of conversations between

Mark and me, then they can hear for themselves that there's no evidence of any kind of complicity.''

"Unless you and Mark talked in a prearranged code," Borbokis said.

"Code? Oh, for God's sake, George." She got up from her chair. Faintly, she could hear the sound of the pneumatic drill from the street ten floors below. The world was in a state of disarray and disintegration.

"Complicity. Codes. He hasn't even established *guilt*. He's gone out and gotten himself a warrant, and he's seized a bunch of papers, that's all he's done.''

Borbokis sat back in silence, plump hands clasped.

Sara asked, "Isn't there some way we can find out what Mark's alleged to have done? The judge who granted the warrant. Can't you ask her? Can't you get to see this affidavit?''

"It isn't that simple, Sara. Basically, the Feds have all the marbles. It's only when they decide to bring charges against Mark that we get a copy of the affidavit. Usually it takes about ten days before we learn anything.''

"So we just sit and *wait* for something to happen?''

"That's the position.''

"But that's outrageous. They have all this power . . .''

"Yes, they do.''

"And they ride all over us.''

Borbokis capped his fountain pen. He asked, "Did McClennan say when he wanted to question you?''

"No.''

"I'll find out when he intends to interview you because I want to be present.''

"What am I supposed to do in the meantime?''

"Go home and wait. Be patient. And when Mark gets in touch with you, have him call me immediately. That's imperative.''

"If you talk to McClennan, you might mention that I don't exactly appreciate being followed. There was one of his men on the train coming in.''

"How did you spot him?''

"I didn't have to. He introduced himself.''

Borbokis looked puzzled. "By name?''

"No. He just started talking to me. He knew who I was. He'd been following me.''

The attorney said, "They don't usually introduce themselves, Sara. In my experience, they like to stay quietly anonymous."

"Not this one. Maybe it's some new technique they're trying. See how clever we Feds are. You're never alone. The walls have ears and eyes."

Borbokis looked preoccupied as he walked with her to the door. "I know it's tough, but try to keep calm."

"I can't promise that."

"I'll be in touch."

She rode the elevator down to street level. The man with the drill was gone. The wind carried the damp unpleasant scent of the river. *Codes*, she thought. *Complicity*.

She walked briskly to shake off the feeling of angry disbelief that had seized her. She felt exhausted, lonesome. On an impulse, she went inside a coffee shop and walked to the pay phone. She dropped a coin in the slot and dialed a number.

"Rosenthal Brothers," a voice said.

"Jennifer Gryce, please," Sara said.

"One moment please."

Sara heard Jennifer Gryce say, "Hello."

"Jen? This is Sara."

"Oh."

"Have you got time for a drink? I'm just around the corner."

"Right now? I'm tied up, Sara."

"A couple of minutes, that's all."

"I don't think I can. You should see my desk."

"Please, Jen. I need somebody to talk to. I really do. I wouldn't ask if I didn't need you."

Jennifer Gryce, who'd joined the company the same month as Sara, who'd become Sara's best friend in the firm and the first to know about her relationship with Mark, was quiet for a long time. The silence was awkward and jagged. Sara remembered flashes of her friendship with Jen—a visit to Chippendales when they'd both laughed themselves into hysteria at the brazen tack of it all, a tour they'd made one night of the meat-market bars just for the general lunacy of the singles scene, a Joe Cocker concert on a hot summer day in Central Park. A montage of shared experiences, secrets, laughter.

"I'm sorry. I can't make it, Sara. I just can't leave the office right now."

"Five minutes, Jen. That's all."

"I can't do it. I'm sorry. Listen, I have to go into a meeting, people are waiting for me. Bye—"

Sara said, "Five minutes, for God's sake. Don't hang up—"

But the line was cut, the receiver dead in her hand.

She walked out of the coffee shop into the long cold gully of the street, where she shivered.

**4**

SHE sat in the car and just stared at the house as if it belonged to somebody else. As dusk gathered, the windows were turning into unwelcoming dark rectangles. The porch was deeply shadowed and lifeless. The house, she thought, had withered.

She got out of the car, climbed onto the porch. She turned the key slowly in the lock, went inside. There was a ponderous, unbearable quiet about the place. *This silence. This dread.* She switched on the TV in the living room. A babble of commercials assailed her. She was aware of visuals—baby's diapers, cans of dog food; and the noise of jingles, the kind of noise she needed. She took off her coat and let it drop to the floor.

She walked to the answering machine. There were two messages. She pressed the Playback button. The first was from her father. *Call me when you can.*

The other was Jennifer Gryce. *Please don't call me, Sara. I hate to sound mean, I really do, but it doesn't help if you call me. I've got to think about my position here . . . I'm sorry, I'm truly sorry.*

"Fuck you, old buddy," Sara said aloud. "You and your position in the fucking company," and she flopped down into an armchair and shut her eyes. Jennifer Gryce didn't want to be associated with her, and this hurt.

And Tony Vandervelt had been abrupt. Conclusion: whatever Mark had done involved the Rosenthal firm. Jennifer knew, and so did Tony. And everyone else. The whole firm would be buzzing with gossip. *Mark Klein, who would ever have thought it of him*? The bright-eyed boy goes wrong. The golden young man tarnished.

*No*, she told herself. *There has to be a very straightforward explanation for all of this. For this quote unquote* fiscal irregularity. *Mark wouldn't screw the firm. He wouldn't do that.*

What to do. What to do. What step to take. She stared at the answering machine. Nothing from Borbokis. And, more importantly, nothing from Mark. *The world is flat*, she thought, *and I am sailing toward the edge.*

Inside her the baby shifted. She wondered what unborn babies could detect of stress, if they felt emotional changes in their environment. She clenched her hands as tightly as she could. Blood drained out of the knuckles. Bone white. *Baby*, she thought. *What is going to become of you? You lie inside me, take nourishment from me, I'm your life-support system and I can't even support myself. And Daddy's gone, and I don't know how to find him.*

Images crowded her head—scuffed sampans floating in Hong Kong harbor, skyscrapers adorned with neon signs in Chinese characters, mazes of narrow streets. But Mark wasn't in any of these pictures.

She pulled her blouse up and looked down at her swollen stomach, running the tips of her fingers over her flesh. The shape of her navel had changed.

*Everything* had changed.

She couldn't sit still. She walked up and down the room for a time. She stopped by the telephone. She wondered if it was worth making the call that had just occurred to her. Why not—she didn't have anything to lose. She couldn't simply wait, as Borbokis had advised her, until the machinery of the FBI cranked into action and brought specific charges against Mark. She dialed a number.

Sol Rosenthal said, "Yeah?"

She hesitated. "Sol?"

"Yeah. Who's this?"

"Sara."

"Sara. My favorite girl," he said.

"Am I still your favorite?"

"The one I got now, you wouldn't believe. Her brain's pickled in aspic."

He didn't sound any different. His rough-edged voice was

the same, his manner the same. She heard him suck on a cigar.
"So. What can I do for you?"

"Sol, you know why I'm calling."

"Yeah. I know."

"I don't know what the hell is going on, Sol. Tell me what
Mark's supposed to have done."

She heard smoke being expelled swiftly. "I used to tell
people, I used to say, this Sara, even when she sneezes, she
don't produce germs."

"Sol, please."

"This girl's got class stamped all over her, I used to say."

"Sol, what the hell has Mark done?"

Sol Rosenthal said, "Trouble with lawyers, kid, they gag
you. They don't allow you to speak. They put you in this kinda
leper colony and tell you, don't speak to anybody, don't prejudice things."

"Prejudice what?"

"That's all I'm saying. All I'm allowed to say."

"Sol, *please*."

"Sara. Do yourself a favor. Don't ask questions."

He hung up. She put the phone down. She remembered the
tap on the line. She imagined a reel-to-reel spinning slowly
somewhere, a darkened room or a parked van, men with ear-
phones. Sol knew, of course he knew, but he wasn't going to
tell her anything. Wasn't allowed to. Silenced by his attorneys.
Gagged.

The telephone rang, and she picked it up at once. It was her
father.

"You got my message?" he asked.

"I just got in," she said. "I was going to call you back."

"I've been anxious. How did it go?"

"Have you eaten yet?" she asked.

"No."

"You fancy going somewhere for food?"

"Sounds good."

"I'll pick you up. Maybe we'll go to Sam's. You like their
seafood, don't you?"

"Sam's is okay. You sure you don't want me to come get
you?"

"No. Just give me half an hour."

"You really up for this? You sound tired."

"I'm famished. See you in thirty minutes." She set the phone down. Stilted talk. When you knew your conversations were being recorded, how could you be natural? She'd have to remember the fact that privacy had gone out of her life.

She looked across the room at the door of Mark's office. Something different, she thought. Something not quite right. Mark's room. She was sure she'd closed the door before she'd left earlier, but now it was slightly ajar. She walked to the threshold of the room, reached in, and flicked on the overhead light. The drawers of the filing cabinets and the desk hung open. The barren white surface of the desk itself reflected the light. In the center was a square of dust where the computer had been.

She'd shut the door this morning; she was certain. And now it was open. Okay, you didn't close it properly. That's all. Perfectly reasonable. Memory flaw. Cells not functioning.

She went inside the room and examined the empty filing cabinets. The agents had taken everything, every folder, every scrap of paper. The desk drawers contained nothing but paper clips and rubber bands, pencils and pens. She looked at Mark's swivel chair, remembered the way he sat there late into the night going through work he brought home with him, shoulders hunched, sleeves rolled up, a distance in his eyes. It seemed to her for a moment that a phantom of her husband still lingered in the room. She turned off the light, closed the door tightly. Something else niggled her—

*The Walther.* Of course. McClennan had taken the gun from her hand as soon as he'd entered the house. Had that been confiscated along with everything else? Was that also to be construed as evidence of Mark's alleged guilt? She looked for the gun in the drawer of the coffee table, on the mantelpiece, between the cushions of the sofa, the armchairs.

She didn't find the Walther.

Instead she discovered, stuck between cushion and upholstery, a creased yellow Post-it note on which she'd written: *Kimberley, Hong Kong.*

She crumpled the note in the palm of her hand and the sticky edge adhered to her skin. She felt dismay, a sense of crashing. An escape route had collapsed in her head.

He'd lied to her. He'd lied to her after all.

5

"**THIS** isn't the way to Sam's," her father said.

"I've changed my mind about Sam's," she said.

"You don't look too good. You're pale."

"Yeah. Well. It's been a long day." She clutched the steering wheel and peered into the darkness ahead of her. The headlights of the car sliced through high shrubbery. She glanced in the rearview mirror. There was no traffic behind her. She wondered if McClennan had already dispatched one of his spies to Sam's Seafood House. One of his eavesdroppers.

"Where are we headed, Sara?"

"There's a bar a few miles from here. They do good burgers."

"Jackson's?"

"Jackson's," she said. Grilled meat, disks of ground beef leaking blood. She couldn't face food. She could still feel the adhesive of the Post-it note against her skin. She could still see her own hasty handwriting.

Her father touched the back of her hand. "What did the attorney say to you?"

"What do attorneys ever say? He said he'd look into it and get back to me." Her mood was black. She didn't want to communicate. She felt isolated, imprisoned in herself.

"This isn't the best way to Jackson's," her father said. "These back roads are slow."

She didn't respond. She knew she'd say something she'd regret. She didn't want to lose her patience with her father. *The importance of honesty*, she thought. *You've concealed a whole life from me, Mark. You've been working away in cracks and crevices. In places I knew nothing about.* She desperately wanted to see him, if only to confront him. And yet— some stubborn pocket of herself *still* refused to believe he'd done anything wrong. There was some good reason for the lie he'd told her; there had to be. She was hanging, against the force of evidence, to a fragile thread. He'd suddenly turn up, he'd explain the anomalies, and how the warrant was all some kind of horrible mistake; he'd talk in his quietly reasonable way, and she'd listen, she'd understand. *I want to believe*, she thought.

Her father said, "You've gone AWOL on me."

"I'm sorry. I was thinking."

"Anything you want to share?"

The parking lot of Jackson's Tavern appeared ahead. An electric sign hung in the dark sky. HAMBURGERS RIBS STEAKS COCKTAILS. "I'm not great company, Dad."

"You don't want to talk, don't talk."

They went inside the bar. It was one of those places trying to be country-western. Sawdust on the floors, rough-hewn wood tables. The waitresses wore short red skirts and boots and leather vests. The air smelled of meat. A jukebox was playing an old Tammy Wynette number. "Stand By Your Man." The last song Sara wanted to hear.

A hostess approached. She smiled as if she were programmed. "Table for two? Follow me." She led them to the back of the room. "Bobby will be your server tonight. Enjoy."

Sara sat facing the door. She wanted to see who came and went. Her father looked round the big room and remarked, "I haven't been here in years. I'd forgotten how enormous this place is." He listened to the jukebox with an expression of distaste. "Those songs are always about guys pining for their women or vice versa. Masochism in three chords."

Sara smiled thinly at him. She'd force conversation out of herself. The music stopped. "Sometimes they're about God and country."

"Ah, yes. Patriotism, Nashville style. Sequins and spangles." He reached across the table and let his fingers rest on her hand. The softness of touch, the concern and sympathy in his eyes: she felt sad. She was linked to him through loneliness. His life had been a solitary one for the last twelve years. Her own solitude, on the other hand, had only begun at dawn. She was a novice when it came to loneliness. She imagined him pottering around his big empty house, and what she heard was the rushing sound of a void, like a wind on a dead landscape. Was that her future, too?

"Hi there. I'm Bobby." The waitress was young, slim, effervescent. She produced two menus and in a high-pitched voice rattled off the night's specials. "I'll have an old-fashioned burger," John Stone said. "Medium rare. No fries."

Sara asked for the same. Bobby smiled and took the menus away. "Drinks?"

Sara ordered scotch and water. Her father asked for a Coors. When the waitress had gone, Sara said, "Don't look at me like that."

"Like what?"

"You know. That professorial frown. I feel like having a drink. I need it. One drink isn't going to damage the baby's brain, Dad."

"I wasn't aware of frowning," he said.

"Take my word for it. You must have terrified whole generations of students with that look."

"I doubt it. I used to wonder if my students were ever really listening to me anyway. Mostly I felt I was talking to myself. Math requires concentration, which implies an attention span of more than thirty seconds. And everything has to be encapsulated in a maximum of two sentences these days. Beyond that—you might as well forget it. Nobody wants complexity."

This was one of his favorite topics. Sometimes he expanded on this theme to include a denunciation of the American educational system. When he was in the mood, he wandered off into tirades against the corruption of politicians, the pernicious influence of lobbyists. She wondered if he'd end up espousing rabid conspiracy theories in his very old age. Listening to his familiar speech, though, gave her a mild sense of comfort. Some things were constant in the world.

Their drinks came. "Cheers," she said. The scotch was smothered in cubes of ice, and weak.

"And to you." He sipped the frosted mug of Coors. Beer left a froth on his upper lip. "You haven't been very forthcoming about the attorney, Sara."

"He said he'd check out a few things, then he'd call me."
She heard impatience in her voice. Why couldn't he see that
she didn't want to talk about the lawyer? She needed to pretend a certain normality existed. The status quo was un-
changed. Because you had to keep going, no matter what.
That's what you had to do.

He persisted. "Did he say he could help?"

"Yes."

"How?"

She bit into the burger and pink juice ran down her fingers.
Her stomach turned. "Lawyers aren't always specific, Dad."

"You're not telling me everything, are you?"

"God, Dad. Just drop it."

"I shouldn't push you."

"Sorry. I shouldn't lose my patience."

"Patience isn't all it's cracked up to be, Sara. Sometimes
it's a good thing to lose." He opened the bun of his burger
and studiously removed the onion slices. "I take it there's no
word from Mark?"

"I would have told you."

She put her hamburger back on the plate, pushed the whole
thing to one side. She sipped the scotch and gazed at her
father's face for a time. "Can I ask you a question?"

"Fire."

"What do you think of Mark?"

"What do I *think* of him?"

"You've never told me."

"That's a tough question, Sara."

"You don't like him."

"I never said that."

"Okay. But you've never really approved of him."

"I guess I don't know him very well . . . I suppose I always
just figured that if you were happy, everything was okay."

"That's an evasion."

"I don't mean to evade, Sara. I'm just trying to think how
I can answer you. I've never had any really personal conversations with him, so I don't have a basis for making a judgment."

"Forget judgment. Tell me about your instincts."

"Instincts. I've lived most of my life in a world of math-

ematical truths. I guess my instincts have become rusty from
not being used.''

"*Dad.*"

John Stone was quiet for a time. "Last spring he asked me
if I was interested in investing in some kind of offshore tax-
exempt scheme. Some loophole he'd found."

"He never told me that. Did you invest?"

"No, and I can't tell you why I didn't. Maybe I thought
fifty grand was too rich for my blood. Maybe I didn't like the
sound of it. I don't know."

"You thought it was . . . what? Illegal?"

"Illegal, no. If I was forced to put my finger on it, I'd say
I didn't really enjoy the sense of being pressured."

"And that's what he was doing?"

"Pretty hard. I figured he worked in a competitive marketplace, and he was trying to sell me something I didn't want."

Sara finished her drink. She hadn't known about Mark's
attempt to get her father to invest money. She couldn't imagine
him pressuring the old man—but there were a lot of things
she apparently couldn't imagine about Mark.

"He had an air of desperation about him," her father said.
"That's the impression I got at the time. He just *had* to get
my signature on the dotted line. It was as if his life depended
on it."

She stared into her glass, where ice melted into crystallized
mounds. An air of desperation. She'd never seen Mark in that
kind of state. He worked too hard, he was eager and ambitious,
he was always trying to draw in new clients, always making
deals. *There are an awful lot of naive people out there*, he'd
once said. *And too many of them are giving their money to
the government because they don't know how to invest it to
their own advantage.* And so the desk lamp burned long after
midnight, and the computer hummed, and the fax machine
beeped, and the telephone rang at all hours with calls from
countries in different time zones. But desperation—no, she'd
never seen that in him.

The waitress appeared at the table. "Hate to interrupt. Are
you Sara Klein? If you are, there's a phone call for you. You
can take it at the bar."

Sara glanced at her father, then rose, and walked across the sawdust-strewn floor to the bar. Puzzled, she picked up the phone.

A man's voice said, "We want to see you, Sara."

"Who is this? McClennan?"

"We need to talk."

"I don't talk to strangers," she said. "And I don't like being followed."

"You'll talk to us," the man said.

"I'm hanging up. Talk to my lawyer. George Borbokis. He's in the book."

"You're not listening. We don't *talk* to lawyers. We prefer face-to-face."

"I don't give a damn what you prefer—"

"You're not paying attention, Sara. We're outside. In the parking lot. Put down the phone. Walk out quietly. Don't make any phone calls, and say nothing to your father. You don't want him upset, do you? At his age. You understand that?"

The caller cut the connection. Sara put the telephone down. She turned and looked back across the room at the table where her father sat. He was sipping his beer. In the dim light he appeared spectral, vulnerable. She looked at the door that led to the parking lot. A green sign glimmered: EXIT.

6

THE night air was cold and smelled of rain. A wind flapped at the hem of Sara's coat. The big electric sign that said HAMBURGERS RIBS STEAKS COCKTAILS cast a red glow across the parking lot. She looked at the stationary cars. She counted seven in all. She heard something hum from the sign, an electric flaw. The B in RIBS sparked a moment. She moved out into the lot and wondered why she hadn't stayed inside the restaurant. But she knew—the menace in the voice had left her no choice, the reference to her father. *You don't want him upset, do you? At his age.* She remembered the young man from the train and the way he'd said *Nice old guy*.

She was suddenly afraid. Fear didn't anesthetize the way people sometimes claimed; it sharpened her senses, honed her perceptions. She could hear blood course to her heart. The wind made her face tingle, and her eyes smarted. Her breathing seemed unusually loud and deep.

*We want to talk to you.*

She passed her own car and saw how it reflected the red sign as if somebody had sprayed the vehicle with blood.

*We don't talk to lawyers. We prefer face-to-face.*

Whoever had phoned had no connection to McClennan, no affiliation with the FBI, she was certain of that much. McClennan wouldn't operate like this. McClennan wouldn't have objected to talking with her lawyer, wouldn't have insisted on this peculiar assignation in a quiet parking lot. But if the caller had no association with McClennan, if he wasn't connected to the federal machine, who was he?

She heard somebody say, "Over here, Sara."

She saw a man emerge from a dark blue Buick, leaving the door open. He wore a black scarf and beige raincoat with epaulettes. His face was bloated and unattractive; the pallor of his skin, tinted by the electric sign, gave him the look of someone with high blood pressure. His hands were in his pockets.

"Over here," he said again.

She was ten yards from the car. She had the impression that there was somebody else inside the Buick. She thought of her father. He'd wonder where she'd gone; her absence would worry him after a few minutes, and he'd come looking for her. She took a few steps forward.

"Who are you?" she asked.

The man took his hands from his pockets. They were large, gloved. "Closer," he said.

She shook her head.

"A quiet word, Sara. That's all we want with you." And now he made the effort of a smile, but it wasn't warm, it wasn't inviting.

She heard the first few drops of rain fall on the bodies of parked cars. The sounds were amplified in her head. The clocklike tick of rain on metal and the way the electric sign crackled again. The B flickered and died this time, leaving a strange hole in the fabric of the sky.

"Sara," the man said. "Just walk toward me. Come over to the car."

"Who are you?" she asked again.

The man shrugged. "You're close to him, right? You're very fond of him. That's the way it ought to be. Father and daughter. Family."

She felt rain against her face. She wondered about her reserves of stubbornness. Being stubborn wasn't enough. Defiance carried you only a short distance before it became depleted. She thought again about her father, and she took a few steps toward the Buick. She remembered the young man on the train. *He'll make a terrific grandfather.*

"It's not so difficult after all, is it, Sara?"

She could see inside the Buick. A figure, locked in shadow, occupied the backseat. Sara paused a few feet from the man in the beige raincoat. This close to him, she saw a maze of broken veins on his nose. His left eyelid was odd, half-closed.

She said, "I don't like threats."

"Who's threatening? Have I made threats?"

"The way you mentioned my father . . ."

"You see that as a threat? I was only saying how nice it is to see a bond between father and daughter in this day and age, when all you ever hear about are damaged families. People alienated from one another. Separated. That kind of thing. You want to interpret *that* as a threat, that's up to you."

The figure in the backseat moved slightly. Sara had the impression of metal glinting. Her first thought was a gun, but that was wrong. She saw through the open rear door of the Buick; the glint came from the aluminum frame of a walker. Two skinny white hands clutched the metal. The man in the beige coat leaned into the car. The figure in the back, whose face Sara couldn't see, whispered something.

The man in the coat turned to Sara. "Get in the car, Sara," he said.

"No way."

"Make this easy on yourself. Just get in the car."

"No!"

He caught her, grabbed her arms, swung her around, and forced her toward the Buick. Shocked by the unexpected physical contact, she struggled. He said, "A few minutes of your time, Sara. That's all. Nobody's going to harm you. Okay?"

She felt herself being pushed forward. She tried to resist by gripping the edge of the open door, but he prised her fingers loose effortlessly and maneuvered her, almost gently now, into the backseat. She found herself sitting alongside the person with the aluminum frame. The air was pierced by the smell of cloves.

The figure in the backseat was a woman.

She had an old face, cheeks hollowed, the mouth a single lipsticked line, the hair dyed yellow and combed back flat to the skull in a mannish way. A yellow carnation was attached to the lapel of her dark fur coat, which was a massive garment in which she seemed tiny.

"You are Sara Klein," the woman said. Her voice was hoarse, throaty.

"Yes," Sara said.

"Are you scared, Sara Klein?"

Sara didn't answer this. She had the feeling the question was asked with no expectation of an answer. The woman opened a small brown bottle, stuck a Q-Tip inside it, then raised the stick to her mouth and slid it between her lips.

"Oil of cloves," she said. "I have a toothache. I also have an irrational fear of dentists. I make my own temporary repairs, Sara Klein. A dentist might want to extract. But I am reluctant to lose a tooth I have had in my head for seventy years, give or take. One comes to value small possessions, however trivial they may seem." She reached out and laid the palm of one skeletal hand on Sara's stomach.

"Small possessions," she said again.

Sara didn't move. She felt the hand make a circular motion across her belly.

"This baby. Boy or girl?"

"I don't know," Sara said.

"Ah. You like the element of surprise."

"Not always."

The woman capped the bottle of clove oil and sighed. "I have come a long way to see you, Sara. From St. Petersburg. Formerly Leningrad. What do you think of my English?"

"I don't know who you are, I don't know what you want—"

"I studied English in Moscow years ago. English is the language of business, am I right? Without English, nothing is possible these days. Commerce. International finance. Tell me. My English. Is it good?"

"Yes. It's good. So what?"

"I am pleased." The woman let her hand fall from Sara's stomach. "You are carrying a girl, by the way. I have an instinct for such things. I can feel certain vibrations. Feminine. Masculine. They emit different signals. In another time, they might have accused me of witchcraft." The woman laughed at this notion. It was like the sound of pebbles shaken inside a shoe box.

"What do you want from me?" Sara asked.

"Surely you know the answer to that."

"If I knew the answer, I wouldn't have asked the question."

The old woman took Sara's hand and pressed it between her palms, which were icy. "Your hand is trembling, Sara. But you have no reason to fear me. I am not a bad woman. On the contrary, I consider myself reasonable and generous. You don't know me well enough, of course."

Sara listened to rain quickening on the roof of the car. She saw another letter pop in the electric sign. HAMB RGERS. The scent of clove oil assaulted her. The woman's cold papery fingers caressed her hand. The night was charged with turmoil, dislocations, inversions. An old woman with toothache and Russian-inflected English. A man who'd clapped a hand around her mouth and bundled her inside this car. Rain breaking the electric circuits of a sign, leaving meaningless words adrift on the darkness. Her father sitting alone, growing impatient, worried by this time. Her husband—

*This is all about Mark.* This situation in the parking lot was related to Mark. She realized he hadn't simply absconded with a single fabrication, he'd left chaos in his wake, fragments of a life he'd abandoned, and she was somehow supposed to deal with them. She slid her hand from the old woman's grasp.

"It's my husband, isn't it," she said.

"Your husband, my dear girl, has presented us with a mystery. If it were only that, it might be fun in a way. A game to play in the drawing room on a dreary afternoon. Unfortunately, the mystery has a serious aspect."

"How? Explain it to me."

"Explain? Surely you know."

"No, I don't know," Sara said.

The woman brought her face very close to Sara. There was an atmosphere of imposed intimacy; for a second Sara anticipated a terrible kiss being pressed upon her cheeks. The stench of cloves failed to conceal the persistent musks of old flesh and the fur of a dead animal.

"I mentioned my generosity," the woman said. "But it has its limits, Sara. There are boundaries. And dishonesty goes far beyond those boundaries."

"Dishonesty? What dishonesty?"

"We need to find your husband."

"And you think *I* know where he is?"

"Call it a working hypothesis."

"It's wrong," Sara said.

The old woman seized Sara's wrist. Her bony grip was unexpectedly strong. "I know when people are lying, Sara. It's one of my gifts."

"You think I'm lying?"

"I'm receiving mixed signals from you. No gift is absolutely infallible. But in the end, I always know. Always. With total clarity.'' She tightened her grip. ''Where is he, Sara?''

''I've told you, I don't know.''

''Try again.''

''You're hurting my wrist, goddammit.''

''You're fragile, Sara Klein. But I wonder if there is something else beneath that surface. Are you hard? Are you tough? Can you last the distance? Where is Mark?''

''Christ, let go of my wrist, I don't know where my husband is—''

''Think before you answer, Sara.''

''What is there to think about, for Christ's sake? I don't know where he is, I don't know how many times I have to tell you.''

''Think, Sara Klein. *Think.*'' The woman's sharp nails dug into Sara's flesh. Sara tried to pull herself away, but the old woman was tenacious. Sara looked into her face, the thick layers of makeup, the determined brightness of the eyes, the scarlet slash of the mouth. You couldn't win a contest with this woman, she thought. The eyes suggested a lifetime of doing battle and emerging victorious from all kinds of conflict.

''Please,'' Sara said.

The old woman sighed and relaxed her fingers. ''There. You are free. Abracadabra. Just like that.''

Sara drew her arm away. She could still feel the nails in her flesh. ''Are you through with me? Do I have your permission to go?''

The woman appeared to shrink inside the fur coat, as if she were drained and had suddenly lost all interest in Sara. ''I'm not through with you. But you can go, my dear girl. You can go.''

Sara stepped out of the car. The man in the beige raincoat was leaning against the Buick, arms folded. He looked at Sara, and said, ''This meeting never took place. I guess I don't have to tell you that, do I?''

Sara's attention was drawn to the sight of her father coming out of the restaurant, drawing his jacket up over his head against the rain. Something in this commonplace gesture touched her, saddened her.

The man nodded in the direction of John Stone, who was

calling out Sara's name. "I guess you already know silence is part of the game, don't you?"

"Yes, I know," Sara said.

"You tell nobody. I mean, nobody. Not your lawyer. Not the Feds. The cops. You understand that, don't you?"

"I understand."

"Pain isn't uppermost on our agenda," the man remarked. He got inside the Buick. The car moved off across the parking lot.

Sara walked toward her father. His jacket, pulled out of shape, created a hood over his scalp.

"Where the devil have you been?" he asked. "I've been worried."

The lie came quickly to her. "I wanted to get something from my car, that's all."

"Let's go back indoors," he said. "You shouldn't be out in this weather. What are you thinking of?"

He put his arm around her waist and together they hurried inside the restaurant. He took off his jacket and shook it. "Who was on the phone?"

The second lie came as quickly as the first. "Just a friend. I'd left the number of this place for her to call."

"And?"

"Nothing, Dad. Unimportant."

He scrutinized her face as if he'd detected falsehood. But he seemed to understand; there were areas in her life he was unable to approach.

"What's that smell?" he asked.

"Oil of cloves," she said.

"You have a toothache?"

"Yes," she answered. But it was another kind of pain, one cloves couldn't alleviate. It was heartache.

**7**

SHE drove her father home from the restaurant. She was silent all the way, dazed. She parked her car in his driveway, and he asked her if she wanted to spend the night. She was tempted. The idea of the empty house over the Sound was unappealing. But she declined because she felt she had to be in her own home, she had to be close to the telephone. Because Mark might call.

Her father was reluctant to get out of the car, as if he were unhappy about going inside his own big silent house.

"I could stay at your place tonight," he said. "I wouldn't mind that at all."

"I'll be okay, Dad."

"I could throw some things in an overnight bag, wouldn't take a minute."

"Really. I'm going to be okay. I'll go home, take a bath, go to bed." She held his hand. Her fingers encountered the wedding band he wore. His skin was smooth, like stone over which water has flowed for years and years. *Silence is part of the game*: the man's words echoed in her head. She understood. She couldn't talk to anyone about the strange, alarming encounter in the parking lot because of what might happen to her father if she did. The threat was vague. The best threats always were. *Fuck you, Mark*, she thought. *Whatever you've done has not only shattered the calm of my life, it's also endangered my father*. And the old man didn't know. And she couldn't bring herself to tell him.

She forced a small smile. "I'll call you first thing in the morning."

He patted her hand. "I'm always available for you, Sara. Day, night, it makes no difference. I'm here for you. I love you."

"And I love you," she said. *She was a kid again, and she was trying to learn the violin, and her father was explaining to her the relationship between music and mathematics, and she didn't understand and he was working patiently to tell her, little building blocks of language, simple phrases, but it was all too complicated because she didn't have that turn of mind.*

He opened the car door. "Drive carefully," he said.

"I always do."

She smiled and backed out of the driveway, watching him. He stood very still in the rain, the porch light feeble behind him. She knew he'd watch until she was gone out of sight, and even then he might linger, listening until the sound of the car faded away. Once, when she'd brought home a report card which carried the comment *Sara doesn't have a grasp of mathematical principles*, her father had looked at it and laughed and said, *Some things just don't run in the family, I guess.* A forgiving man, an undemanding man, gentle and patient. And now there was a shadow across his life, and he didn't know it existed.

She drove dark roads. She didn't want to think. She wanted the blessing of deep sleep. That merciful condition. She listened to the rain, the distant waters of the Sound raked by wind. She had an image of her father at the funeral of her mother. Dark-suited, pale with grief, dignified. She remembered the smell of earth, the long dark coffin going down into the grave, the bleak rage of her own tears, her inexpressible feelings. John Stone, who didn't believe in an afterlife, had taken her aside and said *I could talk to you about God and heaven, but I won't. Try to consider it this way, Sara. Your mother isn't suffering now. Be happy about that.*

Be happy. Yeah, sure.

She saw her house come in sight. She'd left all the lights on earlier, and the windows of the place burned against the darkness. She got out of the car, walked up on the porch, unlocked the front door, went inside. She slipped the bolt in place. The exhaustion she felt was a dead weight in her brain.

She looked at the closed door of Mark's office and experienced an overpowering resentment. You marry a man, you love him, you welcome his sperm inside your body, you carry his child—*and you don't know him*. You hear him on the telephone making deals, you pack his suitcase for his business trips, you give up great chunks of your life for him—*and you don't know him*. And yet you *still* hope you hear his step on the porch, the sound of his voice, the sight of his smile. You hope everything can be clarified and life go on the way it was before, and all this—this ungodly mess—is a monumental mistake.

She checked the answering machine. Nothing. She flicked the Off switch. On the back of her wrist she noticed small marks left by the old woman's fingernails. I have come a long way to see you, Sara. St. Petersburg. Formerly Leningrad. *Get in line,* she thought. *Whoever you are, take your place behind McClennan and the FBI. Behind me. We all want to find Mark Klein.*

She moved to the stairs, began to climb. Halfway up she stopped. The baby suddenly lurched inside her. She clutched her stomach. She had a sense of the baby twisting and dropping. And then it was still again. A girl, the old woman had said.

She continued to the top of the stairs, where she went inside the bathroom, turned on the faucets, listened to the roar of water surge into the tub. She sprinkled bath salts, watched them foam. The water changed to pale blue. She took off her clothes, dipped her hand in the tub, adjusted the flow until the temperature was right, then lowered herself carefully in. She sank up to her neck. The baby stirred again, gently this time. She thought, *If I concentrate on this child, if I think of nothing else, if I build my life around the anticipation of this kid, everything else will be inconsequential.* A load of ifs. She drifted toward sleep, imagined Mark sponging her back, thought she heard him ask, "How does that feel?"

She opened her eyes. *How could he leave me? He wouldn't just disappear.* What if he had? If she never saw him again? What if there was no trace of him for the rest of her life? Off the face of the earth, no explanation. Gone forever. She had a panicky feeling, a sharp sensation in her chest, an obstruction at the back of her throat as tangible as the bone of a chicken.

She reached for a towel and stood up, and soapy glistening water slid from her skin in a series of small popping bubbles.

She dried herself, took a terry robe from the closet and put it on. She strolled wearily inside the bedroom and lay on the bed, but sleep seemed an unreachable distance away. Her mind buzzed. When she shut her eyes she kept seeing the sign in the parking lot flicker. She kept feeling the old woman's hand on her stomach. *Small possessions.*

She sat up. Idly, she reached into the bedside drawer for a nail file.

The Walther lay there beside a packet of Kleenex and a bottle of antacid. She took out the gun and stared at it in surprise, remembering how she'd hunted for it earlier, the way she'd scoured the downstairs rooms. She must have brought it up here just after McClennan had first come to the house. In her stunned state, her mind focused on the warrant, she must have carried it upstairs absentmindedly and shoved it into the drawer, because that was where it was always kept. McClennan might have replaced it, of course—but she couldn't recollect him ever leaving the downstairs rooms. And even if he *had* carried it up, how would he have known to put it in the bedside drawer? Only two people knew the gun belonged in that drawer. Only two. And if *she* hadn't replaced the weapon, which she couldn't recall doing—

She got out of bed. She went quickly downstairs. She stood outside the door of Mark's office. An unlikely expectation made her heart beat a little harder. She'd open the door, he'd be standing beside the desk, puzzled by the missing computer—

The room was empty.

She turned, trying to still the disappointment she felt, even as she knew her hopes were irrational; she hurried toward the front door and stepped out on to the porch. Rain roared in the trees, the wind whined across the waters of the Sound. The night was in a rage all around her.

What in God's name was she doing out here? What stupid groundless desperation had driven her downstairs and out into the darkness? Had she really expected to find Mark inside his office, or see some sign of him outside? Had she really thought he'd come home, found the house empty, spotted the gun lying around, taken it upstairs and replaced it, and then decided to go for a stroll in this dismal rain—

*You're losing it*, she thought. *You're slipping badly.* Sliding down into the chaos of forlorn little hopes, seeing signs where none exist. She shut the door, fastened the bolt. The wind knocked against the house. Her hands trembled.

*Are you scared, Sara Klein?*

Yes.

**8**

SHE dreamed she was walking barefoot on white sands, where she came across the great delicate skeleton of an unidentifiable creature whose bone structure she looked at with wonder. She woke when she heard the phone ringing downstairs. In the shadowland between dreaming and waking she imagined that the sound of the telephone originated from the skeleton, as if it were somehow being galvanized into life. The word "pterodactyl" was in her mind.

She rose slowly. There was a muscular ache in her neck, and she rubbed it as she went down to answer the phone. Mark hadn't wanted a phone in the bedroom. *Who needs to be disturbed when they're asleep*? It had struck her as a reasonable point of view at the time, but now, as she descended sleepily toward the living room, she considered it an inconvenience.

George Borbokis was on the line. "Did I wake you?"

"It's all right," she said. "I had to wake sometime."

"I talked with McClennan. Can you make a noon appointment?"

"Where?"

"My office."

"What time is it now?"

"Nine-thirty."

"I'll make it."

"Sara, one thing. If he asks anything you don't want to answer, you're under no legal obligation as yet. You understand that? And don't let him make you nervous. Don't let anything he asks fluster you. Because he'll try that tack."

"I'll give it my best shot."

"Noon then."

Sara hung up. She wandered inside the kitchen, boiled water for tea, drank it slowly. The idea of being questioned by McClennan wasn't inviting, but it was best to get the interview over and done with. She looked through the window. The morning sky was blue and clear. Last night's rain glistened on shrubbery. *Last night*, she thought—and a concern for her father touched her and she picked up the phone, dialed his number. He answered on the second ring. She felt relief at the sound of his voice, more so than she'd expected.

"How are you this morning?" she asked.

"Funny you should ask," he said.

"Funny how?"

"I just had a visitor," he said.

"And?"

"Well, it was odd."

"What was odd about it?"

"The guy was selling plots of land."

"What's so strange about that?"

"These were burial plots."

"*Burial* plots?"

John Stone laughed. "I've never had anyone come to my door and try to sell me a grave before. Is it a new trend or what? Maybe we can look forward to people selling coffins door-to-door. They'll have all these catalogues filled with glossy pictures of caskets. I'm telling you, Sara, we're living in the Golden Age of Tack."

Sara experienced a sense of decline, a form of eclipse. "Who was he? Did he leave a business card?"

"No, he didn't. He introduced himself as Frederick something or other. But no card."

"What did he look like?"

"Oh. Handsome, I suppose, if you go in for soap-opera looks."

"Was he young?"

"Why are you so interested?"

"Just answer me, Dad."

"Middle twenties. You get to my age, it's hard to tell things like that. Why do you want to know?"

"I think the same man was going around this neighborhood. A few people were suspicious. Maybe they thought he was casing their homes.'' These lies she was obliged to feed her father: was there a place where they finally stopped?

Young. Handsome.

''I told him I already had a plot,'' John Stone said. ''He said advance planning for the business of dying was something more people should do. Sensible, he said. Advance planning for the business of dying—the phrase has a certain ring, don't you think? Investing in your own death, so to speak.''

Sara felt cold. She was remembering the young man on the train, the symmetry of his features, the perfection of his looks. Was this the man that had visited her father? Say it was. Imagine. What was the idea? A warning, a gear shifted upward in the machinery of menace? She'd assumed the young man was associated with McClennan, but now she wasn't certain. *Advance planning for the business of dying.*

She pictured her father alone in his big, morbid house, and she wondered if she should tell him about the encounter outside Jackson's, if she should say that he might be in danger. She owed him that much. She owed him the truth, as far as she understood it. But she couldn't predict how he'd behave if he knew. Outrage? Fear? She just couldn't say. Maybe he'd do something completely foolish. She didn't know. She didn't want to cause him undue alarm, but at the same time he had a right to know.

''Any news on your front?'' he was asking.

''The lawyer called. We're meeting the Feds.''

''Today?''

''Noon. I have to get going. I'll come see you when it's over.''

''I'll be waiting.''

She said good-bye and hung up. She'd deferred the decision for a few hours. But that was all she'd done. She felt as if she were juggling hoops greased with oil. She washed, dressed quickly, applied a small amount of makeup, brushed her hair, then drove to the station in Port Jefferson. She looked in her rearview mirror from time to time, but saw no evidence of anyone following her—although she couldn't be sure.

She parked, bought a round-trip ticket, waited on the platform. A few fellow travelers stood around, a couple of men engaged in conversation, a young girl in dark glasses, a woman clutching the hand of her infant daughter. So ordinary.

The platform, the sunshine, the people waiting. It was hard to connect this commonplace world with the situation into which she'd been plunged. Two different dimensions, two realities that had to intersect somewhere. Sunshine and banality. Rainy parking lots and dread.

She heard the drone of the train in the distance. When it slid to a halt, she boarded, found a seat in a car that was almost empty.

She thought about the young man again. Burial plots. She tried to convince herself that her father's visitor had been on legitimate business, but she'd never heard of burial plots being sold on a door-to-door basis. It was possible, sure. This was America, land of the drive-through funeral, anything was possible.

She closed her eyes, listened to the meter of the train, the click-clack of wheels. At each station she studied the boarding passengers, but saw no sign of the young man, nor of anyone else who might have been tracking her movements. When the train arrived at Penn Station, she was still wondering if she'd tell her father.

**9**

BORBOKIS was waiting in his office for her. Thomas Mc-Clennan was present, and so was the agent with the large mole on his cheek. When Sara came in, she said, "I'm late. Sorry."

Borbokis said, "A few minutes. No big deal, Sara. Take a seat."

She sat down in a chair close to the attorney, facing the two agents. The arrangement of chairs was strategically important. She was nearer to her lawyer than she was to the Feds—a comfort zone.

McClennan said, "This is Special Agent Ross, Sara. You mind me calling you Sara?"

Sara shook her head and glanced at Ross, who looked at her with a frown. He took a notebook and pen from his jacket. It was obviously his function to record. He sat to the right of McClennan and just slightly behind, a minor figure, a walk-on.

Borbokis said, "Sara, as you know, Agent McClennan has some questions for you. Answer them to the best of your ability. If you don't know the answers, fine. Say so."

It was almost like the instructions you got before a college exam, she thought.

McClennan removed a folder from his briefcase and opened it. "There are a couple of little background details I have to get out of the way. Mark has worked with Rosenthal Brothers for the last five years."

"Right."

"And you worked with the same company for six years."

"Is her work history relevant?" Borbokis asked. Like a

52

chess player probing for space in a cramped position, he leaned across his desk with a look of concentration. His unruly eyebrows bunched together. "The warrant, as I read it, limits your activities to documents and other materials at 3242 Midsummer."

"George, Sara's married to the man. She worked in the same firm. Consequently, she may have information relevant to a federal investigation. You know I can walk out of here and be back in less than an hour with an amended warrant. There are two ways to play this, George. Let's take the easier route, what do you say?"

Borbokis said, "I'm just as keen as you are to get this interview over with. I'm sure my client feels the same."

Sara had the sense she'd been forgotten during this brief exchange. The phrase "probable cause" that Borbokis had used yesterday popped into her head. It was baffling, mysterious, like a code that couldn't be broken. Why couldn't McClennan just be straightforward and *say* why the warrant had been issued in the first place? "Probable cause" was an impenetrable stone wall. It allowed the agent certain privileges, one of which was the freedom to ask questions of people ignorant of why they were being questioned in the first place.

She looked round the room, saw the impressive leather-bound volumes of law books. *I don't belong here. I shouldn't be in this place, this position.*

McClennan was staring at her. He appeared less sympathetic than the day before. There was a quality of hard determination in his eyes that had been absent yesterday. This was down-to-business McClennan. No more *when's the baby due* chitchat. "During the last two years, how many trips did your husband make abroad?"

Sara shrugged. "I don't know offhand."

"Six? Seven? A dozen? Fifty?"

"A dozen would be closer, I guess."

"Can you remember the countries he visited?"

"Well, the Far East, at least three times. Hong Kong. Shanghai. I also remember . . . Sydney, Auckland, and somewhere in the Caribbean. Aruba." She wondered if she was telling McClennan anything he didn't already know. He had an air of inscrutability about him.

"What about Europe, Sara?" he asked.

"He went to France once. I remember that."

"What about Russia?"

"I think I would have remembered if he'd gone to Russia."
Her mind drifted to the parking lot at Jackson's. The old
woman's clawlike fingernails. *St. Petersburg. Formerly Leningrad.* Mark had never mentioned a trip to Russia. Never.

McClennan asked, "Are you sure about Russia?"

"I'm sure."

"Yeah? The way you were sure about the hotel in Hong
Kong, Sara?"

Sara felt a hard little kernel of contempt for the agent. She
didn't like the way he'd thrown the hotel business in her face,
the casual swipe of malice. Resentful, she shifted in her chair.
She made no attempt to answer his question.

McClennan continued. "Did you ever accompany Mark on
these business trips?"

"No."

"Did he ever ask you to go along?"

"I was working," she said. "I couldn't get away."

"You weren't working during this last trip. You'd quit your
job."

"Pregant women don't usually feel like sitting on an airplane for twelve hours or whatever."

"Did he ask you to accompany him on this trip?"

"No. He knew I didn't want to go."

"But he was a dutiful husband and always phoned you
when he was abroad," McClennan said.

"Sure." She didn't like the sarcastic way he said "dutiful."

"You had to take his word when he told you where he was
calling from, right? You assumed he was always being truth-
ful. He might have been phoning from Yazoo City for all you
knew."

She looked at Borbokis. "Do I have to put up with that
kind of question?"

"No," Borbokis said. "You don't."

"So I can leave? I can just walk out of here?"

"I wouldn't advise it," the attorney said.

McClennan said, "It would look like you were avoiding
something, Sara. That's what your attorney means."

"I don't have anything to avoid," she said.

"Don't you, Sara?"

"No, I don't."

"What did Mark tell you about his trips?"

"Not much. A few things he'd seen, places . . ."

"Like what? Tourist attractions? Hong Kong harbor, things like that?"

She'd cut McClennan's abrasive manner with calm, she decided. She spoke in an unhurried way. "Mainly he described the insides of hotel rooms. He didn't have much time for touring."

"He never talked about the people he met. The people he did business with?"

"Not often."

"What about business? Did he discuss that?"

"He might have, I don't recall."

"*Might have* isn't helpful."

"I don't know what else to tell you."

"No? Try a little harder, Sara. You can do better."

She understood he wanted to hustle her out of her stride. She was determined to get through this with dignity. It was an effort. Her palms were damp. The baby kicked, and she thought *Please, not now, kid, not right now. Be very still.*

"He never mentioned business deals, Sara. You're positive about that?"

"I don't care for finance," she said. "Most of it is beyond me. So there wouldn't be much point in Mark discussing it with me, would there?"

"You really expect me to buy that? You worked for Rosenthal for six years, Sara. Six years. What did you do there? Brew coffee? Run errands?"

"I was Sol Rosenthal's personal assistant."

"What did that involve?"

"Arranging his schedules. His appointments. Business trips. Sol's life can get hectic, and he doesn't always manage it very well at his age."

"A secretarial position."

She shook her head. "No, it was much more than that."

"In six years, Sara, you must have picked up *some* knowledge of the financial world."

"Look, I wasn't involved in structuring deals, planning investments, advising clients, talking to investors. I didn't get into that side of things."

"You just held Sol Rosenthal's hand."

"I made his life run smoothly, that's what I did. I helped him function."

"Let's backtrack, Sara. Let's see if we can't ransack that reticent memory of yours. Mark never mentioned any names of the people he dealt with?"

"Again, he might have," she said.

"But you don't remember, of course."

"No, I don't. I told you already."

McClennan rose, put his hands on the sides of his hips and bent his body from one side to the other, the swaying motion of a man trying to work a crick out of his back. "What you're telling me is that the man you're married to came back from his overseas trips, and he didn't mention what he'd been doing, the people he'd seen, his work? He didn't share his world with you, that's what you're telling me."

"You make it sound like we never communicated," she answered. McClennan's question had a disturbing resonance. She concentrated on trying to remember what Mark might have told her, but her recollections were vague. The resentment she felt toward the federal agent shifted slightly in Mark's direction. *You landed me in this mess, Mark. You did this.* If he spoke about his overseas experiences, it was always in the form of inconsequential small talk, unmemorable statements. He'd always been glad to get home, as if the business trips had been voyages into the suburbs of purgatory he didn't want to discuss; and she'd accepted that.

She said, "I don't think I ever questioned him."

"Not even casually? Come on, Sara. He comes home from some exotic place, and you don't talk to him about what he's seen or done there? What kind of marriage is that?"

Borbokis interrupted quietly. "I don't think Sara's marriage lies within your sphere of interest."

McClennan ignored the attorney. He didn't take his eyes from Sara. "Married people talk, don't they? They share things, Sara. They don't have secrets from each other, do they?"

She looked at Borbokis, whose expression was hard to read. The atmosphere in the office was stifling. She understood that McClennan's aim was to grind her down. He was working away like some tenacious termite in the fragile woodwork of her marriage. At the same time, he was coming in from another, less direct flank; he was unwilling to accept her claim that Mark hadn't talked much about his business journeys because he thought she was lying to protect him. He was looking, she realized, for evidence of what Borbokis had called complicity, hunting for an indication that she was hiding something.

How had the attorney described McClennan's world? *A murky green pond.* She pictured stagnant water, tendrils of dead plants floating on a greasy surface.

McClennan said, "Are you admitting that Mark had secrets? Are you telling me that?"

"I didn't tell you anything of the sort," she said. The problem with dignity, she thought, was how quickly it decomposed. *Secrets.* Yes, Mark clearly had secrets. Otherwise, she wouldn't be here now. She wouldn't be under assault from an agent of the FBI. She wouldn't have been sitting in a car in a darkened parking lot last night with a strange old woman who said she was from St. Petersburg. Her father wouldn't be threatened.

McClennan said, "I'm not seeing how this hangs together, Sara. Guy goes away, comes home, says nothing much about his experiences, but at the same time he doesn't have secrets. Which is it? You can't have it both ways."

Sara felt a small hammer rise and fall inside her head. "You're twisting my words around. I told you. I didn't really question him. I was always glad to see him when he came back, and he was always happy to be back—"

"But you lacked curiosity, right? Welcome home, Mark. Let's not talk about what you did when you were away. I'm not that interested?"

She felt defensive, menaced. "You keep talking about secrets. Why don't you tell me what yours is, McClennan? Why don't you come out and say what it is Mark's supposed to have done? What's *your* secret?"

"I'm the one asking the questions, Sara."

"Maybe you should be answering a few," she replied.

McClennan said, "It doesn't work that way."

Her mouth was very dry. She said, "I can't tell you any more about my husband. I don't *know* any more. You could

ask me questions until the cows come home, and I still
couldn't answer them."

McClennan sat down. He undid the buttons of his grey
jacket. He was quiet for a while, pressing the tips of his fingers
against the sides of his head. "Maybe he has a mistress," he
said. "You know. Some slim young bimbo on the side. Somebody who isn't pregnant."

Borbokis said, "You're way out of line, Tom."

Sara asked, "A *mistress*? Mark?"

"Why not?" McClennan asked. "These foreign junkets.
His *alleged* lack of communication. Sounds like a guy with
something to hide. So why not a mistress? It happens. Foreign
soil. He's not going to run into anybody he knows."

"That's sleazy. You're not going to get to me that way,"
she complained. A mistress. It was something she'd never considered before. She dismissed the notion out of hand. She
wasn't going to allow McClennan to plant that kind of poi-
soned seed in her head. "I know what you're trying to do,
but I won't let you, McClennan. No way."

McClennan smiled in a strained way. "What am I trying to
do, Sara?"

"Undermine me. Rattle my cage."

"Is that what you think?"

"It's pretty damn obvious."

McClennan leaned forward in his chair, elbows on his
knees. "I'll ask you again, Sara. Do you remember any
names?"

She tried. She felt the peculiar little panic of memory failure. Maybe if she had time, if she wasn't being pressured, she
could sit down and think hard and come up with answers.
Right now, her memory was as empty as a vacated seashell.
She listened to the sound made by Ross's pen on the pages of
his notebook.

McClennan opened his folder and said, "Okay. Let me give
you a refresher course." He read from a sheet inside the
folder. "Last June. June 19 to be precise. Nineteen hundred
hours US Eastern Time. Your husband called you from Sydney, Australia. He said: *I've just come from a meeting with
this guy called Pearson. Three hours in an office and the air-
conditioning unit is broken and I'm dying.* You replied: *Poor
honey, I wish you were back home.* You want me to go on,

Sara? It gets a little intimate at this point. A little hot and heavy, if you know what I mean.''

Last June she thought. As long ago as last June telephone conversations were being recorded. Privacies, intimacies preserved on tapes. She wondered how many Feds had listened to the tapes and whether they'd found a source of crude amusement in the personal exchanges between husband and wife. "You don't need to go on," she said.

"Pearson," McClennan remarked. "You don't remember that name?"

"Why should I? Mark just mentioned it in passing, I guess. I don't even remember that particular conversation. Then again, I don't have the benefit of a tape recorder, do I?"

"I could go through other conversations, Sara. I could quote you other instances when Mark mentioned somebody's name to you. Somebody called Lee in Macao. A guy named Devlin in Auckland. But you wouldn't remember them either, would you?"

She couldn't even say that the names rang faint bells for her. Pearson. Lee. Devlin. None of them had registered strongly enough to lodge in her mind. "Okay, I confess," she said. "I have a bad memory. Or maybe I just edit out stuff that isn't important."

"And maybe you're a bold faced liar, Sara."

"I don't have to listen to this," she said. She heard a shrill little note she didn't like in her own voice.

McClennan said, "Don't get so defensive, Sara. I'm a reasonable guy, I'd understand if you were lying. Mark's your husband, after all. Your partner. The father of your baby. I'd understand if you wanted to protect him."

"You're all compassion, McClennan."

"I have a few virtues," he said.

"I'm sure you do. Being open just isn't one of them. Why don't you say if you're accusing me of something? Because if you are, I wish to God you'd just spit it out."

"Was I accusing you?"

"You just said I was a liar."

"*Maybe*. That's what I said."

"It's not *what* you say, McClennan, it's the way you *say* it. You make me feel like I'm hiding something from you. That I'm a criminal."

"Are you?"

"Jesus," she said. She looked at Borbokis for support, but he was making a note on his legal pad. "As far as I can follow this, nobody's specified any crime that's been committed. You come to my house with a warrant, you haul stuff away, you tap my telephone, your people follow me around, you sit there and insult me, you question my integrity. And you're asking me if *I'm* a *criminal*?"

"And you're not answering."

She leaned back in her chair. She said, "I don't have to answer. It's a stupid question. And you know it."

"You're evading the issue," he said.

"I don't even know what the issue is, McClennan."

"It's simple. I'll say it again. *What do you know about Mark Klein's business affairs*?"

"How can I impress on you I don't know anything?"

"I don't believe that, Sara."

"I don't care. Believe, don't believe."

"Sara, you're not helping yourself. You play a little ball with me, things might start looking up for you. You've got a bad attitude, which isn't going to get you very far."

"I came here today in the hope some things might be clarified," she said. "Instead, all I get are accusations and insults. So my attitude shouldn't come as any great surprise to you, McClennan."

She looked directly at him. Was it only yesterday she'd been asleep in her bed when they came with the warrant, only yesterday when her life had begun to unravel? She felt a fierce animosity toward McClennan; it had all the intensity of a migraine. He was the enemy. An agent of the US government, and her enemy. She thought about the old woman inside the Buick, the man in the beige coat. Also enemies.

She wondered what would happen if she told McClennan about the woman from St. Petersburg. Listen, McClennan, she'd say. You're not the only one looking for my husband. You have competition, she'd say. She remembered her father coming out of the restaurant into the rain, the way his jacket was pulled up over his head for protection. She remembered the odd poignancy of the sight. And she also remembered her instructions: *You tell nobody. I mean, nobody. Not your lawyer. Not the Feds. The cops. You understand that, don't you*?

She heard what sounded like a metronome ticking inside her head. If she mentioned the meeting in the parking lot, how could the woman from St. Petersburg and her charming companion find out anyway? Unless Borbokis or McClennan or Ross passed the information along . . . a notion that left her adrift in complications and puzzles, connections she couldn't make. She had the feeling of being tilted to one side, off-center.

McClennan said, "Here's how I see it, Sara. You know more than you're saying. Which means you're impeding an investigation—"

"You are so full of shit," she said.

Borbokis said, "Tom, are you going to charge my client with something? I'm hearing a lot of innuendo and nothing substantial."

McClennan paid no attention to the attorney. He went on in the manner of a man accustomed to riding across complaints and protestations. He was the one with all the real authority here; he could say what he liked, and he didn't have to listen to other voices. He was secure behind search warrants and probable cause and an FBI badge. "We're not getting anywhere this way, Sara. I suggest you go home and take a little quality time to yourself and reevaluate what you've told me. And then ask yourself: do I need the hassle of going through all this? Do I need the hassle of a trial?"

"Trial?" She hadn't even considered this possibility. It was too remote. She thought of a courtroom, lawyers, a judge, the whole legal circus of a trial.

McClennan said, "And then ask yourself this: Do I want to run the risk of having my baby born behind bars? A jail-baby, Sara. The stigma. Think about that."

A baby behind bars. If McClennan was blowing smoke in her direction, it was strong stuff. If he was bluffing, he'd hit an exposed nerve. She looked at him and thought, *I haven't done anything wrong, I can't let him force me into feeling I have*.

Borbokis stirred to life suddenly and capped his fountain pen. "I think that's more than enough, Tom. I'm going to instruct my client she doesn't need to answer any further questions. She's come here in the spirit of cooperation, and I think she's been as cooperative as you can expect."

"Instruct all you like," McClennan said.

The attorney had risen and was hovering over her. "You're looking pale, Sara. Can I get you something?"

Pale, she thought. Pale with animosity, with anger she'd tried to contain. Any decorum she'd sought to impose on herself had evaporated. A trial. A baby born in prison. Concepts she couldn't entirely grasp. McClennan had conjured them out of thin air, a bit of sleight of hand. She wanted to say something, but words wouldn't shape themselves. McClennan was stuffing his folder back inside his briefcase.

"She's pregnant, Tom. I think that's something you might keep in mind," Borbokis remarked.

"Her condition is about the only thing beyond any doubt in all this business," McClennan said.

Sara stared at the agent in a reproachful way.

He said to her, "I'm only doing my job, Sara."

"Yeah? I'd like to see your job description sometime."

"It's quite simple. I look for the truth," he said.

"Do you ever find it?"

"Oh, I find it all right. The trouble is, sometimes it comes in bits and pieces, and you have to glue them together before you see the big picture." He moved toward the door, where he stopped and looked around at Sara. "One small thing. You mentioned something about being followed around. You actually saw somebody follow you?"

"More than that, McClennan. He spoke to me."

McClennan smiled. "Your paranoia's showing, Sara. One, you wouldn't notice any of my people following you. Believe me. And two, they wouldn't speak to you. Not in a hundred years." He opened the door. "Thanks for your time. We'll talk again."

Sara watched the door close behind the two agents. She should have felt relief, but she didn't. She was thinking of the young man on the train. She was wondering about his affiliation. Disconnected notions tumbled through her head. McClennan. The young man. The woman from St. Petersburg. The disappearance of Mark. Flecks of glass in a kaleidoscope, falling without form.

Borbokis said, "Well, I told you the kind of approach he'd take."

"A jail-baby. That's a spooky phrase, George."

"It was meant to alarm you, Sara. I wouldn't put too much stock in it."

"You know what this whole thing feels like? One of those crazy dreams you have, and you know you're dreaming, except you just can't force yourself awake. It's like that. Things are going on, and they don't make sense, and you're just caught up in the insane flow of it all. And when you *do* wake, you're sweating. Your heart's pounding. You open your eyes and it takes you a minute to remember where you are."

Borbokis said, "If you have nothing to hide, Sara, then nothing's going to harm you."

"You believe that, George? You really believe there's some kind of natural balance, and everything comes out right in the long run?"

"That's how it usually works. Not always. But usually."

"What happens next, George? No, don't tell me. We wait. We still wait."

"That's about the size of it."

Borbokis touched her shoulder in what seemed to her a mechanical gesture of sympathy and went back to his chair. "If he contacts you again, let me know. And if I hear from him, I'll be in touch. Sooner or later, he's got to throw something specific at us. Something I can get my teeth into."

She rose a little unsteadily and went out into the corridor. She walked toward the elevators. McClennan's questions reverberated inside her head. She felt raw, as if she'd just had her scalp hauled back from her skull.

She pressed the button, waited for the elevator to arrive. She knew where she was going when she left this building. Where she had to go.

**10**

THE panhandler on the street was Korean, Vietnamese. Sara wasn't sure. He came forward to block her path along the sidewalk, his palm held out. She normally gave to beggars, but her present mood wasn't charitable. She tried to sidestep the man, but he moved directly in front of her.

She said, "Hey, do you mind?"

He raised his palm up in the direction of her face. His hands were grubby, nails broken and chipped. He wore an old camouflage jacket. His complexion was the color of a newspaper left for years in a hard tropical sun. It was difficult to tell his age. Thirty, thirty-five. She made an attempt to go around him.

"A dulla, lady. Playse, lady. Just one dulla."

"Leave me alone," she said.

"You having a baby. Very nice," he said.

"I'm in a hurry, for God's sake," she said.

"Baby a boy. Grow up strong and healthy like father, huh? Father strong man?"

She looked into the panhandler's face. His eyes were fixed on her with all the hopeful persistence of the beggar. A boy. Strong and healthy like his father. *Father strong man*? She fumbled in the pocket of her coat and produced a bunch of loose change, which she shoved into the man's hand. He closed his fingers around the coins. He shook them in his fist and listened to them rattle.

"Father good man," he said. "Baby be good also."

"Yeah, yeah," she said, and made another effort to slip around him.

"You wait. Present for baby. Here," and he rummaged inside the pockets of his tattered jacket.

"Listen, I don't want anything from you, nothing."

"Favor gets a favor, lady," he said. "Here. Must take."

"I don't *want* anything."

"No, no, must take. Must read. Words of comfort."

It was a crumpled wad of paper. Something out of a fortune cookie, she thought. Some platitude or other. A weirdo religious tract. She'd be polite, if only because she wanted to be rid of the man.

"Okay, I'll take." She shoved the paper inside her coat pocket, next to her car keys.

"Very good. You good mother. Must have happy husband, huh?"

"Happy husband, right," she said.

"Grateful for cash," he said. "Good fortune."

"Have a nice day," and she moved past him, reaching Wall Street. Panhandlers and high finance, contrasts in the system, imbalances. See capitalism at work. Its conquerors and its victims.

She walked purposefully. Even when she reached the entrance to the building she didn't break her stride, didn't yield to doubts and misgivings. She was going to do what she had to do. There was no other way. You couldn't live like this very long. This anger, frustration, all the knots tied tight inside her. They had to be loosened somehow.

She stepped inside the building and headed for the elevators as she'd done thousands of times in the past. She rode to the third floor, and when the doors slid open she stepped out and walked directly past the reception area and the sign that said Rosenthal Brothers. She moved over the familiar grey carpet along the corridor until she came to double glass doors, which she pushed open forcefully. She entered a huge room where secretaries and assorted financial hotshots had their desks and computers, everything arranged in open-plan mode, here and there half partitions for senior personnel. Telephones were ringing, fax machines oozed messages, printers cranked out spreadsheets and data. She kept going, looking straight ahead, conscious now of people staring at her in surprised recognition, aware of whispers, her name being uttered. It didn't matter. She just kept going.

"Sara, what are you doing here?"

Sara glanced at the person who'd asked the question. Linda Brand, in her usual black Donna Karan dress offset at the collar by some kind of brassy brooch, stepped in front of her. Sara brushed past her.

"Sara, wait, you shouldn't be here."

"Call security and have me thrown out," Sara said.

"Sara, be reasonable, what do you think you're doing?"

"Going to see Sol."

"Sol?"

"You heard me."

Jennifer Gryce appeared now. Gryce, hair sculpted into her skull, was too gaunt for her own good.

"Sara, for Christ's sake, this is inappropriate."

"Your aura's grey, Jen. Anybody ever tell you that? You're not eating the right food. Maybe you need a man in your life. You're definitely deprived of something, old pal."

Jennifer Gryce caught her by the wrist.

Sara shook herself free. "Don't touch me, Jen. Pregnant or not, I'm perfectly capable of decking you."

"You're out of your mind, Sara."

"Sure I am. I'm a lunatic." She kept going. She felt good, mad, gathering a deranged momentum as she moved in the direction of Sol's private office. She was aware of Jennifer Gryce and Linda Brand flapping around her, and even when they were joined by other gawking staff members, she just kept going. She had propulsion now. She had a fire burning nicely. She was feeling better than she'd felt at any time during the last thirty-six hours. This was a positive move. This was what you'd call breaking out of your shell with a vengeance.

Tony Vandervelt came out of Sol's office. He looked at her with surprise. "Sara . . ."

"Get out of my way, Tony."

"You can't see Sol, if that's your intention," he said.

"It's my intention all right," she said.

"You can't just go barging in, Sara. Be reasonable." He was trying the gentle approach, taking her arm, stroking the back of her hand.

"I've tried reasonable, and it doesn't work, Tony. So if

you'll kindly let go of my arm, I can get on with my business.''

"No, wait, Sara. It's a bad time. You can't go in there."

"I'm going in. Whether you like it or not."

"This is idiotic. Sol can't talk to you."

"The fuck he can't," she said. She freed herself from Vandervelt, but he came at her again, cupping a hand around her wrist.

"I've had enough of people pawing me, Tony. I warn you."

"You don't look so good," he said quietly.

"I know, I'm more than six months pregnant and I'm pale as a goddam sheet. But don't let appearances deceive you."

"Why don't you and I go off somewhere quiet and have a cup of coffee and talk this thing through?"

"Out of my way, Tony."

Vandervelt looked flustered. He turned to Jen Gryce. "Call a security guard."

Linda Brand said, "I've done that already."

"*I've done that already,*" Sara mimicked Linda Brand's nasal voice, which had always irritated her. "I bet you have. Conscientious bitch."

"He should be here in a moment," Linda Brand said. "He'll deal with *her.*"

Sara said, "Tony, take your hands off me. I'm not going to ask you again."

"Sara," Vandervelt said, "we're all trying very hard to be patient with you."

"I warned you, Tony." She brought her hand up and swiped him directly over the eye. She felt a fingernail puncture his eyelid, drawing blood. She derived wondrous satisfaction from the way he moaned and stepped back from her. A narcotic joy, a high. It was the only act of violence she'd ever committed in her life.

"Jesus, Sara, what the hell was that for?" He touched his eyelid and looked at the blood on his fingers.

She moved quickly, pushed open the door to Sol's office. Inside, she turned the key in the lock just as Sol was raising his face to look at her. His shaven head caught sun from the window at his back. He had a dead cigar in his right hand. The air in the room was foggy from recent smoke. She knew this room. She was flooded with a sense of familiarity that should have been some kind of comfort to her. But it wasn't.

"You're locking us in?" Sol said. "I'm a hostage suddenly?"

"We need to talk without being disturbed, Sol."

"Sit, take the weight off your feet," he said. He relit his cigar with a big lighter designed to look like a golf ball.

"Thanks." She sat down in front of his desk. She looked at the photographs that covered the dark green walls. Sol loved being snapped in the company of showbiz celebrities. He attended high-dollar charity luncheons and dinners, dressed in an old tuxedo he superstitiously refused to replace. She looked at his image—there he was, smiling and bow-tied, in the presence of Bob Hope. Paul Anka. Joan Rivers. He had the same big smile in each of the pictures. One particular photograph drew her attention. It depicted Sol dressed as Santa Claus at an office party five years ago; Mark was visible in the background, his features indistinct. Shadowy. How appropriate, she thought.

She turned her attention back to Sol. "They tried to keep me out," she said.

"So how did you get past them?"

"I scratched Vandervelt's eye."

Sol smiled. "You gotta watch him. He's litigious. He's probably on the phone to his lawyer asking about damages already."

"I wish I'd scratched both eyes," she said.

"Blind employees I don't need, Sara. I got sorrows enough."

"Yeah, we all have those," she said.

He stood slightly hunched. Seventy years of age, seventy-one; he kept his birth date a secret. He had an imposing forehead and pink cheeks; at times she thought he resembled a bald, redundant cherub. His blue double-breasted suit had smudges of ash on the lapels. An untidy man, crumpled, careless with his cigars, mindless of clocks and schedules, but when it came to business he was sharp and exacting. He had an uncanny capacity for making and remembering deals. He could recall in precise detail business transactions made twenty, thirty years ago.

He puffed on his cigar. "You shouldn't have come here,

Sara. I love seeing you, don't get me wrong, but you shouldn't have come here.''

"Listen, Sol. Nobody's telling me anything. The FBI came to the house with a warrant, they took just about everything from Mark's office. I've just been questioned by them. They act like they suspect me of something. Tell me, Sol. Just tell me what's going on.''

"Sara, I got these lawyers, I told you already. I had the Feds here also.''

"Was one of them called McClennan?''

"McClennan, guy with white hair cut like he's at some WASP prep school? Yeah, he was here.''

"He's threatening me,'' she said. "He's talking about a trial. He even mentioned jail. Jail, Sol.''

Rosenthal sighed and shook his head and peered at the lit end of his cigar. "He's jerking your chain. He's full of crap.''

"But he's got a way of making it sound good. And maybe he's got a way of making it stick. I don't know . . .''

Sol Rosenthal dismissed her words. "You got nothing to worry about, Sara.''

She was quiet a moment. "What has Mark done?''

"Sara, please. I ain't supposed to discuss this stuff.''

"Come on, Sol, it's obvious everybody that works here knows something I don't know. Something I have a right to know.''

There was a knock on the door and Tony Vandervelt's voice could be heard. "Sol? Sol, are you okay?''

"I'm okay. Don't worry about me,'' Sol called back.

"She just shoved her way in, Sol.''

"I said I was okay! Chrissakes!''

He came around the desk and took Sara's hand and held it for a while, looking serious. "People think I'm in the money business, Sara. That's half the picture only. I'm also in the people business. I got clients to please, and that involves trust, a lotta trust, and trust's a funny thing. It takes years to build up and maybe five minutes to wreck.''

"And Mark's wrecked you, is that it?''

Sol crushed out his cigar, and said, "Between you and me. There's been damage, Sara.''

"He's screwed the company. He's embezzled funds. Tell me the truth, Sol.''

"We're coming up short."

"How much?"

"A lot, Sara."

"How much?"

"Last count, thirty-two point six million and change, kid. Probably more. A whole lot more. There are guys doing audits. They're like fucking forensics characters going over bodies, slicing veins."

She said, "Thirty-two . . . ?"

"It ain't exactly pocket money."

"Why Mark? What evidence is there against him?"

He took his hand from hers. He patted the pockets of his suit, found a fresh cigar in a silver tube. He stuck the cigar between his lips, but didn't light it at once. "This I'm not at liberty to discuss, Sara."

"The door's locked. Nobody's going to come in. Nobody can hear us."

Sol Rosenthal looked thoughtful for a moment. "Okay. So how much do you want to know? How long have you got, kid? We're talking tricky business. Complexities."

"Make it simple for me."

"It ain't simple, Sara. I'm telling you. Can of goddam worms, is what. Dummy companies, a whole slew of them. Jersey. Isle of Man. Monaco. Liechtenstein. Funds channeled from under my nose into these phony corporations. Cash wired here, then wired there, and from there to someplace else, and God knows where after that. Computer records falsified. Statements doctored like you wouldn't believe. The whole thing. Right under my goddam nose." In his agitation, he'd broken his cigar in half. He dropped it in an ashtray, and said, "I hate the waste of a good cigar."

She thought: *Thirty-two million.* Probably more at the end of the day. The thought went round and round inside her head until it became meaningless.

*Thirtytwomillion.*

"Are you sure—"

"Sure it was Mark? Is that what you were gonna ask? Sara, honey, we're talking about *his* clients. We're talking about people who invested their cash on *his* say-so. They listened to his advice, they acted on it, they wrote checks, then they sat back and thought what a smart guy they got looking after their money. Why not? They're getting tax breaks plus the promise of a good return on their investments, and Mark's got this halo round his head. Smart boy. Charming. Inspires confidence. Can't do no wrong. Guy sitting on his nice boat down in the Keys with a fishing fucking rod in his hand and he's going *my money's safe, it's multiplying nicely.* And what he don't know is, it's gone. Puff. Up in smoke.''

He was talking rapidly. Saliva gathered like tiny balls of cotton at the corners of his mouth. ''This news breaks, it's cardiac arrest for a lotta guys. Drop-dead time. It's also pay dirt for the lawyers, kid. They hear this, and they ain't gonna be coming outta the woodwork with lawsuits? Don't tell me. Me and my brother, God rest his soul, we started this business in nineteen hundred and forty-seven. I can't even go down to his grave no more, this shit going on.''

She sat perfectly still. She seemed to be standing somewhere outside of herself, a distant observer. ''How long has Mark been . . .'' She couldn't locate the word she wanted. *Embezzling* was a tough one. *Swindling* was just as hard to get out.

''That matters?''

''No, I guess not.''

''What matters is he cracked the system like it was a hen's egg. Then he turns into Houdini and leaves us this omelette we can't digest.''

''I'm sorry, Sol. I'm so sorry.''

''For him, you're apologizing?''

''No. Yes. I don't know what I'm trying to say.''

''Say nothing. Go home. Think about your baby. That's all you should have on your mind.''

Tony Vandervelt was knocking on the door again. ''Sol. The security guy's here, and he needs to know you're okay.''

Sol said, ''Tell him to go away.''

''You sure about that?'' Vandervelt asked.

''The natives are restless, Sara,'' Sol said quietly. ''You better go. Otherwise, they'll break down the goddam door. And I got wreckage enough.''

Sara got up from her chair. She reached out and touched Sol Rosenthal's shoulder. She said, ''I hope this turns out to be something else.''

"What? Like Mark's gonna show up and prove his innocence?"

"Something like that."

"Innocence is hard to prove when you left your fingerprints all over the place, honey. Just go home. Think about the baby. And don't take this the wrong way, okay—but don't come back here again. I can't have you poking my people in the eye. Know something? If I was you, I'd think real hard about getting away, taking a trip of some kind, treat yourself to a break, a nice resort someplace, Catskills this time of the year ain't bad. Trees changing color. Pretty. Maybe too cold for you, though."

She pondered this a moment. It was appealing, sure, but she couldn't do it.

"Thanks," she said.

"For what? I should be thanked for telling you your husband's a thief?"

"For being straight with me." She walked to the door.

Sol Rosenthal said, "I'll call you sometime."

"Please," she said.

She turned the key and opened the door. An armed guard in a pale blue shirt swept past her into the room, followed by an anxious Vandervelt. She heard Rosenthal say, "Since when did people start coming in here without knocking? What the fuck's happened to courtesy?"

She walked past the desks and the computers in the direction of the elevators, ignoring the workers who scrutinized her, conscious of them only as a blurred white sea of faces. Inside the elevator she thought: *Your husband's a thief. He stole other people's money.* She thought of his victims, the people who'd invested money, people he'd hurt. She wondered about them, Sol's hypothetical guy on his fishing boat in Florida, others; she conjured up retired physicians, schoolteachers, professors like her own father, people who had put their life savings in Mark's hands. She felt sorry for them. Why hadn't she noticed any peculiarities in his behavior? Why had she never once suspected Mark of anything like this? Blind and trusting, she supposed. Like the people who'd given him money. It was more than blind trust on her part; she loved him.

Face it. She loved him even now. Love didn't just perish overnight.

She reached the street, walked out into the sunshine. The car slid quietly alongside her, the back door opened, a voice she recognized said, "Get in, Sara. We'll go for a drive."

**11**

SHE sat in the back of the Buick with the old woman, who wore a floral dress with a pattern of huge red-and-green flowers. The combination of colors pulsated when Sara looked at it. The man in the beige coat was driving. The smell of cloves lingered in the car. Sara rolled her window down a few inches.

"You look very nice today, Sara Klein. Pregnancy agrees with some women. They bloom. You have such a glow."

Sara looked at the woman's thick makeup. By daylight, it failed to conceal the cracked condition of her skin. Her lips were glossy scarlet, as if she'd just sucked on something heavy with blood.

"I have never had a child myself. In my lifetime I have had many lovers, of course. But I can't remember one with whom I wanted to have a baby. Most men are worthless, do you not agree?"

Sara said, "Some are."

The old woman said, "I think back, and perhaps I regret the fact I have no child. And then I remind myself of the painful business of labor, and I'm glad I didn't go through it. All that effort of pushing a new life from between your thighs. And then this screaming pink thing emerges, making demands, needing to be fed, crying at inconvenient hours."

"I want this baby."

"Of course you do. Some of us are cut out to be mothers. Others not. You are different from me."

The woman did something unsettling; she slowly lowered her face and laid it against Sara's stomach. Sara looked down at the thin dyed-yellow hair, the way it was flattened back in oily strands. This connection of the woman's face to her body was distasteful, sickening.

"What the hell are you doing?"

"Listening for a heartbeat, Sara."

"I don't like this," she said. She wanted to shove the head away from her lap. But she didn't want to touch that yellow hair. That grease.

"Why? Does it upset you?"

"Yes, it does."

"You are easily upset, Sara."

"I also get upset when somebody calls at my father's house and talks about selling him a burial plot. I want him to be left alone, left in peace, do you understand that? He hasn't done anything. He doesn't need any grief."

"None of us needs grief, do we?"

"Leave him alone, that's all I'm asking. Just leave my father out of the whole equation." She inched away from the woman, who raised her face and smiled.

"Total silence. The product of Mark Klein's seed is as silent as Mark Klein himself."

"I haven't heard from Mark. That's what you want to know, right?"

"Ah, Sara. There are so many things I want to know."

Sara felt the ghost of the old woman's face pressed against her stomach. She looked out of the window. The Buick was heading up Amsterdam. The sun flashed intermittently in the cross streets.

Sara said, "I don't know where he is. I keep hoping he'll get in touch with me."

"Hopes are butterflies, Sara. They settle for a short second, then they fly away."

"I can live without the aphorisms," Sara said.

"Can you live without your husband?"

Sara looked at the street, the pedestrians, kids playing basketball. *To live without your husband.* Thirty-two million dollars and counting. She wondered if he'd placed a monetary value on his wife and unborn child, if he'd decided that thirty-two million was worth more than his tiny family unit. She tried to imagine him somewhere in the world—sitting on a sandy beach overlooking an isolated lagoon, or wandering the crowded streets of some grubby city in South America. He'd wear dark glasses and a hat and he'd grow a beard: wasn't that what men did when they wanted to disappear? He'd have a fake passport, maybe more than one.

How long? she wondered. How long had he planned his vanishing? It hadn't been a quick overnight decision, no spur-of-the-moment thing, that much was certain. Months of planning, maybe more. She didn't know. What lay behind it—something as elemental as greed? Why couldn't she remember if he'd shown signs of anything as basic as avarice? What she recalled was how contented he'd always seemed. Ambitious, keen to forge ahead through hard work and long hours, sure. Loving, too, and attentive to her. But now there was another side to him, a dark aspect, an unknown Klein. She pictured his face—irregular good looks, thick black hair he wore brushed back, an electrifyingly honest smile in which all the worries of the world dissolved—and somehow she couldn't relate this image to what Mark Klein was supposed to have done.

The old woman asked, "Do you love him?"

"He's my husband."

"Do you love him?"

She hesitated a beat. "Yes."

"How touching. He disappears from your life, and you still love him. He abandons you, and yet love persists. There is a certain romantic melancholy in all of this that appeals to me."

"I'm happy for you."

"Happiness is not a durable state." The old woman sighed and spoke to the driver. "Play some music. Jazz. I'm in the mood for something quiet. Brubeck."

The driver found a tape, inserted it into the deck. The car was filled with the mellow sound of Brubeck's piano.

"So, Sara, the mystery remains. Where is Klein."

"What has he done to you?" Sara asked.

"Don't you know? You lived with the man. You slept with him. You made this baby together. But you don't know?"

Sara remembered McClennan's interrogation; it was being echoed now in the back of this Buick. She said, "He stole money from you, didn't he?"

The old woman said nothing, just smiled oddly. She tapped her hands on her knees in time to the music.

Sara asked, "Why don't you talk to Mark's firm? Better still, go to the Feds. Why pester me?"

The old woman said, "It's not so simple as that."

"Why? It's the logical thing to do."

"This has nothing to do with logic, Sara."

"You think I'm involved in his scam, don't you? I'm hanging around for the right moment to join him in some remote spot and share the spoils—is that how you see it?" She thought: *McClennan thinks along these same misleading lines.*

"It's a possibility."

"You're way off."

"You're hiding something from me, Sara. I was hoping that by giving you some time to think about your situation, you would be prepared to tell me the truth. But obviously you are not ready to be agreeable. You're stubborn or foolish or both. So. Now I must take other steps."

"What other steps?"

The old woman tapped the shoulder of the man in the beige coat, and said, "Charlie. Drop her here."

"You got it," Charlie said. He turned into a side street and stopped the car. He got out, walked round the car, opened the door for Sara. She looked into his face, the lazy eyelid, the intricate pattern of broken veins on his nose.

"An unpleasant neighborhood," the old woman said. "But you'll find a cab, I'm sure."

Sara stepped out of the Buick. "What other steps?" she asked. "Tell me what you mean."

The woman smiled and turned her face aside. Charlie settled in his seat, slammed the door. The Buick pulled away from the curb. Alone, Sara realized she had no idea where she was, a strange quarter of the city, Hispanic store signs, men sitting on crumbling stoops, arrhythmic Latin American music issuing from a decrepit coffee shop nearby.

She walked a little way. She was conscious of how she was stared at, assessed by sullen faces. This wasn't her New York. This was some distant fringe of the city she'd never visited. She'd been insulated by circumstance from neighborhoods like this. Ignorant of those areas of the city reputed to be dangerous, she'd never visited this part of New York, and now she felt as if she'd passed into another dimension. Gutted build-

ings, windows boarded, graffiti sprayed in mysterious acro-
nyms on walls. She'd been dumped here.

She kept walking. The baby shifted in her womb. This
screaming pink thing. A quick little stab of pain. She had to
stop. She was aware of a cluster of teenagers staring at her
from the next corner. They were passing a crack pipe back
and forth avidly. They appeared to lose interest in her. She
was a stray, no part of their world, no danger to them.

Around her on the sidewalk were scattered crates of rotted
fruit and vegetables—oranges, pawpaws, gourds. Flies buzzed
in clusters. Brought here and abandoned. She needed to sit
down somewhere. She also needed to get to a telephone, call
her father, because she was afraid for him. *Other steps*. What
did other steps mean?

A telephone. Where? She skirted the crates, passed the teenagers. A kid with tattoos of acne on his face said to her, "Oo,
mama," and stuck his belly out to mimic her pregnancy, and
his friends laughed and took up the refrain. *Oo, mama. Oo,
mama*.

She kept going. She stopped outside a store selling fruits
and vegetables. Women fingered the merchandise, grapefruits,
cantaloupes, mangoes. The signs were in Spanish. She looked
for a friendly face; at least one that might be receptive, somebody who might point her to a phone, a kindness. She approached the fruit stalls timidly. Where was that strength, that
uplifting surge of resolve that had enabled her to strut through
the Rosenthal offices and scratch Vandervelt's eye? Where had
that gone?

"You need something, lady? I got some nice passion fruit
just come in. Real tasty."

She saw a hand proffer her a passion fruit. She looked into
the man's face. He wore a bright red bandanna around his
head. Young, Hispanic, a T-shirt with a faded logo that said
*Este Mundo*.

"I need a phone," she said. Her throat was dry.

"A phone? You ain't gonna find no phone round here."

"Do you have one inside?"

"You sick, something?"

She placed her palm to her forehead. "I just need to get to
a telephone."

"Your baby troublesome, something?"

"The baby, yes."

"You come inside. Come in here." A small compassion for which she was grateful. He guided her past the stalls and into the dim interior of the shop. Small, cramped, stacked with crates of produce. She had the impression of hundreds of bunches of bananas hanging all around her, like motionless and unfamiliar tropical creatures. She wondered if she could sit, if she could just settle a moment on one of the crates. The young man was discussing something with an older man, maybe his father. They spoke rapidly in Spanish. She understood that the older man, paunchy and indifferent, was registering some kind of objection. Eventually, he turned away, slapping the air with an upraised hand in a gesture of dismissal.

"Okay, lady," the young man said. "Don't worry about him. He was born suspicious. This a local call?"

"Long Island," she said. "I'll call collect."

"Collect, yeah. Okay. Through here."

He led her inside a boxlike office. The phone was on a desk littered with invoices. Papers were stuck on a spike. She picked up the receiver and asked to make a call to Long Island. Other steps, she thought. Burial plots.

She heard a man's voice say he'd accept the call. It wasn't her father. A wrong number, obviously—but that didn't make sense. Why would anyone accept a collect call from a stranger?

"Who is this?" she asked.

"Who are you trying to reach?" the man asked.

"John Stone."

"Your father can't come to the phone right now, Sara."

"Who are you? Put my father on the goddam line."

The telephone connection was severed.

The young man was watching her from the doorway. "Trouble?"

She gazed past him into the store. She couldn't think of an answer. Her lungs were constricted.

"You wanna sit a while, lady? Rest?"

"A cab. Where can I find a cab?"

"Your best shot, corner next block."

She shook her head, brushed past the young man, stumbled out into the street, pushed her way through the throng of women gathered round the fruit, hurried along the block. You want to go back in time, she thought. You want to turn the clocks back to the time when Mark Klein last stepped out of the house at 3242 Midsummer, to the very moment when—suitcase in one hand, briefcase in the other—he'd climbed inside the taxi that was to take him to the airport. Back to the split second when he smiled and waved and the taxi started forward. Back and back.

And you want to stop it right there, a freeze-frame.

You want to say: *Don't go*.

**12**

THE cab that took her to Penn Station, the train out to Long Island, the drive to her father's house—these experiences were distilled in a series of smudged brushstrokes: a child holding a blue balloon on a railroad bridge, cramped houses overlooking the tracks, a caged cockatoo framed in a window. She went through a turmoil of feelings: impatience, agitation, anger. Whatever force channeled and organized emotions seemed spent inside her. The swindler's wife. The embezzler's wife. This was what Mark Klein had turned her into: somebody she didn't know.

In Port Jefferson, she drove to her father's house, rushed up to the porch, opened the screen door. She went inside, called out. No answer. She stood at the foot of the stairs and listened to her own voice disappear into the gloom of the place.

She moved toward the living room, hesitated on the threshold. "Dad?"

Nothing. The house absorbed light and sound. A dead space.

She went back across the hallway, reached the kitchen. There was an empty cup on the table, a slice of brown bread, a jar of blackcurrant jelly over which a wasp crawled. The door to the backyard was open. She walked outside. The yard was big and overgrown, a fusion of fall colors.

"Dad?"

She went in the direction of the greenhouse at the end of the yard. Illuminated by the fading sun, it resembled lit crystal. Something stirred between the long grass stalks that rose as high as her knees. Her father's cat. Simon, black and silken, rubbed against her legs, then lost interest and drifted away.

"*Dad?*"

The greenhouse was empty. Large overripe tomatoes pressed against the panes. She turned, gazed at the sun-struck rear windows of the house. She had a bad moment. She imagined her father had vanished into the same alternative reality as Mark Klein. Husband and father, both gone into the same blackness.

She went back indoors, still calling out.

He appeared at the top of the stairs. She heard the sound of his feet, a sigh. She rushed up toward him. He said, "I was napping," and she clasped her arms around him, held him a little too tight in the enthusiasm of relief.

"Hey hey," he said. "I love you, but you're making it tough for an old guy to breathe."

She relaxed her hold on him. Her face was pressed to his chest. She was comforted by the familiar smells of her father—the scent of aftershave, the breath that always reminded her somehow of root beer. "You're okay," she said. "You're okay."

"What did you expect?"

"I just don't know."

"You're trembling, Sara. Your heart's sprinting. I can feel it. You need to sit down. I'll make some tea."

"No, I don't want to sit down," she said. "I just want to hold on to you."

"What's behind this sudden fit of affection?" he asked. He stroked the side of her face.

"I was worried."

"Worried? About me? I would think you—"

"Have you been home all day?"

"I went to the grocery store a few hours ago, came back, felt tired, napped, then I heard your voice."

"I phoned this afternoon," she said. She had to tell him; she couldn't keep it to herself any longer. "A man answered. Said you couldn't come to the phone."

"A man? When was this?"

"Between three and four. Later. I'm not sure."

"You're saying somebody came inside the house in my absence and picked up the phone and talked to you." He seemed confused. He rubbed his eyes sleepily.

She nodded. "The back door was open. Did you know that?"

"I didn't know," he said.

"We should check, see if anything's missing."

"Better idea to call the police," he said.

She hesitated. "I don't think we should do that, Dad."

He put his hand under her chin, turned her face up so he could see her eyes. He looked at her a long time. She knew this expression of his, this careful scrutiny. "I've had the uneasy feeling you're keeping something back from me. If you don't want to talk about it, that's your business. But if you want to talk, I'll be happy to listen. More than happy. What's it going to be, Sara?"

She sat on the top step and looked down the flight of stairs to the front door. John Stone sat beside her and put an arm around her shoulder. He asked, "Is it grim, Sara?"

"Yeah, it's grim."

"Talk to me," he said.

She couldn't face him; she felt herself shift the blame for this whole situation from Mark to herself. If she hadn't fallen in love, if she hadn't married Mark, none of this would ever have happened. She'd listened to the promptings of her own heart too quickly. Four years ago she should have approached things with more caution. But she'd been careless and selfish, and now her father was paying. It wasn't Klein's fault alone. She shared in it. There's *complicity* for you, McClennan. The only complicity.

"Talk to me, Sara," he said again.

She took a deep breath, spoke quietly. She told him about the interview with the FBI, the old woman from St. Petersburg, the funds embezzled from Rosenthal Brothers. She left nothing out of her narrative. He listened in silence. Now and then he'd tug on his upper lip, catching it between thumb and forefinger in a characteristic gesture of contemplation. When she'd finished, he didn't say anything immediately. She watched him blink in the dim light at the top of the stairs, the slow closing of his eyelids.

He said, "The Feds want Mark, and this woman from St. Petersburg wants Mark. And they all think you're involved."

"There's this one little difference between the two," she said. "So far, the Feds haven't threatened *you*."

He said, "It's still a hell of a situation, Sara. It isn't the kind of thing an old math professor anticipates in his so-called twilight years, is it?"

"No, it isn't."

"I'm wondering how I'm supposed to respond to the idea that certain people I've never met are making threatening noises about me. It's not a field where I have any experience. There were a couple of students down the years who wanted to punch out my lights because I failed them, but that's hardly comparable." He smiled quietly. "What about you, Sara? How are you holding up?"

"I'm maintaining," she replied.

"Do you believe Mark's a crook?"

She shrugged. "I have phases, Dad. One minute I believe. The next . . . Christ, who knows?"

"Thirty-two million dollars. Is that enough to dump your wife and kid for?"

"Maybe."

"If he's enough of a shit. Is he?"

"I don't know anymore."

"I bet you don't." He leaned down and placed his hand on her head, ruffling her short hair, as if she were still a kid, somebody he needed to look after. "You've been keeping all this to yourself, poor thing."

Poor thing, she thought. Was that going to be the attitude of people when Mark Klein's crime made the newspapers? They'd go around behind her back, whispering *poor thing*. But there would be others who'd whisper with more malice. *She's involved, how could she not be? She didn't know what her husband was doing? She'd have to be pretty dumb*.

She caught her father's wrist. "Forget me for a moment, Dad. Put me to one side. The question is—what do we do? This crone from Russia is using your safety as a bargaining chip to get what she wants. And I don't have what she wants. And she isn't going to believe I don't have it. Which isn't good for you."

"The young guy with the burial-plot routine. He's one of her people?"

"She didn't deny it."

"And the guy who was here when you phoned—he's another?"

"I assume so. Maybe one and the same guy."

"So what was he supposed to achieve by coming to my house, Sara?"

"It could be he expected to find you here. Maybe he was going to get rough."

"Then he'll come back."

"And then what?"

"I used to box middleweight at college."

"I don't think that counts."

"Still got the old gloves up in the attic somewhere." He raised his clenched fists, shuffled his feet, ducked his head down. An old man playacting. He was trying, she knew, to make light of it. He was trying to infuse the situation with normality. This was everyday business. Threats, hell, they were as common as junk mail. He was doing this for her benefit.

"Seriously," she said.

"Why don't we go to the cops? I could explain, and they'd provide their friendly neighborhood protection, and I'd be safe under their vigilance."

"No cops," she said. "They were emphatic about that. No cops. No Feds."

"It would take me a few minutes to call the local gendarmerie, Sara. I could have a uniformed officer round here in a matter of thirty minutes or so. If he was hurrying, that is. How would your Russian woman and her friends find out about that? Unless they've got my phone tapped. Maybe that's what my visitor was doing this afternoon . . . planting a bug on my phone."

There was something inherently wrong with his suggestion that they go the police, only she couldn't quite put her finger on it. On the surface it sounded reasonable enough. But she wasn't convinced. "I don't think we should involve the cops, Dad."

He asked, "Why not? We don't even need to use the phone, Sara. We could drive to the station. It's only a mile or so. Are we going to be prevented if we try to leave the house? Are we under observation at this very moment?"

She moved, grabbed the banister, stood up. She felt heavy. Her father had started to go down the stairs. She followed him into the living room, where he walked to the window and looked out across the front yard. She admired his attitude; the purpose in his stride, the facade of levity. There was an inner strength to the man. There always had been.

"I don't see anybody except Rigby sweeping leaves across the way. Dear old Rigby, deaf as timber. He'd hardly be a candidate for a spy. I don't see anyone else, Sara. Well? Do we go to the cops?"

"Wait. Just think."

"Think about what?"

"What they might do if they find out you've gone to the police. Think, Dad."

"I'm beginning to entertain a general dislike of being threatened," he said. "I consider it a violation of the very few Constitutional rights I have left to me. *Thou shalt not be threatened*. It's one of the unwritten commandments. A man ought to feel safe in his own damn home. He ought to be able to walk the streets of his neighborhood without having to worry his head about people making threats."

"Ought," she said. "I don't think we're discussing moral imperatives, Dad. These people wouldn't have much interest in your opinions."

"I let them run my life, Sara, is that it? I cower silently in my mausoleum and do nothing? I fail to take a stand? You forget. I come from three generations of New England stock, and we're a stubborn iron-headed bunch of bastards when we're pushed."

She wanted to feel he was right. But there was something missing from his argument. Something he hadn't considered. She still wasn't sure what. Maybe her own fears limited the possibilities of taking action. Maybe her dread colored everything.

She stared from the window, watching the neighbor across the street sweep fallen leaves into brittle mounds. She wondered about the Feds, whether McClennan had somebody posted in the vicinity. The thought occurred to her that perhaps McClennan's surveillance wasn't the omnipresent business she'd imagined it to be. Perhaps they didn't watch her all the time. Perhaps the prospect of observation was enough to prevent her from attempting to run. She didn't know.

"Are you ready?" he asked.

"I'm not sure. What would you tell the cops anyway?"

"Your whole story. Start to finish."

"You assume they'll believe it, of course."

"Why wouldn't they?"

"I don't have any proof of these threats, do I? I don't even know the name of this Russian woman. I don't have any evidence of her existence. She might be a figment of an overwrought imagination. Without proof, it's just a sad story. Look at me. I'm pregnant, my husband's embezzled a fortune and vanished; therefore, my emotional state isn't altogether stable. They might view it like that, Dad."

"On the other hand, they might not. It's worth a try. Your car's in the driveway, Sara. There's nobody watching the house as far as I can see. There won't be a better time."

*It's too easy*, she thought. That was what had been bothering her. *It's all too simple.* They were going to be allowed to walk out of the house and get inside her car and drive down to the local police station?

She didn't think so.

She stopped by the telephone. Bugs, listening devices. How would you go about looking for such things? You unscrewed the cap of the mouthpiece and the device just fell out into your hand, right? That's how it happened on cop shows. She had a feeling the reality would be very different. On TV, the bugs were always instantly evident, little plastic limpets stuck to the base of a lamp, something like that—but she didn't know what kind of high-tech advances might have been made lately; the world of electronic surveillance was sophisticated. She was out of her depth. She wouldn't know what she was supposed to be looking for.

"Well?" her father asked.

"Okay. We'll do it your way, Dad. We'll try. But even if the cops believe my story, they'll probably contact the Feds anyway, and the whole thing will go all the way back to McClennan, and I don't know if *he's* going to believe me."

"Never create problems before they happen," her father said. "It's a waste of time."

He clasped his hand round her elbow and smiled. They walked in the direction of the front door.

They didn't get that far.

"I'd think twice in your shoes," the young man said.

**13**

HE must have come in from the backyard. He stood in the kitchen doorway. His smile was glacial, his eyes were dead. He reminded Sara of a beautiful young man embalmed.

"Don't tell me," John Stone said. "You've got another burial plot I might be interested in? Some halcyon little strip of land with a river view?"

The young man, dressed in an expensive single-breasted suit, shrugged. "Not this time, Mr. Stone. Pardon the joke, that was a dead-end career."

"The joke's pardoned," John Stone said. "You're trespassing."

"Guilty as charged. I was eavesdropping in the kitchen. Bad manners, I know. But you were saying something about running to the cops, right? Don't let me stop you."

Sara felt the atmosphere around her change. Before, it had been fraught with uncertainty and some fragile little hope that maybe, just maybe, the cops would provide protection, an escape route. Now it was charged with particles of potential violence. She wasn't breathing well. Shallow.

"Cops," the young man said. "They don't have eyes in the back of their heads. Also, they're never around when you really need them. You ever notice that? Same with the Feds. The bottom line is, they can't be everywhere at one time."

"I take your point," John Stone remarked.

Sara wondered how her father could sound so calm. He might have been discussing a mathematical theorem, something abstract that had no relationship to life and how it was lived.

"You think I'm gonna smash things around, don't you?" the man asked. "You think I'm gonna bust your head, something like that?"

"It crossed my mind, I admit."

The young man laughed. He had a pleasant laugh, light and musical. "Funny what people sometimes think."

"You're telling us we can just step out the door and go about our business, I suppose," John Stone said.

"Free country. Come, go. As you please. I don't see no time clocks you got to punch."

"Then we'll go," John Stone said.

Sara thought: *No, too easy.* She felt her father propel her toward the door. She had a sense of disaster. They'd go out through the screen door and something would happen to them, something vicious.

The young man said, "Before you go, I got a question for you, Mr. Stone."

John Stone said, "I'm listening."

"You want to be a grandfather, don't you?"

"I have every intention—"

"Yes or no, Mr. Stone. Just like in a courtroom. Yes or no."

"Of course I want to be a grandfather."

"Terrific." The young man looked at Sara. "This baby . . ." he said.

She waited for the rest of it. She was tense and light-headed. *This baby*, she thought. She felt as if she were hanging in midair.

"You intend having it in a hospital?"

"Yes," she said. He was getting at—what? She couldn't think.

The young man stroked his chin, and said, "Hospitals worry me, Sara. You know what I mean."

"No, I don't know what you mean," she said.

"You hear horror stories. Kids get mixed up with other kids. They get the wrong tags on them, end up in the wrong homes, wrong parents. Worse than that even . . . You hear now and again about kids that just don't make the cut. Something wrong with their breathing. Their heart, maybe. What do they call it? Crib death? Is that the term?"

"Crib death," she said. She couldn't get these words to form a picture in her head.

"Yeah. I mean, it's never anyone's fault. You know what hospitals are like. They can get chaotic. Nurses make mistakes. They're too busy, too many things going on, they sometimes take their eye off the ball."

John Stone stepped toward the young man. "Are you . . . Are you actually *threatening* this child in some way?"

"I'm just pointing out some of the deficiencies in the hospital system, Mr. Stone. That's all. Fact. Babies die. Fact. Sometimes some psycho walks in right off the street and just steals a kid straight out of the nursery. That's the kinda stuff that sometimes happens in hospitals. That's why they worry me."

"Jesus, you're a cheapshit piece of work," John Stone said.

"I been called worse, Mr. Stone."

Sara closed her eyes. She heard the voices of the two men as if they were poorly tuned radio stations. This unborn child. Crib death. Somebody walks in off the street and just steals a kid. Her mind was flying like a kite in a gale. She heard her father say *I've never heard of anything so goddam monstrous in my life.*

She opened her eyes. She'd been upright before, but now she was sitting down. She couldn't remember moving to a chair, the passage of her body through space.

John Stone was standing close to the young man, hands clenched.

The young man said, "You gonna hit me, Mr. Stone?"

John Stone didn't speak. His expression was one of anger and frustration. He held his head in an attitude of belligerence, jaw thrust forward in a way Sara had never seen before.

"I could," he said. "I could—"

"You could what, Mr. Stone?"

Sara's father raised one hand to strike. He tried to bring his fist down in the direction of the young man's face, but he was slow and old and the young man simply smothered the fist in the palm of his hand and caught it.

"You could what, Mr. Stone? Don't make me hurt you."

The young man twisted John Stone's hand back at the wrist. Sara's father, his whole life changed utterly in the last fifteen minutes, struggled a moment against the other man's strength, then he sagged to his knees.

The young man released the fist and smiled. "You're out of your league, Pops."

Sara moved to her father, bending over him, stroking his shoulders as if to console him for his failure. "Dad," she said.

The young man stepped back toward the kitchen. "Don't bother to see me out, Sara. I know the way."

Sara didn't look at him. She heard him move through the kitchen, the sound of the back door closing. She smoothed the few strands that remained of her father's hair, and he raised his face to look at her.

"Some hero," he said quietly.

"I don't need a hero, Dad." She was overwhelmed by love and pity. She took his hand and looked at it. The bones felt brittle, fragile. His skin was freckled by the rust-colored spots of time. "Did he hurt you?"

"It's more than physical, Sara," he answered.

"I know," she said.

John Stone got to his feet slowly. He drew his fingertips across his eyes. "Age is a curse," he said. "One time, I . . ."

"It's okay, Dad."

"No, it isn't okay. It's a long way from okay."

She saw it in his expression: despair, humiliation at his inability to protect not only his daughter, but also his grandchild—the baby that just then lunged inside her, stretching perhaps an arm, a leg, as if it were trying to defend itself against a danger it couldn't see, but could sense.

John Stone rubbed his wrist, flexed his fingers. "Godammit, Sara, it's one thing to threaten me, but it's something else when . . ." He didn't complete the sentence. He walked round in slow, pointless circles. He resembled a creature caged and restless.

He said, "It's monstrous, monstrous, I don't have a word for it. What kind of people are they, for fuck's sake?"

She realized she'd never heard him swear in his entire life until now. He walked to the mantelpiece and surveyed the collection of family photographs, as if he were trying to resurrect better times, seeking reassurance that his life had once been measured by ordinary matters—getting up in the morning, going to classes, grading papers. The tenured professor, a quiet man leading a respectable life. There had never been disturbances in his world, except for the death of his wife and a period of grief. *Thank you, Klein*, Sara thought. *Thank you again. Thank you for all of this.*

He said, ''Your mother was sick and in pain for more years than I can remember. And I never heard her complain. Not *once* did she ever say she was suffering, Sara.''

''I remember.''

''Smiled through the whole damn sickness,'' he said. ''Laughed. Even when her hair was falling out, she'd make jokes about the wigs she had to wear. Thatches, she called them. What thatch should I put on my head today, John, she'd ask. You fancy blond or brunette. Where did she get that courage from, Sara?''

''She just had it, Dad. She was gutsy.''

''She was that all right.''

''So are you,'' she said.

''I'm not a patch on your mother.''

She said, ''But you are, Dad. You are.''

''I don't have her reserves of bravery,'' he said. ''What do we do, Sara? What the hell do we do?''

''You could go away,'' she said.

''Run?''

''I didn't mean *run*—''

''I don't run, Sara.''

''You could go to Florida, or California, anywhere, and you could stay away until all this is over.''

''Over? When is that likely to be?''

''If you went somewhere they couldn't find you, that's all I'm saying. Somewhere you'd be safe.''

''Do you honestly expect me to walk out on you?''

''I'm thinking about your safety, Dad.''

''My safety? What about *yours*? What about the baby?''

''Look, you're in a situation you're not responsible for. You didn't ask for this shit to happen—''

''Did you?''

''Dad, I'm the one married to Klein. Not you.''

''You're also my daughter, for God's sake. You heard the man, Sara. He's not just threatening *me* . . . it's not just *my* head he's holding a gun to. How could you even imagine I'd walk away? It wouldn't enter my mind. I'm a stubborn old fart, and I'm your father, and you're stuck with me. I don't want to discuss it anymore. It's unproductive.''

She had to sit down. The baby was working up a small fury of movement, turning, pushing, stretching. This child was an essential part of herself, as important to her life as her own heart, even more important. She was tethered to this child through her own blood and oxygen. She existed so that the baby could exist. It was as simple as that. She placed her hands on her stomach. She'd never felt quite this force of motion before. She took a few deep breaths, tried hard to relax. She wouldn't let anyone harm this child. No matter what, this child would come through unscathed.

She gazed at her father's troubled look and her thoughts drifted to Klein and she tried to bring his face to mind, but it was strange how his features had suddenly disintegrated. In the back of the old woman's Buick she'd envisaged him perfectly, but now she had to reconstruct him from memories that were already beginning to blur. He was a sketch in her head. It was as if he'd been missing for years, the casualty of a foreign war, dead and rotted beyond recognition in a rice paddy, a swamp. She got out of the chair and laid her head against her father's shoulder.

''If I knew where to find Mark,'' she said quietly.

''What would you do?''

''I'd tell them. That's what I'd do.''

''You'd trade him off. You're sure of that?''

*I'm not sure of anything*, she thought. ''I'd smile and I'd say, here he is, here's the man you want, now get out of my life and get out of my father's life. Leave us alone.''

''If you knew where he was. But you don't.''

''I just wonder if there's something he left behind. Some little clue. Some kind of hint. Something he overlooked. Some small thing he forgot. I don't know what.''

''Where would you even begin to look?''

She considered this question. She thought of Mark's suits hanging in a closet, the drawers that contained his shirts, underwear, socks. The things he'd left behind. She was touched by a little stab of unexpected sadness at the idea of his abandoned possessions.

''Come with me,'' she said.

''Where are we going?''

"My house."

"You think you might find—"

"I don't honestly know if I'm thinking anything, Dad. I'm just reacting. I can't sit round and wait for things to happen. I have to do something."

The prospect of escaping from the gloomy entrapment of his house seemed to energize him. "Okay. Let's go."

She took her car keys from the pocket of her raincoat. A piece of paper caught up in the key chain dropped to the floor. She remembered the panhandler on the street, the wadded sheet he'd insisted on giving her. She bent, very slowly, and picked it up. She opened it and saw in smudged, cheap print the capitalized words *NOTHING CAN SERIOUSLY UPSET YOU OR MAKE YOU AFRAID, IF GOD IS TRULY YOUR REFUGE.*

Great, she thought. Wonderful. Here, read these words and take succor from them. God, be truly my refuge. Please. She started to screw the paper up when she noticed that something else had been written on the sheet with a pale lead pencil.

**14**

**SHE** drove through the streets of Port Jefferson as the sun was beginning to slide out of the sky. Her father was in the passenger seat, examining the piece of paper. "What exactly did this panhandler say to you?"

"Something about the baby. How my husband must be a happy man. I can't remember his exact words."

John Stone read the message aloud. " 'Nothing can seriously upset you or make you afraid, if God is truly your refuge.' Comforting little thought, if you like that kind of thing." He smoothed the paper between his fingers. "*Call 213-456-8453*. I don't see it's anything to get thrilled about, Sara. Okay, so there's a phone number scribbled in the margin, but what does that mean?"

"Probably nothing at all," she said. "But why was he so damned insistent I take the paper when it must have been obvious to him I didn't want it? He practically forced it on me."

"You think he wanted you to have this number?"

"It's a possibility, that's all."

"He was a beggar on the street, somebody you never saw before."

"I know, I know . . ."

"But you think he might have had some hidden agenda for giving you the number?"

Hidden agenda. Sara stopped the car at a traffic light. She glanced in the rearview mirror. Immediately behind her was a big refrigerated truck. The cab was too high for her to see the driver's face. This was the condition of her life now. Looking

95

over her shoulder, scanning sidewalks, watching faces, wondering: perfectly innocent people filled her with doubt. Nothing was the way it seemed to be. Nothing was the way it had been before. It was a world of skewed reflections, mirages, people with hidden agendas.

John Stone said, "Okay. Assume he meant you to have the phone number. He meant you to call it. Why? Given the sentiment of the words, I'd say it's probably the number of some kind of religious group. You call them up, and they ask for a donation. They use beggars as conduits for getting their phone number into circulation."

"Dad. The number's been scribbled in pencil, like an afterthought. If it came from a religious group, they'd put the name of their organization on the paper."

"Maybe not. It's written in pencil to provoke your interest. And so you phone the number because you're intrigued and a nice lady asks you for money."

This didn't convince her. Sometimes her father had an irritatingly practical approach to life, a mathematician's attitude; he didn't seem to realize that certain areas of experience were so ill defined they couldn't be clarified by an accumulation of commonsense statements.

"There's one way to find out," she said. She ran a hand through her hair.

The light changed. The refrigerated truck behind her made a right turn, replaced in the rearview mirror by a pale green sedan. She observed this car for a time. She couldn't see the faces of the people in the front seat. The hood of the car gleamed in the dying sun.

Up ahead on the right was a bar. She turned the car into the parking lot. The green sedan didn't follow her.

*This is nonsense*, she thought. A man comes up to you on the street and forces you to take a slip of paper and because there's a telephone number written on it, you leap to the notion that it's intended for you personally, it means something, it becomes a rage in your head, you have to call the number, it's important. She didn't move out of the car. She gazed at the doorway to the bar. A Schlitz beer sign was lit in the window. She took the paper from her father's hand and thought, *My state of mind is askew*. She was poised between tearing the paper up and going into the bar to make the call.

A delicate balance this; a fragile little hinge barely holding things together.

"Wait here. I'll only be a minute," she said.

"I'm coming with you," he said.

"You don't have to."

"Maybe I don't have to, but I want to."

She kissed him on his forehead. He held her hand a moment. Then they stepped out of the car, crossed the parking lot. She had an unfocused feeling of being watched. Two men, laughing at something, lounged near the door of the bar. She moved past them, went inside. Her father followed. The room was dark and long, the far side in deep shadow. The woman behind the bar looked at her.

Sara asked, "Do you have a pay phone?"

"Back there, honey," the woman said. She stared at Sara's belly.

A drunk man on a barstool, the only customer in the place, remarked, "It's out of order."

The woman said, "It's been fixed, Billy."

"Yeah, so how come it always eats my quarters?"

The woman, a gaunt redhead of about sixty, smiled at Sara. "Pay no attention to him. He ain't made a phone call since Eisenhower was in the White House. He don't know anybody with a phone anyhow."

The drunk said, "That phone's on the fritz, I tell you. Everything's fucked round here."

"Wash your mouth out," the woman said, and turned to Sara. "Just go back there, honey. Outside the toilets. Can't miss it."

Sara thanked the woman.

John Stone said, "I'll wait right here," and he moved toward a table at the side of the room. He wasn't going to let her out of his sight.

She made her way past a silent jukebox and into the shadows. She heard the drunk say, "I got a whole buncha friends with phones, Bernice."

"And I'm the sex goddess of your dreams," Bernice said.

Sara kept moving until she came to a sign that said REST ROOMS FOR CUSTOMERS ONLY. Outside the door of the men's room she found the phone. A smell of disinfectant hung in the air. There was barely any light, just a low-wattage bulb over-

head. She looked at the number. The 213 prefix was California, the Los Angeles area. She fed a bunch of coins into the
slot without counting them—nine or ten quarters. Then she
pressed the digits. *Nothing can seriously upset you or make
you afraid*: but why was God always in hiding when you really
needed him? The ringing stopped, a man answered.

"Hello."

"Who am I calling?" she asked.

"This is the Cresta Vista Motor Lodge, LA, and I'm Eric.
How can I help?" The voice was that of a well-trained polite
desk clerk.

"Let me explain," she said. "Your number was on my
telephone statement and I didn't recognize it when I saw it."

"So you want to know if somebody might have made an
unauthorized call on your phone."

"Right. I know I never called this number," she said.

"Phone company's mistake. Happens all the time."

She didn't want to hang up. She was holding a thin, slippery
thread. "Eric," she said.

"Yes?"

She wasn't sure what she wanted to say, how to keep him
on the line; she wasn't sure why she even thought it important.
*A panhandler gives you a phone number in LA—why*? It turns
out to be a hotel. Why would a beggar have the number of a
hotel in Los Angeles?

"This is a weird question, Eric. But do you have some kind
of religious outfit working out of your hotel? Some kind of
charity?"

"Charity? Uh-huh. What's this got to do with your phone
bill?"

"I'm not sure." She'd run out of questions. She'd come to
a dead end. But still she was reluctant to cut the connection.
*Call 213-456-8453*. That word *call*: what was it—a reminder
that meant something only to the person who'd written it? Or
an instruction intended for her and her alone? Her thoughts
scattered away from her like small frightened fish in a tank.

"One last thing." She hesitated. "Has anyone left a message for me?"

"What's your name?"

She told him. She heard the phone being placed down on a

hard surface, imagined Eric shuffling through a drawer of envelopes. He came back on the line.

"Mrs. Klein," he said. "Mrs. Mark Klein."

"Yes," she said.

"There's an envelope."

An envelope. She experienced an odd weakness, a subsidence. "Would you open it, please?"

"Will do," he said.

She heard the sound of the envelope being opened.

"Tell me what it says."

"One word. *Wait.* That's all. No signature."

"Do you remember who gave you the envelope?"

"We get hundreds of people coming through here all the time. Bunches of them leave messages."

"And you don't remember getting this one?"

"No, I don't. Sorry."

A pulse beat at the side of her head. "Have you had a guest called Mark Klein recently?"

"I'd have to check the computer."

"Can you do that? Please?"

"Sure."

There was the sound of a keyboard being tapped.

A message. One word. No signature. She blinked at the overhead lightbulb. Dead moths adhered to the opaque glass.

Eric said, "No. There's no record of anyone by that name. Sorry."

She wasn't sure what she felt. Disappointment, puzzlement, an amalgam of the two. But if Mark had stayed in the hotel, would he have used his own name anyway? Fugitives didn't. They used fake names.

"Thanks for your help." She put the receiver back in place. She didn't move from the telephone, almost as if she expected Eric to call her back and say he'd found Mark Klein on the computer after all.

*Wait.* What did that mean? Somebody leaves a one-word message for her in an LA hotel, somebody makes sure a panhandler gets the phone number to her—an elaborate business, an intricate charade. She still didn't move from the telephone. She laid her head against the wall. She wondered about going to Wall Street to look for the Asian and question him, but the chances of finding him were slim. He wouldn't be there; he'd been used as a courier and his job was over.

Used by whom?

*Wait.* Wait for what?

Who else but Mark would leave her a message?

Wait. *Be patient.* Was that what he was telling her?

Maybe the message wasn't from Mark. Somebody else. A source unknown. But that didn't add up. Just this one tantalizing word: "wait." *Wait for you to come back, Klein? Wait for you to return with some nice cool explanation for the shit you've put me through? Is that what you mean?* She was angry even as she still entertained some misbegotten hope. Hope for what? That he'd return? Come back into her life with reasonable excuses and explanations? They'd have to be good, goddam good.

She wandered back toward the bar.

The drunk twisted round on his stool. "Phone working?"

"Yes," she said.

"See, what did I tell you," said the woman behind the bar, and she reached out to shove the drunk's elbow in a gesture of friendly admonition.

Sara looked at the table where her father had been sitting. There was no sign of him. His absence jolted her. She glanced round the room. He'd gone. She thought he must have decided to step outside, get some air; maybe the dark atmosphere of the bar had depressed him.

*No,* she thought. *That isn't right.* She knew he wouldn't have abandoned his post. He wouldn't have just walked away from sentry duty.

She turned to the counter, and asked, "Did my father leave?"

The red-haired woman said, "Tell you the truth, honey, I didn't notice."

"He was sitting right here."

"I remember him coming in with you, but I wasn't paying much attention, to be honest."

The drunk belched quietly. "What this place needs is more lights. This goddam dark."

She went outside where the sun had all but faded. What remained of it was distilled in disintegrating little scars of light in a darkening sky. She looked across the parking lot. Maybe he'd walked back to the car for some reason. Why, though? What reason?

She put her hands in her pockets. The air was turning chill. You could smell winter, the onslaught of long nights, icy winds, snow.

She reached her car. Stopped. The passenger seat was empty.

**THE** trick was not to panic, to remain perfectly calm. Her father had gone for a stroll, he'd decided to stretch his legs, he'd be back in a moment. She leaned against the car and waited. And waited. There was no sign of him. Darkness was descending with deadening finality.

She wandered up and down the parking lot for a while. A stroll, stretch his legs—but these possibilities were no longer holding water. She crossed her arms, hugged herself; a wind sloughed through the darkness.

She gazed at the front of the bar again. The blue Schlitz sign emitted a solid glow. She couldn't just stand here and wait. She had to move if only to keep the cold out of her bones.

She walked away from the car, wandered round the side of the bar, found herself in an alley. A black plastic Dumpster was situated at the back door of the tavern. It looked malignant under the pallid light falling through a rear window of the bar.

A Dumpster. Where you tossed things, trash, castoffs, dead items. The air smelled bad with the scent of decay. She didn't want to think what she was thinking. The inside of her head was burning. The trick was to ignore the burning—but the small sharp flame in her head wouldn't be extinguished. She stared at the Dumpster. What she felt was dread.

She didn't want to touch it, raise the lid, look inside. *You want to be a grandfather, don't you*? She remembered the question the young man had asked, she remembered the way he'd snapped her father's hand back at the wrist and how John Stone had slumped to his knees. She stood very still.

A man materialized at the entrance to the alley. She recognized him as the one the old Russian woman had called Charlie, the beige coat with the epaulettes, the drooping eyelid.

"You're thinking about it," he said, and he nodded at the Dumpster. "You're thinking he's in the Dumpster, right?" He moved a little way toward her.

Sara turned her face to the side. The night pressed against her, confined her.

"You're thinking he's dead, Sara. Dead and discarded. Trashed. Like something you read in the newspapers."

She looked back at Charlie's face. The wind conjured smells out of the darkness. Brine, rotted vegetable matter, wet cardboard. "You wouldn't," she said.

"Wouldn't what, Sara?"

"Harm him."

"I told you before. Pain isn't high on our agenda. But things change, Sara, they change when you aren't getting the results you want. You need to take a fresh approach. Understand me?"

"I don't know anything," she said, and her voice was shrill. "I can't help you. I keep saying it. Why in God's name don't you believe me?"

"Look in the Dumpster. Open the lid, Sara. Go on."

"No."

"Go on, Sara."

She clenched her fists. Every muscle in her body was locked tight.

"Satisfy your curiosity," Charlie said. "Why don't you."

She didn't move. She couldn't bring herself to do what he was asking.

He said, "There's different kinds of burial plots, Sara. They're not all nice and grassy. They're not all located under some picturesque tree."

"What have you done to him?"

"Open the lid, Sara."

"*No.*"

He came directly toward her. He brought his bloated face very close to hers. "Open the goddam thing, Sara."

"Just raise your hand, Sara. Open the lid."

She touched the underside of the lid.

"Now open it," he said.

She resisted. She felt his big strong hand cover her own. "Need an assist, huh?"

He pushed her hand upward. The lid of the Dumpster swung up and open, flapped on its hinges. She closed her eyes. The rancid perfumes of garbage assaulted her.

"Now look, Sara," he said. "Open your goddam eyes and look."

She kept her eyes shut. She tried not to breathe. The offensive smell was trapped in the back of her throat, like something bad she'd eaten.

He said, "It's a treasure trove, Sara. Let's see what we got here. Some nice old pizza slices. Some chunks of stale cheese and—what's this?—yeah, a whole gang of maggots working overtime. We got old newspapers, a couple of cardboard boxes, some milk past its shelf life. We got a whole lot of very interesting stuff here, Sara. Look. *Look*."

She felt a sticky liquid flood her mouth. It ran between her lips, slid over her chin. She had a sensation of suffocating. She opened her eyes and tried to focus on a point beyond the contents of the Dumpster.

"Don't avoid," he said. "Just look."

She turned her eyes downward quickly. Slimy brown stalks of spinach, milk cartons, rotted cheese, a slow-wriggling clump of maggots illuminated by the pale light from the nearby window. But not—

Not what she'd expected. Not that.

Charlie said, "See what happens when you fear the worst, Sara. See what happens when you let your imagination run riot."

She gasped, slumped back from the Dumpster, leaned against the wall. She felt depleted. Punctured. She felt as if she'd gone to the edge of a precipice where she'd almost lost her balance. Where the drop was long and black. She ran the palm of her hand across her mouth.

"Where is he?" she asked.

"He's safe, Sara."

"You're not answering my question."

"He's safe, all you need to know."

"How do I know he's safe?"

"Take my word."

"I want to speak to him."

Charlie laid one hand comfortingly on her shoulder. "You'll get the opportunity, I'm sure."

"When?"

"When the time comes."

"When the old bag tells you."

Charlie smiled. "It's her show. She runs it any way she likes."

"And you're just a hired gun?"

"Hired. I don't know about the gun bit."

"Who is she? Does she have a name?"

"Get real, Sara."

"She knows about me. I don't know the first thing about her."

"We prefer it like that."

"She wants her money back. That's all I know."

"You sure that's all you know?"

"Damn sure."

The wind rifled the alley. She shivered.

"You'll catch cold here. Go home, Sara. Just go home."

"And then what?"

"Take a good long bath or something."

"Try to relax? Unwind a little? Is that what you're suggesting?"

"I'm suggesting you think," he said. "Think real hard." He turned from her and walked in the direction of the entrance to the alley.

Another figure appeared there. It was the young man, the burial-plot salesman. He was smiling at her in his glassy way. He said, "You heard the man, Sara. Just do what he tells you. Just think. Got it?" He winked. He winked, the slow closing and opening of an eye, as if all this were a lighthearted conspiracy between Sara and him. Some fun they shared.

She watched them go out of sight. She wanted to call them back and ask about her father, but they wouldn't answer anyway: what was the point? He'd been abducted. Spirited away. She didn't know where, and she didn't know how to get him back.

She walked to her car. She sat for a time behind the wheel. Her clothes, her skin, carried the faint smell of the garbage to which she'd been exposed. *This is the bottom*, she thought. Rock bottom, a bitter place to be. She adjusted the rearview mirror and looked at her reflection and what she saw was a specter, a shadow of self, as if the real Sara had been replaced by a waxen replica, and the face Mark Klein had described as elfin had become shrunken in defeat.

**16**

THIRTY-two forty-two Midsummer was in darkness when she arrived. A ragged fog was drifting up from the Sound. It swirled around the lower part of the house; only the upper floor could be seen. The fractured fog created the illusion that the house stood on stilts, an unlikely edifice.

She unlocked the door, went in, turned on lights. She immediately climbed the stairs to the bedroom, switching on lights as she moved. She didn't want darkness, pockets of shadow. She wanted bright illumination, the harshness of electricity. Everything exposed.

She yanked open the door of the closet that contained Mark's suits. He had eight suits in a variety of somber colors. Dark greys, dark blues, black with a pinstripe. They were all well made. Hugo Boss. Klein. She started going through the pockets, although she wasn't sure what she expected to find.

She thought of her father, wondered how his abduction had been orchestrated: lured out of the bar, arm twisted behind his back, forced inside another vehicle and driven away—had it happened that way? She had tears in her eyes, and her throat hurt; crying was useless. She had to keep busy, busy digging through his clothes. She had to search for something. People didn't move through the world without leaving at least some traces in their wake, did they? An envelope in an LA hotel wasn't enough. A message on a piece of paper added up to nothing.

She went through pocket after pocket, sifting lint, threads, finding a half-empty packet of Camel Lights in the Boss pinstripe, a Visa receipt for a purchase made at a Doubleday bookshop in Manhattan. She remembered: he'd brought home a book of baby's names, and they'd read it together, savoring certain names, laughing over others. Esmeralda had been funny. Euphemia had caused Klein a convulsion of mirth. Emma he liked. The simplicity of it. Roger amused him, Roland was dismissed as too English, the kind of name to which a cigarette holder might be attached, Robert was ordinary. He hadn't acted that day like an embezzler about to abscond. No trace of nervousness, no silent withdrawals—just a father-to-be considering names for his future child. He had to be two people, she thought. A split personality or a damn good actor, it didn't make a difference which.

She kept rummaging in a hyperactive manner. She had the feeling she'd collapse if she just stopped. Doing this prevented her from thinking. She didn't want to think. She found matchbooks from midtown restaurants where he presumably had business lunches with his unfortunate clients. She discovered a couple of tickets from an offtrack betting office, two months old. The occasional flutter on a horse—something else she didn't know about. She found a wadded Kleenex, a Vicks nasal inhaler, a Zippo lighter. The stuff of her husband's life.

She closed the closet door, opened the drawer where he kept his underwear. Silk boxer shorts, briefs in an unopened plastic cylinder. What could you tell about a man from his underwear? She opened the plastic tube and pulled out the briefs—red, yellow, sky blue. *What do I expect to find in all this, this marital archeology?* She dragged out the entire drawer, dumped the contents on the floor. Ludicrous to be sitting in the middle of the bedroom surrounded by your husband's underwear. She sifted through them, found nothing unusual.

The sock drawer next. Greys and blacks and navy blues—she was struck by the absence of color in his choice of socks. Conservative: were they meant to provide reassurance to clients, an impression of carefulness? *I will be thoughtful with your money, sir. I will see that it is invested well. Trust me.*

Suddenly she buried her face in her hands. She felt like a widow exploring the garments of her recently deceased husband. Klein, Klein. All this wreckage. She lay back on the floor, hands limp at her sides, and gazed at the ceiling. How easy it would be to stay this way, catatonic, removed from the stringent demands of a world out of control. But she couldn't, she had to get up. She half rose, moved on her knees to the bureau where he kept his watches and cuff links in a tiny drawer. She pulled it open, tipped the contents on the floor.

A broken Rolex he always said he was going to have repaired. A comic watch with a Donald Duck face he'd bought impulsively from a street trader one Sunday morning in the Village. When life was fun. When impulses ruled. When she'd walked with her arm round his waist across Washington Square and stopped every so often to watch old patzers play chess. When he'd do funny animal impressions to make her laugh, causing the chess players to complain at having their concentration broken. When the world was sweet and her father was safe in his house in Port Jefferson.

*Dad*, she thought. She remembered how he'd insisted on coming inside the bar with her.

And now he was gone.

She rummaged under the Donald Duck watch, discovered an assortment of cuff links and tiepins. There was nothing extraordinary here. Nothing she didn't recognize. No hidden significances. What did she expect to find anyway—a signed document attesting to his crimes?

She entered the bathroom, opened the cabinet. Razor blades, toothpaste, dental floss, a bottle of aftershave, aspirins, Band-Aids. She moved all this stuff around as if she might come upon something concealed beneath it, but there was nothing. Stripped of ownership, possessions were like books written in a foreign language. She closed the cabinet door, returned to the bedroom, sat on the edge of the bed with her hands placed together in an attitude of prayer. *Nothing can seriously upset you or make you afraid . . .*

The doorbell rang, startling her. She didn't move. It rang again. She walked to the bedroom doorway and looked down the stairs. The bell continued to ring. She descended. Through glass, she could see the outline of a man on the porch.

"Who is it?" she asked.

"Tony. I need to speak to you, Sara."

She opened the door. What did he want? What had brought him all the way out here?

"Can I come in?" Vandervelt asked.

"Why not."

He followed her into the living room. He tugged his grey cashmere scarf from his neck.

She sat facing him. "I'm surprised to see you."

"I figured you would be." He smiled and touched his eyelid, which was red and slightly swollen. "You need to cut your fingernails, Sara. They're lethal weapons."

She felt toward Vandervelt a certain hostility. "Do you have the firm's permission to be here?"

"Oh, Sara," he said.

"After all, this might be construed as collaborating with the enemy," she said.

"I came here to apologize."

"For what?"

"For being a shit."

He leaned across the space that separated them and took her hand and clasped it between his own. His palms were cold.

"I haven't been sympathetic, and I don't like myself for it," he said. "I thought about you being out here on your own—"

"And you felt sorry?" She pulled her hand away.

"Sorry and sad," he said. "Mark's disappearance, your condition . . ."

"This is a pity trip."

"Christ, Sara. I only want to say I'm sorry. I should have contacted you before. But I just let it drift, and that was careless of me."

"You were afraid how it might look," she said. "Thirty-two forty-two Midsummer is off-limits to you. The house of plague."

"We were instructed that contact with you wouldn't be advisable in the circumstances," he said.

"Toeing the party line."

"You might say." He undid the buttons of his coat and sat back in his chair. "The whole business has made everyone nervous. I'm not proud of my own behavior, you know."

*Nervous*, she thought. Now there was a good word. That covered it all. The missing husband. The kidnapped father. *Nervous*. She said, "So you've come all the way out here just to wave the flag of personal loyalty."

"We're old friends, Sara," he said.

Old friends. She let this phrase tumble through her head.

"Tell me something, Tony. How long has Klein allegedly been embezzling funds?"

"I don't have an answer for that. There was an audit about four months ago. Discrepancies showed up. Biggies. Big enough for the Feds to get involved. So another audit was ordered."

"When was the second audit done?"

"It was begun, let's see, three weeks ago. It isn't entirely finished with yet. It's a deep one."

"Three weeks ago? The Feds have had a tap on our telephone for at least three months. Which means they must have had grounds for suspicion long *before* that second audit. So why didn't Sol at least suspend him after the first audit?"

"I don't think Sol wanted to believe Mark was capable of any wrongdoing. You know how he is."

Yes. She knew. Sol sometimes had a tendency to hide from unacceptable truths; he had a wide streak of sentimentality and loyalty when it came to his employees. He'd hired Mark himself, and he liked to think he was a great judge of character: ergo, Mark couldn't possibly betray him. It figured.

"Do you think Mark suspected he was being targeted after that first audit?" she asked.

"I seriously doubt it. If he'd thought so back then, he wouldn't have waited until last week before taking a hike. It was the second audit that panicked him."

"Why did it take so long to begin the second audit anyway?"

"Sol again. He didn't believe the figures. First, he blamed the computer system. Then he blamed the programmers. Then he blamed the original audit team. He blamed everything and everybody. Except Mark."

"Do you believe Mark stole the money?"

"I don't want to believe, Sara. But the evidence is damning. All the missing funds are from the accounts of his clients. He was the only one with the computer password for those accounts. And if he was innocent, he'd have hung around long enough to defend himself. If you've got nothing to hide, you don't skip."

"Unless you're scared of something else," she said.

"Like what?"

"Maybe he's being blamed for something he didn't do, and

he knows he can't come back until the real culprit is caught.''

"I'd love to believe that," Tony said.

She was quiet for a time. Her father kept drifting in and out of her mind. Not knowing where he was: that was the worst of it. She was aware of Vandervelt watching her with eager sympathy.

"Has Mark tried to contact you, Sara?"

She said, "No."

"Somehow I can't imagine him vanishing without getting in touch with you. Walking away without a word . . . You two were always so damned *close*."

"Yeah, we were close. We were tight. I always thought so anyway."

"Have you ever considered taking a break? Getting out of here for a while?"

"Running away, you mean?"

"Taking a holiday," he said.

"And burying myself somewhere? I don't see what that would achieve." She remembered Sol had made the same suggestion.

"It's just an idea," he said. There was silence. He fidgeted with the fringe of his scarf.

"Sara, is there anything I can do?" he asked eventually.

"Like what?"

"Help in some way?"

*For starters you can get my father back*, she thought. *Then you can locate my husband.* "I don't think so, Tony."

"You only have to ask. You know that. I should have been a better friend to you, Sara. And I'm genuinely sorry."

She saw the contrition on his angular face. She remembered the few times they'd gone out to dinner years ago. She recalled how, on one particular evening, he'd fumblingly tried to kiss her in his car. She'd had to explain she didn't feel anything of a romantic nature toward him. He'd been embarrassed and apologetic.

"Have the Feds talked to you?" she asked.

"Somebody called McClennan."

"Did he ask about me?"

"As a matter of fact, yeah. He had this notion you might have been involved in Mark's . . . well, okay, swindle."

"And what did you tell him?"

"I told him the idea was totally absurd."

"Did he believe you?"

"You can't tell what those guys are thinking. They play hard poker."

"Which is one damn good reason I have to stay where I am," she said. "I go somewhere, and what does it look like?"

She rose. She walked around the room. She stopped at the door to Mark's office and leaned against it, arms folded. An image of the black plastic Dumpster came into her mind. She forced it aside, but the picture kept shimmering just beneath the surface.

She asked, "What do you know about Mark's clients?"

"How do you mean, Sara?"

"Did you ever meet any of them?"

"Well, sure. If they came to the office, Mark sometimes introduced them. Generally, though, he was protective of his own clients. We might work for the same firm, but you tend to guard your personal clients jealously. You know how it is. Commissions are involved."

"Did you ever meet a woman from Russia?"

"Russia?"

"Old woman, dyed-yellow hair. Ugly."

Vandervelt frowned, seemed to think about this a moment. "I can't say I did. Why?"

"It's nothing."

"You can't ask a question like that and then just brush it aside," he said. "You've met this woman?"

"I've met her," she answered.

"Was she a client?"

Sara wondered how far she should go. She was tempted by the idea of telling Vandervelt everything—from the arrival of the Feds to the disappearance of her father, and everything else in between—but she resisted. She wanted a confidant, but she understood she had to be careful. She had to be wary. Tony might have come here on a fishing expedition, for all she knew. He might be digging, for reasons of his own, for information he'd pass on to the Feds. She couldn't know. Trust had seeped out of her life.

"It's not important," she said. "Why don't we drop it?"

Tony Vandervelt shrugged. "If that's what you want."

"That's what I want," she said.

She saw him get out of his chair and walk slowly toward her. He extended his arms, and said, "You know what you need, Sara?"

"You tell me."

"A hug. A big hug."

"A *hug*?"

Then, preposterously, he was embracing her. She felt his arms around her shoulders, his body pressed against hers. She smelled mint on his breath.

"I've always been fond of you. Remember that."

"I'll remember," she said.

He released her. "You need anything, you know my home number."

"I've got it somewhere," she said. The physical contact had disturbed her, though she wasn't sure why. Was it conceivable that Tony was making some kind of underhanded pass at her? She was pregnant, for God's sake. She was swollen and unattractive. And she felt nothing for Vandervelt anyway, even if she had been available. Which she wasn't. No, she thought. She'd misconstrued his action. That was all. He turned away from her and picked up his scarf, which he'd draped over the arm of a chair.

An unexpected impulse caused her to ask, "Would you lie to me, Tony?"

"Lie? No. Why do you ask? Do you *think* I've lied to you about something, Sara?"

"I'm not sure." And she wasn't: the question had popped into her mind like a bubble bursting.

"Sara, clear the air," he said.

"Okay. The Russian woman . . ."

"What about her?"

"You've never met her?"

"Never."

"You're sure."

"I told you, Sara. Never. Why would I lie?"

This tattered life of hers: nobody was telling the truth, and even if they were it was because they had ulterior motives. The world was a shifting cluster of fabrications and disappearances. And yet she needed a friend. She didn't like solitude, and the way she'd come to doubt everybody and everything was contrary to her nature. Tony was here because he was ashamed of the way he'd acted in the office. There was no more to it than that.

He kissed her lightly on the cheek. She found herself gazing at his swollen red eyelid. "I'm sorry I scratched you, Tony," she said.

"I heal fast." He smiled. "You need me, call me."

"But not at the office," she said.

"That's a toughie."

She walked behind him to the front door. He stepped out on to the porch, wrapping the scarf about his neck. She said good night and shut the door and went back upstairs, where she surveyed Klein's belongings strewn in disarray—parts of a puzzle she didn't know how to assemble.

She lay down on the bed, closed her eyes. Sleep was a galaxy away. Her father's image was embossed behind her eyelids, and she could still feel Vandervelt's kiss on the side of her face, a clammy memory.

**17**

THE sound of the telephone woke her from a shallow, dreamless sleep. The sky was beginning to turn from black to slate grey. Sleepily, she got out of bed and padded downstairs to answer the phone.

George Borbokis was on the line. "I hope I didn't wake you, Sara."

"I was just getting up anyway, George."

"I called to ask if you'd heard anything more from our friend McClennan."

"Nothing. Have you?"

"Not a word. The man likes to keep us waiting," Borbokis said. "I guess he'll just spring out at us one day soon."

"You make that sound ominous," she said.

Borbokis asked, "What about Mark? Anything?"

"You'd be the first to know, George."

"I discovered one small thing, Sara. I had one of my people check the airlines and, sure enough, Mark had round-trip business-class tickets from JFK to Hong Kong. But he didn't show for the flight. That leaves us two options. Either the tickets were a decoy. Or something happened to him when he got to the airport. Something that made him change his mind."

"Like what?"

Borbokis said, "I couldn't even begin to guess. The only sure thing is he didn't make the flight. My investigator checked the cab companies and found the driver who took him to Kennedy. Dropped him off there, no problem, then drove away. Far as the driver knows, Mark went inside the terminal building. Whether he caught some other flight, or whether he just turned round and walked back out of the terminal—I can't say.''

''If he flew to another destination outside the contintental US, there would be some record, wouldn't there?'' she asked.

''Sure. Unless—and I hate to say this—he had access to a false passport. But if he didn't have fake documentation, Sara, then he didn't fly out of the United States at JFK, or anywhere else for that matter. The Feds have presumably been over this same territory and come to the same conclusion.''

''Mark could still be in the country.''

''He could be. My investigator is still scratching around, Sara. If I hear anything new, I'll be in touch.''

''Thanks, George.''

She hung up. *Mark goes inside the terminal and is never seen again*. She was left with the same mystery. The same vanishing. He had tickets but hadn't used them. Decoy tickets. Unless, as Borbokis had suggested, something had happened to prevent him from using them. But what? She couldn't think. Had he gone to California, to the Cresta Vista Motor Lodge? You didn't need a passport to travel from JFK to LAX. He could have hopped on another plane, given a false name, paid cash—nobody would have questioned him. She considered the notion of going at once to the airport and catching a flight to Los Angeles, but the enormity of the undertaking overwhelmed her. What would she do? Hang out at the Cresta Vista, watch people come and go, spend hours just sitting and waiting and watching and hoping in the lobby?

She thought of her father. She wondered if she'd dreamed all that, the Dumpster, the disappearance. No, this was reality. This was the way things were. She couldn't go anywhere, she couldn't abandon whatever fragile link she still had to her father.

She walked inside the kitchen and sat at the table and held her head between her hands. She watched dawn streak the dark; tire tracks of dull light. A soft rain was falling, slipping down the windowpane. She thought of going back upstairs to bed, but she was awake now even if she wasn't alert. She brewed a pot of coffee and listened to it drip through the basket, and the sound of the coffee became commingled with the pattering of the rain to the point where she couldn't tell the difference between the two.

She poured herself a cup and took it to the table. She sipped the coffee and forced her mind into action. This was the beginning of the third day since McClennan had entered the house and altered her world beyond recognition. The third day. She couldn't go through it like some useless piece of driftwood at the ocean's mercy.

She slammed her cup down in the saucer and screwed up her hands and noticed how the veins in her wrists darkened. She stared at the determined bone white ridge of her knuckles. She finished her coffee and dressed, then, hurriedly, she left the house.

## 18

SHE took an early train to the city. Packed with commuters, airless, the car smelled of damp clothes and wet umbrellas. Rain coursed against the windows, and the view was bleak. At Penn Station she found a cab to take her to the upper East Side. Central Park was shrouded in misty rain. She got out of the cab at an address on East Seventy-sixth Street.

The entrance to the building had a wine-colored canopy under which a sour-faced doorman stood. She ignored the doorman, stepped inside a marbled hallway where a security man in a blue blazer sat behind a desk. He rose as she attempted to go past him.

"Where are you going?" he asked.

She told him.

"You expected?"

She said she was.

"Don't mind if I call upstairs, do you," he said.

"Feel free."

"Your name?"

"Sara Klein."

He picked up a phone and turned away from her and mumbled so that she couldn't hear what he was saying. She waited. The rhythm of her heart was strange, as if it were out of sync. A few slicks of rainwater dripped from her coat.

The security guard said, "Okay. You can go up."

She walked to the elevator, rode to the sixth floor, walked down the carpeted corridor. How long was it since she'd been here? Just after her wedding, a drinks reception, staff from the office. Jennifer Gryce had been a bridesmaid, attired in a peach-colored dress. Jennifer Gryce, who wanted no further part in Sara's life. The memory of the wedding was a dull ache, and her rejection by Jennifer hurt, even if she didn't want to admit it to herself.

Sol Rosenthal was standing at the door of his apartment, dressed in a maroon velvet robe. He was smoking a cigar.

He said, "First of the day," and nodded at the cigar as if he detested his dependence. "Come in, come in."

He ushered her inside the apartment, which was large and furnished with antiques, heavy Victorian pieces, massive brocade drapes at the tall windows. The walls were painted in deep browns, navy blues, reds that had deepened to burgundy with the passage of time. Sol's wife, Alice, who spent part of each year in Florida because she didn't like New York weather—winters too cold, summers too humid—had chosen the furnishings. Her function in Sol's life was to introduce a certain refinement into the old man's world. She bought his shirts and shoes, chose his suits and ties. There was a rumor she'd once tried unsuccessfully to convince him to take elocution lessons. But you could no more refine Sol Rosenthal than you could transmute lead into gold.

"Coffee?" he asked.

"No, I'm fine." The high ceilings and elaborate cornices made her feel small.

Sol picked up a silver jug from a table and poured coffee into a floral china cup. "Gotta have my coffee, jump-start the heart. My age, you need a good jolt first thing." He sipped, set the cup down, drew on the cigar so hard that his cheeks deflated, then he blew smoke away from her in a considerate manner.

"The early bird," he said.

"I haven't been sleeping well, Sol."

"And you can't take pills either, your condition."

He got up, drew back one of the curtains, and an uncertain light filtered inside the sitting room. He came back to his chair and sat facing her, crushed out his cigar, then wiped small tobacco flakes from his hands.

"So, sweetie. What brings you down here this time of day?"

She said, "I don't have anywhere else to turn, Sol."

"Get outta that wet coat and talk to me."

She removed the coat and said, ''My father . . .''

''Yeah?''

''They have my father, Sol.''

''Whoa. Back up. Who has your father?''

''People that did some business with Mark, and they think I know where he is, and so they snatched my father.''

''Snatched? As in abduct?''

''Right.'' Abduct. The word was sonorous, an iron bell in some impregnable steeple.

''Jesus Christ,'' Sol said.

''And I can't go to the authorities. If I do . . . Well, it's obvious. I don't see my father again.''

Sol's face was tinted with anger. ''These people, you don't know anything about them?''

''One's Russian. An old woman.''

''Russian? But you don't know her name.''

Sara shook her head. ''She didn't exactly introduce herself, Sol. She was one of Mark's clients, I guess, and she's anxious to know what's become of her money.''

''So why doesn't she go to the Feds? Or why doesn't she come to me if she's worried about her investments?''

''I've been wondering about that,'' she said.

Sol looked thoughtful a moment. Then he snapped his middle finger against his thumb and his expression was one of shock. ''There's only one reason I can think, and I don't want to think it—the money's illegal, and she's been laundering it through Mark. There's a whole shitload of highly dubious Russian money floating round these days. From drugs, gambling, hookers, you name it. What they do is, they try and filter it through connections in New York—and I ain't talking about guys in white hats working for old, established finance houses. I'm talking about the other side of the coin, kid. Bagmen. Guys that specialize in trying to hide illicit earnings.''

''The *mob*?''

''That's one name. These guys, you don't steal from them. Uh-huh. You don't get caught with your hand in *their* fucking pockets.''

Sara was silent a moment. What was this lunatic world she'd been plunged into? This craziness? The mob. Russian gangsters. The laundering of money. It was all so far removed from any reality she'd ever known that Sol might have been

talking in a foreign tongue. Okay, if that was the situation, if
it involved gangsters and members of some Russian mafia, if
that's how things were, somehow she'd find a way to deal
with it, to absorb this knowledge into her life. She had to. She
was weary of being excluded, weary of mysteries she couldn't
solve.

She said, "They made other threats, Sol. The baby . . ."

"The baby? They threatened the baby? You gotta be jok-
ing."

"I wouldn't make that kind of joke, Sol."

"Fucking Christ, they're scum, kid. Lowlife. Lower than
lowlife. Such . . . I don't have words." He made a tiny de-
spairing motion with his hands. "I seen some bad customers
in my time, Sara. I seen all kinds. But usually there's a place
where even the worst of them draw some kinda line. This
bunch, they don't know from lines."

She said, "What do I do, Sol?"

"You could talk to the Feds, except you'd be slicing your
father's throat."

"I'm in a bind. And it's tight. Too tight. And the FBI—
they don't believe anything I tell them. They've got me
pegged as a liar."

He finished his coffee, tapped his long white fingers on the
surface of the coffee table. "I don't know, for the life of me.
All this shit, breaks my heart. I been aware for some time
there's heavy Russian cash coming into the city, and some of
it's being filtered through respectable financial houses, but you
just never think any of it's gonna come your way. You try to
take a few precautions when it comes to new clients, but you
have to trust them, bottom line. Where their money comes
from—end of the day, that's their own business." He took a
fresh cigar from a box on the coffee table. "So, our bright
boy got his hand in the Russian mob's cash register. Bad, bad
news. Funny money coming through my own fucking company. This I don't wanna hear. This I don't even wanna know
about. It's tough enough having the Feds around the place
without this extra grief."

She leaned forward, elbows on her knees. "Is there some
way you can find out this woman's name?"

"Go through Mark's client list, you mean?"

"Right—"

"And give you the name of this woman?"

"Yes—"

"And what would you do with it, Sara?"

She thought for a moment. "It would be something, Sol. One little snippet of information. Something."

"Some kinds of information you don't need. You're asking me to endanger you?"

"I'm only asking you to get me a name."

"I don't like the look in your eye, Sara."

"Screw the look in my eye," she said. "Get me a name."

Sol smiled a little forlornly. "It ain't that easy. Starters, it's one hundred percent certain her name wouldn't show up on your husband's client list. The money woulda been buried inside some corporate entity, and this woman—you think she's going to be listed as a director? The funds woulda been invested by the corporate entity. The woman wouldn't have been involved by name."

"You don't know that for sure."

"Two, kid. Even if I got her name, you think I'd gift-wrap it and give it to you? Gravedigging I don't do."

"Help me, Sol. That's all I ask."

"No fucking way."

"Sol . . ."

"You know what you oughta do? Find that husband of yours and throw him to the goddam wolves. Say, here's the sorry asshole, take him off my hands, now please can I have my father back. That's what you oughta do."

*Throw Mark to the goddam wolves*, she thought. She didn't mention the message left in LA. It was a vague area to her still, a distant conundrum. She was focused on getting information out of Sol, didn't want to be sidetracked. She said, "I'm not asking for much."

"Oh, kid. You're asking way too much."

She listened to rain slap against the windows. A small gold clock on the mantelpiece chimed the half hour. It was seven-thirty.

"You won't help," she said.

"I *can't* help. Chrissakes, you can be stubborn."

"You once said you admired that quality in me."

"Yeah, when you were turning people away that I didn't

want to see, sure, you were great at that. But this is a different kinda stubborn, Sara. This is the lethal kind.''

She stood up. ''I guess it's pointless to persist?''

''You got that right.''

She grabbed her raincoat, put it on.

''Where you headed now?'' Sol asked.

She shrugged. ''Thanks for your time, Sol.''

''Hey.'' He caught her by the arm. ''I'm truly sorry about your father. You know I am. Jesus, I have to tell you that? But what the hell do you expect of me? So long as they got your father, the best thing we can do is hope it turns out okay. I mean . . .''

''I don't put much credence in hope,'' she said.

''Sara, listen, don't rush off. Maybe you oughta tell McClennan, take your chances. Maybe he can do something to help. He's got resources, he's got this and that, he could find where your father is—''

''I'm not going to take that kind of chance, Sol.''

''This is causing me heartache, kid,'' he said.

''That's something you learn to live with. Quickly.''

''I don't need this aggravation.''

She moved toward the door.

''Go back home, Sara. Go home. Just wait. It's gonna work out okay. You'll see.''

*Go home*, she thought. *Wait.* She was sick of these useless platitudes of advice. Home was the last place she needed to go. Waiting was the last thing she wanted to do. She was burning all at once with a kind of fever. She opened the door. Sol, robe flapping, was hurrying after her. He tracked her out into the corridor. ''Sara, listen to me.''

She pressed the button for the elevator.

''Don't do nothing stupid, you hear me?''

''Double negative, Sol,'' she said.

''Double what?''

The doors slid open and she stepped inside the elevator. She rode to the ground floor and walked out to the street, where she waited only a few minutes before a taxi came smoking and hissing through the rain.

**19**

SHE was on Wall Street a few minutes before eight. The rainy sidewalks were already crowded with traders, dealers, bean counters, financial consultants of varying degrees of credibility, con men, secretaries, all the servants and manipulators of the system. She paid the cabby and entered the building.

She took an elevator to the third floor. She knew the earliest arrivals at Rosenthal Brothers didn't get there until just before eight-thirty on a normal day. Occasionally you might find some eager new employee in place at eight, and sometimes Tony Vandervelt arrived at quarter past—but these were chances she had to take.

She reached the empty reception area. Two men in red uniforms were running vacuum cleaners over the carpet in the corridor. They glanced at her. A pregnant woman, therefore harmless. She walked confidently past them and entered the main office.

Nobody was present. She was struck by the silence of the place. Printers silent, computer screens dead. The only functioning item was the big bright console that flickered with financial data, share prices from Tokyo, Bonn, London. This ran continuously even if there was nobody around to see it. Sol had been known to come down to his office at 3:00 A.M. if he was having an insomniac attack, and he liked the buzz of the big screen at those times. Vigilant Sol, studying the numbers, calculating, wondering where he could put his clients' money to work to its best advantage.

She was tense. She didn't know if she had enough time to find what she needed. She didn't even know if she could still find her way around—things might have changed, systems might have been amended as a consequence of the audits. She just wasn't sure. She knew only that she had to move quickly. She walked in the direction of Mark's desk, which was located behind a half partition in the corner of the large room.

She took her reading glasses from her raincoat pocket. The lenses were smudged. She looked at the computer terminal, turned the power switch on, heard the drive crank into life, saw the screen flood with letters. ROSENTHAL BROTHERS NUMBER 6–8. Six-eight was the number allocated to Mark's terminal. That hadn't changed at least.

She wondered if the files had been wiped from the hard disc by the auditors or the Feds, taken away to be used as evidence against Klein. She realized she'd been expecting some kind of crime-scene tape to be surrounding his desk, spidery strands of yellow plastic, a sign to indicate that the desk was off-limits, a padlock even—but everything appeared normal, right down to the photograph he kept of her on the desk. She gazed briefly at her own image, which had been snapped a year ago when she wore her hair long, when she smiled at the world and the smile was the genuine article.

ENTER PASSWORD.

She held her fingers poised above the keyboard. She heard the sound of vacuums buzzing out in the corridor, the faint hum created by the computer.

ENTER PASSWORD.

She wondered if the password had been altered. The letters blinked. There was a time limit programmed into the machine, and if you didn't type the password within twenty seconds, the computer shut down, denying you access.

She heard one of the cleaners shout above the noise of the vacuum cleaners. "You done the johns yet, Andy?"

ENTER PASSWORD. The words flickered persistently.

She had nothing to lose. She placed her fingertips on the keyboard and typed the letters: SARA JOAN 2 25 62. Klein, like so many computer users, had used as a password a name and number familiar to him, something he wasn't likely to forget. Sara Joan: her full name, her date of birth. He'd once said to her, *Hope you don't mind, but I borrowed your name, S J*. Of course she hadn't minded. She'd even enjoyed the idea that he used her name as his private password; there was an intimacy about it she'd liked, a secret shared.

The name worked. ENTER PASSWORD faded. The screen blanked a moment, then a menu exploded in front of her. She scanned the list of items.

PROJECTIONS.

PLANNING.

CLOSED.

Something called PROBABLES.

Something else named CONTACTS.

FOLLOW-UPS.

STATUS QUO.

REFER.

CORRESPONDENCE.

MODEM.

DEAD.

The private business world of Mark Klein distilled in a series of staccato headings. DEAD.

She was conscious of time evaporating, sands running through her head. It would be impossible to bring up all the files under these headings and examine them. She looked at the big digital clock on the wall—8:10.

CURRENT.

She wondered if this was the directory she needed. But she couldn't just draw up a chair and sit here and casually go through the files. It would take too long. She stared at the word CURRENT, then decided to give the computer the print instruction. She pressed the appropriate keys and expected to hear the printer kick into life.

But nothing happened. The printer, a laser device, was situated on the corner of the desk. Was it broken? Had it been disabled? She typed again, and still nothing happened; and then she saw that the cable linking the printer to the computer was disconnected. She picked up the end of the cable, plugged it into a socket at the back of the computer, then gave the print instruction again, and this time the printer mechanism whirred and green lights flashed on the cover. She heard the first sheet emerge.

Eight-fifteen.

How many sheets had to be printed? How extensive were the files contained in the CURRENT directory? She had no way of knowing. She tapped her fingers on the desk, watched more sheets slide out of the printer. The machine printed at a rate of one sheet every ten seconds. If there were a hundred pages, say, she'd be here for—how long? She was too stressed to make even a simple calculation.

She stared across the big room in the direction of the doorway. Any second somebody might come through. Vandervelt, perhaps. One of the assistants. A secretary. She drew her hands to her sides and turned back to look at the printer. *It's too goddam slow*, she thought. *Hurry, hurry.* The sheets came out facedown. Every so often the computer made a clicking sound as it fed data along the cable to the printer. She willed it to work faster, but electronic devices were dispassionate things, you couldn't hurry them beyond their programmed capacity. You could only wait. She gazed at the word CURRENT on the screen. There was a second word flashing in the bottom right corner of the screen. PRINTING . . .

*Yes*, she thought, *I know you're printing. Please be quick.* Eight-nineteen. Eight-twenty. The clock was her enemy. Time was against her. And she had no way of knowing if what she was printing was relevant to her needs.

Eight-twenty-two.

The printer stopped, and for a moment she thought the process was finished, but the pause was brief, caused by a buffer inside the computer drive as it slowed the traffic of data being transmitted. Then the printer kicked in again, and the sheets kept coming.

She turned and looked back in the direction of the door. The vacuum cleaners had quit. The only sound now was the low buzz of the printer.

The printer died again.

It was flashing a red light. PAPER OUT. She couldn't afford to start hunting around for more paper. Even if she found some immediately, she'd have to go through the process of loading it into the printer, and more precious time would be consumed.

Eight-twenty-four.

She'd take what she had, and she'd leave.

"I don't know what the hell to make of it," somebody said.

Sara grabbed the stack of papers from the printer tray just as Thomas McClennan entered the big room, followed by Special Agent Ross.

Ross said, "You work an angle, then before you know it, Christ, there's another one."

"It's all angles," McClennan said. "And they're crooked. Every one of them."

They were moving in the direction of Sol's office. Sara ducked her head, concealed herself behind the partition. If the agents were going to Sol's office, they'd pass a few yards away from her. She went down on her knees. She tried to make herself very small and very quiet. She wanted to be invisible.

McClennan said, "I can't figure her, Jack."

"Yeah, well," Ross remarked.

"Rosenthal swears she's on the level."

"Depends on whether you consider Rosenthal a good judge of character, Tom."

"Maybe she's just smart. Plays dumb, but bright as hell. Pulled the wool over Rosenthal's eyes for years."

"Could be," Ross said.

Sara held her breath. She heard all her pulses thud inside her, like tiny missiles exploding in the distance. Her heart was surely audible.

McClennan had stopped a few feet from the partition, and was saying, "I'd like to just break her, Jack."

"Sometimes I think we need nightsticks and baseball bats in this job," Ross remarked.

McClennan said, "You could make out a damn good case for that."

Sara, huddled behind the partition, felt a jab of cramp in her stomach so painful it made her want to gasp. She opened her mouth and struggled to stay silent. *Nightsticks and baseball bats*, she thought. *I'd like to just break her, Jack.* She shut her eyes and willed the agents to vanish, to dematerialize. What time was it now? Soon the first workers would be coming in. Soon the computers would be humming and the phones ringing and the fax machines beeping. *Go away, McClennan*, she thought. *Just go the hell away.*

"I think we need more surveillance," McClennan said. "She's wise to the phone, so she isn't making any useful calls. And the only person she ever seems to spend time with is her father. We're missing something. I don't like that feeling."

"I'll arrange it," Ross said.

"You do that. What time's our appointment with the old man?"

"Eight-thirty."

"Eight-thirty. You think we should go in his office and wait for him?"

*Yes*, Sara thought.

"He won't like it," Ross said.

"I'm at a stage where I don't give a shit *what* he likes," McClennan said.

Sara heard McClennan walk into Sol Rosenthal's office, and Ross went after him a little reluctantly. She raised her face, saw that the door of Sol's office was open. The two agents had their backs to her.

It was now, or it was never.

She rose to a half crouch and, clutching the papers, scurried toward the exit. She made it out into the reception area, stuffed the papers inside her coat, and walked to the elevator. The number 3 was lit up on the panel. She could hear the cage rise in the shaft. She'd take the stairs, she had no choice. She moved past the reception desk just as the elevator chimed and the doors slip open and the sound of Jennifer Gryce's voice could be heard. "He was nice, sort of old-fashioned."

Linda Brand said, "Gimme rough any old time. Flowers and flash dinners don't ring my bells."

*"Chacun à son gout,"* Jen Gryce said.

"One woman's meat," said Linda Brand. "And I do mean *meat*."

Jennifer Gryce said, "You're something else."

Sara turned the corner to the stairwell, where she pushed the metal bar on the exit door. She was halfway down the stairs before she realized she was breathless. She paused, leaned against the wall. Spots shimmied in front of her eyes. There was pressure in her chest. The baby dropped, turned over, a small acrobat in its sac. She found herself succumbing to an assortment of prenatal anxieties: premature birth, webbed feet, deformities. A kind of mutant. The consequence of stress, of panic. You imagined a monster growing in your womb.

She kept descending. When she reached the ground floor she left by an alley at the back of the building. The clutch of papers was secure under her coat.

She went to the end of the alley. She was impatient now.

She wanted to know exactly what she'd plundered from Mark's files.

We're missing something, McClennan had said.

*Yes, you are.* But if she felt good about slipping away unnoticed from McClennan and Ross, then the prospect of the Feds increasing their surveillance undermined her sense of achievement. She wondered how often they watched her anyway. Obviously not enough, not if McClennan was complaining about it.

She crossed the street at a red light. She saw Sol Rosenthal, half-hidden under a yellow-and-black umbrella, come toward her. She stepped into a doorway, and he went gliding past without noticing her. She watched him go, wondering if he'd tell McClennan about the abduction of her father—no, he wouldn't, he wouldn't take that risk. Sol, who knew when to speak and when to keep quiet, the soul of discretion, wouldn't do anything to endanger John Stone.

Sara walked to the corner of the block where only yesterday she'd encountered the panhandler. She didn't expect to see him again—but there he was, standing under the awning of a coffee shop, his hand held out to pedestrians who ignored him. "A dulla," he kept saying. "One dulla, playse." On and on, a monotonous litany.

He turned his face, his eyes met those of Sara, but he showed no sign of recognition, not even when she was within a few feet of him. He shoved his hand toward her, and said, "Got a dulla, lady?"

She took change from her pocket and dropped the coins in his dirty hand. "Don't remember me?" she asked.

"You nice lady. Blessings on you."

"No papers to hand out today? No little messages for me?"

He swayed, shuffled on his toes, wiped a streak of mucus from his upper lip. "Messages?" he asked.

"Yesterday you gave me a piece of paper," she said.

He looked blank. She wondered if his mind was gone, drugged out, snuffed like a candle. "You gave me a message yesterday. You really don't remember?"

He shook his head. In his closed fist the coins rattled. "You nice lady. Have good baby. Big strong baby."

"Yeah, yeah, strong baby."

"Healthy and strong, make husband proud."

"Tell me about the paper. Tell me who gave it to you."

"Paper, lady?"

"Paper," she said. "It had a religious message. And a phone number. And all I want to know is who told you to give it to me."

He shuffled some more, like a man hearing little tunes audible to nobody else. "No, lady wrong, Sammy don't give no papers."

She dangled a five-dollar bill in front of him. "You want this?"

"Sure thing. Wow. Sure thing."

"Then give me the information I want, and you can have the money."

He couldn't take his eyes from the bill. "Remind me. Remind Sammy. I gave you paper yesterday?"

*"Yes."*

"Paper. Yeah."

She made as if to return the money to her pocket. He reached for it, and she pulled her hand away. "Sammy, you need to earn this. You don't get something for nothing."

He looked furtively here and there. He slapped his hands together, rubbed the palms.

"Somebody told you to give me the paper, didn't they? Just tell me who."

His face contorted in furious concentration. He had the look of a man trawling the dead oceans of his brain for flickers of life-forms. "I don't remember, lady. Honest. I don't."

She stuck the bill back in her coat pocket and walked a few paces away from him. He shuffled after her. The sole of his right shoe was loose, and it flopped against the sidewalk.

"Lady, don't run," he said.

She turned to him. "Well?"

He said, "Lissen. I don't remember. Truth."

"Okay, too bad, you don't remember." And she walked away from him, moving toward the next corner of the block. He kept coming after her. She stepped off the sidewalk to cross the street. Halfway across the street he caught up with her, seized her wrist.

Oblivious to traffic and the sound of horns, he said, "Guy gave me photograph of you. Said to look out for lady with baby." He rubbed his stomach.

"A guy gave you a *photograph*? Describe him."

"Don't know what guy, don't know name, he gave me photograph and twenty-dulla bill and he say look for the lady in the photo, give her this piece of paper—"

"Let's get out of the street," she said. "We can't talk here." She dodged between vehicles and headed for the sidewalk. The panhandler, weaving through traffic, followed. He was calling out, "Look. Show you picture. I still got it. Here, lady. See. Show you picture—"

She turned, saw his outstretched hand with a creased photograph lying in the palm, a plaintive little offering. She was about to reach for this rain-streaked rectangle when a car, storming round the corner, struck the panhandler, and he flew up across the hood and was thrown sideways, flipping over on his back in the center of the street. She heard the windshield crack and the terrible sound of concrete against his skull, bone thudding stone, saw the way one leg was broken and buckled underneath his body, watched the photograph drift out of his fingers and slither toward the gutter, swirled by the stream of rain.

For a moment she was too shocked to move. The driver, a stout man in a dark coat with an astrakhan collar, stepped out of his vehicle and hurried to the panhandler. "Holy fuck, he just stepped out in fronta me," the guy said. And suddenly there was a crowd around the scene, and a cop appeared out of nowhere trying to make space for himself so that he could get to the victim, and the driver kept repeating the same phrase. "I braked soon's I saw him."

Sara experienced a glaze, as if some kind of transparent screen had formed to shield her from the hard reality of the scene. Blood, diluted by rain, ran from the man's open mouth. His eyes were shut. Arms limp, grubby palms upturned. She heard rain drum on the roofs of cars. She heard the cop say, "Anybody see this happen?" There was some jabbering from the spectators. The driver was describing yet again what had happened. "I braked soon's as I saw him."

Somebody with a shivering Afghan on a chain said, "I know the guy. I seen him around a few times. He's a bum."

*A bum*, Sara thought. *Just a bum. Put it on his gravestone.* The cop said, "Somebody call an ambulance."

A voice in the crowd said, "He's past that."

The driver said again, "I braked soon's as I saw him, swear to God."

Another voice said, "Check his veins. He's a junkie."

The cop said, "Would one of you make yourself useful and call a goddam ambulance?"

Sara felt a black cloud move through her head. She had the thought: This is theater, all theater, the victim, the shell-shocked driver, the uniformed cop, the extras standing around. Even the rain was the creation of a special-effects team. Nothing is real here. Not even the photograph floating down the gutter.

She moved slowly toward it; it was facedown in water. Nobody saw her stoop to pick it up. She stuck it in her pocket just as the sound of an ambulance could be heard, like some animal, unclassified as yet by zoology, screeching through the rain.

**20**

**SHE** walked and walked. When she reached the intersection of Forty-second Street and Fifth Avenue she was exhausted. She went inside a coffee shop, where she spread the sheets of computer paper on the table. The photograph she placed facedown on top of the papers. A moment of lethargy overwhelmed her; the stack from Mark's files, the panhandler's photograph—she was too weary to touch them. It was as if the accident had drained her of all curiosity, and the nervous energy she'd used up inside Rosenthal Brothers had sucked her dry.

She ordered black coffee and watched steam rise from the cup and tried to stir herself into life. She kept seeing the panhandler tossed through the air, kept having images of her father's face as she'd last seen him in Port Jefferson. She sipped the coffee, glanced out at the street, watched traffic froth through the dismal rain.

The photograph, the stack of papers; dampness had infiltrated her coat, and the papers had begun to curl at the edges. The back of the photograph was streaked with water. She didn't want to look at it yet. Didn't want to turn the goddam thing over and see whatever image the panhandler had given her. She just didn't want to look at herself because—

Because she was afraid. Because she didn't want to see herself, didn't want to know where and when the picture had been taken, and by whom. Afraid of what the picture might reveal. Afraid of the connections she might make when she looked at it.

She picked it up, held it a moment in one hand, then set it to the side, and turned over the first sheet of paper. There were about sixty in all. Sixty sheets to peruse, and no guarantee of finding anything.

She looked at the first and saw: BETELMAN, HERBERT, 3570 HACIENDA AVENUE, LITTLE ROCK, ARK. This was followed by a list of Herbert Betelman's investments. $100,000 had been placed in something called Dagenham Properties, Lexington, Kentucky. A sum of $850,000 had been put in CDs in a bank by the name of Jackson Alliance Trust, Mississippi. She turned to the second sheet.

BRIERLEY, JANE, NEW HOPE HOUSE, WILLIAMSBURG VA. Jane Brierley's money, $1.3 million, had been invested in a corporation called Weinstock Holdings GmbH, whose address was given as 37 Geblerstrasse, Munich, Germany. The third sheet detailed the investments of a company called BROSE, INC., PENSACOLA FLORIDA—$2.44 million, half of it invested in Weinstock of Munich, the other half in an organization named Futuraki Mining, Cape Town, South Africa.

She finished her coffee, ordered another. She wondered how long it would take her to go through everything. Were these some of the monies Klein had dipped into? Had he siphoned off funds from Betelman and Jane Brierley and Brose, Inc. and scores of others, and wired them to the dummy corporations Sol had mentioned? He must have lived in terror of an audit. He must have been impaled on the fear of discovery. Why hadn't she seen any of that anxiety about him?

He came home from work, chatted about his day as if it were all very ordinary and didn't involve the responsibility of investing massive sums of money on behalf of other people. Sometimes he brought home a bottle of good wine and they'd drink it and make love, which he'd always done wholeheartedly, passionately, with the kind of attention that made him—for her—a good lover. Remembered intimacies flooded her. His hands, his lips, the touch of his tongue on her breasts. Had she simply been *blind* to the other side of him? Had she been that unaware?

She drank from the second coffee. She glanced at the photograph. She'd been postponing the moment of turning it over and looking at it. Sooner or later, you have to do it. She touched the edge of it; a crease ran across the word KODAK. She took her fingers from it and thought, Wait. You're not ready to see your own face stare back at you, not ready for the whole *environment* of the photograph and what it might reveal. She left it lying facedown and turned her attention to the papers again.

*CHARLES, DONALD, 66 PRESSMAN, ITHACA, NEW YORK.* Six hundred thousand dollars of his money had gone into a pension plan run by Fidelissima Futures, with an address on Fifty-seventh Street, New York City. Another $500,000 had been tucked away in an entity called Starlight Holdings, Inc., of Gary, Indiana. A further $500,000 was in a trust account administered by Guzman & Brothers in Costa Rica.

*CRAWFORD, DEE DEE, 5700 FOUNTAIN HILLS DRIVE, FOUNTAIN HILLS, ARIZ.* Dee Dee's investments, which totalled $2.7 million, were all over the place—Rio, Cape Town, Liechtenstein, Dublin, Guernsey, Munich.

Klein had smooth-talked all these rich people into parting with their cash, praising the tax advantages of this investment, the returns on that. He must have had them sipping nectar out of his palms. Charm and confidence, that buoyancy he had. They bought it; just as she'd bought it. She'd been embezzled, just as Mark Klein's clients had been embezzled. The only difference was that her wallet hadn't been plundered; it was her heart that had been emptied.

She rubbed her eyelids, went back to the sheets, flicked through them. So much cash, and so easily accessed. She wondered if day after day greed had just grown inside Klein, a wicked flowering, a tempting plant that in the end he couldn't resist plucking. She stared through the window at the street. Rain smeared the glass, obscured the buildings. The city had a moribund look. She could see the panhandler's blood flowing into the gutters of this dead city.

She flipped the papers quickly now. She decided to eliminate investors with less than three million dollars—an arbitrary line, she knew; but she couldn't imagine the woman from St. Petersburg going to the trouble of abducting John Stone because relatively small amounts of money had been misappropriated. No, she guessed it would be large sums, a big operation—what was the point in trying to launder a couple of hundred thousand grand here, another couple there? The Russian woman would want it done quickly and smoothly. Money created its own urgent demands. It had to be buried fast and resurrected before it began to smell, because any kind of unusual stench would draw the wrong sort of attention.

She sifted the papers, eliminated all but three. A corporate entity called Tri-City Designs, Inc., with an address in Scranton, had $9.8 million invested in a variety of different money funds overseas. The corporate directors weren't named. Alba Services, Inc., located in Bridgeport, Connecticut, had a total investment of $8 million, some of it in the Cayman Islands, some of it Belize, some in Luxembourg. The directors of Alba Services weren't listed. She wondered briefly what services Alba provided.

The third candidate was situated here in New York, a company called White Sky Industries with an address in the upper West Side. White Sky had $15.9 million in various investments, mainly in the Far East—Hong Kong, Shanghai, Beijing. One company director was named: Theodore Pacific. She thought the name somehow had a fake ring to it.

She placed her hands on top of the sheets. White Sky, she thought. A nice name. What did White Sky do for its money?

It was time. She couldn't stall the moment.

She picked up the photograph now.

Turned it over, Looked at it.

Saw her own face.

Saw Mark Klein standing alongside her, an arm around her waist. The shadow of the photographer fell like a dark bloom against them. She held the picture a long time. She remembered the photographer saying *I gotta get you both in the shot, so get closer together*. The picture slid from her hands and fluttered to the floor. She remembered that day, she remembered the chill in the April morning air, and the way their breath fogged up. She remembered the photographer saying *One for the album, kids*.

The photograph had fallen right side up and as she bent awkwardly to retrieve it, she felt that whole morning come back to her in a rush of cold, frost on the grass, the cameraman's cajoling words. *For posterity, Mr. and Mrs. Klein. Smile*!

**21**

SHE took a cab to the upper West Side. The rain was beginning to let up and a milky sun was visible now and then through slits in the clouds. The street where she got out of the taxi was lined with old buildings undergoing renovation. Scaffolding clung to the sides of walls, heavy machinery roared behind wooden hoardings plastered with all kinds of posters—rock concerts, political slogans, bits of meaningless punk.

She wandered along the street. She had the computer sheets under her arm. Where there was a sidewalk she kept to it, but every so often it vanished behind protective barriers, forcing pedestrians back onto the street. Overhead, a massive orange crane dangled a slab of precast concrete.

Less than a few blocks away was Fordham University. Mark, she remembered, had once spent a semester there. Or so he'd said. She wondered about his history, how much of it had been fabricated—the parents he claimed had died in a plane crash, the young sister allegedly dancing in Las Vegas, the degree in business studies he'd received from the State University of New York at Albany. How much of that was true? How much of anything was?

She fingered the photograph in her pocket as she walked. She felt the ridged crease against her fingertips. How appropriate, she thought, the way the crease bisected the picture, creating a boundary between her face and his. She remembered when Tony Vandervelt had presented them with a copy of this snapshot he'd taken that April morning in Central Park. *Not exactly Karsh of Ottawa*, he'd said.

She'd stuck it in one of her photo albums anyway. How

could she have predicted then that Klein would take Tony's artless picture from the family album and give it to a panhandler he'd used as a messenger? She tried to picture this. Mark talking to the panhandler, pressing money into the guy's grubby hand, then a photograph. Keep your eyes open for this woman and when you see her give her this message.

And such a *useless* message, too, and so elaborately delivered. *Wait.*

*Is that all you have to say to me, Klein? Is that the only word you could find? No promises, nothing like I can explain all this, I can clear everything up, just hang on. No verbal flotation devices. Just one stupid four-letter two-cent word you took a whole lot of trouble to get to me.*

She passed into a covered walkway, the slatted wood ceiling of which supported scaffolding. Nearby, machinery gouged earth.

She stopped. On the other side of the street was a newly refurbished redbrick building where, according to the address on the computer printout, White Sky had its offices. She stood in the walkway, listening to rainwater drip through the planks overhead. White Sky. Theodore Pacific. What was she supposed to do—just go inside and ask to see this guy Pacific and demand the return of her father?

In your dreams.

She gazed at the windows of the building. Okay. She'd cross the street, go in, what options did she have? She'd think up some pretext, see this Theodore Pacific. Sometimes pregnancy helped. Sometimes it won you tiny concessions—a seat on a bus, a train, somebody opening a door for you. It also allowed you the luxury of mild eccentricities, because nobody held you responsible for odd behavior caused by the hormonal bedlam going on inside your body. Pregnancy was a license to behave in slightly unusual ways. She emerged from the walkway and crossed the street.

She entered the redbrick building and studied the directory on the wall by the elevators. White Sky was on the fourth floor, one floor above something called Ludex Enterprises and one floor below an outfit named—Weinstock (Germany) Holdings. *Weinstock*: it was one of the companies where Klein had invested the funds of certain clients. *Weinstock GmbH of Munich*. A coincidence too far, she thought. White Sky, Weinstock—had Klein come here one day and canvassed the companies in the building, looking both for investors and places where they might invest? She was no great believer in such confluences.

She stepped into the elevator. She fought against the tension she'd begun to feel. Her scalp prickled and her fingertips tingled. What was she going to do when the elevator stopped on the fourth floor? What story, what excuse, what kind of bluff? Her mind stuttered in the wrong gear. She considered getting out on the third floor and walking the rest of the way up, giving herself time to think.

She watched the number 4 blink on the panel, then the door slid open, and she stepped out. She found herself in a reception area, an unfinished place of loose wires, sockets that hadn't been fixed to the walls, pots of paint, paintbrushes, canvas covers stuck over furniture. The air was rich with the smell of paint thinner. The reception desk, wrapped in plastic and sealing tape, was unoccupied.

A corridor stretched off to her right, and she followed it, crossing brand-new carpet that hadn't been tacked into place. She noticed electric wires dangling from between the tiles of the suspended ceiling. Doors on either side of her were open; empty offices, unfurnished. More paint pots, stepladders, bare floorboards, unattached power cords.

"You looking for somebody?"

The man had appeared in a doorway at the end of the corridor. He wore paint-splashed coveralls. He was in his mid-thirties and overweight. His neck was red, his face flushed. She was too surprised by his sudden appearance to think of anything to say.

He was staring at her impatiently. He had a paintbrush in his hand and thick drips slid over his wrists.

"Is this White Sky?" she asked.

"You got the right place," he said. "But if you're looking for somebody in particular, you come on the wrong day."

"I was looking for Mr. Pacific," she said.

The man said, "Him, you never see."

"He doesn't come in?"

"Once in a blue moon maybe. Just sorta looks around, says he wants the walls a different color, then he leaves. Like that." The man snapped his fingers.

''What about other employees?''

''*What* other employees? Nobody comes here excepting me and the electrician, and the electrician don't come more than once a week, and he don't do jack shit even when he appears. Fiddles with a plug, then calls it a day.''

She felt a little dizzy. The smell of paint thinner, of fresh paint. An assault on her senses.

''I mean,'' the guy said, ''I work here on my own mosta the time. I paint the walls. Pacific comes in and says he's changed his mind. First it was pale blue. Then it was eggshell. Then it all had to be changed to white. It ain't no skin off my nose. I get paid.''

''What kind of business is White Sky?'' she asked.

''Plastics, far as I know. Trash-can liners. And those doodahs they wrap sandwiches in. They got a plant in the Bronx, I understand.''

''The Bronx,'' she said. Trash-can liners. Plastic doodahs. Did they also manufacture Dumpsters? she wondered.

''Pacific's the one that pays you,'' she said.

The man's expression became guarded. He looked at her with his face a little tilted. ''You from the IRS?''

''Do I look like IRS?''

''Can't tell these days, lady.''

''I work for the company upstairs. Ludex? And I just wanted to come down and say hello.''

''Neighborly,'' he said.

''Right, neighborly.''

''Well, you gonna have a hard time finding *these* neighbors.'' He wiped a white-streaked hand upon his coveralls. ''Between you and me, I don't know what the hell's going on around this place. Half the power sockets don't work. There's like one overhead light. I mean. I know this is a new building and all, just the same . . . You'd think they'd be anxious to get things under way.''

''Strange,'' she said.

''I ain't never been on a job like it, that's all I can tell you.''

She shrugged, looked through open doorways into the vacant offices. ''Maybe they're in no hurry. Maybe they're being careful with their budget.''

''Budget? I seen Pacific drive up in this brand-new Porsche.

Suits he wears—gotta be eight hundred dollars at least. More. I don't think he's worrying over no budget.''

"What does he look like?" she asked.

"Look like?"

"Yeah. In case I happen to run into him in the elevator."

"Young guy. Always well turned out." The painter pinched his nostrils between thumb and index finger and suppressed a sneeze. "Gotta laugh. A painter that's allergic to paint. Heh, heh."

"Can't be convenient for you," she said. "So Pacific's young and well dressed. What else? Any distinguishing features? Warts? Moles?" She'd decided on a light approach, casual, not too prying.

"*Warts and moles? This guy*? No way. Hair always just combed. Suits always look like they just been pressed. If this guy saw a hint of goddam dandruff on his collar, he'd have cardiac failure." The painter squeezed his nostrils again. His eyes watered. "I gotta find a new profession one day soon."

"So if I see a well-dressed young man in the elevator, it's going to be Mr. Pacific," she said.

"That'd be him all right."

She said nothing for a moment. *A well-dressed young man*, she thought. "If they don't have any budget worries, then I guess they're just not in any rush to open these offices."

The painter rubbed his eyes with his knuckles. "My wife, who watches too much TV, says this place sounds like a scam. Like a tax write-off. Know what I mean?"

Sara nodded. "A front, you mean."

"Kinda. You know. You don't actually open the office, you just keep redecorating the goddam place, and you go on doing it until the IRS guys smell a dead mackerel."

*A front*, she thought. She said, "I guess I'll look in some other time."

"You want I should tell Mr. Pacific you come by?"

"No big deal," she said.

"I'll see you out."

He walked with her to the elevator and pressed the call button for her. "You ever need trash-can liners, you know what brand to buy," he said, just as the elevator arrived.

"Nice to have met you," she said.

"High point of my day," he remarked. "Believe me."

She stepped inside the elevator, watched his face as the door slid shut. The elevator began its descent. A front. She wondered if the plant in the Bronx even existed or if it was just something that Pacific, this well-dressed young man, had told the painter.

Something in the enclosed space of the elevator disturbed her. It was faint, but it took her only a moment to realize what it was, the fading aroma of something she'd smelled before. Clove oil.

**22**

SHE went into the street. She watched three men in hard hats perched high on the scaffolding. A balancing act of cold nerve.

The scent of clove oil in the elevator; the Russian woman had been in the building—a few minutes before her? Or had she just entered the place immediately after?

Sara crossed the street and looked up at the redbrick facade of the place. If the woman hadn't been in the offices of White Sky, then she must have visited some other floor: Weinstock Holdings, possibly. Sara strolled to the end of the block. She considered the prospect of reentering the building and going to the premises of Weinstock, but she couldn't see she had anything to gain from such a move. If she went back, and if the woman was still in there, what could come of an encounter with her? She didn't want to look at that ancient face, the yellow hair, the cruel slit of that mouth. She didn't want to look into the eyes of the person responsible for the abduction of her father. She sensed violent possibilities within herself— but what would it achieve to claw the crone's painted mask with your fingernails? She had the feeling skin would peel from bone like corrupt, mummified flesh.

Besides, Sara had something else in mind, something that might ultimately be more constructive than a run-in with the old woman, which would be disagreeable at the very least.

She walked quickly in the direction of Amsterdam Avenue. She entered the first restaurant she found, a vegetarian place with scrubbed wood tables and a massive array of plants and waitresses who smiled as if they were stoned on some derivative of valerian root. She ordered a glass of papaya juice and asked to see the phone book. She took the directory to a table and flipped the pages until she found what she was looking for and jotted an address and phone number down on the back of one of the printout sheets. She left the place. She walked until she found a cab, which she rode as far as Madison and Forty-third.

The day felt like a rubber band stretched behind her to breaking point. She wanted to lie down somewhere and sleep, but she had to keep going because she didn't have any choices. You move, keep moving, you don't need to think, you don't have to entertain images of your father, you go beyond contemplation of all your limited options, you just goddam go, you don't wilt because of anything as inconvenient as an affliction of weariness.

She walked east along Forty-third. When she came to the address she was looking for, an elegantly restored town house, she paused, saw drapes bunched back neatly at windows, security alarms and video cameras placed over a glossy black front door. Now: either she climbed the steps and rang the doorbell or she turned and walked away. She kept gazing at the windows, wondering if this were the place where her father was being kept. Her reaction, based on nothing more substantial than a daughter's intuition, was that John Stone wasn't inside this house.

She hesitated. It would be foolhardy to go directly up to the door and announce herself, which would be exposure she didn't need. For the moment, she'd just content herself with the location of the house and store it away for future reference. It was a little nugget of knowledge, and maybe it didn't amount to much, but it was something more than she'd had before—a physical address for somebody who might have a connection with the Russian woman.

She was about to continue along the sidewalk when a car slid into view. It was a dark blue, low-slung MG and it backed into a parking spot a few doors down from the town house. She watched the driver step out and move along the sidewalk to the stairway of the house. He didn't look in her direction; his focus was elsewhere. He hurried up the steps and took a key from his pocket and opened the front door. He went inside, slamming the door. She lingered a moment, saw him pass in front of a window, watched him pick up a telephone, and then he moved into shadow and out of her line of vision.

*Mr. Theodore Pacific*, she thought. Young, well dressed, everything the painter had described.

The last time she'd seen Theodore Pacific was in the alley behind the bar in Port Jefferson, when he'd winked at her.

She walked to the end of the block. The baby turned fiercely inside her and knocked the breath out of her. At the heart of all her anxieties and fears, she felt a love of such primal intensity that it transcended all the limits of language. And love, she understood, was a reservoir from which you could draw all kinds of resolve, all manner of courage.

# 23

IT was late afternoon by the time she returned to 3242 Midsummer. She entered the empty house, checked the answering machine, found no messages. She wadded the computer sheets and stuck them in the drawer of the telephone table. She lay down on the sofa in the living room and closed her eyes: the day swirled through her mind, the meeting with Sol, the theft of data from Klein's computer, the car slamming into the hapless panhandler, blood in the rain, the slick photograph, the empty offices of White Sky and the smell of cloves, the town house where Theodore Pacific lived. These images coagulated into one formless whole. She shut her eyes—but her brain, on overload, was still restless.

She heard the sound of the doorbell. She rose, saw Thomas McClennan on the porch. She opened the door.

"Can I come in?"

"Why not," she said.

He followed her into the living room. She couldn't tell from his expression what mode he was in. Was this the avuncular Fed? Or the other McClennan who longed for nightsticks and baseball bats? *I'd like to just break her.*

He stood near the fireplace.

"Checking up on me?" she asked.

"You might say. How's the package?" He nodded at her stomach.

"The package is fine."

He wandered the room, idly touching surfaces, glancing at the answering machine. "No word, I suppose?"

"From my husband? Why ask? You already know the calls I receive."

"The calls you receive *here*," he said. "You might take phone calls someplace else."

"I might," she said.

"And you might make them someplace else too."

She said, "I thought you were keeping tabs on me, Mc-Clennan."

"Yeah. We do that."

"But you're afraid you might miss something."

"We pride ourselves on missing very little, Sara. I have to say, though, that was a nifty little switch you did with the restaurant the other night. Sam's Seafood House. Very tricky."

"I believe in privacy," she said.

He smiled and ran a palm across his hair. "We all believe in privacy, Sara. Trouble is, sometimes people use it as a curtain they draw across activities of an illegal nature."

"I changed my mind about a restaurant. Is that activity of an illegal nature, McClennan?"

"You weren't breaking any law," he said.

"So we can still choose where we go to eat in America. Hallelujah."

McClennan perched on the arm of the sofa. "You make me feel like I'm the kind of guy who doesn't approve of personal freedom. I see it differently. I uphold the law. Which means I'm one of those people that ensure the preservation of our basic freedoms. No law, and you've got anarchy, Sara. Which isn't a working philosophy. Guys like me—we protect people."

"You'd be a laugh a minute except you're a little too scary for that. This fixation you have about me concealing information from you. That's a long way from being funny. And what you put me through at Borbokis's office wasn't remotely entertaining."

McClennan said, "I turn over stones. Sometimes I find what I'm looking for."

She stared at him. She had the feeling he was in some kind of holding pattern, circling a target he was going to hit only when it suited him.

He said, "You know by now why we're looking for Mark, don't you?"

She said nothing.

"I hear you made a scene yesterday at Rosenthal's. You barged into Sol's office. I guess he felt an obligation to inform you about what was going on."

"Did Sol tell you that?"

"Sol's a discreet old guy. You need forceps to get anything out of him. Anyway, if he didn't clue you in, your old pal Vandervelt probably did. When was it he came to see you? Last night?"

"Was it only last night? Time flies," she said. She turned her face away from McClennan and wondered why his surveillance teams hadn't picked up on her encounter with the Russian woman, hadn't seen her step inside the Buick yesterday afternoon. Because they couldn't watch her every minute of every day. Because surveillance was never one hundred percent. You lost sight of people on crowded streets. You couldn't always track them. Why hadn't they been around when John Stone had disappeared? Why had they taken their eye off the ball at that particular point in time?

"Thirty-two million big ones," McClennan said.

"Find Mark, maybe you'll find the money," she said.

"And you've heard nothing from him?"

"How many times can you ask the same question, McClennan?" Did he know about the message from the beggar? she wondered. Had he somehow discovered this? She realized she was meant to feel that she was hiding information from him. This was the way he worked.

She said, "I know what you think, that I'm Mark's accomplice—"

"Maybe. Maybe not. All I do is explore every avenue of possibility—"

"You believe I'm about to pack my bag and run off and join him somewhere in the sun."

He smiled, held his hand up to interrupt her. "You can't run anywhere, Sara. You couldn't even get a boarding ticket on any airplane with a foreign destination."

"Why not?"

"Because you need a passport."

"I've got a—wait, you've nullified it, whatever you call it. Is that it?"

"Right, it's no longer valid," he said.

"You worked this out with the Justice Department, did you?"

"A string was pulled, yeah."

"A string was pulled. Didn't I hear you say a minute ago you were this great believer in personal freedom? Or did I just imagine that?"

"Freedom's a privilege, Sara. A reward you get for being a good citizen."

She got up from the sofa. What was the point in telling him that she'd always been a good citizen? He wasn't about to listen. He heard only what he wanted to hear. So: no passport. No freedom of movement. She was landlocked. Good citizen, but a prisoner of the system anyway. There might just as well have been bars around the house.

He asked, "Why did you go to the Rosenthal offices this morning?"

She caught her breath. She knew she'd slipped away unobserved. He hadn't seen her leave. This was a bluff, a trick question. "I didn't," she said.

"What if I tell you you were seen there? Even guys with vacuum cleaners notice things, Sara."

Guys with vacuum cleaners, she thought. The buzz of machines, men in uniforms. They'd hardly glanced at her.

"Well?" he asked.

"There's been some mistake," she said.

"A mistake? A pregnant woman was observed entering the offices just after 8:00 A.M. Dark blue raincoat. You got a dark blue raincoat, Sara?"

"Doesn't everybody?"

"Short hair."

"So what?"

"Sounds very familiar to me," he said.

"I wasn't there, McClennan," she said.

"There's more."

She waited. Rain lashed around the house all at once. The wind drove through shrubbery and raked trees and whipped crisscrossing eddies across the tiled roof.

"Klein's computer."

"What about it?"

"Somebody broke into it this morning."

"Broke into it? What does that mean?"

"Data was printed from it."

"And?"

"You tell me."

"Tell you what? I wasn't there. I didn't touch any damn computer."

"The computer's tagged, Sara. Anybody touches it without authorization, it's recorded on the mainframe. Somebody entered the computer this morning, and printed data from the files marked CURRENT."

"It wasn't me," she said. Was she giving anything away by her expression, by some inflection in her voice?

"Okay, it was some other short-haired pregnant woman in a blue raincoat," he said. "And this woman, who happens to bear an uncanny resemblance to you, goes to Klein's computer and prints out some information—why would she do such a thing, Sara? And how did this phantom woman know the password?"

Sara made no reply. She remembered tapping the keyboard. Her mind jumped to the idea that she'd left her fingerprints behind.

"See how black it all looks, Sara. A pregnant woman comes in, keys in the password, makes off with some data. The way things stand, you're the only pregnant woman in the whole goddam scenario."

"I don't know the password," she said.

"For argument's sake, let's say you're lying. Let's say you know the password—"

"But I don't—"

"Let's just imagine for the moment that you do, okay? Now this opens a real can of worms, Sara. Not only did *Klein* have access to his accounts, but so had *you*. Are you getting my drift?"

"You're still harping on the idea of my involvement in Klein's alleged embezzlement, and I'm getting tired of that, McClennan."

"Well, hell, I apologize for bothering you. Forgive me. The problem is, we have to confront some hard facts sooner or later, Sara, troublesome as they might be to you. If you knew the password, you knew how to get into the accounts. And if you knew how to do that, you also knew how to manipulate the numbers.''

"Right," she said. "Klein and I, we were a team, we masterminded the whole thing together, I confess, so get out your cuffs and take me downtown or wherever it is you take criminals.''

She bungled this attempt at levity. She shouldn't even have tried it. McClennan wasn't in the mood. His face flushed angrily. "Don't fucking tempt me, Sara. I'm already *this* close to nailing you on suspicion of tampering with evidence.''

She heard something snap inside her head, some little twig of resolve. She had a powerful urge to throw herself on McClennan's mercy, to tell him everything from beginning to end and implore him to find John Stone. She struggled with the temptation. McClennan wouldn't go for it; the Russian woman, the mob, the kidnapping of John Stone—he'd accuse her of making up ridiculous fictions, tales to cover her complicity. He might even go as far as to suggest that her own father was just another player in Mark Klein's scam. She didn't know. And she didn't want to take the chance of finding out. John Stone was out there somewhere, a tiny dot on a big map. And McClennan wasn't the one to find him. Besides, she'd read stories about how the Feds botched kidnap cases, victims they never recovered until it was too late, shoot-outs, wholesale disasters.

"Why did you want the information, Sara?" he asked.

"I don't want to talk to you again unless Borbokis is present.''

"Did Klein ask you to find something out for him? Something he'd overlooked? Was it like that, Sara?"

"I'm saying nothing."

"Something he'd forgotten?"

She said, "Talk to my lawyer."

She strode quickly to the door, opened it, pointed to the porch. McClennan moved toward the door slowly; he wanted to irritate her, to agitate her.

"Go," she said. "Just go."

"It doesn't end here, Sara."

"Does it have an end?"

''Sure. Everything has an end. Sometimes the journey's a little difficult, that's all.''

He stepped on to the porch where the rainy wind curled under the roof and blew at him. She saw his car parked at the end of the driveway.

''Like all journeys, there's always a destination,'' he said. ''Remember that. And I have a feeling this particular destination is coming up real fast. One other thing to keep in mind: you can't hide behind a lawyer forever.''

She shut the door on him. She'd behaved without cool, she knew that. She'd acted guilty. He'd have to have been blind not to have noticed her alarm. She trudged upstairs to the bedroom, lay down on the bed. Two men with vacuum cleaners, for Christ's sake. And she'd thought she was being so goddam smart. Stupid, stupid and desperate. Foundering in rough waters. Pilfering stuff from the computer, going to the offices of White Sky, tracking down the address of Theodore Pacific. Bright girl. You don't even know what you're doing, do you? It isn't good sense that drives you, it's blind panic, which has its own lunatic momentum. She imagined fingerprint men going over the keyboard, dusting the keys. How long would it take them before they found hers?

She rolled over on her side. It was only then she noticed the thick padded brown envelope propped against the base of the lamp on the bedside table. She picked it up, ripped it open. It contained an unlabeled videocassette. Somebody had come here in her absence. Somebody had entered the house and climbed the stairs to the bedroom to leave this envelope. She held the cassette in one hand, quickly opened the bedside drawer with the other.

The Walther was still where she'd left it.

Whoever had come to the house had been a delivery boy, not a thief.

**24**

*A seashore. A gull in sunlight. Her father, around the age of forty, is troweling a channel in wet sand. He works diligently. The foaming tide is receding. Sara appears in the margin of the shot. A skinny kid, barely a teenager. Her one-piece bathing suit is damp and gritted with sand. Her father laughs, catches her arm, pulls her down. She lies flat, pretending to complain, but she's laughing along with her father. There's no sound. No voices, no whimper of tide. The colors are all a little off, bleached. The whole scene is dreamy. Her father makes her lie down in the channel he's dug and then begins to spade sand over her. And the same silent laughter goes on. The sand covers her until only her face is visible—*

The picture jumps. A time leap. The same beach, later.

*Her mother is wrapped in a towel. She looks pinched and unwell. Her face is parchment stretched over bone, her eyes are unnaturally large. John Stone is sitting alongside her, his hand laid lightly against her hipbone. Her mother's hair is glistening.*

The camerawork is shaky. Sara remembers: *I took this sequence. I held the camera. How many years ago?*

*John Stone puts his arm around his wife's shoulder because she's shivering. He draws her very close to his body, protectively, gently. He does this as if the woman were fragile, as if any excess pressure of touch will pain her. The woman lays her face against John Stone's shoulder. They sit motionless this way, husband and wife clinging together in an intimacy they both know is doomed. Because the woman is sick. Because there are not going to be many more days like this one.*

155

*Because love is a limited commodity, a transient blessing.*

The picture dissolves into a few brief images, none of them lasting more than a couple of seconds. *Sara in a sand grave, laughing. Sara's mother staring without expression into the lens. John Stone slurping an ice-cream cone and making a great messy moustache of it. And everything silent. Everything soundless. Life and laughter and a dying woman and a man eating an ice-cream cone in total silence.*

The picture stops. A series of numbers flicker across the TV screen. An ending, Sara thinks, remembering how her father had had all his old home movies transferred to videocassettes—but it isn't quite an ending, not yet.

The screen is filled with a close-up of John Stone's face. He's no longer a man of forty. He looks exactly the way he looked the last time she saw him in the bar in Port Jefferson.

And now there's sound, words coming from his lips.

In a flat expressionless voice, he says, ''I want you to know I am fine. I want you to know I am in good health. You need have no concern for me, Sara.''

The tape ends in a series of hissing noises, almost as if it were an image beamed from an extraterrestrial source, one that has been destroyed by interference before reaching ground control.

She gets the remote. Sea and sand. A sand grave. She rewinds the tape a little way, back through the hissing, back to the image of her father. The close-up.

''You need have no concern for me.'' The clipped diction, the lips that hardly move. He seems to be speaking from a prepared statement, something he's been forced to memorize. The stilted phraseology, the perfect enunciation of each word. This isn't John Stone's way of speaking.

She studies his face again. She presses Pause and the image, though unsteady, like a picture in the early stages of deterioration, stays on the screen. She gets up from her knees and goes closer, because now she's exploring the edges of the picture, as if she might make out a background detail, an indication of where this epilogue to the original home movie was shot. But all around John Stone's face, in the dark narrow margins, are impenetrable shadows. You could stare long enough and imagine you see shapes there, people lingering behind him, marks on a wall—but this is all fancy.

She rewinds the tape back to the shot of her father with his arm around her mother. She watches it again, her heart fissured by a deep ache. She watches it disintegrate into the rapid flashing of disconnected cameos, her mother's eyes, the ice-cream mess on her father's face. She can smell ocean and sand and suntan lotion and vanilla. But this is more fancy. She thinks: *a few days after these pictures were shot, my mother was dead.*

She freezes John Stone's face again. She touches the TV screen with her fingertips, as if she might actually reach inside and feel her father's face. She hears static crackle against her skin, pulls back her hand from the surface of the glass.

She slumps. The motionless image looks at her in a haunted way: is her father blaming her for his plight? is that accusation in his eyes? She can't tell. She turns from the screen, lets the remote drop to the floor. She can still feel the way sand clung to her bare legs, the way it got in her hair and made her scalp itch.

She closes her eyes. The tape is a malicious kind of souvenir, she realizes, sent to remind her not only of her father's predicament, but also of the fragility of family life. Of human life.

Especially John Stone's.

She stands, kills the picture with the Off button. She climbs upstairs. The muscles in her calves are unsteady. She sits on the bed. What washes over her is a vast sense of sadness. Of times past and lost.

The uncertainty of tomorrow.

The empty bedroom dismays her.

She can't sit still.

She rises, opens a closet, pulls out a stack of family photograph albums and leafs through them. Whether she expects to find some comfort by flipping through these images, she doesn't know. She understands she just needs to dip into the waters of the past. Faces flutter, phantoms rise from their graves behind sheets of transparent plastic.

Her father and mother on their wedding day.

Herself at a barbecue in somebody's gloriously sunny backyard, July 4, circa 1973.

Herself and Klein snapped at Coney Island, he munching gleefully into a hot dog, she in baseball cap with a DODGERS logo. Herself and Klein snapped in Central Park one chill morning—

She feels a little knot of air compressed at the back of her throat. It takes her many seconds before she understands something is wrong here, something is out of place, badly so.

## 25

SHE drove through relentless rain. The car windows fogged up, the wipers scratched at the hard-falling rain with the screech of nails on a blackboard. Traffic signals, signposts, other cars: these seemed to exist in a dimension where she didn't belong. She'd remained in the bedroom for a long time before she'd rushed from the house because it was no longer a place where she felt any comfort or security. It wasn't 3242 Midsummer anymore, it wasn't the house over whose threshold Mark Klein had carried her years before.

She passed through Port Jefferson, dreary in the wet darkness. Somewhere along the highway she drove into a filling station and switched off the engine. She was unraveling. She laid her face against the wheel, a slumped position.

She stayed that way for a long time. She thought of her father's image on the videocassette. She thought of the photograph Tony Vandervelt had taken of her and Mark in Central Park. When she moved at last she went to the pay phone and listened to rain make crazy music on glass and she called Vandervelt's number. There was no answer. Where was he? She needed to talk to him.

But it wasn't just Tony she needed. She had a desire for a general human connection, a grounding in some kind of companionship. She tried Sol's number, but when she heard his gruff voice on his answering machine, she left no message. Friends—where were all her friends? Jennifer Gryce was lost to her. Her old high-school friends had joined the great American diaspora, disappearing into the heartland or to the Far West in search of new lives. They sent Christmas cards from

Santa Barbara, or Albuquerque, and promised visits that never materialized.

She went inside the coffee shop of the filling station, bought a can of Dr Pepper. A security camera scanned the store. She saw herself on a black-and-white monitor behind the counter. She saw herself going through the motions of paying for the soda. She was reflected everywhere—in the monitor, the glass-fronted door of the soda cooler, the small digital display of the cash register, the window. A multiplicity of pregnant Saras. She tore the tab from the can and drank quickly. Her thirst was demanding.

"Refreshing," the voice said.

Sara didn't turn. She recognized the voice, she didn't need to look. She stared straight ahead at the monitor. She could see the old woman immediately behind her. Charlie was there, too, dipping his big hands into a bag of potato chips. Sara still didn't turn. She crumpled the empty can in her hand. She felt the old woman's breath against the back of her neck.

"Some TV is quite entertaining, I find. Don't you, Sara?"

Sara cut her hand on the jagged opening of the crushed soda can. She didn't feel the pain.

"But often there is too much rubbish. Too much mindless nonsense. Don't you think so?"

The picture on the monitor changed as the camera panned away from the counter. Now there were views of shelves, mountains of candy bars, a stack of disposable diapers. Sara turned round. She was unpleasantly surprised to see the old woman in color; she preferred the monochromatic image.

She moved, made an attempt to step past the woman, but Charlie, nimble for such a big man, blocked her way.

"Sara, dear girl, have you nothing to say?" the woman asked. She adjusted the position of her aluminum walker with a gesture of irritation that she had to rely on such a contraption.

Sara was aware of the clerk behind the counter filling the reservoir of a coffeepot. The sound of water, the whiff of ground coffee. Her cut finger leaked blood over the crumpled soda can. It trickled down into her palm.

"What is the saying? Cat has your tongue?" the woman asked.

Charlie said, "Cat *got* your tongue."

"Charlie. Why do you try to correct me? My English isn't up to your enviable standard?"

Sara stared across the store. Water had begun to drip through coffee grounds. *Dad*, she thought. *My father is filtering away from me.* She stared at the woman, who was smiling, her face angled to one side. She resembled an arthritic old bird with ruined plumage.

"Of course, television can have educational functions," she said. "It doesn't always have to be mindless."

"You fucking bitch," Sara said.

"Ah, you see, Charlie. She speaks. Profanity, unfortunately. But at least she speaks."

"Did you write my father's script for him? Did you hold a card in front of his face for him to read?" Sara let the soda can drop inside a trash container. She didn't take her eyes from the woman. She felt her heart fill with rage. She saw nothing beyond the woman. Everything else was out of focus and meaningless except every little detail of the woman's features. Pink lines in the whites of the eyes, a wart that hadn't quite been covered by the plaster of makeup, the multitude of furrows that resembled small incisions made by a razorblade around the lips.

"Such an intense look, Charlie. Do you see how she stares at me? Would you call that loathing?"

"I'd call it that," said Charlie.

"Even worse than loathing," the woman said. She was dressed in the green-and-red pulsating nightmare of a dress she'd worn before. "Is there a word for that, Charlie?"

"Beats me," said Charlie.

The woman reached out to touch Sara's arm. Sara stepped back and finally looked elsewhere. But it didn't break the stranglehold of her hatred, which was so wild, so overwhelming, there was no room inside her for anything else. But what good was such intensity unless you could channel it and make it work for you? If you didn't direct it, it controlled you; and then it was useless. She had to rein her rage in, corral it.

The woman said, "Are you ready now to discuss certain matters with me now, Sara?"

"I want my father back," she said.

"Of course, you want your father back. This is perfectly understandable. Daughters need their fathers, after all. And yours is an especially nice example of the species. But what do I get in return?''

"Anything in my power to give you."

"Anything? Does that include Klein? Can you give me Klein?''

*Klein*, she thought. "I need time." It was a statement born out of anxiety, a lie of desperation. Klein might as well have been lost in space, imprisoned in a capsule beyond the reach of recovery.

The woman said, "And how much time are you asking for, Sara?''

"I don't know."

"You don't know. Always the same thing, Sara. You don't know. You don't know anything, do you? I do not have the patience of a saint." The words were delivered in a series of furious little serpentine hisses. Sara felt a spray of spit. The woman scrutinized Sara's face, and her expression altered, became suddenly mellow. "But you're pregnant, of course. And pregnancy often leads to some mental confusion, I imagine. Let me ask you again, more quietly. How much time?''

"I can't answer that."

The woman glanced at Charlie and asked, "How much time can we give her?''

Charlie shrugged his wide shoulders. "That's your decision.''

"Can you deliver Klein by tomorrow morning, Sara?''

Sara said, "I need longer than that." How long? she wondered. A month? A year? The rest of her life?

"Your father has been complaining of abdominal pains. Is that not so, Charlie?''

"Absolutely," Charlie said.

"Abdominal pains?" Sara asked. "How? What have you done to him?''

"Done to him? Nothing. Nothing at all. The pains are stress-related, I would say. He doesn't care for his present situation.''

"I don't want him harmed in any way," Sara said. "Do you understand that?''

"Nobody wants that, let me assure you, Sara.''

"If you hurt him . . .''

"What will you do, Sara?''

"I'll look for you, and I'll find you."

"And then? Tell me. You'll kill me?"

"*Yes*." Sara listened to the surprising ferocity in this simple little response. She realized in all her life she'd never entertained the notion of killing another person. The idea, once so foreign to her nature as to be unthinkable, struck her then as the most reasonable thing in the world.

The old woman smiled. "So there is iron in you, after all. There is flint, Sara Klein. Wonderful. I appreciate a woman who will not simply lie down and roll over. You and I have something in common, it seems."

"I doubt it," Sara said. "I seriously doubt if we even breathe the same air."

"Sara, listen to me. All my life I have resisted the attempts of people, usually men, to suppress me. You're too weak to control complex business affairs, they said. Your enemies will demolish you. On and on. But they were very much mistaken. And those who underestimated me paid a very high price."

*You and I have something in common, it seems.* Sara saw in the woman's eyes the kind of focused determination that wouldn't be interrupted by fruitless moral debate when it came to eliminating her enemies. What would it be like to kill somebody, to take another life? She wondered if the old woman recognized a murderous look in her own eyes just then, a faint mirror image of herself in Sara's face. It wasn't a thought Sara entertained for long. There was no affinity, no likeness. There could never be.

The old woman said, "I will tell you this, Sara. If you're obliged to quarry deep enough into your own heart, you sometimes come across a black seam you may not like. But there is nothing you can do about it. Absolutely nothing."

"I don't believe that," Sara said.

"Believe, don't believe. I am telling you a simple fact of life. My God, who do you imagine yourself to be, Sara Klein? A pregnant little suburban housewife? Somebody meek at heart? Somebody who thinks twice before swatting a housefly? Is this how you perceive yourself? Are those your pathetic limits?"

"No, I'm not like that."

"Of course you are not like that. This is what I have been telling you. Iron and flint. Flint and iron. And I am the same."

The old woman patted the back of Sara's hand in a gesture that might have been one of gentle encouragement.

Sara, repelled by the touch, quickly drew away her hand. "We're not remotely alike," she said. "We don't live on the same planet. We don't have a single goddam thing in common."

"You think so now, of course. But things have a way of changing." The old woman, altering the position of her metal frame, stumped toward the door. She looked back at Sara.

"By the way," she said. "It would be quite pointless to show the videotape to anyone, Sara. What would they see in any event? A home movie, sweet in its way, but badly made. A father's declaration of love and an announcement of his good health. That's all. So. You will hear from us by, let's say, noon?"

Sara watched the old woman, followed by Charlie, go outside. The stalks of the frame made clicking sounds. Charlie opened an umbrella for the woman, and they passed close to the gas pumps where neon illuminated them briefly before they moved into the shadows to their car.

Sara lingered a time inside the shop. Find Klein. By noon. She knew she couldn't unless in some inscrutable heaven a miracle might be manufactured. And this wasn't the age of miracles. Prayers weren't answered anymore. You prayed, you were talking only to yourself. God no longer gave you quality time.

She went outside and hurried to her car. The rain, falling from that same heaven where prayers ascended hopelessly, came crashing down through blue neon and slammed like thumbtacks against her face. She got inside her car and laid her wet hands on the wheel and felt cold rainwater slick from her scalp and run down the back of her neck. *Flint and iron*, she thought. *Iron and flint*.

Maybe. Maybe so.

# 26

**SHE** drove to Manhattan. Clouds, gorged with rainwater, choked the moon. She parked in a street in the Village. She locked the car and walked less than half a block. She was soaked, but no longer felt the rain. When she reached an old house that had been carved up into a series of apartments, she pressed one of the bells and heard Tony Vandervelt's voice from the intercom. She announced herself. Tony sounded surprised.

"Sara?"

"Can I come up?" she asked.

"Yeah, sure you can." The front door buzzed open and she stepped into the hallway. She climbed the stairs to the second floor where Vandervelt, dressed in a long dark green robe, was waiting for her at the open door to his apartment. She went inside.

"You'll need a towel," Tony said. "Dry your hair."

She took off her raincoat and watched him vanish inside the bathroom. She looked around. The walls were hung with paintings. Tony collected the works of unknown artists in the hope that sooner or later at least one of them would become big-bucks famous. An eclectic gathering altogether. One Gothic piece bothered her a little. It depicted a batlike creature devouring a dark shape similar to itself; it was all blackness and blood and sharp little fangs.

Tony came back, pressed a towel into her hands and said, "Here. Dry off before you catch cold."

She rubbed her hair vigorously with the towel.

"I'm surprised to see you," he said.

*165*

"I'm not interrupting anything?" she asked.

"Nothing." He made an empty gesture with his hand.

"I phoned earlier."

He took the towel from her and laid it carefully over a radiator. "Let me make you some tea."

"Really. I don't want anything."

He sat on a sofa facing her. He looked, she thought, just a touch uneasy. Maybe her unexpected arrival disturbed him. She glanced around the room again. One door led to a bathroom. Another, halfway open, to the kitchen. Copper-bottom saucepans hung on hooks. A third led, presumably, to Tony's bedroom. She saw a pale slit of lamplight under this door.

"What brings you down here?" he asked.

"A question," she said. "A simple little question."

"You've come all this way to ask a simple little question?" He looked at her doubtfully. He crossed his legs, the robe parted. His legs were pale.

She reached for her wet raincoat, which she'd dropped on the floor. She took out the creased photograph and passed it to him.

He studied it a moment. "I remember this," he said. "Central Park. March, April this year."

"April. A cold day."

"Bitter," he said. "We all went to lunch at some Indian place on Forty-sixth Street, didn't we? Mark insisted on spicy food."

"I'd forgotten that," she said. "Tandoori lamb."

He fingered the photograph. "This has been through the wars."

"You made a copy of it for us. Did you keep one for yourself?"

"Did you come all the way into the city to ask about an old photograph?"

"Can I see your copy?" she asked.

"Whatever for? It would look like this one—except in better condition."

"I'd just like to see it." She wasn't sure how much she wanted to explain to him. It came back again to a question of trust.

He shrugged. "I don't know where it is exactly."

"Find it for me, Tony."

He turned his face and looked in the direction of the closed bedroom door. He was quiet a moment. "Usually I just toss snapshots into shoe boxes. I don't put them in albums. I'd have to sift through God knows how many boxes to find that one."

"Try. For me. A small favor."

He didn't move. He shut his eyes and said, "I'm concentrating. They say if you can visualize a thing you can usually locate it. Let me visualize a moment."

His expression was one of mute concentration. Sara watched him with a sense of impatience. Then her attention drifted around the room, floated across the furniture—minimalist stuff, chrome and glass—and came finally to rest upon the bar of pale light visible under the bedroom door.

"Okay," Tony said. "I'll see if I can find it. Be patient."

She watched him go inside the bedroom. He shut the door behind himself. She gazed at the murderous bat, then turned her face elsewhere. She could hear Tony rummage inside the bedroom, going through the contents of a closet.

She thought she heard a voice that wasn't his, somebody whispering at him, perhaps a woman. Had she interrupted Tony entertaining in his bedroom? Then why hadn't he just said so? Why hadn't he told her she'd come at an awkward time and could she return later? Maybe she'd only imagined the whisper anyway. She heard clothes hangers sliding along rails, then the sound of something toppling, boxes perhaps.

She stood up. She walked around. She thought of her father. Abdominal pains. She saw his face on the videocassette. She thought of the word *noon*, but its precise meaning managed to elude her. And there it was again—that persistent nudge of panic she'd been foolish enough to imagine had left her. But it wasn't so easy to conquer after all. She fought it. She took long deep breaths. She imagined her limbs submerged in warm soothing water.

She heard the whisper from behind the bedroom door. *God's sake, Tony.* She was certain this time. Tony had a woman inside the bedroom and he didn't want Sara to know. She heard Tony say *Ssshh.* Then there was silence. She went back to her seat, stretched her legs. She wondered about Tony's visitor, about his apparent need for secrecy. Shyness? When he came back, he was carrying an old shoe box. He

set it down on the coffee table, removed the lid. "If it's anywhere, it's in this lot," he said. He began to sift quickly. "I
wish you'd tell me why this is so important, Sara."

She watched him flip through a series of glossy shots. Dis-
embodied faces, edges of landscapes, street scenes, all contained in yellow envelopes. She thought of the beggar, the way
the car had clattered against him, how the photograph had
fluttered down into the gutter.

"There you are. Come to Poppa," Tony said. He teased a
photograph from one of the yellow envelopes and slid it across
the table toward her. She picked it up, stared at it. It was the
same image that had been in the possession of the panhandler.
She held it a moment, compared it to the creased copy; she
set both pictures down alongside each other and examined
them as if she were determined to find some small difference
between the two. But they were exactly the same. Exactly.

"What's the big mystery?" Tony asked.

"I can't explain."

"Can't? Or won't?"

"Can't."

"How come your copy is in such a terrible condition? Did
it go accidentally through a washing machine or something?"

She shook her head. "You made two copies. Right?"

"Right. One for you and Mark. One for me. Where is this
leading, Sara?"

"But not a third copy?"

"No. What would I want with another copy?"

"Did you give the negative to somebody?"

"Who'd want the neg of a casual snapshot, Sara?"

"You still have it then?"

"I guess so."

"Would it be in that same envelope?"

"Why is this so important?"

She said nothing, reached for the box, removed the yellow
envelope in which Tony had found the snapshot, then withdrew strips of negatives. She held them up to the light, scanning the reverse images slowly. And there it was: herself and
Mark Klein. Undeniably a negative of the photograph taken
in Central Park.

Fact. A third print had been made, and it had been given to
the panhandler.

She stared at Tony Vandervelt a moment. "You're *positive* you didn't order a third print?"

"I'm one hundred percent certain."

"And you didn't give the negative to anybody?"

"I'd remember if I did, Sara. It would be a pretty peculiar request for somebody to make, don't you think? Say, Tony, can I borrow that negative for a couple of hours. I'd remember something like that."

"Yes. You would," she said. She gazed down at the two prints on the table. Mark Klein stared back at her. What was there about his look—some kind of challenge? Come on, sweetheart, find me. You only have until noon. What happens when noon comes and goes? She thought of the sun at its highest point. Stark and dreadful.

She wondered if Tony was lying to her, if he'd ordered a third print and given it to the beggar—but she couldn't find reasons to explain why he'd do anything like that. There was one narrow avenue of possibility—that Tony had embezzled the funds and Mark was being made the fall guy. But even if that were true, why the rigmarole with the photograph? why the message left at the Cresta Vista in Los Angeles? Why all of that? Why anything? Maybe it was simpler—somebody had broken into Tony's apartment and borrowed the negative and had a print made from it, then returned the negative without Tony ever knowing. Simpler? Did that scenario make anything *simpler*?

She stood up. She took the creased print and stuck it in the pocket of her coat. "I've wasted your time," she said.

"No, no," he said. "It's always good to see you. Even if it's a little puzzling this time."

"I don't mean to be puzzling," she said. "That's just the way my world is these days." She turned her face in the direction of the bedroom door. A shadow obscured the strip of light; somebody was standing immediately behind the door. Sara had the compelling urge to step toward the door and haul it open. But she didn't.

"You sure you don't want tea?" he asked.

"Thanks anyway."

Tony walked with her to the door. He kissed her briefly on the cheek.

"Drive carefully," he said.

"I will."

She went downstairs and into the street. The rain had stopped. She walked to her car and sat behind the wheel and waited. She wondered how long she'd have to wait. She pushed the seat all the way back and stretched her legs and clasped her hands over her stomach. A third print, she thought. Somebody makes a third print and gives it to the beggar and—

Her eyelids were leaden. She imagined Tony and the woman coupling feverishly in Tony's bed. It was a tough image to conjure. Vandervelt was one of those men she couldn't imagine in the act of sex. Long-limbed, clumsy and angular— she couldn't see him in a contortion of passion. She remembered the time when he'd tried to kiss her in his car. The geography of his mouth was all wrong. The way he shaped his lips was more amusing than seductive. She closed her eyes, felt sleep buzz inside her head. She forced her seat forward and sat upright. She'd wait another thirty minutes, then she'd leave. What business was it of hers anyway to spy on Tony?

Anything to do with Klein was her business.

Twenty minutes and counting.

She saw the door of the building open. The woman who stepped out was lit a moment by a lamp over the door. Sara leaned forward, her face close to the windshield, her quickening breath misting glass.

**27**

THE woman drove a late-model white BMW, an easy car to track in the dark. Even when it managed to overtake a slower vehicle, Sara was still able to keep it in sight. Buses threw up oily slicks of rainwater, and gypsy cabs driven by desperadoes swiveled in and out of the traffic flow—but the white BMW, four or five cars in front of Sara, was still a good target to spot.

It was an odd feeling to be following somebody across a city at night, like a high, as if you were no longer a prisoner of events around you; as if finally you had some kind of grip on the slick ladder of your destiny. *Iron and flint*, she thought. She'd follow the white car through a river of sludge if that's what it took.

The BMW slipped in front of a truck and was lost a moment to Sara, but when the truck made a turn the white car reappeared. Sara thought: *If I was going about some sneaky nocturnal business, the last thing I'd want is a white car. I'd want something dreary and anonymous. Something that couldn't be picked out like a beacon.*

Steam billowed out of subway vents. John Stone had once told her a story that dragons lived deep under the streets of Manhattan, and the steam you saw was from their fiery breath. A nice little fable she'd believed for years. Gullible Sara, fed on a diet of fables.

Red traffic signal. Stop. Go. The BMW was a block away now. Sara pressed a little harder on the gas. The lights from storefronts zipped past. Mannequins in bright windows were

weird and otherworldly. Rain dripped from the canopies of
hotels and apartment blocks.

Another red signal, this time outside a funeral parlor. Burial
plots, she realized, turning her face away from the establish-
ment. She focused on the BMW, continued to drive, remembered the strip of light under the door of Tony Vandervelt's
bedroom, the shadow of the woman, Tony's little secret, his
eavesdropper. How many keys were there to those locked
boxes marked Duplicity and Treachery?

The BMW made a left turn. Sara followed. There was no
other vehicle now between herself and the other car. The
BMW slowed, brake lights a flash of sudden red. What cross
street was this? Forty-fourth? Forty-third? She hadn't been
paying attention to signs. She understood she was in the vicinity of Madison, but her mental map of the city was in disarray.

The driver of the BMW had found a parking space and was
backing the car into it. Such a tidy little maneuver. Sara had
no choice but to drive straight past; she could hardly block
the middle of the street. She glanced in her rearview mirror.
The woman was getting out of the white car. An interior light
glowed a moment.

Sara searched for a place to park and found one in front of
a fire hydrant. Illegal, so what? She was in a scofflaw frame
of mind. She was determined not to lose sight of the woman.
She got out of the car and moved along the darkened sidewalk.

The woman was about fifty yards away, passing under a
tree in a cautious manner—afraid, no doubt, of fouling her
shoes in soggy dead leaves and dog shit. Or worse, slipping,
losing her balance, coming buttocks down in fecal matter and
dirtying her expensive coat.

But the woman recovered her poise and was walking with
an easy confidence. *How well she moves*, Sara thought. *How
elegant she looks*. Sara kept going, clinging to the shadows
just beyond the reach of the lamps. The woman stopped outside a town house, lingered a second at the foot of the steps,
then climbed to the door and rang the bell. Over her head a
security camera panned almost imperceptibly.

Sara thought: *I know this place.*

The door opened, and Theodore Pacific appeared. He smiled
his handsome smile and with an exaggerated gesture of welcome, a bow almost theatrical, admitted Jennifer Gryce inside.

And then he shut the door.

**28**

SHE dozed off in the car for a few minutes. The sound of somebody tapping on the window startled her. She opened her eyes, saw McClennan on the dark sidewalk. She rolled down the window and gazed at him in a bleary way.

"I know, I'm parked illegally," she said.

"Illegal parking isn't my province, Sara," McClennan said. He looked at her a moment, assessing her. "Busy evening for you. You leave home, you go visit your old friend Tony Vandervelt, you stay maybe fifteen minutes with him, you sit in your parked car for another twenty minutes, then you drive across town and for some reason you park here—you're all over the place tonight, Sara."

"You're observant, McClennan."

"The question is: what's the bee up your ass, Sara? Why all this running around?"

"I got lost. I'm not accustomed to driving in the city. I pulled over, fell fast asleep. Guilty as charged."

McClennan looked up and down the sidewalk, as if he were trying to figure a good reason for Sara parking in this particular street. "Why is it I have this problem buying anything you say? Every time you open your mouth, I get the feeling another lie is about to pop out."

"You have an unfortunate flaw in your nature," she said. "You don't trust anyone."

"Who's the old woman, Sara?"

"What old woman?"

"The one with the walker."

"Walker?"

"You went inside a gas station on the Island. You had a conversation with this woman."

"Oh, yeah, right, I remember now. She was asking for directions." Sara felt the night air, cold now, flutter against her face. McClennan has been working overtime, she thought. She wondered if he'd noticed Jennifer Gryce leaving Vandervelt's apartment building. But why would he? If he was watching Sara, he probably hadn't seen Gryce get inside the white BMW. He wouldn't have grasped the fact that Sara was following Jennifer Gryce across town.

"Must have been complicated directions, Sara. Took you a while to relay them to the old woman."

"She didn't speak good English. Some kind of tourist from Europe. I admire your cloak of invisibility, McClennan. You must have been parked right outside the gas station, and I never noticed a thing."

McClennan sighed. "What are you up to?" he asked. "Why did you go see Vandervelt?"

"I'm a woman abandoned, remember? I needed a shoulder to cry on," she said.

"Why not your father's?" he asked.

She wanted to tell him why not. It was the same compulsion she'd felt in his presence before. He allegedly represented law and order, but in her life these words had become drained of meaning. She couldn't trust law and order, nor the men who stood for it. She was walking a high tightrope all alone, and there was no safety net to catch her when she fell.

"I don't like to burden my father with everything," she said.

McClennan changed the subject suddenly. "What did you do with the printed data, Sara?"

"I told you before, McClennan. You want to discuss that accusation, I'll be happy to talk with you—but only in the presence of George Borbokis."

"You know, it really bothers me you have this need to consult a lawyer before you say anything. It implies you're hiding something. Why can't we just discuss it between ourselves?"

"It's my Constitutional right to have legal representation," she said.

"God bless the Founding Fathers." McClennan smiled in a bleak way. "We dusted the keyboard."

"Dusted?"

"As in fingerprints, Sara."

She felt a little shadow form in her head. "And?"

"We're checking," he said.

"I guess you found a whole bunch of prints. Mark's. The guys that did the audit. Your own people. Must have been hundreds of prints."

McClennan said, "I need a set of yours, Sara."

"Talk to Borbokis," she said.

McClennan stepped back from the car. "Fine. I'll call good old George first thing in the morning. I'm sure he'll have no objection to me fingerprinting his client."

First thing in the morning. She turned the key in the ignition. She took a quick look behind her and saw Gryce's BMW parked down the block. What did they talk about, Gryce and Pacific? What was that connection? She thought of strands, vague and sinewy, perplexing. She tried to figure out where these strands touched each other, the places where they became interwoven—but the pattern evaded her.

"I'm going home," she said.

"Think you can make it? It's a long drive."

She nodded. "I can make it."

"Don't fall asleep at the wheel," he said.

She slid the car away from the curb and watched McClennan in the rearview mirror. A set of prints. But that was in the future, and she could postpone thinking about it for the moment. She wondered if the Feds were going to escort her all the way back to Long Island—where she had no intention of going.

**29**

SHE drove through midtown. The dashboard clock read 12:05. After midnight, and the city was humming; sidewalk drifters, people in the windows of restaurants, kids hanging out on corners. An insomniac city. She checked the rearview mirror every few minutes. But she couldn't tell if McClennan was following her. There was too much traffic behind her.

She reached Times Square, gloriously gaudy, then headed down a side street that led from Broadway in the direction of the river. She parked the car, waited, studied the view in her mirror. FBI cars—what did they look like? The ones that had come to her house at dawn a few days ago had been dull and anonymous. She couldn't even remember them properly. Chunky, American, bland gas-guzzlers, designed to be utterly forgettable.

She stepped out of the car. She smelled the timber-rotted scent of the river in the night. She crossed the street quickly, moved away from the Hudson. She entered a narrow thoroughfare, a place of long shadows and few streetlamps. Old buildings had been upgraded and turned into apartments, but there was still an unenticing quality to the place.

She found the building she wanted. On a navy blue canopy were the words HUDSON VIEW. She unbuttoned her coat, stepped under the canopy, and approached the glass doors. Inside, a man in a dark green uniform was seated at a desk reading a copy of the *New York Post*. She tried to push the doors open. Locked. The man behind the desk didn't see her. She took a quarter from her pocket and rapped firmly on the glass, and only then did he raise his face.

She pressed her swollen stomach against the glass. A pregnant woman seeking admission, she thought. Who but the most mean-hearted could resist? The uniformed man got up, opened the door, stepped to one side and let her enter. He had a big Irish face, beefy red jowls. He was in his mid-fifties and wore a wedding ring. She saw softness and good humor in his features. *Play the pregnancy card*, she thought. *Play the whole deck if you have to.*

"Catch your death out there," he said. He shut the glass doors. Sara held her hands across her stomach and moved slowly toward the desk. She leaned against it, slightly slumped.

"You all right?" he asked.

"It's just one of those wonderfully nauseating maternal moments," she remarked.

"Yeah. I know all about those."

She forced out a pathetic little smile. She realized she was learning guile quickly. It was all a matter of looking despondently vulnerable while you still maintained some little touch of stoic cheer. The human condition. Procreation may be a goddam nuisance, but where would we be without it? The doorman, who wore a lapel badge identifying him as Sean, hovered near her elbow.

"You want a glass of water, something?"

She shook her head. "I'll be fine. This usually passes in a minute or so. If I'm lucky." She glanced at the buttons on Sean's uniform. Brassy, shiny.

"How far along are you?" he asked.

"Over six months."

"Third trimester," Sean said. "Sometimes tricky."

"Sometimes," she said.

"Why don't you sit a moment? Here, go behind the desk, take my chair. God knows, I sit too much anyway." He helped her toward the chair and looked at her solicitously. It hadn't yet occurred to him to ask what she was doing here. He'd get around to it sooner or later, of course. Meantime, though, he was going on about trimesters in the manner of a man who has spent many hours in the waiting rooms of maternity hospitals. Apparently he had six children of his own, none of them easy births. He was something of an expert on birthing and physicians, most of whom he held in low regard.

"You feeling any better?"

"I'm getting there," she answered.

"Sure about the water?"

"Well, maybe a small glass would be nice."

He wandered off, came back a minute or so later with a Dixie cup of water. She was more thirsty than she'd realized. She drained the cup in two gulps.

"Thanks," she said. She screwed up her eyes, peered at his badge. "*Sean.* You wouldn't be Irish by any chance?"

"Second generation. County Kerry. You know it?"

"My great grandparents came over from Kildare," she said. She didn't like lying to the man, but sometimes expediency was everything.

"You been there?"

"I wish," she said.

"I was back one time. Grandmother's funeral. I'll say this. They sure know how to die in style over there."

Sara made a tiny grimace. Sean, like a night nurse attending a sick patient, didn't miss it. "You sure you're okay?"

"A twinge," she said.

She tilted her head back. She needed to pull off another stunt, now that she'd gained access to the building. The question was how. She had Sean's sympathy, willingly given, but how far could that be stretched? He might be a nice guy, but he still had a job to do, and it involved the security of this place. She closed her eyes, frowned. "I hope I'm not being a nuisance to you," she said.

"Listen, glad to be of assistance. Nights get boring round here. Read the paper. Do the crossword. Check the corridors. Check the elevators. Read the paper again. It's stimulating stuff."

She bit on her lower lip. She uttered a tiny moan, barely audible. But Sean, experienced father, was attuned to even the smallest signals of distress. He placed his big hand on her forehead. "You might have a slight temperature, you know. It's this weather. Rain one minute, sun the next."

"Yeah, it's been changeable all right," she said.

Sean took his hand away. "Just sit there long as you like. Take it easy."

"You're very kind," she said.

"Kindness begets kindness," he remarked.

She remembered the panhandler saying *Favor gets a favor, lady*. She glanced past Sean in the direction of a series of small cubbyholes that contained keys, obviously spares kept for forgetful tenants. How to pull off this next bit? She had to exploit Sean's natural generosity—but if that was what it took, then that was what she'd do. She needed cunning. She needed the ability to prey on the kindness of other people. She had no choices.

"Would you do something for me?" she asked.

"Sure."

"Would you mind . . ." She held out the empty Dixie cup, and he took it.

"Still thirsty, huh? No problem. Back in a flash."

A flash. Was a flash going to be long enough? She watched him move along the corridor. As soon as he was out of sight she hurried up out her chair, slipped the key she wanted from the cubbyhole, rushed toward the stairs. She couldn't risk the elevator because he'd notice the numbers lit on the panel when he returned. Two floors—that was all she had to climb.

*Sean, I'm sorry. I'm very very sorry. You've been betrayed.*

She climbed quietly. Breathless. She'd been playacting before, but now she felt genuinely out of sorts. Weak, limbs heavy, stomach uncertain. She clutched the key in the palm of her hand and kept moving. She entered a corridor, hurrying, still breathless. She slipped the key in the lock of door number 202, then stepped inside the apartment, closing the door behind her. She found a lightswitch, flicked it on.

It was about two years since she'd been in this apartment, but it hadn't changed. The living room was big; the dominant color motif was black and red gloss paint—walls, bookshelves, candlesticks, even the expensive secondhand furniture, which had been carefully stripped down and repainted. The room gleamed. She realized she'd always found this place unwelcoming, as if the colors were designed to repel rather than attract. She crossed the floor, glanced inside the kitchen— messy, dishes stacked in the sink, the table littered with newspapers, magazines. She moved toward the bedroom, opened the door, paused: what did she think she was going to find in this place anyway?

The bed was unmade. Costly black-satin sheets hung to the floor. Red pillows had slipped from the bed. Everywhere, the same black and red gloss dominated. One corner of the bedroom had been transformed into an office nook, separated from the rest of the room by thick red-and-black blocks of wood. A typewriter, a PC, a phone, a fax, an answering machine, sheets of paper, bills that had been opened and stacked to one side of the desk. No photographs, she noticed. No pictorial souvenirs of a life.

She pulled the chair from the desk and sat down and took her glasses from her pocket. She sifted quickly through the bills, even if she had no idea what she was really looking for. American Express. MasterCard. Macy's. Bloomingdale's. She saw nothing out of the ordinary. Items of clothing, mainly. A few restaurant bills. She set the credit-card statements back in place, then she opened the middle drawer of the desk.

Paperclips, a staple gun, pencils, an unused scratch pad. There was also a phone bill consisting of several sheets of itemized calls. She wanted to read through those on the chance that she might come across a familiar number, but she didn't have the luxury of time. She stuffed the bill in her pocket and thought: *Later*.

She opened one of the side drawers of the desk. Manila folders, neatly arranged, each one color-tagged. Blues, yellows, greens. There was some kind of system here. She took out one of the blue-tagged folders. It contained bank statements and canceled checks; everything very orderly, everything stapled together according to the month of payment. She flicked through the checks. One had been made out to a paint store for ninety-eight dollars, another to a credit-card company for six hundred even. It would take too long to examine all the checks, and even if she had all the time in the world she might find nothing useful anyway.

She pulled out a yellow-tagged folder. Insurance policies. Endowment policies. Details of pension plans. Home insurance. Auto insurance. The print was impossibly small.

She put this folder back, withdrew one with a green tag, opened it. It was stuffed with hundreds of sheets of paper, each embossed with the Rosenthal logo—a stern-faced eagle with wings folded, something designed long ago by Sol to reassure his clients that Rosenthal Brothers was an all-American kind of place where your money would always be safe. *The great bird of trust*, she thought.

She skimmed through the sheets. They contained the names and addresses of clients, and data concerning their investments.

She saw: BROSE, INC., PENSACOLA, FLORIDA.

BROSE, INC. was one of Mark's clients. She remembered the name from the sheets she'd printed herself from Klein's computer. And there were others. JANE BRIERLEY. DEE DEE CRAWFORD. What was this information doing here?

The telephone rang on the desk, surprising her. She heard the answering machine click into action on the fourth ring, the recorded message, *please leave your name and number*.

A man's voice said, ''We need to talk. Call me as soon as you get in.''

The line went dead. Sara pressed the Playback button. She listened to the message, concentrated on the voice. She knew it. She knew it well. She was tempted to play back the message again, just to be certain. Before she could reach out to punch the button, she realized somebody had entered the bedroom and she'd run out of time.

She turned.

''This is the kind of thing that can get you arrested, Sara.''

**30**

SARA felt blood flow to her head, a reaction to discovery; an intruder apprehended by outraged householder. The folder slipped out of her hands and all the sheets with the Rosenthal logo spilled across the floor.

Jennifer Gryce asked, "Do I call the cops now, or do I listen to your explanation first?"

Sara said, "I don't really have much in the way of an explanation, Jen. Maybe you should just call the cops. Wait—phone McClennan instead. This could be his big chance to haul me in. God knows, he's been waiting for one. Breaking and entering. Serious business."

Jennifer Gryce took off her coat. She wore a sleeveless blouse and a short skirt. Her arms were pale and skinny. A tiny tattoo of a lily was visible on her upper left arm. "No explanation, Sara? Nothing to say for yourself? You just had this bizarre impulse to break into my apartment? You were just kinda breezing through the neighborhood and you thought—why not break into Jen's place? What fun."

Sara looked at the woman's skeletal face, the thin, perfectly straight nose. Jennifer Gryce was almost pretty in an emaciated way. Sara had the impression that if you were to hold her up to the light, you could see through her.

"I'm pregnant," Sara said. "My hormones are out of control. I'm not responsible for my actions. I'm given to incomprehensible behavior. Kleptomania. Home violation. All kinds of things."

"Hormones, my ass," Jen Gryce said. She took a step forward, surveyed the litter of sheets on the floor.

"Sorry about the mess," Sara said. "But it goes with the general ambience of the place, don't you think? It fits nicely."

"Yeah, well, we can't all be pampered homemakers living in expensive houses overlooking Long Island Sound, can we? Some of us have a living to make. Some of us just don't have the time to drag out the trusty vacuum cleaner or go down on our knees with a jar of floor polish. Or maybe you've got a maid that comes in to do all your chores for you."

"Her name's Lila," Sara said. "She comes Tuesdays and Thursdays. Mark insisted on hiring her, not me. You want her number? Maybe she can fit you in."

"The way things are going for you, Sara, I don't think you'll be able to afford Lila much longer."

"I'd be sorry to lose her," Sara said.

"Get used to the idea." Jen Gryce, whose voice was hard and cutting, looked down at the mess of papers. Sara thought—you can see it in the calculating look, you can almost hear her think: *What has Sara found here?*

"I'll clean up this mess for you," Sara said. "That would give me some practice for the future."

"Touch nothing," Jen Gryce said.

"Trying to help, that's all."

*"Just don't touch anything."* Jennifer Gryce folded her arms across her chest in a defensive gesture.

"Interesting stuff," Sara said. "Details of Rosenthal clients. Where the money's invested. You bring your work home with you, Jen?"

Gryce nudged the sheets of paper with her foot, edging them back into a tidy pile. "Everybody at Rosenthal's works hard, Sara. We all bring work home with us. You should know that."

Sara leaned back against the desk. "Why do you have Mark's client list, Jen? Why did you bring *his* stuff home with you?"

"I don't have to answer your questions, Sara. You're the one who broke in here. If anyone should be answering questions, it's you."

Sara said, "So why don't you call McClennan?"

Jennifer Gryce bent down, gathered the sheets, crammed them back inside the folder. "Because I'm trying to spare you the goddam embarrassment, that's why."

"That's very generous of you, Jen. Very sweet. But I've broken the law, right? And I deserve to be punished. I'll tell you what—I'll phone him personally, turn myself in, do the right thing," and she reached for the receiver.

"I think that would be rash, Sara."

"Oh?"

"You're pregnant. Your husband's absconded with his clients' funds. You don't need any more stress than you've already got."

"I think I can handle it, Jen. Don't worry about me." She raised the receiver to her mouth and wondered how long it would take for Jennifer Gryce to intervene.

A moment, no more. Gryce stretched out her hand and pulled the phone away from Sara, who didn't struggle. There was a silence; Sara felt Gryce's tension, like static in the air.

"Tell me something, Jen. What are you hiding?"

"I've got nothing to hide," Jennifer Gryce said.

"You don't want me to call the law, which I find very odd. Because here I am, an intruder, a self-confessed violator of your home, and I'm quite prepared to turn myself in—but you don't want me to. Which leads me to the conclusion that you've got something to conceal."

Jennifer Gryce made a derisive sound. "I call the Feds, what happens? They arrest you, and it's just one more potential scandal for Rosenthal's. Which Sol doesn't really need right now. *Desperate wife of discredited Rosenthal dealer accused of burglary*. Terrific stuff. Great publicity."

Slick. Even passably plausible, if you were in an uncritical frame of mind.

"Go home, Sara. I'll forget this ever happened."

"I'm sick and tired of people telling me to go home, Jen."

Jennifer Gryce lit a cigarette and blew smoke at Sara. "I hope smoke isn't harmful to you. Or the baby."

"I think I can cope," Sara said.

"Good. Then go home. You'll cope even better there."

"But you haven't answered me yet. Why do you have Mark's list?"

"Okay. You want an answer, I'll give you one. I've been involved in the audit process. I've had access to everything. Every file. Every transaction Mark ever made. It's long and it's complicated and I've been obliged to work at home late into the night. There. Happy with that?''

A lie. As casual as a flick of the wrist. No Rosenthal employee would be involved in an internal audit. Auditors were *always* brought in from outside, independent operators.

''Happy enough,'' Sara said.

''Fine. Now you can split. And we'll pretend this breaking and entering never happened.'' Jennifer Gryce exhaled another cloud of smoke.

Sara remembered her going inside Pacific's town house. She juggled names, conjured up possible connections. Pacific and the man called Charlie worked for the Russian woman. Jennifer Gryce was associated somehow with Pacific. Could you go from there to the conclusion that Gryce was also in the Russian's employ? It was a leap. It was also a hand she wasn't ready to play. Not now. You didn't expose all your information in one shot. You held some back—because it was the smart thing to do for your own safety. For your father's. She thought of the voice on the answering machine. *We have to talk. Call me as soon as you get in.* That voice. Another connection—but of what kind?

She asked, ''How long have you been sleeping with Tony?''

''Sleeping with *Tony*?''

''Yeah. How long?''

Jennifer Gryce stubbed her cigarette out, but it continued to smolder in the ashtray on the desk. ''He's not my type, Sara.''

''That's what I would have guessed. So what were you doing in his bedroom tonight?''

Jen Gryce smiled without mirth. ''Quite the little detective, aren't we?''

''Not so little these days,'' Sara said, and patted her stomach.

Gryce lit another cigarette. ''Not so little is right on. You're fat, actually. Your ankles are swollen. Your fingers are all thick. Look at that bulge round your wedding ring. Too tight for you, is it? And you've got the makings of a second chin. Are you keeping an eye out for stretch marks?''

''Oh, I'm a regular balloon, Jen. I'm going to apply for a job as a Goodyear blimp any day now. But my appearance is beside the point, old pal. I was wondering how long you've been screwing Tony, that's all.''

"It's an occasional thing, if you really must know."

"I assume from your tone of voice that we're not talking about a love made in heaven."

"Don't make me laugh. Love."

"So the earth isn't quite moving under your feet?"

"Tony's irrelevant, Sara."

"Somebody you use."

Gryce shrugged. "There's this thing called loneliness, Sara. You heard of that condition?"

"Loneliness? I don't think it's that, Jen."

"No? You've got some special insight into human relationships, have you?"

"A photograph," Sara said.

"Photograph?"

"One particular negative."

"What the *fuck* are you talking about?"

"You pilfered a negative from Tony. It was a shot of Mark and me. You had a print made of it—"

"What for? To frame? Hang on my wall? Here's my former best friend and her thieving husband? You're out of your tree, Sara."

*Out of my tree*, Sara thought. *Maybe*. Maybe she'd fallen from a very high branch. But she didn't think so. Jen Gryce had access to Vandervelt's bedroom, and Sara was sure that very few people had or even wanted to have that particular privilege—so why not? "You had a print made from this negative. You got somebody to give it to a panhandler on Wall Street, who was paid to get a message to me. A pointless message. A cryptic message. But a message anyway."

"Dingdong. Bellevue time," Jen Gryce said.

"I don't think so."

"Do yourself a favor, sweetie. See a shrink."

"What was the reason behind the message, Jen?"

"Oh, for Christ's sake—"

"I was supposed to think Mark was in Los Angeles, was that it? I was supposed to go scurrying off there to find him— was that the scheme? Because I was an inconvenience hanging around the scene of Mark's alleged crime? Or because somebody wanted me to vanish the way Mark did so it would look like I was involved in his scam? Was it something along those lines? Just say if I'm getting warm." She was stringing onrushing thoughts together. She heard a shrill note in her own voice, a slackening of self-control. This wouldn't cut it. Getting angry at Gryce wasn't the way to go. If she pushed too hard—how could she know she wasn't signing her father's death warrant? As soon as she left this building, how could she know Gryce wouldn't be on the telephone immediately to one of her associates? To the menacing Pacific, for example? And from him a series of concentric circles would flow out, ripples that reached the Russian woman—*Okay, this is madness*, Sara thought. *Complete lunacy*. So why did it feel so goddam good? She was flying. Breaking the chains and soaring free.

Gryce said, "I really think you're falling to pieces, Sara. I honestly do. Photographs. Panhandlers. Messages. Listen to yourself. Listen to the way you're babbling. I'm no specialist in the subject, dear, but I'd say you were wandering pretty damn near the border of paranoia."

Paranoia. Sara thought about the town house again, the sight of Jen Gryce going inside. She thought about the voice on the telephone. All right, if this was paranoia, it wasn't really so bad.

"Where's Mark?" she asked. It wasn't a question she'd planned to ask. It popped out of nowhere. She wasn't sure why she should even *imagine* Jen Gryce would know the answer. But in a world where everything was tricky, anything was possible.

"Mark? Let me guess. Bora Bora? Panama? Wherever fugitives gather."

"Try again, Jennifer."

"You know what I think? You've just taken a big step across the border, babe. You're out there in the badlands now. And it's not hospitable terrain."

"You know where he is, don't you?"

"No, I don't know—"

"*Don't you?*"

"Piss off, Sara—"

Sara reached forward all at once and, despite her resolve to remain in control, caught Jen Gryce's wrist. She remembered the old schoolyard torture, the twisting of the skin round the wrist, the burn of friction. Some actions were irresistible. For a second she had the hallucinatory feeling that it wasn't Jennifer Gryce's wrist she was squeezing, but the wrinkled, papery skin of the Russian woman.

"Let go, Sara, Jesus, you're hurting me."

*"Where's Mark?"*

Gryce struggled, twisted, but Sara held firmly to her.

"Where is he, Jen?"

"Let go, this is stupid—"

"Just tell me where he is."

"I don't fucking *know* where he is!"

Sara felt the baby explode then, felt it kick like a small enraged mule, felt all the air forced out of her body. She groaned and bent forward, her hands flattened against her stomach. The kicking was sharp, persistent. She backed away from Gryce and bent ever lower, as if to find some relief from the tattoo of blows inside her womb. *This is what happens*, she thought. *This is what happens when you push yourself beyond your limits. The baby wakes from sweet amniotic slumber and lashes out at you in annoyance.* She bit her lip, moaned, moved toward the bed and sat on the edge of the mattress.

"Baby being bad?" Gryce asked.

Sara's eyes watered.

"Just grin and bear it, Sara. The joys of motherhood. You're a saint. You deserve a medal."

Sara shut her eyes. What had possessed her to attack Gryce? The answer to that question could be traced back to the moment in time when Mark Klein had stepped inside a taxicab outside 3242 Midsummer on his way to JFK. Or it could be tracked down to the sight of McClennan's badge flattened against the glass pane of her front door at dawn, the darkened lot of a restaurant outside Port Jefferson, the smell of clove oil on an old woman's breath, the disappearance of her father, the way her entire life had been shaken and reshaped as if by a series of hurricanes. And she'd snapped. She'd become unhinged.

Jen Gryce was looking down at her. "Do you need a doctor?"

Sara shook her head. She moved tentatively, gripping the side of the bed. Shakily, she stood up. When she needed dignity, she couldn't find it. Her legs trembled. The pain seemed to have coagulated in her throat.

"Go back to your nice view of Long Island Sound," Gryce said. "Give up this new career as a burglar. You're in no condition for it."

Sara didn't speak. The roof of her mouth was ashen. Her gums ached. Babies took nutrition from every part of your body. They devoured you, protein by protein. They drew sustenance from the marrow of your bones. She moved a few unsteady steps away from the bed, her hands held in front of her in the manner of a blind person feeling for obstacles. "I need to get my strength back before I go anywhere," she said.

"You need more than your strength back," Jennifer Gryce said. "You need your head examined."

"Maybe."

"Seriously, Sara. You break in, you talk a bunch of nonsense, then you physically *assault* me. I don't call that rational behavior."

"I'm not rational these days."

"Understatement."

Sara fumbled against the wall. The baby was dormant again; her insides felt bruised, punched-out. She leaned against the slabs of wood that surrounded Jen Gryce's small office compartment. She glanced at the answering machine, saw the single red light flashing, wondered if Jen Gryce had heard her listening to the incoming call earlier.

Jennifer Gryce said, "We used to be friends."

What was this? Sara wondered. The new, soft approach? Was a hug of reconciliation about to be offered?

"We had some great times, Sara."

"Didn't we," Sara said.

"We don't have to be enemies, you know. It doesn't need to be this way."

Sara shrugged. "Maybe not."

"Whatever Mark's done—it doesn't have to come between us, does it? Not in the long run."

Sara said, "You made the choice, Jen. Not me. I called you. I *needed* you. But no, you were too busy, remember? You didn't have time for your old friend. Your position in the firm was too precious for friendships."

Jennifer Gryce said, "Be reasonable. I didn't have much in the way of options. How is it going to look if I stay on close terms with you? Besides, this god-awful situation isn't going to go on forever.''

''You're an ambitious girl,'' Sara said. ''And me—I'm just a pampered homemaker soon to pop forth the fruit of my absentee husband's loins. What the hell have *we* got in common?''

Sara moved out of the bedroom. She turned, looked back; Jennifer Gryce was watching her from the doorway, stroking her hair with her fingers.

''Sorry about the break-in,'' Sara said, and she went out, closing the door behind her.

She walked halfway down the corridor, turned round, moved back. She wasn't ready to go yet. She had one more thing to do here. She waited outside Jennifer Gryce's door. When she was sure she'd given Gryce enough time, she slid the key in the lock and turned it—gently, gently. It made a small clicking sound. She pushed the door open, entered the apartment, held her breath, heard her heart stop, listened to Jen Gryce speaking on the telephone in the bedroom.

''Yeah, I got your message . . . No, I don't see I'm being unreasonable . . . I know, I know . . . You know what you stand to lose . . . Yeah, I know we had an agreement, but sometimes arrangements change . . . No, I don't, I don't . . . I won't back down . . . You know I won't . . . No . . . Stubborn is a compliment in my book . . . right . . .''

There was a long silence. Sara barely breathed. Stillness was the essence of eavesdropping. You pretended you no longer existed.

Jen Gryce said, ''You see it my way, fine . . . See you tomorrow.''

The receiver was replaced. Sara moved swiftly in the direction of the door. She closed it softly and went back into the corridor and hurried toward the stairs.

In the foyer, Sean was looking at his newspaper. He raised his face when he saw her, and said, ''Hey, hang on there,'' but she was already past him and heading through the glass doors to the street.

**31**

**THE** doorman said, "He's not at home. He stepped out."

Sara blinked. The light from the chandelier in the lobby was harsh. "When?"

"Ten, fifteen minutes ago."

"Did he say where he was going?" she asked.

"He's under no obligation to inform me of his movements, madam." The doorman was tight-faced and stern, a man in love with the authority imposed upon him by a uniform that might once have been worn by a functionary in a bankrupt Stalinist republic. "He goes for a walk around this hour sometimes. That's all I know."

Sara left the building. She stood indecisively on the sidewalk. Which direction would he have taken? Toss a coin. She could choose one way, and be wrong. On the other hand, she could wait in the lobby until he came back. But the doorman, who wore his misogyny like a medal on his chest, wouldn't take kindly to her hanging around.

She turned right, strolled to the end of the block. There she paused, looked this way and that along an unpromising street of dark-shuttered storefronts, then walked back the way she'd come. She kept going until she reached the next intersection.

Think. Where would he go at one-thirty in the morning? If he was on foot, probably not very far. Taking the air. Turning things over in his mind. She made a left turn, heading toward a cluster of lights a block away.

The night was a dark wrap all around her. Fatigue had ceased to bother her. She was running on some form of reserve adrenalin that kicked in when the regular supply ran out.

She reached the source of the lights; a late-night delicatessen. This was exactly the kind of place where he'd come. She was sure of it. She went inside. She was assailed by the scents of cheeses and pastrami and herbs.

She looked around the room. A couple of old geezers were arguing in a corner booth; they were the only occupants of the deli, except for the man behind the counter. For a moment she was disappointed. The two old guys stopped yakking and glanced at her indifferently before they picked up on their argument again. The counterman barely looked at her.

She moved toward a booth, sat down, asked for coffee. It was black, stewed. She heaped sugar into it; anything to maintain her revival.

She sat at the window, watched the street. If he was only strolling a few blocks, he might pass here on his way home. She drank half the coffee, listened to the two old guys, who'd switched to Yiddish. She caught her reflection in the window. Her hair was untidy, and her eyes were wild in the fashion of somebody who has been fighting sleep for a long time.

She continued to watch the street, saw nothing. She slipped her hand in her pocket and took out Jennifer Gryce's phone bill, set the sheets on the table. She didn't examine them at once. Her mind was flooded with a memory of her struggle with Gryce, that moment of unexpectedly exhilarating violence, the need that had surfaced inside her to inflict hurt. She saw it all in a series of badly focused stills, out of sequence. It wasn't really herself in these images—it was some second-rate actress auditioning for a part she was never going to get, because she couldn't do violence with the necessary conviction. It was the same bad actress who'd clawed Tony Vandervelt's eyelid.

She leaned her face against the surface of the window. Glass iced her forehead. She considered the abnormality of her life. This nocturnal journey through the dark tunnel of city. This sense she had of chains and links, of unreal connections, of lies and suspicions. Jen Gryce had lied outright about one thing at least, and that was her reason for having Klein's client list in her possession. Part of the audit team: no way. And then there was the matter of the phone call, the way Gryce had said *Yeah, I know we had an agreement, but sometimes arrange-*

*ments change . . .* in a tone that suggested bargaining. What agreement? Sara wondered.

*I don't see I'm being unreasonable*, Jen Gryce had said. Unreasonable about what? The timbre of her speech had been either petulant or greedy, maybe even both.

Okay. So Jennifer Gryce was a liar, and she lived a secret, divided life. Rosenthals by day, Theodore Pacific by night. Wall Street on the one hand, and some murky associations on the other. What else? What else was she hiding? Sara stared at the sheets of the phone bill. Local calls were not itemized. Long-distance calls, though, were detailed—number, place, date and time, duration of call. She ran her finger down the list.

Calls had been made in the past month to Las Vegas, Atlantic City—casino towns, fast-action joints; was she placing bets long-distance? Sara had never known Gryce to gamble. Maybe she knew people in Vegas and Atlantic City. But what kind of people? Unsavory characters gravitated to those cities, but it didn't follow that Gryce had any connections with them.

She returned to the list. *Clovis, New Mexico*. Jen had an aunt out there, Sara remembered vaguely. Fine. *Boise, Idaho*. Sara couldn't imagine a reason for anyone to call Boise, Idaho. Pass on that one. The next two were more intriguing. *San Jose, Costa Rica. Forteleza, Brazil*. What were these? Vacation plans? Did Gryce foresee a holiday on her horizon? Or was it more than that? A skip, say. A Big Vanishing Act? No, Sara thought; she had no grounds for wild speculation.

She kept running her finger down the list.

She was getting toward the end when it hit her, and she sat back in her seat, feeling the unmistakable shudder of recognition. She gazed round the room—slow-motion time, the two old boys arguing in draggy sentences, the counterman cleaning a meat slicer, a fly lazily gliding round a fat, hanging cylinder of salami.

She looked back at the number again. As she did so, she was aware of the glass door flashing open, somebody entering the deli—Sol Rosenthal, mournful in a black coat and scarf and gloves, his shaved head covered with an old-fashioned soft hat. He moved toward her table, slid into the seat facing her.

"Himmler says you were looking for me," he said.

"Himmler?"

"The Nazi doorman. The guy who looks like he might have sold truckloads of Zyklon-B to the crematorium at Bergen-Belsen. I figured you might have come here." He took off his gloves and reached for her hands and held them, and for a long time he said nothing, just gazed at her in a distant way.

"You want to tell me what's going on, Sol?" she asked.

"Life's a misery, what's new with you?"

"Gryce and you. Tell me about it."

"Gryce and me?" He turned his face to the side, nodded at the counterman, who came over with a cup of hot chocolate. Sol's raised the cup to his lips.

"I want to know," she said.

"What's to know?"

"Fuck you, Sol. Don't fob me off with shit like that. I want to know."

"I never heard you swear before, all the time I knew you. It don't suit you, kid." He took off his hat and laid it on the table.

"Consider it a release valve, Sol. Talk to me about you and Gryce."

He shrugged. He looked infinitely sad. She squeezed his hands. She felt a stiffening in his bones, a resistance. "Listen, kid, you got the wrong end of the carrot. You're coming up with some very odd shit all of a sudden. Gryce and me? What are you trying to say?"

She said, "I was in her apartment when you left the message, Sol. I was also present when she returned your call. I heard. You know what I'm saying? I *heard*."

"So you're a spy now, huh? My Sara, Mata fucking Hari." He sipped his chocolate, leaving a circle of froth around his mouth.

"Sol, my life's been turned around. It's been wrenched out by the roots and it's been shaken and everything is upside-down and I want as much of it back as I can get—and all I'm asking you is a simple question: what the hell is going on with you and Gryce?"

Sol raised a paper napkin to his lips. "Nothing's going on. Leave it like that."

"Leave it like that?"

"Yeah, godammit, leave it, just leave it."

"Tell me to run along home, Sol."

He stared at her. There was moisture in his eyes. Whether they were tears of an emotion that had caught him unexpectedly, whether they were caused by the sharp night air through which he'd been walking, she didn't know. He didn't look too good. Pallid, sunken. A man carrying a tiresome burden.

He said, "You're playing among scorpions, kid. You shouldn't be down in the gutter. Not you. Not my Sara." And he stretched his arm across the table and lightly stroked the side of her face, a gesture that was more than one of avuncular concern. She thought of her father. She thought of his tenderness. Sol was touching her that way. Like John Stone did.

She caught his fingers in her palm. "Tell me, Sol." Quietly now. Patiently. "Gryce has some kind of hold over you, doesn't she? She's got something on you, hasn't she, Sol?"

"She's not the nicest person I ever met, granted."

"What's the lock, Sol?"

"It can't be picked, Sara. Forget it."

"Fuck you again," she said.

Sol leaned across the table, propped on his elbows. "I wish you'd drop that kinda language. Coming from me, okay, it's acceptable. Only person I never cuss in front of is my wife. I keep a zipper on my mouth when she's around. Which ain't often."

"Sol," she said, "don't change the subject on me."

"What is with you? You attracted to trouble? You out cruising the night for grief?"

"If I'm cruising for anything, Sol, it's for somebody to tell me the truth."

"Truth? In a world of scorpions and liars, the girl's looking for truth? Okay. You want truth?" He gazed at the two men arguing in the corner. "See that pair. Sherman and Morris, brothers, rich as Getty the pair of them, and every night they come down here and they have the same fight, and you know what they fight about? Huh? Who's gonna pick up the tab. The tab! They come *this* close to fisticuffs over a few bucks, five tops."

"And?"

"How would they behave if it was millions of bucks at stake? Want me to tell you? They'd fucking *nuke* each other. They'd have rocket launchers and nuclear submarines, the whole schmear."

"What's the point of the story, Sol?"

"The point, she asks. The point is always the same. Money. More money. It's what people do to each other for money, kid. It goes beyond blood and family. It's a whole fucking law unto itself—it's like gravity, the speed of light, electricity, it's a law of nature. Flash for you: People do bad things for money."

"And Gryce comes into that category," she said.

"We *all* come into that category. Show me a saint, I'll show you his fucking Swiss bank account, Jesus Christ. Show me a charity saving the asses of Romanian orphans, I'll show you millions of bucks stashed away in funny-money accounts in goddam Monaco."

He took his hand away.

"Cynicism's not my thing," she said. "Too easy."

"Easy? I worked a lifetime to earn mine. You, you got a way to go."

"I've never heard you talk like this before," she said.

"You're hearing me now."

She was silent a moment. Then she said, "This lock that can't be picked. What is it?"

"Leave it alone, Sara. You don't need any more crap in your life."

"That's it? End of story?"

Sol drained his drink. "Yeah. End of story."

"I'll pester you, Sol. I'll bug the hell out of you."

He shrugged, looked up at the ceiling. She watched his face, but she couldn't read the expression. Impassive, inscrutable. He took out a cigar and struck a match. He vanished behind smoke, like an amateur's simple illusion.

She said, "Gryce's got some odd friends, Sol. Did you know that?"

"Surprise me."

"You ever meet a man by the name of Theodore Pacific?"

Sol shook his head. "Never heard of the guy."

"Pacific's heavily involved in the Russian money."

"Yeah? Where does your information come from?"

"That's not important. Take my word for it. Earlier this evening Gryce met with Pacific. She went to his house. She was there maybe an hour or more. Ask yourself, Sol. Ask yourself what Jennifer Gryce's doing associating with a guy who's actively pursuing the missing Russian money. A strange connection, wouldn't you say? Jen Gryce, your employee, in league with a guy who's mob-connected—why, Sol? Why?''

Sol Rosenthal puffed on his cigar quickly a couple of times. Sara knew this gesture: he was thinking, mind racing, figuring the angles from behind a screen of thick smoke. He wafted the fumes with a motion of his hand. He didn't say anything.

She said, "Pacific's also one of the people involved in the disappearance of my father.''

"And this is the same guy Gryce knows?''

"The same.''

"You sure of that?''

"Positive. He's working with the Russian woman I told you about this morning when I came to your apartment. Where does Jennifer Gryce fit? What kind of footsie is she playing with that gang, Sol?''

Rosenthal stacked sugar lumps in a small column. The cigar, stuck between his lips, had gone out. He worked the cubes into a high stack before they finally collapsed across the table. He stared at the wreckage of this edifice as if it depressed him.

"Help me, Sol,'' she said. She covered his hands with her own. "That's all I'm asking. Give me some kind of help.''

"Sara, Sara,'' he said. "How can I help you? I can't help myself even.''

She was leaning forward across the table. "What do you mean you can't help yourself?''

"I need to explain something simple? I can't help myself, I can't help you. I close my eyes nights and I hear the demolition ball, kid. That's on good nights. Bad nights, what I hear is the whisper of the ax.''

She was silent a time. The demolition ball. The whisper of the ax. She gazed at his troubled expression, the slack set of his lips, the lack of luster in his eyes. He had the look of a man fading into another dimension.

"Tell me the truth,'' she said. "How deep is the shit you're in?''

"You got a way of asking hard questions,'' he remarked.

"The missing funds—you're accountable for them, right? Rosenthal Brothers stand behind their clients. Rock-steady, reliable, the good old American eagle on the notepaper. Your money's safe with Rosenthal's. Climb on board, everybody.

We're leaving the station right on schedule with bags of gold bullion, which will multiply bounteously overnight to your benefit. Now it's gone wrong, and the Rosenthal train is off the tracks, and you don't know how to get it rolling again.''

He gazed at her, then shut his eyes. "You understand anything about shame, kid? You know what shame is like?"

"Tell me about shame," she said.

"You've come to the guy that wrote the book, kid. You're sitting down with the numero uno expert on the subject. Shame eats you from the inside out. It's a fucking cancer. Worse. You can't take drugs for it. You can't go for chemotherapy. You don't sleep nights. You wander the streets. I worked years to . . ." He opened his eyes, yanked the dead cigar from his mouth, and pounded it in the ashtray.

He covered his face with his hands. "What you see before you ain't human, it's a piece of shit. Smell the air, kid. Just smell the air."

"I smell salami and cheese, Sol. That's all."

He lowered his hands. He stared at his palms. He didn't look at her. "It's gone, Sara. You understand that?"

"Gone? What's gone?"

"Everything. You name it."

"You're talking in riddles, Sol."

"It's all riddles, kid. Start to finish. That's money for you. That's what I was saying to you. What money does to people. It befuddles their heads. It screws up their senses. Nothing makes sense except it has a dollar sign in front of it. And what you're left with is this fucking shame. I worked for that all these years? Day and goddam night? To end up with a barrel load of shame? Stick it on my gravestone. Sol Rosenthal. Died of shame. Don't feel sorry for him. Don't send flowers."

"You're getting away from me," she said.

"Yeah, well, you ought to be happy. There's safety in distance," he said.

She fidgeted with her empty coffee cup, ran a fingertip round the rim, glanced at the sheets of Jennifer Gryce's telephone bill. She focused on the phone number that had galvanized her attention just as Sol had come into the deli. Jennifer Gryce had made the call the same day Mark Klein had stepped inside the cab to take him to the airport. She remembered the smile, the blown kiss, the last wave of his hand, good-bye.

"Mark ruined you," she said. "It's Mark's fault. He embezzled the funds, he left you stranded like this."

Sol Rosenthal smiled in a thin, curious way. "The last thing I wanted, kid, was you to get hurt. I mean that."

"I don't follow you, Sol. If it's Mark's fault, you don't have to feel any responsibility for me."

Sol Rosenthal reached for his hat. He suddenly stood up. He shrugged; a tiny gesture of—what? defeat? disappointment? bitterness?

He said, "You're a good kid. You deserve better."

She rose. "Don't walk away from me, Sol."

"Better this way."

She caught his coat sleeve. "I want some goddam clarity, Sol."

"Clarity? Last thing you need."

She wouldn't let go of his sleeve. She had the feeling that if he slipped away from her, so would everything else—any chance of understanding, of unraveling the intricacies, the elaborations. He looked irritated at the way she was grasping the material of his coat. She'd never seen this expression on his face before, at least never directed at her. When he spoke, his voice was raised in annoyance.

"You know your biggest fucking problem, Sara? Sheer goddam stubbornness. I tried to get you to leave. I gave it my best shot. I didn't want you round, having to see you, having you plague me, I didn't want to look at your face, see your pain. But you, you just wouldn't go. You wouldn't leave the goddam thing alone."

She thought a moment. The images in her head were like spilled quicksilver. "I don't like the Catskills," she said.

"Catskills," he said. "Anywhere. What difference?"

"And I don't like Los Angeles either, Sol."

He tried to move away from her. She waved a sheet from Gryce's phone bill in his face. "Gryce phoned a place called the Cresta Vista Motor Lodge in Los Angeles the day Mark left for the airport. The way I see it, she arranged for a message to be left there for me. I was supposed to think it was from Mark. And you, you got the picture from Gryce, you gave it to the beggar, you arranged all that, and I was supposed to be intrigued enough to jump on the first available plane—''

"Beggars, photographs. Enough, Sara."

"What was the idea? I was to fly off to Los Angeles and wait for Mark to show? Maybe the occasional cryptic message would reach me now and again and keep me sufficiently intrigued to stay out there? Sent out of harm's way, so I wouldn't be a hangnail in your conscience?"

Sol yanked his arm away and turned toward the door. She went after him, caught him again in the doorway as he opened it. He sighed, stared at her, frowned.

"You should have gone, kid. That's all I can say. It would have been easier all round."

"Easier for who? You? Gryce?"

He stepped out into the street. She followed him. He hurried along the sidewalk and she rushed to keep up with him. He wouldn't turn when she called his name. When she was close enough to him she grabbed the back of his overcoat.

He spun around, stared at her. "I look at you, I see my shame," he said. "Go away. Leave me alone."

"This shame, Sol. Explain it to me."

He sighed. He stuck his hands in his pockets. "I never knew," he said quietly.

"Never knew what?"

"It was Russian money. Mob money. I never knew that."

"Mark? Did he know?"

"Mark?"

"*Did he know*? Yes or no?"

"Boy's a law unto himself, Sara."

"What does that mean?"

Rosenthal gazed in the direction of the delicatessen. His voice was soft, almost a whisper, when he spoke. "I lived in this neighborhood twenty-three years. Long time. I came all the way up here from a cold-water walk-up in Brooklyn. It's quite a distance when you don't have a fast track and a fancy education. A long haul, lotta sweat, lotta hours, you can't imagine. But finally you make the big time, your own company, all this dough is just pouring in from people that want to get rich and avoid as much tax as they can, and you want the best for your clients because you're proud of your rep, so you look for terrific opportunities, and you hit this real lucky

streak, and then you think, fuck, everything I touch just turns
to gold, I must be some kinda Midas, so you believe the gods
are looking over you and the sun just shines outta your butt.
And you're thinking, I can do *anything*, I can turn a hundred
bucks into a thousand in the blink of an eye, no sweat, so
you're making deals, the phone's attached to your ear twenty-
three hours a day every day, everybody's your buddy from
Sacramento to Switzerland—and suddenly, zippedy-doo, it
crashes, it comes down all around your head, because the gods
have turned on you. And when *they* turn, Jesus Christ, they
really *turn*. Earthquakes in Japan. Floods in the Philippines.
Crop failures. Pension funds that collapse like a house of
cards. Savings and Loans with Out of Business signs hanging
on their doors and executives absconding to Rio with brief-
cases bulging. And you realize you've reached the end of your
string, you got all this money belonging to other people and
it's out there in some accursed places, and it ain't coming
back, it's vanished inside a black hole, and you can hear this
bell of doom ringing inside your head . . .''

He stopped. He might have been talking to himself. ''So,
you start playing it cute. You try to pull off a few moves to
cover that tender region known as your ass. But what you're
using to cover your ass is what you lost in the first place—
other people's money. And that doesn't work, and so you're
becoming desperate . . . and desperation, Christ, that leads you
in all directions. Usually the gallows.'' He stopped talking.
There were little flecks of spit in the corners of his mouth. He
looked depleted.

''Where does Mark come into all this?'' she asked.

Sol Rosenthal ignored the question. ''I wanted you out of
the way. For your safety. And for my own sense of well-being.
I didn't want to see that face of yours. You understand me?
But you wouldn't go.''

''I asked about Mark, Sol.''

''Yeah, you did.''

''Well?''

Rosenthal walked a few paces away. Once again, she went
after him.

''Mark,'' she said. ''Where does he fit into all this?''

''Used to be this hit tune, I remember. How did it go? *I see
a bad moon rising*. Like that. Well, I see all kinds of bad

moons rising, kid. And I don't like any of them. Jap earthquakes. Floods. All bad moons. Jesus Christ.''

She thought: *He's losing it. He's just coming apart.* She
rubbed his arm gently. "Sol, relax. Take it easy. Please. This
isn't doing you any good.''

He inclined his face to her shoulder. He made a choking
sound. He spoke her name a number of times in a hoarse
whisper. She remembered all the times she'd covered for him,
canceled appointments he didn't want to keep, stalled people
who wanted to see him, she remembered the small gifts he
gave her, he called them tokens of gratitude—orchids regu-
larly, a silver brooch once, an expensive diary embossed with
her initials in gold. *You're my lifesaver, kid*, he used to say.
*God bless you.* And now he stood shivering against her body,
a husk of the man she'd admired.

"I fucked up royal,'' he said.

"Sol,'' she said, and she stroked his back softly.

"I fucked everything royal.''

"I'll walk you home,'' she said. "Take my arm.''

"You've got too much heart in you, kid. You got this heart
the size of fucking St. Patrick's. People asked me, I always
told them that. Too much goodness in that girl. One day she's
gonna get badly hurt . . . and, God help me, that's what happened.''

He was crying openly. He stepped away from her and drew
his hand across his eyes. "You oughta hate me, Sara.''

She looked at him curiously.

"You oughta despise me. What I did.''

"I don't despise you, Sol.''

He drew the cuff of his sleeve against his face. "See, when
a guy realizes he's got no future, what he does, he looks round
for somebody else to blame. When his honor's on the line, he
acts without any. And Gryce knew. She knew.''

"What did she know, Sol?''

"She found out. I want this, she'd say. Or I want that.
Money in this account. Money in that. I wouldn't mind a new
car, come to think of it. Nothing too obvious. Tasteful. She
doesn't like ostentation, not Gryce.''

*"What did she know, Sol?''*

"Know? Everything. You name it.''

"Such as what?''

Sol Rosenthal was silent for a time. "She knew Mark hadn't done a goddam thing wrong."

Sara held her breath. The city was very still all around her. Traffic sounds had been vacuumed out of the damp night. She felt an alteration in the rhythm of her heart.

Sol Rosenthal forced a smile through his tears and said, "She knew it was me."

**SOL** Rosenthal's big apartment was cold. He stood by the dead fire, rubbed his hands together, and said, "An icebox, this place. So why do I keep it? It don't feel like a home." He shivered, sniffed, took out a handkerchief, blew his nose hard. "What I should do is go down to Florida and live with Alice and drink these rum doodahs on the beach." He rubbed his hands ever more briskly.

Sara sat on the sofa and looked into the flickering embers of a charred log. She felt stunned, as if she'd been slammed to the side of the head. She might have been an instrument that was flat, in need of tuning. There were things to say, but they weren't being said. Sol Rosenthal's fraud, Mark being blamed, Gryce's blackmail. She listened to the crackle of wood, watched a dying spark float into the blackness of the chimney. There were still more questions than answers. Where was Mark? And her father? And Gryce—what linked her to Theodore Pacific?

Sol Rosenthal stuck his hands in his pockets. "This talk of Florida. Hate the goddam place. Too many old Jews like me retired down there. Shuffleboard and checkers all the livelong day. I'd get roped into going to *shul*. Functions and fundraisers, all these old guys talking about their hemorrhoids and prostate surgery and showing me pictures of their grandkids and waiting for me to show them mine, which I ain't got . . ."

His voice drifted off. He moved toward the sofa. He looked down at Sara. He reached for her hand, but she drew it away.

Sol said, "I understand. I understand how you feel, kid."

"Do you, Sol? Do you really know what you put me

through? You know what I'm still going through?''

He sat beside her. He didn't touch her, didn't look at her. "Don't," he said.

"Don't what? Don't remind you?"

"I been carrying this . . ." He made an inarticulate gesture.

"Why did you choose to blame Mark?" she asked. "Was it some kind of lottery? You picked his name out of a hat? Why him?"

"He had more money going through his accounts than any-one else in the firm. I figured I could dip into it because there was so much of it. And I also figured I could turn the situation around before it was too late, and get the cash back in place, but the hole kept getting deeper and deeper—and then the shit hit, and the audit guys were swarming like fucking horseflies, then the Feds came in. And I panicked."

"You didn't think about me," she said.

"You got that wrong—I never quit thinking about you, I swear, I just never dreamed it would go this far."

"And Gryce?"

"Gryce, yeah. She confronts me. She's a sharp cookie, brain like a machete. She figures Klein wasn't a likely candidate for doing anything underhand with his client's cash. So she asks herself—who else has the password? Who else has the op-portunities? It's my goddam company, Sara. I got the keys to the fucking city. Nothing happens in that firm I don't know about. So I'm an obvious mark. She asks for a cut. I'm buying her silence. Then the ante goes up. And it goes up again. And now I'm really scrambling. You gotta understand. She's got it all on paper and she keeps copies in her apartment and other copies stuffed inside some bank vault as a precaution, mean-while I'm digging real deep to meet her demands—"

"I don't *gotta* understand anything, Sol. You screwed with my life."

"Did I know about that Russian money? Did I know dirty money was coming into the firm? I could predict that? I could predict they'd grab your father? Threaten your baby? Jesus Christ." He inclined his head, flattened his hands against his cheeks. "If I could turn the fucking clocks back . . ."

Sara said nothing. Sol was still trying to make excuses, fum-bling for absolution, muttering more to himself than to her.

His words had all the force of rain falling on another continent. They meant nothing to her.

He said, "The only thing I don't feel bad about in all this is I tried to get you outta the picture. Gryce, she was real gung ho for you to take the fall along with Mark. I don't know what she's got against you, Sara—envy maybe. You're married, what's she got to go home to nights? A cold bed? I drew a line. I told her no way is Sara gonna take any heat over this. I had a scheme figured. It was a tease, I thought you'd jump at it. I thought you'd be intrigued. The message. The panhandler . . ." His voice faded again. He drummed the palms of his hands on his knees and looked around the room with the expression of a man trying to locate something important, something fixed and absolute.

She remembered the sad unkempt man in the rain, the way he'd shuffled carelessly after her through traffic, the sound of his bones breaking when the car hit him. And it struck her with the force of a mallet. She stared at Sol, and said, "You had him killed, didn't you?"

Sol flapped his handkerchief as if at some imaginary fly. "He was supposed to go away, that guy. Deliver the message, split, vanish. But his brain's scrambled, he don't know the time of day, so he keeps working the same pitch, and he's still got the fucking photo I gave him, also he's in a position to describe me . . ."

The photo. Stolen by Gryce, given to Sol. "So you had him killed."

"I know some bad guys from the old days, do anything for a coupla thousand, no questions asked. I figured, take the beggar out the frame—"

"You had that poor bastard killed."

She imagined Sol, fear-driven, panicked, making a phone call, arranging a killing. She imagined him saying *We gotta remove that shitting panhandler for keeps*—and whatever pity she might have felt for him dissipated in a fog of anger. But anger, she knew, disrupted her judgment, taxed her body. She had to maintain a form of control, come up with a cold plan of action, something she could execute in fast easy steps.

She rose from the sofa and paced the room, conscious of Sol following her movements with a sad, wary expression. "You really had it figured, Sol. You really worked it out, didn't you? My husband's gone. My father's God knows where. The Feds would love to clap me in irons. You owe me. You owe me big-time. And it's payback time.''

"Name it, you just name it.''

"Call Gryce. Tell her you want to see her.''

"When? Like now?''

"Now. Make up a story. Anything. I don't need to coach you, I'm sure.''

"She's gonna jump in a cab and come over here at—what? Two-thirty in the morning? Sara, she's bright—''

"She's also greedy—''

"She'll smell something.''

"Convince her, Sol. Make it worth her while. You can do it.''

He didn't move for a time. He just kept drumming his open hands on his knees, like some sad tattoo.

"Then you call McClennan. Tell him the truth. Tell him Mark's innocent. Tell him to get his ass over here.''

Sol Rosenthal shut his eyes, tilted his head back. "Yeah, I was waiting for that one. The biggie.''

"Do it, Sol. Make the calls. Gryce first. Then McClennan. I want them here together. I figure Gryce will take her time. McClennan won't. He'll be here as soon as you hang up the phone. I want him to question her. I want to be around for that. Believe me.''

He got to his feet very slowly. "You know what this means to me, telling McClennan the truth.''

"You know what it means to *me*, Sol?''

He looked round the big room. He blew his nose, crumpled the handkerchief and stuck it in his pocket. "I guess Florida's a no,'' he said, then he smiled in a pale way and moved toward the desk, the telephone. She watched him, conscious of the weariness in his body, the reluctance in his stride. His whole life goes down the tubes, she thought. Everything he worked for. Everything. Everything that motivated him: gone. And because of what? Japanese earthquakes. Floods in the Philippines. Crop failures. Pension plans that folded. All the delicate little struts on which the world of investments depend had collapsed under him.

She had to fight off any lingering trace of compassion. She had to be hard. A world of scorpions and liars, she couldn't be weak. She wanted to see McClennan turn the screw on Gryce. She wanted to see him twist it hard and watch her squirm. She wanted the satisfaction of seeing Gryce nailed to a cross.

Sol sat at the desk, reached for the telephone. She didn't take her eyes away from him. He picked up the receiver. She stood directly behind him and watched him punch in numbers.

"Jen? I wake you? I gotta see you . . . Yeah, now . . . No, sweetie, it can't wait . . . No, it can't goddam wait . . . You think I'm calling this time of night for the sake of my . . . No, it's nothing bad, sweetie, it's just something you oughta know about . . . What stunt? How could I pull a stunt when you got incriminating documentation stashed inside some fucking bank vault . . . Yeah. Twenty minutes. Fine." He put the receiver down and looked at Sara.

"There," he said. He was sweating. Even in this cold room, he was sweating. She looked at the ice-blue veins visible under the surface of his shaved scalp.

"Now McClennan," she said.

"Right. McClennan. You know his number?"

"Call the operator. Ask for the FBI."

"The operator, yeah, right . . . wait, I think I got the Fed's number written down someplace," and he slid open the drawer of the desk before she could move, slid open the drawer and took out the gun, and said, "Call McClennan, no way, no fucking way. Sorry, kid, I can't hang around for that," and for a second she was alarmed because she thought he was about to train the gun on her, but he had another intention, he parted his lips, raised the gun, shoved the barrel inside his open mouth, tipped his head back and pulled the trigger, all this in one swift, anguished moment—and she gasped, turning her face away, hearing the explosion, hearing him slump back in the chair.

She didn't know how long she remained standing, her face turned aside. She had no means of measuring this kind of time. This blood time. Seconds, minutes, she was paralyzed, the clock ticked stupidly on the mantelpiece, registering a time outside of time, irregular passages beyond the measurement of any device, and even when the clock chimed the sound meant nothing to her. Her legs lost strength, buckled under her. She went down on her knees and placed her face against the side of an easy chair. Velvet against her skin. She wanted to drift off inside a safe dream. *What money does to people,* he'd said. *It befuddles their heads. It screws up their senses. Nothing makes sense except it has a dollar sign in front of it.* She listened to the noise of something dripping, and at first she associated it with the motion of clockwork, but then she understood that what she was hearing was Sol Rosenthal's blood running out of him.

She still couldn't look at him. But she knew she'd have to. She'd have to get up and go to the phone and call McClennan and she'd have to be tough enough to ignore the blood on the instrument. She halfway turned her head. She saw his feet under the desk. Black shoes. The cuffs of his pants. She didn't want Gryce coming here unless McClennan was present too—

The realization struck her now: She had nothing to give McClennan. Not now. She had nothing but a dead man's story. She had absolutely nothing to convince McClennan of Klein's innocence. She was empty-handed. Sol had shut the book. Sol had locked the safe and died with the combination. *She had nothing.* What was she supposed to tell McClennan? Klein's innocent, Sol was the embezzler, the trouble is he shot himself through the head before he could tell you? Very persuasive. McClennan would buy that one, yeah.

Gryce knew the truth, of course. But she'd deny it. *Black-mail? I never heard such crap.* Sure, Gryce would deny it; and Sara had no way of refuting her.

She pulled herself to a standing position. She couldn't stop herself from looking at Sol now. His chair had wheeled a few feet back from the desk and his head hung to one side and his lips were· gone and what she was reminded of was some kind of latex horror mask. But this was Sol Rosenthal. This was what remained of the man.

She moved a little closer. But she didn't have the stomach to look. She didn't have any ghoulish curiosity. She stared at the gun that had fallen from his hand to the desk. It was small and brutal and it had the words Desert Industries stamped on the barrel. She picked it up without knowing why. She was compelled to move, she couldn't stand still, she had to go through little pieces of behavior·because the sight of death had that effect on her, the bizarre urge to clean up, sponge the bloodstains, clear everything away—this was a panic reaction, and even though she recognized it she couldn't stall it. She stared at the gun in her hand. Sol's blood. Sol's blood—*her* fingerprints. Her fingerprints on his gun, her fingerprints on Klein's keyboard. All the traces she left of herself were small forms of conspiracy. She'd clean the gun, she'd find a rag and clean it immediately. She'd clean everything.

"What a pretty sight, Sara."

Sara turned to face the door.

"My, my. Why did you shoot him?"

Sara stood with her back to the desk, as if in some futile attempt to hide Rosenthal's body. Gryce strolled toward the desk and shook her head and sighed.

"The goose is dead," she said.

The goose, the golden egg, Rosenthal is dead.

Sara heard Gryce say, "They'll keep you a night or two at the Bellevue Hotel where they'll process you, a few psychiatric tests, some questioning. The pregnancy's going to help you a little. And your circumstances, of course. Mitigating factors. It might not be so bad, Sara. You never know, I could be quite a useful character witness for you if you play your cards right. I'll take the gun, you don't mind."

*Take the gun*, Sara thought. She weighed the object in her hand. "Okay," she said.

Gryce held her hand out for the weapon.

Sara raised it and stuck the barrel against Jennifer Gryce's forehead and held it there.

She said, "Okay. I'm ready. Let's play, Gryce."

**33**

"UNWISE, Sara. Not smart, this journey."

The streetlamps of the city flickered past, lit windows burned against the fringes of darkness. The back of the cab was cold and smelled of previous occupants. Damp clothing, sweat, ash. The driver, protected from deranged passengers by a metal grid and a reinforced window shut tight, had the letter Z cut out of his thick hair, as if he were a member of some odd cult. The night was filled with strangeness, Sara thought. Strangeness and tragedy. Cruel disruptions. The night had a savagery about it.

"Nobody's going to believe he shot himself," Gryce said.

"Don't talk. I don't want to hear anything out of you." Sara held Sol Rosenthal's gun concealed under her raincoat.

"And nobody's going to believe Sol robbed his own firm," Gryce said. "As for this blackmail yarn." She shrugged. "If you really thought that one was watertight, you'd be taking me to the Feds. Instead of which . . ." She made a loose, all-embracing gesture.

Sara said, "Shut up, Gryce."

Jennifer Gryce said, "What, you don't like the sound of my voice?"

"I don't like anything about you."

"You want to watch your stress levels, Sara. The baby. Remember what happened before?"

The baby was still, perfectly so. Slumbering in blissful security. Sara didn't like the proximity of the gun to her stomach. She didn't like the gun, period. Think of it as an instrument, nothing more. A means of reinforcement. She gazed at the street. Storefronts covered by steel shutters, fortresses. Here and there a shambling homeless figure, a shape hunched in a dark doorway, a sleeper on the sidewalk. The city was filled with the dross of humanity, the sad and the mad, the disenfranchised, the dying.

"You're in a bind, dear," Gryce said. "This scheme of yours doesn't have legs. You're dealing with people who don't give a whole lot of consideration to the sanctity of life."

The sanctity of life. Sara felt a tiny flare-up of anger again. She wanted some of Gryce's icy calm. She needed something less volatile than blood to flow in her veins right now. *This scheme of yours doesn't have legs.* She was going through with it anyway, because she couldn't think of other options. Because she had to. Because. *Nothing can seriously upset you or make you afraid, if God is truly your refuge. But God isn't my refuge,* she thought. She'd inherited John Stone's agnosticism. In the end, you rely on yourself. You make your own decisions. Right, wrong, but your own. There's nobody in the sky looking down.

The cab was getting closer to its destination.

"Not far," Gryce said, with irritating cheer.

"You and Pacific," Sara said. "What's the deal?"

"Ah, now there's a story," Gryce said.

"Jut give me the condensed version."

"Ted ran into me in a singles bar," Gryce said. "I should say, he sought me out. It was no accident."

A singles bar. Gryce in the marketplace, trawling for bodies. "And?"

"He made me a proposition. In return for a generous consideration, all I had to do was supply him with information."

"What kind of information?"

"Use your head, Sara. I work at Rosenthal's. I know what's going on there."

"You were—what? His person on the inside?"

"That's a way of putting it. He wanted me to keep him posted on what the Feds were doing. He needed to know what kind of progress they were making, what areas they were investigating, whether they'd tracked the missing money. I provided the bulletins. I was his News at Eleven. If there was a flash, I told him."

"You sold information."

"I was back and forth more times than a crosstown bus," Gryce said. "He also wanted to know if the Feds had found out anything about Mark, of course."

Sara was silent a moment. She tried to imagine Gryce zigzagging to and fro with information for Pacific. The Feds are doing this, the Feds are doing that. The idea depressed her, not because of Gryce's bottomless treachery, which was no longer anything to cause surprise—but because she'd still somehow been clinging to the notion that Gryce knew where Klein was, that Gryce and her friends had been involved in Klein's disappearance. And now she'd just learned otherwise. Pacific and the Russian woman wouldn't have wasted time pressuring her for information on Klein if they'd known where to find him, they wouldn't have paid Gryce to dig out information from the Feds, and they wouldn't have abducted John Stone either. Nobody knew where Klein was: the simple, terrible truth. Not Gryce, not Pacific, not the Russian woman, not McClennan—nobody. He'd stepped out of a taxi at JFK and gone inside the terminal building and that, that was the last of him. The thought was profoundly depressing.

The cab was slowing. The driver was looking for the address. "Drop us here," Gryce said, tapping the glass. She took some bills from her coat pocket and slid them through an opening in the partition to the cabby. She said to Sara, "My treat, honey."

They stepped out of the cab. The sidewalk was deserted. Streetlamps glistened in damp trees. Sara heard a faint wind rattle leaves, the occasional drip of leftover rain.

"Last chance," Gryce said. "You can back down right here."

"I'm not backing down," Sara said.

Gryce shook her head and smiled. "You want me to walk in front of you, I guess."

"That would be the best arrangement."

"Okay, boss lady. Enjoy your time in the sun."

They moved across the sidewalk to the foot of the steps. The security camera panned the area. A light was burning over the door. Gryce put her foot on the first step. "Let's do it," she said.

Sara hesitated. It wasn't too late to turn and walk away. Gryce, goddam her, was right. This scheme didn't have legs.

This scheme was crippled from birth. But she'd do it. She'd do it. She followed Gryce up the flight of steps to the door, glancing at the camera lens, a malevolent automatic eye scanning the night.

"This is the moment," Gryce said. She raised her hand to the bell, stretched out an index finger, left it hanging in the air. "You're one hundred percent sure?"

"Just ring the bell," Sara said.

Gryce pressed the button. "There. Done."

Done, Sara thought. What exactly has been done? She was beyond tension. She'd been elevated into another state, transformed into a ragged bundle of perceptions and sensations, none of them glued together to create a whole person.

She heard a sound from inside, footsteps. The door opened. Theodore Pacific appeared. He was unflustered, smiling. "Jennifer. And you brought Sara. Nice. Very nice."

Gryce said, "She's got a gun, Ted."

"Not so nice," Pacific said. "Ah, what the hell. We're all friends here. Come in. Both of you." He stepped back, allowing Gryce to enter. Wary, Sara followed. Pacific shut the door with his foot.

"Drinks?" he asked. "Nightcap, something like that?"

"Sure," Gryce said.

"Sara? You?"

Sara shook her head.

Pacific looked understanding. "The baby, course. Alcohol and pregnancy don't mix. Wise precaution." He moved toward the open doorway of the living room and said, "This way," and Gryce went after him.

Sara followed. This is wrong, she thought. This is like some late-night social call. This isn't right. She watched Pacific go to a drinks trolley. He made two screwdrivers, one for himself, one for Gryce. Cubes of ice fizzed in the glasses.

He looked at Sara. "Coke? Ginger ale? I've got mineral water, if you like."

Sara refused. She was aware of the room in a peripheral sense. Oil paintings of landscapes, still lifes. Expensive, tasteful.

Pacific handed Gryce her drink, and said, "Cheers."

"Cheers," said Gryce.

There was a period of silence. Sara thought again, *This is wrong*. The drinks. Pacific's smile. Gryce's calm. The ordinariness of things. Three o'clock in the morning. The dead hour. Her hand clutched the gun under her coat. The feel of the gun was the only real thing in the whole situation. She'd imagined all this differently. She'd foreseen herself producing the gun, pointing it at Pacific, making—what? Threats? Tough demands for the return of her father?

She watched Pacific, in a white-silk shirt and black jeans, move to an armchair. He sat down. "No news of the missing husband, Sara?"

"No news," she said.

"Too bad. Some guys don't take their responsibilities seriously, I guess."

Gryce said, "I think Sara has a story for you, Ted."

"A story? That right, Sara? You got a story for me?"

"A fairy tale, actually," said Gryce. "Something about how Sol Rosenthal embezzled the funds and Mark took the fall. Sounds desperate, doesn't it?"

Pacific sipped his drink. "Rosenthal stole from his clients and blamed Mark?"

"Yeah. According to Sara."

"Human nature being what it is, I could buy that—except for the one serious flaw in it. Why did Klein take a hike? You got a plausible answer, Sara? You any idea why Mark split—if he was innocent?"

"He was afraid," Sara said. "He was backed into a corner. Nowhere to turn." Even as she uttered these words, she wasn't convinced. Mark walking out. Vanishing, even though he knew he was innocent. She had the unsettling feeling, a tumbling in her gut, that she'd never see him again. He was dead, buried in a place she'd never find, dead and decaying. She couldn't fix this image in her head. She let it drift away and fall apart.

Pacific said, "He could have hung around, told his story to the Feds. Sounds like a fairy tale all right," he said. He gazed into his drink, then looked back at Sara. "The gun under your coat, Sara?"

Sara nodded.

"You forced Jennifer to bring you here?"

"She didn't give me a choice, Ted," Gryce said.

"Yeah, guns make people do things they don't always want

to do.'' Pacific frowned briefly, as if a dark thought had just crossed his mind. Then he smiled and finished his drink and sighed. ''So, Sara. You got plans for the gun or what?''

Sara had a moment of dizziness. The paintings on the walls seemed to stray from their gilt frames and float in midair. ''I want my father back,'' she said.

''And you expect what? You gonna force me to tell you where he is? With the gun?'' Pacific smiled, winked at Gryce, who made a sniggering sound and looked down into her glass. A big private joke. ''You want me to take you to him, is that it, Sara? Take you straight to him and say—'Here he is, why don't you just drive him home?' ''

''What's the point in keeping him?'' she asked. ''He can't help you. I can't help you. And Mark . . .''

''And Klein can't help me either, huh?''

''No, he can't help you. He doesn't know anything. Even if you could find him, he doesn't know anything.''

''Rosenthal confessed all this to you, did he? Told you Mark was pure as the driven snow. Told you he'd embezzled millions out of his own company himself.''

''Yes,'' she said.

Pacific got up, mixed himself a second drink. ''I guess you could ask Rosenthal if this is true,'' he said to Gryce. ''Call him.''

Gryce said, ''Whoops. Insuperable problem with that one. Tell him what the problem is, Sara. You were there. You know the story better than anyone.''

''Sol's dead,'' Sara said quietly.

''Dead?''

''He shot himself.''

Pacific remarked, ''You don't say.''

Gryce said, ''That point's highly debatable, Ted. I stepped inside Sol's apartment and our pregnant princess was standing next to him with a gun in her hand, and Sol's brains were all over the wall.''

Pacific savored his drink, swirling it thoughtfully around in his mouth before swallowing it. ''It doesn't matter in the long run whether Rosenthal iced himself or Sara did it for him. The plain fact is, it doesn't leave us with anyone to substantiate your story, Sara. I can see maybe Rosenthal was depressed about his business and took the quick way out. Happens. Guy can't face ruin, loss of reputation. Same time, I can just as easily imagine you getting into an argument with him, maybe you were too upset about this business with your husband and Rosenthal wasn't being sympathetic and you went over the edge and some spur-of-the-moment madness just rushes into your head, the old red mist descends . . .''

"It wasn't like that," Sara said.

"It doesn't matter," Pacific said. "It just doesn't matter. It changes nothing. Far as I'm concerned, I'm still looking for Klein."

Sol was dead, and it didn't matter. Sara looked into Pacific's face, those black nonreflecting eyes. They were cold and impossibly hard. She couldn't imagine the inside of this man's heart. She couldn't imagine him having feelings.

Gryce was watching her with a quiet look of satisfaction. Pacific was squeaking a fingertip round the rim of his glass. What happened now? Did it stay like this, a frozen tableau? Three people locked together in unproductive silence. No. She took the gun from under her coat.

"Ah, the piece emerges," Pacific said. "You gonna use it?"

Sara said nothing. Use it, she didn't know.

"Let's say you use it, Sara. It won't bring you any closer to your father, will it? Think it through. You shoot me, how does that help you? Or you shoot Jennifer here, it just compounds your problems. See, here's the way it is, Sara. You got nowhere to turn. You got no knight on a white charger hoofing up the street to save you. In any case, flashing a gun fails to impress me, I'm sorry to say.''

Gryce made the ice chink in her glass. "Put the gun away, Sara. Goddam thing makes me nervous."

Sara shook her head. "All I want is my father," she said.

"I'd love to give him back to you, Sara. It would do wonders for my feel-good factor," Pacific said. "But it's not exactly my decision. You understand what I'm saying? I got associates. Colleagues. People to consult. Even if I wanted to, I couldn't hand him over on a platter, Sara. Am I getting through to you?"

"It's her decision," Sara said. "The Russian's."

Pacific smiled. "She's in charge all right."

"And you're the hired hand."

"I have a mercenary heart," Pacific said. "I also got a lifestyle to support."

"She says jump through fire, you jump. The good little Teddy Pacific."

"Is this some kinda tactic designed to annoy me, Sara? You trying to make me feel bad about working for a woman? We're deep into the postfeminist age, baby. I work for anybody. Man, woman, I don't give a shit so long's they pay. If that's your angle, you're wasting your time."

Wasting her time. Sara couldn't just turn around and walk out of here without accomplishing something. She'd come this far. She couldn't go back now. She had to think, and think fast, but the harder she tried to marshal her thoughts the quicker they scattered. She'd walked in here with a foolish hope. The sight of the gun would unnerve Pacific, he'd lead her to John Stone, there, take your dad back, Sara, no hard feelings—this was the idiot script she must have deceived herself into imagining. But it wasn't playing; and there hadn't been a chance in hell it would ever play. And now she was foundering.

He got out of his chair and walked toward her. "Here I am," he said. "A target, Sara. You can't miss."

She thought about it. She thought about the very simple act of just squeezing the trigger. The easiest thing in the world, also the most difficult. She remembered what Klein had always told her: *If you're going to use the gun, just point it and don't think twice.* Klein, poor Klein, whom she'd begun to think of with contempt, hadn't done a damn thing wrong. An innocent man.

"Shoot me," Pacific said.

Seated at the other side of the room, Gryce said, "Don't push her, Ted. Her clutch is slipping."

"You wouldn't shoot me, would you, Sara?" He stood still, spread his arms. For the first time since she'd encountered him on the train, she saw something alive in his dark eyes, she wasn't sure what, some kind of concern, some form of message. *I'm mistaken,* she thought. *He's worried I'm going to pull the trigger, that's all. That's what I see in his eyes. Nothing else. He's dead inside. His mind's a black chamber, locked against feelings.*

"Lower the gun, Sara," he said.

"No." And she shook her head.

"Slowly," he said. He was frowning now.

Gryce said, "Ted, don't go too far, you can't take her at face value. She's unhinged."

Pacific said, "She isn't the kind, Gryce. She isn't the kind to shoot people. She doesn't have it in her. Do you, Sara? You don't have it in you."

"I," she said. *Dear God, don't let me falter now*. Just point it and don't think twice. Yes. It was that easy. Yes.

"She wouldn't kill a soul," Pacific said.

Sara thought: *Do it*.

Pacific stretched out his hand. "Some of us, we're born to kill. Others don't have that kind of chill in their head. That murderous chill. That real cold mist."

"Ted," Gryce said. "Don't fuck *around* with her like this."

Sara looked into Pacific's eyes. She watched his hand hover over the gun. She understood she was wilting. She didn't want it to happen, but she was withering.

"You just weren't born to kill, Sara," he said. He stretched his hand closer.

She shut her eyes.

There. He had the gun. She folded. She closed her empty hand. She was lost. Iron and flint. Flint and iron. She didn't have them, not when it counted. But somehow she knew she'd done the right thing, handing over the weapon. An instinct, persistent and audible as a pulse, and yet as incomprehensible as a word in a lost language, had convinced her. And something else—an odd look in Pacific's eye, a strained expression of reassurance.

Pacific said, "I'm different from you, Sara, I don't have any qualms, none at all," and he turned and fired the gun with quick concentrated accuracy, and Gryce, who had no time to register shock, no time to move, dropped her glass and slithered from her chair to the floor, where she lay with her mouth slack and open and her eyes rolled back in her head.

Sara felt the room tilt, the building slide out of kilter. A bad taste filled her mouth, a flood of hot bitter saliva suggestive of rancid fruit. Lights danced and quivered in her vision, zigzagging streaks like the color show before the onslaught of a migraine.

Pacific walked to the body and looked down at it. "She was

fond of dangerous games,'' he said. ''Something like yourself, Mrs. Klein. But with this difference. She had no humanity to speak of.'' He turned back to Sara. ''Stay right where you are. I got a couple of phone calls to make.''

**34**

He said, "Don't ask any questions, because chances are good I won't answer them."

Sara sat in the passenger seat of the sports car, listened to the rasping of the engine, felt how it vibrated under her body, watched Theodore Pacific's face. The rigidity of his expression, eyes focused on the road, jaw tensed. The perfect symmetry of his good looks had gone, and there was no trace of that terrifying affability he worked so well. Now he was terrifying, period. She thought of Jennifer Gryce, remembered the day she'd acted as bridesmaid, the peach-colored dress, flowers gathered in her arms, smiling Jen, friend for life. Who could have predicted then that the bridesmaid would end her life on the floor of a town house in Manhattan with a bullet in her head? Sara thought: *I feel numb, no sense of loss, just a weird disembodiment.*

She looked at Pacific. "How can you expect me not to ask questions?"

"Asking questions is like smoking, bad for your health. Somebody should have told you that when you were a kid."

"Who are you, Pacific?"

"Who do you think I am?"

"I haven't got a clue."

"Then leave it that way. Because I don't know either."

"Meaning what?"

"Meaning I shed skins. Meaning I've lost sight of myself. Meaning anything you like." He glanced at her quickly. "You shouldn't have forced Gryce into that situation, Sara. You should have stayed the hell out of it. I was sailing along smoothly, I was putting it all together. What I didn't take into account was your really annoying persistence. My fault."

"Why did you have to shoot her?"

"Because I couldn't think of any other way to get you safely out of that house without making her suspicious of me. What the hell, she'd served her purpose anyway." He uttered the last sentence with no inflection in his voice, no trace of regret or conscience. Just a cold statement of fact. She'd served her purpose.

Sara was silent a second. "You wanted me to be safe."

"That's right."

"Why?"

"More goddam questions," he said. He looked back at the road for a while, then once again glanced at her. The collision of eyes was swift, but long enough for her to see hard determination in his face.

She said, "You frighten me."

"Yeah, well, I frighten myself," he said.

She tried to alter her cramped position, shifted her body a little. She stared at the road. She had no idea where the car was headed. The neighborhood was unfamiliar to her, and Pacific drove circuitously anyway, like a man alert to the possibility of being followed. *I frighten myself*, he'd said. Who was he? where had he come from? She thought of the clinical manner in which he'd fired the gun at Jennifer Gryce: the action of a natural killer. The night was fraught with death and puzzling alliances. He hadn't wanted Gryce to become suspicious. But of what? That he wasn't the man he appeared to be, the man she thought he was?

She said, "You paid Gryce money for information. Who did she think you were working for?"

"Criminal elements," he said vaguely. "Who cares what she thought? She wasn't told everything. Only as much as she needed to know. What did it matter to her anyhow? Money overcame any misgivings she might have had, if she had any."

"Who do you really work for?"

He didn't answer. He was driving deeper into the city, into nightmare areas, ruined apartment blocks, wastegrounds where fires burned in battered old oil drums and shadowy figures lingered in the shifting fringes of flame.

"Is it McClennan?" she asked.

Pacific said, "McClennan's a glorified clerk. Give him papers to shuffle, and he's happy as a pig in shit. Give him judges he can suck up to for warrants, and he's like a kid at a circus. Better still, give him somebody he can push around, and he's in his element."

"Somebody like me?"

Pacific said, "A bit like you. Maybe."

She stared at a column of fire, saw how it illuminated a gutted building, flickered on rotted rafters. She wanted to ask where Pacific was headed, but she didn't.

"You seem to know McClennan pretty well," she said.

"Don't dig, Sara. You're not gonna strike oil."

The fires receded; darkness overwhelmed the city again. She said, "You're not really working for the Russian woman."

"I still hear your spade, Sara."

"You only pretend to be working for her. Is that it?"

He revved the car, as if he wanted the engine to do his talking for him.

"You're working undercover," she said.

"Undercover." He said the word with contempt. "There are shades of meaning to that term." Green light from the dash colored his eyelids, gave him an alien appearance. He might have been sculpted out of weathered copper.

"Look," he said. "I work for the Russian. Let's be clear about that. She pays me. She pays me well. And the reason she pays me well is because she trusts me. She trusts the advice I give her. And it's taken a long time to win that trust. A long time. Years."

"And she doesn't suspect?"

"What's to suspect?"

Sara shrugged. "That you're not who you seem to be."

"And who would that be?"

"This . . . this Theodore Pacific character."

He stopped the car on the edge of wasteland, kept the engine running. He turned to look at her. "Let's get a few things straight. My name's Theodore Pacific. You want to see a birth certificate? I run a few companies. I make some investments. Some of them might not be strictly legit, but that's my affair. I have some disreputable and pretty mean-spirited associates because I'm obliged to mix in certain circles. Beyond that, you don't need to know anything. Okay?"

She put her hand out, clamped it around his where it rested on the wheel. "No, you're something else. You're somebody else."

"What the fuck do you think this is, Sara? If you're looking for a hero, don't come in my direction. I'm not the one. I'm not in the business of saving asses, unless it's my own. And if that happens to benefit you, terrific."

"I think it's more than that, Pacific," she said.

"You know your problem? You don't live in the real world, Sara. You got that nice house overlooking the water. That's where you belong. Grow your roses, have your babies, that's your life. The world I live in is a different place. It's unpleasant, it stinks, it's dangerous, it's filled with scum, and I'm probably contaminated by it. But I live in it, and I intend to go on living in it for as long as I need to."

"How long is that?" she asked.

"As long as it takes."

"Takes to do what?"

He slipped the car into gear, drove off. Her question went unanswered. She wondered about him, his denials, his affiliations. He knew McClennan and held him in low esteem: was he connected to the Feds in some way? Was he working angles that McClennan didn't know about? Was he operating on some deep level of which McClennan was utterly unaware?

"Understand one thing," he said. "There's the law, and there's different ways of making it work. Sometimes it's straightforward. A guy steals something out of a five-and-dime and security nabs him as he steps out the door. Easy. No ambiguities. Then you go along a spectrum, and somewhere it starts to get grey. You get this mesh, and you can't tell where law enforcement ends and the shit begins. And sometimes, you can't tell if there's any difference anyway. Maybe there is. Maybe there isn't. It doesn't matter. Speech over."

"You're telling me that's the place where you work. This grey area."

"I'm not trying to tell you anything. Like I said. Speech over."

"So I have to imagine the rest."

"I don't care what you imagine. Whatever it is, it ain't gonna be accurate."

She turned her face from him. She tried to imagine his life, and thought of it as a delicate balancing act between the expensive town house with the tasteful paintings, and places like this, places beyond the reach of security cameras, this sinister hinterland where urban life had ceased, and nothing functioned, and weeds flourished where once people had lived and worked. *I don't care what you imagine*, he'd said. *It ain't gonna be accurate.* Maybe so. Maybe he wasn't Pacific, maybe he'd only become Pacific somewhere along the way, and because he'd been doing it for years he no longer had any conception of who he really was. Trapped inside his own invention. The self extinguished. And for what?

That was the question, and he wasn't going to answer it.

He drove until Sara could no longer tell where blocks had begun and ended. Rubble and waste. She didn't like this place. She didn't want to be here.

"Where are we headed?"

"You want John Stone back, don't you?"

"Yes," she said.

"You want your life," he said.

"Yes. I want my life."

"I got a flash for you. Your wishes are about to come true."

"How?"

"Think about it. John Stone's no good to us now. If Rosenthal embezzled from his own company, there's no future in holding your father. We don't need him, because we don't need a lock on you."

"And Mark. What about Mark?"

"He's off the hook, isn't he?"

"What does that mean exactly?"

"Family-reunion time. It's Thanksgiving and Christmas all rolled into one, Mrs. Klein."

"You know where Mark is?"

"I think I can locate him."

"There's a price to pay for this service, I suppose."

"There's always a price."

"How much?"

"You think I'm interested in money?"

"I don't know what I think. Or what you're interested in."

"Your money's no good. The price is something else. Silence."

"Silence?"

"You don't know me. You never met me. You see me on the street, you walk on. You don't smile. You don't wave. You don't blink an eye. McClennan ever asks, you never heard of me. Same for anyone else. Clear?"

"He's going to ask," she said.

"You've got nothing to tell him, Sara. In any case, certain arrangements will be made. You'll be covered."

"What arrangements?"

Instead of answering, he said, "We're almost there."

She looked out, saw nothing. The same wasteland. The same dead relics of civilization. And then, out of nowhere, a chain-link fence appeared in the lights of the car. Pacific parked, pulled on the emergency brake, took the keys from the ignition.

"Give me ten minutes. You stay here. Don't move. Don't even think about moving."

He got out of the car. She watched him go to a gate in the fence. He stuck a key in a padlock, opened the gate, walked through. She couldn't follow his movements with any clarity in the absence of light. She had the impression of a one-story building beyond the chain-link fence. He was going toward it, visible at times, at other times not. She waited in the car, felt the emptiness of the night press against the vehicle. Family-reunion time. Thanksgiving and Christmas. Mark off the hook.

*Wait*, he'd said. But she felt vulnerable in this awful place. All around her was rubble, shapes she couldn't identify, half-formed entities that might have been people, stunted night creatures, she didn't know.

She tapped her knees apprehensively. *Wait*, he'd said. *Don't even think about moving. Give me ten minutes.* What was he doing in there?

She turned her head, looked out, saw the glow of Manhattan in the far sky as if it were a corrupt star exploding. *Your wishes are about to come true*, she thought. Your life back.

The dark created a carapace of menace around the car. She didn't think she could sit there, didn't think she could wait for him to return. The place was spooky. *No,* Sara thought. *Do what he told you to do. Don't move. You're safer in the car with the doors locked. The shadows can't get to you.* She tried to still her thoughts and fears. Pacific had said he was bringing her life back to her, the greatest gift—

*Could she trust him?*

She hadn't asked herself this before. She'd gone along with him, a mysterious man, a killer, and she'd allowed him to drive her to this isolated place, then she'd accepted without question his demand that she stay in the car and wait ten minutes. And she was supposed to obey. Do nothing. She peered through the windshield. *You have to trust him,* she thought. *You have no other choices left. This man you don't know—you have to put your faith in him.*

She opened the passenger door. A folly. *Stay where you are. Trust Pacific. Trust the man who threatened your baby, who abused your father, who shot Gryce without even a blink of an eye, a sigh of regret—*

She stepped out of the car. The air was dense with the smell of chemical solvents. The scent choked her. She gazed across the acres of rubble, then turned and looked at the chain-link fence. *Go back inside the car, Sara. Just do what you were told. Pacific will come back, bringing your life with him.*

Somehow.

She listened to a breeze waft across the landscape, scattering discarded papers, shaking weeds, bending dandelion stalks. The chemical odor was dispersed a moment by the breeze, but then it came back—harsh, toxic. It caused her eyes to smart. It entered her nostrils, clogged the back of her throat. In the car, with the windows shut, she'd be able to breathe better—

*Contrary Sara. You always have to go against the grain. You don't know when to be still and wait.*

She went closer to the fence. She studied the gate, the unhinged padlock, she looked at the building, saw a light in a window. She pushed the gate open. There was gravel underfoot, and it crunched. She moved off the path, walked through damp weeds. She went toward the light.

She heard what she assumed were voices, but it might have been the breeze coming up again. The air was hardly worth breathing. She imagined vats of chemicals, noxious fumes. She tasted them in her mouth, felt their effect on her bronchial passages, imagined them going down inside her lungs and being dispersed through her blood cells to the baby. The light from the window struck her face. She stood very still. The back of her throat was raw.

She peered through the window.

What she saw at first was plastic, massive uncut sheets stacked in heaps or piled against the walls, tons of the stuff. She edged her face closer to the glass. It was the plastic that smelled, she realized. It released all its overwhelming constituent chemical scents.

She saw Pacific. He appeared between the great flat slats of plastic. He looked small under the high ceiling of the place. He was talking to somebody who wasn't visible to Sara, somebody just out of sight behind the plastic. He was making slow gestures with his hands, shrugging occasionally, sometimes shaking his head. Now and again, as if overwhelmed by the stench, he made a funnel of his hand and raised it to his mouth and appeared to cough.

Every so often, by some acoustic quirk, she caught a word or two of what he was saying. She heard Sol Rosenthal's name being mentioned. The words were muted, like whispers at a seance. She heard him say *There's not much point* . . . and then the remainder of his sentence was lost to her, caught and deadened by the masses of plastic. He was silent now, hands at his sides. He'd said whatever he'd come here to say. The figure to whom he'd been talking was still concealed. A shadow fell, a movement from behind the slats. Then the shadow was motionless, the figure still hidden from sight.

Sara thought, *the Russian woman, who else?* She expected to see the aluminum frame, the yellow hair, the lipsticked face. The shadow moved again. Pacific raised his hand back to his mouth. He appeared to be waiting for something—what? a decision?

Waiting, just waiting.

The world was very silent, very still.

The shadow moved into full view.

Sara saw the florid features, the tangled grey clump of eyebrows. She saw the flash of turquoise rings on the plump fingers, the brown double-breasted suit. She saw Pacific reach out and take something from the other man's hand, and both men smiled as if they were suddenly relaxed because an agreement had been reached.

George Borbokis. Attorney. Licensed by the state of New York to practice law.

Law and deception. And what else besides? It was as if all

the struts that supported social order had been kicked away and she was falling.

She turned away from the window and hurried, stumbling a little, in the direction of the chain-link fence, the open gate, the car beyond. She lost her balance, twisted her ankle, almost fell, reached the gate, pulled it open, moved toward the car. She thought of allegiances within allegiances, alliances within alliances, everything interlinked like the hoops in a magic show. Now they're joined, now they're split apart, and you don't see the seams, the secret openings.

She thought she understood now. She'd been lured to this place to die. She'd been tricked into coming all the way out to this forgotten edge of the city because Pacific intended to kill her. Maybe all he needed was the sanction of George Borbokis, and now he had it, a few quiet words, the shake of a hand, an agreement sealed—

She reached the car, grabbed for the door handle, then remembered Pacific had taken the keys with him, she couldn't get in and drive away, she was stuck there, she was stuck in a godforsaken place with nowhere to go, and out beyond her was nothing but tumbledown wreckage, charred stumps of buildings, all those wasted spaces, and she was alone in a world of treacherous confederations. She opened the passenger side door and saw Pacific coming through the gate toward the car. She slid into the passenger seat and stared through the windshield at him as she locked her door. Her fear was hideous. All her thoughts were misshapen.

He opened the door on the driver's side even as she was thinking of reaching across to press down the lock, and he said, "Done."

"Done?" she asked. The word scared her. "What's done?"

"The business." Pacific started the engine. He drove in silence a little way before he added, "Something troubling you?"

"I thought . . ."

"What did you think?"

"I don't know . . ." She withdrew into a silence. She liked it, the quiet of this inner darkness. It was a placid place where fears didn't erupt inside your head. She wasn't about to die. She let this realization flow through her. She wasn't about to die. Pacific had no intention of killing her. She'd dreamed that.

"Not much of a view, I guess."

"View?"

"From that window."

"You saw me?"

"More to the point, you saw me. And you also saw somebody else."

She said nothing.

"George Borbokis may be the personification of avarice," Pacific said. "But he knows when he's flogging a dead horse. He knows when to use the whip, and he knows when to stop."

Sara said, "Explain it to me. Explain these connections. Borbokis. The Russian woman. Strip it down and give it to me in language I can understand."

Pacific didn't speak for a while. The lights of Manhattan became brighter. "Some things you don't need to know. Other people's business. Who does what for whom. Who's associated with whom. Who scratches whose back. That kind of thing. You with me? There's a lot at stake here."

"I'm supposed to remain in a state of blessed ignorance," she said.

"I can't make it any simpler, Sara. But I got a suggestion for you. More than a suggestion. It's an imperative. It goes back to our agreement."

"The silence?"

"The silence. Precisely."

"I never saw Borbokis."

"Good girl. You never saw Borbokis."

She slumped back in her seat as far as she could. She wanted to be silent, but she couldn't help saying, "Borbokis is involved with the Russian and her money. He's got to be. It's the only thing that makes sense. He's involved in that whole scam. Maybe he even sent the business Mark's way, maybe he—"

"Sara," Pacific said, and his voice was unfriendly. "Let me rearrange your memory. You never saw Borbokis. You never saw any Russian woman. None of it ever happened. I stress that. None of it ever happened. You don't share it with your father. You don't share it with your husband. Unless you agree to that . . . you can kiss off a happy ending. Follow?"

She was quiet for a time. Her thoughts stampeded. She'd have to control them. From now on she'd have to round them

up and stable them and silence them. "I want a happy ending," she said.

"Yeah, most of the world wants that," said Pacific.

They were heading back toward Manhattan. Sara began to
recognize buildings, street signs, landmarks.

Pacific parked in front of a dilapidated brownstone on
Seventy-third Street. He produced a key from his pocket, and
said, "Courtesy of George Borbokis, a guy you never saw.
Second floor, Sara. You want to go up? Or you want me to
do it?"

"I'll do it," she said. She opened her door.

Pacific was quiet a moment. "Keep this in mind, Sara.
When you have those inquisitive moments, when you can't
keep certain thoughts out of your head, think kids and growing
roses and looking out over that nice view of the water."

"Yeah. I will."

"I mean it. It's dangerous to remember certain things.
You're a nice woman, and in a funny sort of way I like you."

Pacific sighed. She couldn't interpret the sound. The fatigue
of a man who'd been fighting too long a battle, the tiredness
of somebody who'd come to the conclusion that you righted
the wrongs of this world by doing anything it took. Anything.
Whatever lay behind the sigh, it was a lonesome sound.

"One last thing."

She waited.

"Next time you need a lawyer, skip the letter B in the Yellow Pages," was all he said. And he winked as he'd done
once before, when he'd been another person in another time
and place, in an alley behind a bar in Port Jefferson.

She reached out to touch his hand, maybe a gesture of gratitude, but he was stepping back to his car already. He turned
once when he was behind the seat and he smiled at her, and
it wasn't the glossy dead smile she'd seen him use before, it
was genuine and open, as if he were allowing her one quick
glimpse of his real self, of the man who hadn't always lived
in slits and fissures and shadows.

He drove away. She went inside the building, a gloomy
place that had been allowed to deteriorate. She climbed to the
second floor. The air was sour. She slid the key in the lock.
The room was bare save for a mattress, a videocamera on a

tripod, a chair. The curtains were drawn shut. The overhead light was an unshaded low-wattage bulb.

John Stone was sitting on the edge of the mattress. His hands were tied, his ankles tethered by rope, his eyes shut.

She gently nudged his shoulder. He opened his eyes, and said, ''Funny thing. I was dreaming about you.''

She held her father against her body, rocking him as if he were a child returned after a long time lost in a wilderness.

**35**

IT was dawn by the time they reached John Stone's house in Port Jefferson. Stone slept in the car most of the way. She led him inside the living room, where she made him lie down on the sofa. She took off his shoes and socks and looked at his familiar gnarled feet, marbled with veins. She sat beside him, stroked his forehead, gazed at him.

He slept intermittently. He woke once, and said, "They treated me pretty well, all things considered, except for that mattress I couldn't get comfortable on, and the tranquilizers they made me swallow." Another time, he remarked, "They made me read that stupid message to you. I told them you wouldn't go for it in a hundred years. I said you were too bright for that."

She said he needed to sleep, everything was going to be fine. She sat for a long time by the sofa, just watching him.

Once, when the sun was fully up over the quiet neighborhood, she went out on the porch, listening to birdsong, thinking about Pacific, who he was, why he'd done the things he'd done. She was having what Pacific had called one of those "inquisitive" moments—but how could she not? She couldn't just button down her mind, restrict her speculations. She'd think about Pacific for a long time, his peculiar world, that odd dangerous place he appeared to occupy between crime and justice. She'd think about wheels grinding within wheels: George Borbokis, the woman from St. Petersburg, Sol Rosenthal, Jennifer Gryce. It was a catalogue whose pages she might flip through and wonder exactly where all the pieces fit. Some of them she knew. Others she could only guess. Others still faded out into mysteries.

She thought, Perhaps it happened like this: The Russian woman comes to Borbokis. Perhaps because Borbokis is known in certain circles as the man to turn to when you need some tricky financial transactions done. He knows his way around the regulations. Knows how to prepare the documents so they look sound.

*Perhaps.*

The Russian wants to invest large amounts of cash. Twenty million, say. Twenty-five. Maybe more. Just for openers. Plenty to follow.

*Perhaps.*

Borbokis approaches Mark, introduces the woman or one of her aides. Perhaps this aide is Pacific himself. Perhaps not. Mark doesn't know the source of the money. But a client is a client, and commission is commission, and Mark's keen, and money changes hands, investment accounts are opened here and there in the world. It all looks very bright. Aboveboard.

*Perhaps.*

And Pacific is watching, waiting, keeping track of the cash, because he's trying to put together a case on his own. He's trying to keep trace of this influx of illicit Russian money. And it's going along nicely, he's got a very smooth inside track, until Rosenthal dips illegally into the funds, and suddenly McClennan and his people are all over the place like scavenging dogs, and Pacific's case is threatened, so he uses Gryce as a source of information to report on McClennan's progress, because he needs to keep abreast of the official federal investigation, and he has to get Mark out of the way because he wants McClennan to go off at all the wrong tangents, because because—

She stopped there. She couldn't take it any further. Her head ached. She was trying to make a solid edifice out of fragile blocks of building material. And it all came down to one thing in the end: she didn't know who Theodore Pacific was.

She didn't know, and maybe she'd never know.

But she did know this much: Pacific had promised to give her back her life. And so far he'd restored John Stone to her. She thought about the rest of the equation. Her whole life. Her husband. Where he was. She watched the sun slide up over rooftops, webs of light strung in the branches of trees like very pale Christmas bulbs. She listened to the drone of her father snoring from the house. A peaceful, ordinary sound. Miraculously familiar. She was tired, but she knew sleep would be a hard trick to accomplish.

She stretched her legs. She felt the sun on her face, bright and just a little chill. She didn't mind the touch of cold. Shortly, the neighborhood would begin to stir in that slow, grudging way of all neighborhoods rising to a new day, alarm clocks, percolators plugged into sockets, cereal bowls filled, milk spilled, kids moaning. Commonplace things. Everyday life.

She stood up. She'd go back inside. She turned and started up the porch steps when she heard a car moving along the street. It came to a halt outside the house.

She saw McClennan emerge from the driver's side. He looked up the driveway at her. There was hesitation in his manner. She stood, arms folded. She wasn't going to give him the small satisfaction of going down the steps to meet him. He'd have to come to her. That was the way she wanted it.

He walked to the foot of the porch. Shielding his eyes from the rising sun, he said, "I expect you haven't heard the news yet."

"What news?"

McClennan said, "About Rosenthal."

He told her. She pretended it was the first she'd heard of it. But her pretence was tempered by a genuine sense of shock, as if for the first time she fully realized Sol was gone. The understanding pained her. She could never have sustained a hatred for Rosenthal, no matter what he'd done. She remembered the way he'd shot himself, she imagined him arranging a murder, but it was a picture already disintegrating around the edges. One day, she had the feeling she'd inter it entirely. One day, far in the future. And the future was the only place she could look.

McClennan said, "Stuck a gun in his own mouth. Pulled the trigger. The end."

The gun, she thought. She'd taken Sol's gun with her from the apartment. She'd left it at Pacific's house.

McClennan said, "Gun was right there on his desk. And the suicide note. The whole confession."

The gun on the desk, the suicide note.

"What did the note say?"

"Usual. He was sorry. He hoped people would understand and forgive him. He regretted any trouble he'd caused innocent people. He regretted the fraud. He'd dug himself into a bad place. And he exonerated your husband. That was about it."

"He wrote all this down?"

"Typed it, signed it."

Sol had never been able to type anything. Whenever he wrote, he used a crabbed longhand, then gave it to somebody else to type. More often, he dictated material. A gun, a typed suicide note: Pacific, of course. Providing a service. Cleaning up the loose ends like a specialized janitor.

"I guess it puts your husband in the clear," McClennan said.

She heard a measure of doubt in his voice. Maybe he was still clinging to the idea he could nail Mark for something. There was an element in McClennan's character she could never accommodate, a tenacity that transgressed reason. He wasn't a man who'd surrender his convictions easily, no matter how unfounded they were. She supposed he needed this attitude for the work he did. It was engraved on his brain. She should forgive him. It was a morning for amnesty.

McClennan said, "If he hadn't decided, for whatever inscrutable reason, to take a hike, it would have saved me a lot of time."

"Would you have believed him if he'd told you he was innocent? You weren't exactly receptive to the notion of *my* innocence, were you?"

"Doing my job," he said.

She turned and pushed open the screen door. She gazed back at McClennan. "I don't suppose I'll be seeing much of you from now on."

"There's no good reason. I'll need to have a few words with your husband the minute he surfaces. Whenever that is. Some loose ends, that's all. Like why he vanished. You hear from him, I want to be the first to know. Here's a number where he can reach me any time."

She took a card from the agent's outstretched hand, and said, "One last thing. I'd like to think the next time I use my telephone, there won't be any eavesdroppers on the line.''

"What eavesdroppers?" he responded.

She went inside the house and shut the door and watched McClennan through the grids of the screen as he walked back to his car. Then she wandered inside the living room, where her father had wakened. She sat on the edge of the sofa and caressed his hand.

"How are you?" she asked.

"Okay," he said. "Except for this feeling I have of being very goddam stupid."

"Stupid?"

"Letting those guys take me the way they did. It was such a simple stunt, and I fell for it. This big guy approaches. He says he needs a word in my ear. It's about your son-in-law, he tells me. Outside, of course. That was the first mistake. I should have stayed where I was. Anyway, I went along with him. Surprise surprise. The burial plot salesman, so-called, was waiting in the parking lot. They grab me, hustle me inside a car. I struggled, sure . . . But you can't put up much of a fight against chloroform, can you? Next time I open my eyes, I'm inside that room where you found me, and they want me to say a few words to a camera, they have this card in front of me with a silly speech . . ." He raised his head up from the pillow. "They fed me terrible food. Hot dogs. French fries from a fast-food place."

"Who brought you the food?"

"Different men. Once or twice the young guy . . . Funny thing about him, though."

"What was funny?"

"I can't quite put my finger on it," John Stone said. "I had this feeling he was playing a role. I never got any real sense he was ever going to harm me."

She said nothing.

"What have I missed in my enforced absence?"

"This and that," she answered.

"Your mother always used to say that when she had something she was never going to tell me. You're the same, Sara. Is there any news of Mark?"

She shook her head. "I expect we'll hear something soon."

"You sound optimistic."

"Why not? Pessimism's a dead end."

He stuck his hands in the pockets of his pants, rattled a few coins. "One thing puzzles me."

She knew what he was going to say.

"How did you manage to find me?" he asked.

"It's a long story, Dad."

"And you're not ready to tell it, are you?"

She smiled at him, said nothing.

"Why did they decide to release me?" he asked.

"I guess they got fed up feeding you."

"No, it's more than that, isn't it?"

She went inside the kitchen, where she brewed coffee. She drank it looking out across the backyard at the greenhouse, which reflected the morning sun. Her father appeared, barefoot, in the doorway. The light made him seem frail.

"You know what the worst thing was? The thought I'd die in that goddam room. They'd keep me there, and they'd forget all about me after a time. And I'd just sit there, wasting away."

She went to him. She put her arms around his neck. She said, "You're precious."

"That's me," he said. "An old treasure."

"Priceless."

"And slightly flawed."

"Old treasures usually are."

She embraced him, kissed the side of his face, felt the rough edge of stubble around his jaw. She realized he was crying very quietly into her hair. She held him harder, and when finally he stepped back from her, she saw his eyes were red and damp.

"Worse than the idea of dying in that room . . ." He paused, raised the cuff of his shirt to his eyes. "Worse was the idea of never seeing you again."

Never again. It was the most dreadful coupling of words in the language. She looked at him, and there was some kind of stricture in her throat as she said, "You'll be seeing lots of me, Dad."

She lay for a time in her former bedroom. She didn't draw the curtains. She wanted the sun to enter the room. She wanted to see the oak tree and the relics of the swing in the branches when she opened her eyes. She slept, dreamed of Mark. Something to do with water, tides, turbulence.

She woke when she heard the telephone ring, and she hurried downstairs to answer it before her father could reach it. She picked up the receiver.

"I don't know where to start," he said.

"Start by coming home," she answered.

**36**

SHE was waiting anxiously in the house overlooking Long Island Sound when the taxi appeared and Mark stepped out, leather bag in hand. She went outside and watched him pay the driver, then he turned and moved toward the porch. She rushed down the steps toward him, and he dropped his bag at his feet. She held him for a time in silence, feeling his face with her fingertips, seeing in his eyes a weariness, a shell-shocked quality. She took his hand and led him inside the house where he paused and looked around in the fashion of a man who finds himself in a place only faintly familiar.

They went into the living room. He ran his fingers slowly across her stomach, then he drew her to the sofa and for a time sat with his head against her shoulder, his palm flattened against the mound made by the baby. It was, she thought, a delicate moment. He was touching her, stroking her, as if he needed to begin the process of familiarization all over again. Her body, the baby, this house.

She brushed his dark hair from his forehead. She kissed his mouth, the side of his face, his eyelids. His eyes, she noticed, were a little bloodshot. As she touched him, she remembered all the doubts she'd entertained about him in his absence, all the fissures she'd seen open up in their relationship; she thought of them now as small betrayals on her part, acts of disloyalty. She'd put them aside, cast them out of her mind. She had to create a new beginning. He was back. He was home. He was innocent. The strands of a life could be picked up and rewoven.

"How's the baby?" he asked.

His first words. His voice was hoarse.

"Growing by the minute," she said.

He pulled her dress up and placed both hands on her hips. He inclined his head and pressed his lips against her navel. She clasped her hands together at the back of his neck. There would be silences and hesitations, she thought. Before the fact of the reunion struck them, there would be fumbling, broken little phrases, awkwardness even. "I thought . . ." he said.

"What did you think?"

"I'd never see you again."

The same words her father had used. She'd left John Stone in his house in Port Jefferson, telling him to make sure he kept his doors locked and his windows fastened, *for your own peace of mind*, she'd said, and he'd obeyed like a small child.

"I went inside the airport," Mark said. His lips were dry, cracked.

"You don't have to talk about this right now," she said. "It can wait."

"No, I don't mind talking. I need to talk. I need . . ." He waved his hand in an indeterminate way. "As soon as I stepped inside the terminal, I was paged on a courtesy phone. And this guy I never heard before in my life tells me you've been involved in an accident, nothing serious, but they're taking you to a hospital. Would I meet him at the information desk, he'll explain it to me . . ."

He looked into her eyes. She wondered if it was fear she saw there; distress, certainly. He was silent a second. "Somebody's waiting at the desk for me. A young man. Very pleasant, concerned, plausible. Your wife took a fall, he tells me. She was on a stepladder, and she lost her balance. And he's come from the emergency room to take me straight to the hospital. I was alarmed, I didn't know your condition. I mean, he was very reassuring, kept saying it wasn't serious, just this slight concussion, the baby's all right, but Jesus . . . There was no way I was catching a flight to Hong Kong if you were lying in some hospital bed. Business could wait."

A young man. Very plausible. Yes. He knew how to be plausible. He knew how to be many things.

"He has a car outside. I get in. I'm worried, obviously. I'm not thinking clearly."

He paused, closed his eyes.

"Suddenly he produces a gun. My first thought is kidnap. He drives me out into the countryside. I'm pleading with him. He isn't listening. How much does he want? I ask. He doesn't answer. He drives me to this wreck of a house—I couldn't find it again if I tried. The back of nowhere. Somewhere in the boondocks of Jersey, I can't be sure. He takes me down inside the cellar, locks the door, leaves. No windows. No way out. Just this dank cellar."

He raised his face, looked at her. "He comes once, maybe twice a day, brings me something to eat and drink, asks me all these questions. Nothing about any ransom money. Nothing about kidnap demands. Just questions. He wants to know about *Rosenthal's*. He wants details of my clients. Where I've invested their funds. How much. What kind of clients have I got. I can't figure it out. Is he a competitor? Is this some kind of financial espionage? I don't know what to think . . . I lose track of time. Do I know money is being embezzled from Rosenthal's? Do I know where it's gone? Christ, of course I knew *something* was going on at the firm, I'd have to be blind not to notice. The auditors working into the night, then all these characters in well-pressed suits examining documents. I figured maybe a serious accounting discrepancy at the worst, I don't know. An oversight. These things happen sometimes. Somebody presses the wrong key on a computer, the human factor. I didn't really give serious consideration to embezzlement. I didn't have any answers for him, and I don't know what he's really after . . ."

She thought: *I could tell you.* She remembered the commitment she'd made to silence.

"At one point, I don't remember exactly when, he brings a cellular phone. Call your wife, he says. Tell her you're in Hong Kong and you're fine and the Kimberley Hotel's a nice place. Make it sound convincing. Don't say anything to alarm her . . ." He frowned. He looked pale. "Then he turns up at dawn this morning and tells me I can go. Just like that. Out of the blue. No explanation. He's finished with me. I'm free. Walk two miles in a certain direction, he says, you'll come to a gas station where there's a phone. Call your wife, he says. She's probably anxious to hear from you. And he drives away."

Mark Klein smiled for the first time since he'd entered the house. But there was strain in the look.

She took his hand, and said, "Let's go upstairs."

They made love quietly, and Klein—afraid of hurting the baby—was considerate and slow, his movements gentle. Sara saw through half-shut eyes the way reflected water made dappled patterns on the ceiling. After, Klein lay at her side, idly touching her breasts.

"I thought you'd abandoned me," she said.

"You thought *what*?" He propped himself up on an elbow, looked down at her. He moved a hand from her breast to the side of her face and studied her with a serious expression.

"You'd gone. Stepped out of my life. Vanished completely."

"You imagine I'm capable of that?"

"I didn't *want* to think that, Mark. Believe me. Consider my situation. I hadn't heard from you—"

"How could you even *think* I'd walk out on you?"

"Because the Feds came here looking for you. Because they had a search warrant. And you weren't in Hong Kong where you were supposed to be, I phoned the hotel, you weren't registered there—"

"Wait. Back up. The Feds came here with a *search warrant*?"

"They took everything from your office. And they suspected me, they thought I was part of this big scam you had to embezzle money from Rosenthal's, what was I supposed to think?"

"A scam? Me?"

"You," she said. "That's what they thought."

"And they really believed *you* were involved?"

She nodded. "Yeah. That's exactly what they believed. Until Sol . . ."

"Until Sol what?" he asked.

"He shot himself, Mark."

"Sol *killed* himself?"

"He couldn't cope with the fact he'd embezzled the company, destroyed his clients, his reputation."

"Sol . . ." Mark looked white, his face an image in a bleached-out photo.

"Millions," she said. "Millions of dollars."

"I can't believe he killed himself. Dear Christ."

*There's stuff you don't know*, she thought. *Stuff I can't tell you. I made a deal with the devil, a fallen angel, whatever Pacific is.*

She listened to the tide in the distance. "This is all that matters," she said. "That's the only thing I know."

He put his ear to her stomach and just for a moment she had an uneasy feeling, an uncomfortable memory. But then she relaxed.

"It kicks," he said.

"Yeah, it kicks. Tell me."

They lay together in silence. She shut her eyes and felt safe. She listened to the steady rhythm of his breathing, and she tried to imagine him a prisoner in a dark basement. There must have been bad moments when he'd wondered if his memories were nothing more than dreams. Wife, baby, home, all fictions. There would have been despair and frustration. Anxiety and black despondency. *The things I went through*, she thought, *so did Mark.*

He rose, went inside the shower. She listened to the drumming of water. He reemerged with a towel wrapped round his waist. His chest hairs were damp, and glistened. He lay down on the bed beside her, and said, "I can't get my head round the fact Sol killed himself. It hasn't sunk in yet."

She pressed her face against his chest, smelling familiar scents of soap and cologne. A breeze fluttered the curtains at the open window. Outside, the sun had gone and a soft rain was falling. She listened to it rattle in the shrubbery. She had a sense of a circle closing, a completion; a feeling that death and treachery belonged in another world.

Later, they went downstairs together to his office. He stared at the filing cabinets. He slid drawers open, shut them again. He did this in a distracted way, like a man with a nervous tic of which he is unaware. Open then close. Open then close.

"They left me some paper clips, I see," he said.

"You'll get everything back," she said. "They don't have any reason to keep your stuff now."

She put her arms around him, held him a moment. She was

aware of a slight uneasiness in him, as if he were upset by the violation of this place.

"You poor thing," he said. "Having all this shit happen when I wasn't here . . ." He gestured around the room. "Alone, pregnant. No sign of me. Going through crap, search warrants, God knows."

He scrutinized her face. With the tip of a finger he gently brushed a stray strand of hair from her forehead. He did this as if he were inscribing a subtle pattern on her brow.

"There's an agent called McClennan you're supposed to contact," she said. "He's the one who served the warrant. He's been looking for you."

"I'll call him."

"The sooner we bury the past, the better. We move on from here, Mark. The future. The baby. Everything."

He turned away from her, wandered the room. He was playing with paper clips, linking them together. "This McClennan. He was the one who suspected you?"

"Yeah, he suspected me."

"He put you through a hard time."

"You might say that." *Harder than hard*, she thought.

He stood with his back to the window, arms folded, his hands made into fists. "I'll talk to him," he said. "I'll do it now."

Mark went first thing the following morning to meet McClennan on Wall Street. Alone, Sara telephoned her father. She told him Mark had returned. She summarized, because details were doors she didn't want to open. John Stone said, "So everything's fine. Everything's back in place."

"Yes. Everything."

"Except the money, of course," he said. "I've been watching the news. Sol Rosenthal's a hot story. The current figure missing from his company stands at thirty-seven point five mil, give or take. That's a conservative estimate, they say. It's a hell of a lot of money, and a whole bunch of people are going to be hurt."

"Yes," she said. Rain had fallen all through the night. There was mist out on the Sound. The landscape was dreary and secretive. "I was thinking of driving over."

John Stone said he'd welcome that.

She hung up, stepped out on the porch. Through shreds of mist, a sailboat was visible. She watched it for a time, then went indoors. She thought about Mark's meeting with McClennan, wondered what they were talking about. Mark would have to explain his disappearance. It was a world of abductions, she thought. A world of puzzles and vanishings.

She drove to her father's house at noon. They sat together in the kitchen. John Stone blew across the surface of his hot black tea, then said, "The man who held Mark captive—I assume he's connected to the people who dragged me away."

"I would think so," she said.

"And it's all wrapped up with the embezzlement, of course."

She nodded. She watched her father set his cup down in the saucer. Outside, rain swirled around the greenhouse, which looked forlorn. The greenhouse door swung back and forward, hinges squealing.

"And Mark had nothing to do with the missing money," he said.

"Absolutely nothing."

"I have a small confession," he said. "For a time there, I guess I thought the opposite."

"You're not the only one."

"I feel your relief. I really do. But it's strange."

"What's strange?"

"The way we sometimes find ourselves entertaining suspicions that turn out to be unfounded. Maybe there's something in human nature that makes us think the worst even when we don't want to. It's an unpleasant notion."

"The evidence was all against Mark," she said. "You couldn't help thinking the worst."

He reached across the table and touched her wedding ring. "How is Mark anyway?"

"A little on the shocked side. But he'll be okay. He's meeting with the Feds. It's a formality. He'll answer some questions, and that's it."

He drew his hand back and said, "I was thinking about heading down to the local gendarmerie and making out a report about my own little misadventure. Then I decided against it. What could I tell them? I was dragged away and drugged and held against my will? Then they'd ask me about the mechanics of my release—and what could I say? My intrepid daughter freed me? And how did she manage to do that? they'd ask. And I wouldn't know how to answer. What could I say? That she won't tell me? She prefers to keep it a secret? Next thing, they'd be pounding on your door. And I figure you don't want to hear any more pounding, do you? You want peace and quiet."

"Peace and quiet sounds good to me," she said. She looked at him with gratitude. "You're a very understanding man, John Stone."

"I try."

She turned her face and looked out across the rain. The greenhouse door kept slamming back and forth in the breeze. John Stone stood up, pulled on a battered old raincoat. "That's driving me up the wall," and he went out the back door and she watched him trudge through long stalks of grass. Her eye drifted absently to a copy of that morning's *New York Times*, which lay open on the table. She saw Sol Rosenthal's photograph on the bottom half of the front page. An old picture, showing Sol in a tuxedo. She didn't want to look at it. She flicked the page over.

The story jumped out at her. A woman called Olga Vaskenaya, an alleged member of a Moscow crime syndicate, had been arrested the previous night in Brooklyn following lengthy inquiries by "special investigators." She was accused of charges that included money-laundering. There was no photograph of the woman to accompany the article. Sara felt a surge of relief, as if on some unexplored level of awareness she'd been thinking about the Russian, and wondering where she'd gone, wondering if she was likely to surface ever again in her life.

Not now. Olga Vaskenaya was out of the picture.

Beneath the article was a related report warning of the perils of the "Russian Mafia" and the rapid expansion of its territory and how a new breed of investigator had to be trained to counter this form of "financial terrorism." *A new breed*, she thought. People who played rough games. People who were young and ruthless and took risks. Who didn't always know where to locate the borderlines that delineated the extent of their lawful influence. Who lived their shadowy lives on raw nerves alone. A new breed who wrote their own rules.

Like Pacific.

Her father came back inside the kitchen, shaking rain from his coat. He sat at the table and finished his tea. ''Perhaps one day you'll tell me everything,'' he said.

''Perhaps,'' she said. But she doubted it.

She drove home in the middle of the afternoon. Mark was in the rear yard, standing in front of the young silver birch tree. It was about seven feet tall.

He had a glass of scotch in his hand. ''She's looking good,'' he said. He patted the slender trunk with his palm. ''Probably needs feeding, though.''

She stared at the tree without really seeing it. ''How did it go?'' she asked.

''With McClennan you mean? You have to wonder if federal agents take courses in bad manners. Maybe there's some kind of night school where they study the basics of how to be offensive. Then they do graduate work in plain fucking rude.'' He turned from the tree, sipped his drink.

''He gives a whole abrasive new spin to the word sceptical. How could I work at Rosenthal's and *not* know Sol was plundering my clients' accounts? How could I fail to see what was going on?''

He swiveled his drink and an ice cube knocked against the glass. ''He made me feel pretty damn stupid. He also made me feel I'd committed a crime. Was I working with Rosenthal? Did we have a scam we were running together? The guy just keeps pushing and pushing until you feel you must have a dirty secret deeply buried somewhere. He specializes in making people feel guilty.''

Sara said, ''He has Sol's suicide note. What more can he possibly want?''

Mark shrugged. ''Scalps, I guess. And then he has all these questions about the guy who picked me up at the airport. How am I supposed to answer them? I don't know the guy. I don't know his name. I don't even know the reason he dragged me off and locked me in his goddam basement. McClennan has this smirk I don't like. I can tell he doesn't believe my kidnap story, but because he can't prove otherwise, and he can't prove I was involved in embezzling from Rosenthal's, he's thoroughly pissed off. He said he'd be in touch if he needed to see me again. Which I sincerely hope isn't necessary.''

He gazed up into the spidery branches of the birch. ''Meantime, the firm's in a state of total collapse. Writs are already thundering in from the lawyers of disgruntled clients. I can't say I blame them. They've been robbed, so they want to pick something off the carcass—if there's anything left to pick, which I seriously doubt. And the place is swarming with Treasury guys. It's a madhouse. People coming and going, documents seized by the truckload, computers taken away. Half the staff didn't even bother to come in today. I guess they read about Sol in the morning paper and figured it was best to stay home.''

''What happens next?''

''There's no next. The Rosenthal doors are shut and bolted. The firm is ancient history. It's not the only company going down either, from what I understand. Financial houses in the Far East, London, Bonn—there's been a whole goddam network of illegal wire transfers, investments in corporations that existed only on paper, illicit tax-evasion schemes, fabricated statements. You name it.''

Sara felt the baby kick. ''You're unemployed,'' she said.

''In a word.''

''Does that worry you?''

''Not particularly.''

''We've got savings, haven't we?'' she asked. She'd never really thought about this before. She'd always assumed Mark, who cloistered her from what he called the drudgery of domestic finances, had savings accounts somewhere. Certificates of deposit, building and loan societies, banks, investments.

''Sure. We can get by,'' he said.

''How much have we got anyway?''

''Enough.''

''Give me a rough figure.''

''There's forty thou in CDs. I could cash them in, and incur penalties, but that doesn't matter. There's another twenty-five grand in a deposit account. We've got about twenty thousand in checking and eighteen thousand and change I invested in a mutual fund.''

''That's more than a hundred thousand dollars,'' she said.

The figure surprised her. If she'd been asked to make a guess, she'd have come in with a lower estimate.

"Right. It sounds like a lot, but if you set monthly expenses against it, it isn't going to last forever. Mortgage, life insurance, health insurance, those kind of things eat your savings away pretty damn fast."

"But it's enough to live on until you find something else," she said. "More than enough."

"Yeah, it's enough."

She sensed a slight distance in him, which she attributed to the effect of his abduction, the news of Rosenthal's suicide, the termination of his job. Too many collapses all at once. He touched the trunk of the birch, snapped off a leaf, closed a fist around it. Then he sniffed the crushed leaf. "Yeah. Definitely needs feeding."

Next morning there was a newspaper item that commanded her attention. George Borbokis had been arrested on charges of unlawful currency transactions. Pacific had been working fast, she thought. There was a picture in the *New York Times* of Borbokis looking perplexed and sweaty as he came down the steps of a courtroom after his arraignment. The caption read: *Prominent Manhattan Lawyer Vows to Prove Innocence.* She showed it to Mark, who read it slowly, then was silent for a time.

"I always thought George was on the level," he said finally. "What the hell. I thought the same about Sol. I guess I'm not the greatest judge of character that ever came down the pike."

She watched him fold the newspaper and set it aside. She was remembering George Borbokis as she'd last seen him. The stench of chemicals. The wasteland. She remembered wondering about the relationship between Borbokis and the Russian woman. She asked, "Did Borbokis ever send you potential investors?"

"George never introduced me to anyone in person. A couple of times he'd call me up and tell me one of his clients was looking for a sound investment. I'd make a suggestion or two, and he'd show them to his clients. Sometimes they went for them, sometimes not. He has a bunch of rich clients. And the rich always need investment advice because what they want more than anything else is to get even richer. Makes them feel smarter than anyone else.''

She wondered if the Russian woman or some representative of hers had come, even indirectly, into Mark's orbit, but then she remembered what Pacific had said. *You never saw any Russian woman.*

Mark got up from his chair and stood directly behind her and massaged her shoulders.

''I love you,'' he told her.

She shut her eyes, felt his fingertips in her muscles, soothing. She was drowsy with a clinging midday sleepiness that drained her of energy.

''I think I'll lie down for a while,'' she said. ''You want to keep me company?''

She woke in the late afternoon. She was alone in the bed. She rose, wandered out of the room, stood at the top of the stairs. Apart from the whisper of rain, the house was silent. She started to descend. She went from room to room looking for Mark. Eventually she found him on the porch. He looked around when he heard the door open. His expression was one of fatigue, a kind of emptiness in his eyes.

She sat in the deck chair alongside him.

''What are you thinking about?'' she asked.

He lit a cigarette, cupping the flame from his Zippo against the breeze. ''I think it would be good for both of us to get away for a while.''

''Away? What have you got in mind, Mark?''

''A vacation. Two weeks at one of those resorts where people wait on your every whim. One of those places where you don't have to do anything except lie by the pool and flunkeys massage you, and you have dinner served by candlelight in your suite. That's what we need, to treat ourselves after all the crap that's gone on.''

A vacation. But she didn't want to go anywhere. She wanted to stay right there. She wanted everything the way it had been before. Mark, the house, everything. She also felt the need to be close to her father. She didn't want to take a trip, go through the hassle of packing, traveling, reaching some destination where she didn't want to be, lying on a beach and looking bloated in a swimsuit, her skin turning pink under a foreign sun.

"The idea doesn't appeal to you?" he asked.

"I don't like the prospect of flying at this stage of my pregnancy, I guess."

"Pregnant women fly all the time, Sara. You're being overcautious." He reached down, picked up a stack of vacation supplements from newspapers. "I've been flicking through these. Cancún. Acapulco. Puerto Vallarta. There are some terrific resort hotels in those places. And they're not all ludicrously expensive. Think sunshine. Relaxation."

"I'm thinking," she replied.

He handed her the wad of glossy sheets. She glanced at them. She had a fleeting impression of bronzed flesh, pools of an unlikely blue, white-jacketed waiters, sunlight, palm trees. She raised her face, saw Mark's expectant expression. He was trying to please her. Trying to tell her that everything was normal again. They could take a vacation. The eggshell fragments were being glued back in place.

"Maybe later," she said. "After the baby's born." She didn't want to deflate his sudden enthusiasm. She didn't want to be a drag. She clasped her hands in her lap. The wind, sloughing off water, blew rain at an angle under the porch roof, leaving a few slick drops on the glossy surfaces of the travel magazines.

"The Regina in Puerto Vallarta sounds good," he said. "Beachfront. Deep-sea fishing. Golf. The whole thing."

"Mark," she said.

"Look, if you don't want to go—"

"It's just unexpected . . ."

"Spontaneity, babe. The key to fun. We could fly as far as San Diego, spend a couple of nights there so you can rest, then hire a car and drive down the coast, which means we avoid some tinpot charter flight down to Puerto Vallarta. That way you spend less time in the air, which ought to ease your concerns about flying a little." He made an expansive gesture, spreading his hands. "I'm back and everything is going to be all right." He gripped her shoulders lightly with his hands and laughed.

She said, "Let me sleep on the idea."

"Don't sleep on it too long."

She looked into his eyes. Yes, he was back. The old Mark, with his great enthusiasms, his energy, his spontaneity, was back. There was air inside the house, and life. The bad stuff was gone. All gone.

**37**

SHE woke, checked the luminous amber dial of the bedside clock. Five past midnight. She wasn't sure what had stirred her out of sleep—the wind rushing against the house, a motion of the baby, a dream, she wasn't certain. She sat upright, heard the sound of Mark's steady breathing. The wind was scatter-shot and wanton, swirling around the house, whistling in the chimney pots. The tide was surging. Cold, she shivered, rubbed her hands together for warmth.

She stared at the window where a decayed moonlight lay like tarnished silver against the glass. The wind drew back with a huge sigh, came again, a spout of wild air spraying the house, rattling a window frame downstairs, making the porch creak. Phantoms, creatures fabricated by that formidable amal-gamation of darkness and wind and imagination.

She reached for her robe, drew it across her shoulders. She touched Mark, whose skin radiated warmth. He didn't move. Her throat was dry. She needed water. She swung her legs from the bed, placed her feet on the floor. She thought of going inside the bathroom and filling a glass at the sink, then decided it wasn't water she wanted at all, she had a craving for some-thing sweet, something packed with ice cubes, cranberry juice, apple juice.

The kitchen. She'd have to go downstairs. She rose, stepped away from the bed, tied the cord of her robe. Mark stirred in his sleep, muttered an incomprehensible word that belonged inside a dreamer's lexicon, then was silent again. She moved quietly to the door, opened it, looked down the dark flight of steps, flicked a light switch. The wind, filled with night sounds, raged anew. The tremor of branches, shiver of leaves, the scurry of something blown across the porch—a twig, a scrap of paper, perhaps one of the vacation brochures. Cancún or Puerto Vallarta scattered into the night.

She began to descend. Halfway down the stairs she felt the draft, a shaft of fresh air that flapped the hem of her robe. A window was open somewhere. She reached the foot of the stairs and turned in the direction of the kitchen, switching on lights as she moved. The living-room window had been blown open. A curtain flapped. She hurried, shut the window, shivered again. The house felt fragile around her, a place constructed out of cardboard and about to be uprooted from its frail foundations by the blast roaring from the Sound.

She passed near the lacquered black piano and caught a reflection of herself in the upraised lid. A ghost of Sara, a specter drifting across polished wood. She went inside the kitchen, turned on the light, opened the refrigerator, removed a carton of cranberry juice and filled a glass. She held it under the ice dispenser and cubes shuddered down the chute into the drink. Then she drank thirstily, noticing how the light from the kitchen reached as far as Mark's tree, whose pale slim trunk swayed.

She finished her drink, put the empty glass in the sink, left the kitchen. That was when she caught it.

*No—I imagine it*, she thought.

But it was there, it hung in the air, invisible, palpable, vile. She wanted this to be a dream, she wanted to wake in bed and turn for comfort to Mark, but the smell was suddenly stronger. She stood motionless, conscious of the odd rhythms of her frazzled heart.

The perfume of crushed cloves.

She heard the sound next, the tap-tap-tap she thought she'd never hear again. She didn't move. The house was off-center all at once, buckled, as if finally the wind had torn asunder the structure.

She turned her face.

Light was reflected from the aluminium frame of the walker and from the woman's glassy red lips. The man, Charlie, leaned against the piano, his hands in the pockets of his overcoat. His big florid face seemed curiously indifferent.

"There is this wonderful system in the United States," the

woman said. "Bail. They arrest you, then you give them money, and they allow you to leave so long as you promise to return. Of course, one has no intention of keeping such a ludicrous promise. Wonderful system, Sara."

Sara looked at the Russian woman. She wore a fur coat, a scarf, gloves. Inside the frame of the walker, she had the appearance of a small vicious animal only half-trapped.

"Nothing to say, Sara?"

Formless sentences went around inside Sara's head. But there were blockages, messages weren't being relayed to her tongue. This was a dream. This would go away. This was something she'd wake from.

"Of course, I surprise you. This is understandable. I come to your home in the dead of night—such a terrible night—and you are astonished to see me. Yes? If you read newspapers, you think I am behind bars. But no, here I am."

Sara was aware of Charlie moving very slightly, pushing himself from the support of the piano, coming out of his slouch. She thought of Mark asleep upstairs.

"Why are you here?" she asked.

"We understand your husband has been returned to you, Sara. Don't we, Charlie?"

Charlie nodded.

"A reunion. And your father is home, too. How sweet." The woman smiled. "I am touched by such things. They move me. But I am easily moved. What is the word? Sentimental?"

*As sentimental as a fucking chain saw*, Sara thought. In a hoarse voice she said, "Mark hasn't done anything. He didn't take your money. Rosenthal did that. Not Mark."

The woman shrugged. "Perhaps."

"There's no perhaps about it, no maybes, Mark didn't have a goddam thing to do with it."

The woman came closer. Her hair, pulled tightly to the back of her skull, gave her the hideous rictus of somebody with a bad face-lift. She reached for Sara's arm and gripped it, and her hold was talonlike. The smell of cloves was overwhelming, acrid, stinging.

"Perhaps I am not as ready as you are to believe the Rosenthal version of the story, Sara. Perhaps I am a little more skeptical by nature."

"There's nothing to be skeptical about." And Sara broke

loose, moved toward the telephone. "Screw this, I'm going to call McClennan—"

Charlie stepped in front of the phone.

"No phone calls," the woman said.

Sara turned, looked at the old woman. "Sol left a note. He confessed what he'd done. Before he killed himself, he even *told* me Mark had nothing to do with the theft of any money, so what the hell do you want? There's nothing here for you. Don't you understand that? How can I make it any goddam clearer for you?"

The old woman said, "This suicide note. Very convenient for you. For your husband. For your father. But this note, I do not trust its provenance."

"I don't know what you're talking about. Provenance. What's that supposed to mean?"

"Come. Step outside. Only as far as the porch. Let me show you something."

Sara shook her head. "No way. I'm not going anywhere with you. I've done that before, and I'm not doing it again."

"Charlie. Make her less stubborn."

The big man's hand struck the side of Sara's face. It wasn't a hard blow, but the slap of his open palm echoed inside her head, and the shock of it filled her with dread. Charlie had her by the elbow and was forcing her to the door. He reached ahead of her, wrenched open the door, drew her out onto the porch. The wind made it hard to breath, sucked at her, gusted against her robe.

"Look," Charlie said.

A figure sat in one of the deck chairs. Because it was in shadow, Sara couldn't see the face. The Russian woman threw a light switch. The yellow bulb cast a dim glow across the porch.

"You see," said the woman.

Sara looked, then looked away, but the old woman caught her chin and forced her to turn her face back in the direction of the deck chair.

She felt bilious. The night swarmed with chaotic noises, and she imagined bats, distressed birds, rodents, a world of uncontrolled creatures and unanchored objects buzzing randomly about her. *What had they done to him. What had they done.*

She took a slow step toward the chair. His arms hung limp

at his sides. His face had been destroyed. Eyelids swollen, lips split and puffy, a mass of contusions across his forehead. His throat had been cut and all the color had gone out of his flesh. Blackened blood crusted his ears. His eyes were flat and dead and without dimension. Human wreckage, a lifeless ruin.

She felt something yield deep inside her. Emotions she couldn't identify. Feelings she'd never had. She slumped against the rail of the porch. Charlie caught her, made her stand upright, turned her around once again toward the figure in the chair.

"He betrayed us," the old woman said. "He played a very dangerous game, Sara. He was clever, but I was never one hundred percent *certain* of him. I always had this tiny instinct, this persistent *feeling*, the kind that never quite goes away, the kind I always pay attention to—and then, when I was arrested in my hotel room, which was a mortifying experience, I realized: somebody had to be in a position to betray me. Somebody had to point the way to me. He was the logical candidate. The only one."

She stumped a little closer to Sara. "It took considerable persuasion, as you can see. But in the end, there's always a limit to the pain any human being can tolerate. He knew the risk he was running, of course. He lived with that. It was the job he did. It's very difficult to keep pretending that you are someone else. It's taxing and stressful. And it's always a high-wire act. And sometimes the wire snaps. You fall. A long way down."

*Torture*, Sara thought. *They tortured him. They found out who he was and they beat him to death and they brought him here to this porch where the yellow light makes him seem waxy and unreal.*

"He told us in the end, Sara. How he wrote the suicide note for the late Mr. Rosenthal. How he exonerated your husband in this note. If the note was forged, who knows what other untruths remain? I want to see Mark Klein for myself."

Sara said, "This . . ." But she had no idea where the sentence was going, and her voice faded away. Her thoughts were scattered. All she could think of was Pacific's pain, as if it were her own. She felt brutalized. Violated. She wondered how prolonged Pacific's resistance had been. To the limits, she imagined. And beyond.

"This is what?" the woman asked. "Unpleasant for you? A body on the porch of your nice little house. How unsettling. How untidy. This mess."

Sara turned her face from the sight of Pacific. She tried to imagine the strata of his life, the secrets he kept, the bluffs, the facade he'd had to maintain. In the end, it had all broken down for him. In the end, he was uncovered. And now this, this monstrosity. The night, even though the wind had dropped briefly, was alien to her. She didn't belong in this place. It could never be the same here. Not in a hundred years. Not if you suffered the worst kind of amnesia, this place could never be the same. Pacific would always be on the porch, an unexorcised spirit. Pacific would always be somewhere in her head, a cinder in her memory.

"Let us wake your husband, Sara. I want to ask him some questions."

"Mark hasn't done anything." And she imagined him being forced to undergo the same torture as Pacific and the thought was like lava in her skull.

"I would like to judge for myself." The Russian woman pushed the door open and stepped back inside the house, and Charlie shoved Sara forward, forcing her indoors. Sara protested mildly, but Charlie raised his hand and she flinched, because she didn't want to be struck again.

"Charlie," the woman said. "Go upstairs. Bring me Mark Klein."

Charlie started to climb. For a big man, he moved with stealth. Sara had the urge to go after him, claw him back, maybe prevent him from reaching the bedroom. But the old woman had a grip on her wrist.

"Listen to me, Sara. In my experience, deceptions are not singular events. You find one, and when you dig a little deeper, you always find others. The unfortunate Pacific practiced deception for many years."

Sara was watching Charlie climb the stairs. She wondered how she could warn Mark. A shout? a scream? But Charlie was already approaching the landing, and the wind was rising again, and if she shouted now there was every chance that Mark, in profound sleep, wouldn't hear her anyway. And even if he did, Charlie would be inside the bedroom before Mark was properly awake. She glanced at the woman, and said,

"Mark's innocent, for Christ's sake. Why can't I get that through to you? Okay, maybe Sol didn't write the note himself, but he *stole the goddam money*, he told me—"

"I have only your word for what Rosenthal told you, Sara. I have asked you to be quiet. I am in no mood for listening to you."

"Please," Sara said.

"Don't whine."

Sara watched Charlie vanish at the top of the stairs.

*He's heading toward the bedroom. Opening the door quietly. Going inside. Mark is dead to the world. Charlie grabs him, drags him from the bed, drags him down the stairs.* And then what?

She couldn't just do nothing. She couldn't let Charlie harm Mark. Nothing must happen to him. She moved, stirred by a rush of impulse, and kicked out hard at the aluminium walker, causing it to list to one side, then it collapsed entirely and the old woman went down with it in a flurry of fur, a gasp of surprise.

"Foolish child." She scrambled, gripped the frame, tried to rise, even as Sara began to climb the stairs. She reached the landing, where she glanced back down quickly, seeing the old woman labor to get herself and the frame in an upright position.

Then Sara kept going, although she had no idea what she could accomplish, the only thought in her head was to help Mark, warn him, if there was still time to do that, save him somehow. She heard herself utter his name, she heard the violent wind ram the framework of the house and the old woman shout after her in an angry voice, but these were sounds that originated in another world. She was all movement, hurrying, calling Mark's name, forgetting the sluggishness of her own physical condition, the child inside her body. She saw the bedroom door ahead of her at the end of the corridor. It lay open. A dark rectangle.

She heard a voice. Mark's, Charlie's, she couldn't be sure.

Then she stopped dead when the gunshot cracked the fabric of the house. A sudden rent in the walls, a fissure in the roof, lightning gashing a chimney.

She felt life go out of her, vapor escaping. And then there was the sound of something heavy falling to the floor and she waited, she couldn't bring herself to step inside the darkened bedroom. She waited in a place outside her senses. Her heart altered. Her impressions came to her through a fractured prism. The gunshot rang and rang in her head.

**38**

**SHE** took a slow small step toward the bedroom door. There was no gravity in this world she occupied. Nothing was fixed in space. The baby was dropping in her womb. She imagined she heard its heartbeat, saw the pulsing of its small lungs.

A figure appeared in the bedroom doorway.

She was aware of the gun in his hand, the paleness of his face, the way his robe was loosely tied at the waist. The relief she felt was bottomless.

"*Mark*—"

He said, "I'm all right. I'm fine. There's nothing to worry about. Absolutely nothing. Believe me."

She reached out to touch him, mentioned the woman downstairs, the money she'd come to ask about. He listened, then quickly moved past her. She went after him, still conscious of the echo of the gun, as if it were a sound destined to reverberate forever until doomsday inside these walls.

The old woman, clinging to her frame, stood at the foot of the stairs, her face turned upward. Mark began to descend, and Sara followed, an object sucked into her husband's slipstream. Mark reached the bottom step.

The woman said, "You took Charlie by surprise. Very quick, Mark Klein. Very quick. Your agility is admirable."

Mark said, "I heard him coming. I was ready. He didn't leave me any alternative."

Sara paused halfway down, a hand on the rail. She watched Mark approach the old woman, the Walther in his fist.

"There are others," the old woman said. "You dispose of Charlie—so what? He is only one soldier in an army. You an't dispose of them all.'' She shrugged her shoulders. She'd covered her composure. She was controlled again. *Iron and int*, Sara thought. Broken glass and gravel. Something other an blood ran in her veins.

"Mark," Sara said. "Tell her, for Christ's sake. Tell her ou had nothing to do with her money. Tell her to leave us e hell alone. Tell her to get out of here."

"Yes, Mark. Tell me. Let me hear it from your own lips." he old woman moved her frame slightly, and sighed in a eary way.

"Sol confessed," Mark said. "I'm sorry if you lost money. /hat more do you want?"

"Twenty-eight million dollars," the woman said.

"Sol embezzled it," Mark said. "It's a matter of record. on't believe me, ask the Feds. Ask the Treasury guys."

The woman smiled. "After me, others will come. I am only ne foreign investor who has been wronged. But there are thers, and they are inquisitive people. And they will blame e for this loss, because I was the one they trusted with their apital. I was the one with the connection in this country. And is blame is something I am not prepared to accept, believe e."

"Rosenthal's dead. The money's gone. The company's ust. If you think I can help, you're way off. Way off."

The woman said, "Tell that to the others, Mark Klein. They ill have questions for you. Many questions. They will want ) make sure for themselves."

"I have nothing to tell them."

"They may not understand that," she said.

"They'll have to understand, Olga."

*Olga*? Sara felt a tiny pulse flicker in her eyelid. This didn't ell. This didn't hang together. *Olga*. There must have been meeting, something arranged by Borbokis. Yes. *Mark, this Olga, she has some money to invest, do you have any won-erful suggestions*? Yes. Something like that. Perhaps in Bor-okis's office. Perhaps a restaurant. A hotel room. Perhaps. 'erhaps more than one meeting.

But: *George never introduced me to anyone in person*, Mark ad said.

But: they met. They talked. They agreed on a deal. Mark nd Olga.

Borbokis brought them together and they came to a busines
arrangement. Money changed hands. Money went into the Ro
senthal machine, and vanished there.

Sara had the impression she was hearing a conversation tha
was taking place inside another room in another house, mile
away from here. *George never.* She thought of Charlie upstair
in the darkened bedroom, perhaps sprawled across the floo
She thought of Pacific on the porch, white and motionless i
the deck chair. This house of death.

She came down the stairs. *George never.* A lie, a simpl
lie. And yet it was infinitely complex, because it implied
maze of concealed motives and impenetrable schemes. It im
plied silences and secrets.

And then she thought: *No, I just misheard Mark, I wasn*
*paying close attention when he spoke, I skipped over h*
*words, simple as that.* Nothing sinister. No cause for alarm
None. But she heard a quiet buzzing sound in her brain, lik
that of a log being sawed in the distance. Then there was pain
the start of a headache, a dizziness. She put a hand to he
forehead. The air around her vibrated.

She moved past the woman, past Mark, headed for the tele
phone, which shimmered in her vision. She said, "I'm goin
to call McClennan. Let him deal with this bitch once and fo
all." She picked up the receiver.

Mark took the phone from her hand. "Wait. We need t
think this whole thing through before we call McClennan."

"What is there to think about?"

The pain in her skull was becoming tidal. Don't faint, sh
thought. But she had a strange swooning sensation, everythin
rushing rapidly away from her.

The Russian woman said, "Well, Mark? Your wife ha
asked you a straightforward question. What's wrong with cal
ing McClennan now? Why waste time? Get it over with. O
are you unwilling to make the call?"

Mark ran the back of his hand across his lips then h
reached out, drew Sara's face against his shoulder, held he
tightly against him.

"It's complicated, babe."

"Complicated? It's the easiest thing in the world. I pick u
the phone and call McClennan, and he comes here and h
deals with this situation." She felt Mark stroke her hair. Hi

and was cold. Its contours were peculiar for some reason. Like the hand of somebody she didn't know.

"Sara, listen, listen to me."

"Listen to what?" she asked. Her voice had an echo. She might have been talking inside a vast cathedral.

"McClennan's just looking for any chance he can get to implicate me, Sara. You know the way he thinks. You call him, okay, he comes out here, he finds a guy upstairs with a bullet in his chest from my goddam gun, then maybe Olga here spins a nice little story that he's quite happy to believe, maybe she convinces him I had something to do with the embezzlement after all—don't you see that? Don't you see how problematic that might be?"

"No, I don't see that at all. Somebody threatened you, and you were forced to use a gun. And even if McClennan wants to construe the situation the wrong way, he isn't going to believe a woman who's facing criminal proceedings. Especially when he finds . . ." And she gestured limply toward the front door, the porch, the sinister yellow stretch of light.

"Finds what?" Mark asked.

The Russian woman said, "Look on the porch, Mark Klein."

"Why?" he asked.

"Who knows? The night air may clarify your thoughts."

Frowning, Mark opened the door. Sara watched him, the way the light yellowed his features. She watched the wind savage his hair, blowing it this way and that. She thought: *George never.* And the thought was like a scab inside her head, something she couldn't resist picking at no matter that it was bound to bleed. *I want to believe in my husband.*

Mark was gone—how long? Ten, twenty seconds? She wasn't sure. When he came back inside, he shut the door. His face was expressionless. Sara looked at him, couldn't read his reaction. A stranger. Her husband.

The woman said, "You recognize the unfortunate Mr. Pacific, of course. He led what you might describe as a very interesting double life, Mark Klein. By his own admission, he was apparently some kind of special agent from the Justice Department, even as he involved himself in less than legal activities. I assume he was telling the truth, given the circumstances in which he was obliged to talk. Double lives can be very costly. Don't you agree?''

*Double lives*, Sara thought, and studied her husband. He was elsewhere, a distance in his eyes, thinking. She knew the look. She'd seen it a thousand times when he sat in his office late into the night and pored over spreadsheets or read incoming faxes or talked into the telephone. It was concentration—no it was more than that, and she remembered something her father had said: *He had an air of desperation about him.* And perhaps that was what she saw in his face now, as if conflicting pressures were converging on him, and he was trying to sift through them, looking for the correct course of action. But there was only one course of action, and that was to call McClennan. And he wasn't doing it, because—

But she wasn't going down that rocky road. She had Mark back home, and he had only to pick up the telephone and everything would be fine, and McClennan would come, and the mist would clear from her head, and the pain go away.

She said, ''Mark,'' and her voice seemed very tiny. ''The phone. Call McClennan.''

He smiled suddenly and walked to the telephone and for a moment it seemed to her that he was about to pick it up, but his hand lingered only a second on the receiver before he drew it away again. ''I need time to think,'' he said.

''About what?'' she asked.

''Yes,'' said the Russian woman. ''About what, Mark Klein?''

Mark rattled the keyboard of the piano with his knuckles. He stared at the keys. Sara had the feeling he was lost to her just then, that he'd slipped inside a labyrinth she couldn't enter. She wanted to go to him and hold him and tell him he only had to make one phone call, one miserable goddam phone call, and everything would be over. But she didn't move. Outside, the night screamed, the wind was breaking the world apart. She felt breathless, as if she were exposed to the violent rush of air arising from the Sound. She leaned on the side of the piano, which vibrated faintly against her body.

Mark walked across the room to the woman. ''He was from the Justice Department, you say.''

''So he informed me,'' she said. ''I have no reason to disbelieve him.''

"Working undercover."

"Deep. Very deep. And for a long time. But not deep enough."

"He infiltrated you."

"That would be an accurate assessment," she said.

Mark was quiet a moment. "What have you done with this information?"

"I passed it along to my associates in Russia, naturally. Did not say this already?"

"What precisely have you passed along?"

"His name. His fate. His allegiance. The matter concerning Rosenthal and the missing money." She shrugged. "And, of course, your name."

"Why did you give them my name?"

"As your wife will tell you, I listen to my instincts—in this case, one that concerns you. That you are not as you seem to be on the surface, this hardworking, ambitious family man, this company man. But when the others come, they will find the truth for themselves. And I was not bluffing when I said this before. They *will* come. They will most *certainly* come. And they are brutal people. Especially when they have been cheated."

Sara was listening to their conversation, but there was a hissing in her head, like background noise on a bad tape. *They will come*, she thought. *They will most certainly come.*

She made her hands into tense fists. "Why the hell are you wasting time, Mark? Pick up the fucking phone!"

The Russian woman said, "Yes, why are you wasting time, Mark? Are you afraid? Panicked? Worried about what might emerge from the darkness? Or worried about McClennan? Or is it the truth that worries you most?"

Mark said, "Why don't you shut up."

The old woman laughed at him. "I am impossible to shut up, Klein. Silence my voice, you achieve nothing. You'll only hear other voices, heavy Russian accents, men with very bad manners—"

"*Shut the fuck up*," he said.

Surprised by the sharpness in Mark's tone, Sara took a step in the direction of the telephone. If Mark wasn't going to call, then she'd do it. McClennan might be a suspicious hard-ass, but he'd understand. He'd grasp the situation. In the end, he'd

see it clearly. Because he had to. Because Sol had exonerated
Mark. McClennan would understand everything.

She saw Mark point the gun at the woman.

She smiled. "Kill me and you gain only a narrow margin
of time. Because they'll find you no matter where you go in
the world, and they'll torture you, they'll torture your wife
they may do some quite unthinkable thing to the unborn child
These are not charitable people, Klein. These are savages."

Sara heard the reference to her unborn child and it clanged
in her head like the sound of a locomotive spinning off a
bridge and crashing in a gulley far below. Giddy, she watched
Mark raise the gun, hold it forward.

The woman said, "I have never been afraid of death, Klein.
I've lived with it too long. Shoot me. Murder me. Show your
wife what you really are, Klein. Show her the stuff you're
really made of. Go on. Do it. Remember this. After I'm gone,
your nightmare is only just beginning," and she smiled, taunt-
ing, daring, her expression one of mockery. "*Do it*, Klein.
Who knows? There may be a better world on the other side,
even for someone such as myself—"

Mark fired the gun, and Olga Vaskenaya, looking as if she
were momentarily *pleased*, slid down inside her frame, her
skull shattered, her small gloved hands clutching the aluminum
tubes as she slithered toward the floor, and then the device
toppled and she became weirdly entangled with it, one leg
twisted around the frame, the other splayed to the side, her fur
coat bloodied, her dress hitched back, her thighs the color of
school chalk above the elastic of her brown stockings, and
then Mark was standing over her, the gun slack in his hand.
Sara slumped on the piano stool, frozen, shaking her head,
feeling pressure at the back of her throat, a raw and awful
throbbing in her heart.

Mark stepped toward her. "It was the only way," he said.
"Believe me."

"Believe . . ." She clutched her stomach, fought a feeling
of sickness.

"This is hard to explain," he said.

"Liar," she said. "You fucking liar. I don't want to hear."
And she clamped her hands over her ears.

His words were audible anyway. "Look, I knew what Sol
was doing. I knew it long before anyone else."

*And you reported it, didn't you*, she thought. *You went immediately to the Feds and told them, didn't you. Like the honest man you are.* She turned and gazed at the dead woman in disbelief. *Show her the stuff you're really made of.* Worlds imploded in distant galaxies, nothing in the cosmos made sense. She saw herself from an impossibly high place and she was a speck drifting defenseless through icy darkness and meteor showers and shooting stars.

"We're talking about millions of dollars," he said. "I knew Sol was moving it around, trying to cover his ass. He was siphoning it out of my accounts. It was a situation that couldn't go on forever."

She thought, *But you're not an honest man.*

"I figured there was enough for me to skim. Sol was going to take the fall anyway. I knew that was inevitable. I just wanted a share before everything completely collapsed. That's all. I dipped a little. I couldn't let the opportunity go past, Sara, because I knew Sol would get the blame for everything."

*Dipped a little*, she thought. She kept her hands to her ears. She didn't want to ask what a little meant. She didn't want to know. She needed to erect a screen between herself and Mark Klein. He's going to say *I did it for us, for you, for the baby.* Please God don't let him say that.

What had Sol said on the night of his death? People do bad things for money.

Bad things.

Understatement.

She got up from the piano stool. She felt the bleak hollows of despair. Mark caught her, wheeled her round, embraced her, wouldn't let her go. He was whispering in her ear. "Eight million bucks. We have eight million dollars, and none of it can be traced to me. Not a cent. Eight million dollars, enough for a lifetime."

"What kind of lifetime?" she asked. "What kind of life, Mark?"

"A good one," he said.

*He means it*, she thought. *He believes it.* She pulled herself away from him. "You're a real piece of shit, Klein."

"You say that now. But you'll change."

"Change how? Change my name? Change my identity?

Dye my hair, wear a fucking wig, go into hiding, is that the kind of change you have in mind?''

"Yeah, well, certain adjustments need to be made, babe.''

"Certain *adjustments*? You heard her, Mark. They'll come looking for you. Brutal people, she said. Brutal, Mark. What do we do for the rest of our lives? Look over our goddam shoulders?'' She knelt on the floor by the foot of the stairs. She had no strength. "Stay away from me. Don't come near me. I don't want you to touch me.''

"Give it some time," he said. "That's all you need. Some time.''

"Time? Where? Puerto Vallarta? Or is that just the beginning? We stay there a day or two, then we have to move on. Next stop, where, Asunción? A secluded valley in goddam Patagonia? Then where? You fucking bastard, Klein. You lied to me, you cheated me. And the worst goddam thing is that I believed you. Until five minutes ago, I believed you. I would have sworn on a mountain of Bibles about you. I'm an idiot. I should have seen through you long ago.''

"Babe," he said. And he bent down and stroked the side of her face.

*Babe*. She hated that. An affection he'd cheapened.

"What was it, Mark? Greed? A window of opportunity you just couldn't pass over? No, don't tell me. I wouldn't understand anyway. I don't want to understand. I don't want to hear the sound of your goddam voice." She pushed his hand away. She shut her eyes. She listened to the wind.

"It was easy money," he said. "You know how many years of work it would have taken to earn that kind of cash? A lifetime. Two lifetimes. Count them. Flying here, there, airports, schedules, meetings, hotel rooms, smiling at people I didn't feel like smiling at, selling my advice for a lousy commission, seeing other people benefit from my work. One day, I just thought: enough. That's it. No more. I was tired. I wanted to stay home with you.''

His words were dross. She wasn't going to listen. She preferred the noise made by the wind. She preferred the faraway roar of the tide. She lay with her cheek pressed to the floor. She looked through half-shut eyes at the staircase. The room smelled of cloves and fur. She heard Klein kneel beside her, felt his hand on her shoulder. She shrugged it away. She

wanted to be numb. Catatonic. She just wanted to drift, floating in random patterns through the dark, ferried out across the
waters of the Sound, out and out into the blackness of the
ocean beyond.

"Get up," he said.

She shook her head.

"We need to get away from here," he said.

She said nothing.

"Sara, babe, we need to go. The sooner the better. I don't
know how long we'll be safe here. I don't want to stick around
and find out. We'll throw a few things into a bag. We'll travel
light. We have to."

She didn't speak. She was going to make herself invisible.
Her husband was a thief and a killer. She was Sara Klein,
married to a monster. She wanted to be somebody else.

Mark placed his hand over hers. "Let me help you up."

She felt herself being drawn to her feet. She reached for the
banister rail, held it for support. She didn't look at him,
couldn't look. She felt withered by betrayals and lies and violence.

"I love you," he said. He laid the palm of a hand against
her cheek. "That's one thing beyond any doubt, Sara. I love
you."

*Love,* she thought. *If you love somebody, Mark Klein, you
don't hurt them. You don't lie to them, you don't cheat, and
you don't bring chaos and death into their lives.* Love was
profoundly simple for her, direct as a laser. Love was a means
of living. It was a set of standards. It was a light that burned
constantly. Love wasn't cobwebs and shadows and new iden-
tities and funny passports and fleeing through godforsaken
border towns on your way to a safety you were never going
to find. Suddenly she saw her world as one of peculiar maps
across which she'd be forced forever to travel, remote dusty
places, rented haciendas, hotel rooms where you spent an ap-
prehensive night or two under a creaking ceiling fan before
you moved on, sweaty journeys in grubby, crowded trains or
overheated cars. And always, always glancing back the way
you'd come, afraid of echoes, suspicious of strangers in restaurants and cafés and street corners.

Mark took her by the hand. "We're rich, Sara. Think about
that. Come with me. I'll show you." He smiled at her. She

turned her face aside. He led her across the room and inside the kitchen, where he unlocked the back door. He took a flash-light from a shelf.

"I don't want to go anywhere with you," she said.

"Come on."

He tugged her arm, drew her outside into the avid wind. She didn't have the energy to resist him. She didn't have the energy for anything. Her robe was caught and blown. All around her shrubbery and trees shook in the shattered night. The moon was cluttered by a mass of clouds that scudded in disarray across the sky. Mark took her elbow, turned on the flashlight. He directed her to the lawn and toward the shrub-bery. He shone the flashlight into the shrubbery, found what he was looking for, a spade, a simple garden spade. He tucked it under his arm and moved a few yards more across the lawn, drawing her with him.

He stopped beside the young silver birch. The marriage tree, whose leaves danced and flapped. He set the flashlight on the ground. "This is it," he said.

He grinned, and it was as if nothing had ever happened, no embezzlement, no murders. She wondered what kind of world Klein lived in. He glossed his way through it, and nothing touched him. He sailed smoothly, and nothing disturbed him. There was no morality in his universe. There was no adhesive that connected him to a code of behavior. This insight sad-dened her a moment, but she turned the feeling aside, because she had no space in her heart for any kind of yearning.

He picked up the spade and, lit by the beam of the flashlight, dug forcefully into the earth around the base of the young tree. "This is it," he said. "You'll see." He turned once to look at her, and in the angled glow of the flashlight she thought he looked demented. He was digging, oblivious to the wind that billowed his robe and raced through his hair.

"There." He dropped the spade and picked up the flashlight and went down on his knees on the edge of the small cavity he'd dug. He scrabbled loose earth aside with his fingertips and brought out a package wrapped in green oilskin. "This is it, babe. This is it."

*Under the marriage tree*, she thought. She watched him shine his light on the package. He ripped it open carefully, pulled back the folds. "Negotiable bonds. Eight million bucks in negotiable bonds. Look."

She saw a bundle of paper in the oilskin. She had an impression of Gothic script, expensive linen paper. She stared at it a moment, then she looked out in the direction of the Sound. Paper. Eight million bucks' worth of paper.

Only paper. And people died for it.

Mark, still on his knees, was holding the package as if it were really precious. But he didn't know what precious was, didn't understand, he lacked a human dimension, and she'd been blind to this for years.

"Now what," she said. "We run."

"For a while."

"How long is a while, Mark?"

"Until we find somewhere safe."

"You think such a place exists."

"Sure it does. And we'll find it. We'll find it."

"And the baby?"

"The baby? He'll be fine."

He, she. Where would the child be born? In a broken-down hospital in a provincial Guatemalan city, attended by harassed, overburdened physicians? In some isolated peeling sun-cooked house, assisted by a rustic midwife with dirty broken fingernails? What would this child's future be?

She felt the wind rush across the darkness. She heard a voice in the wind carrying a message in a language she didn't know, but that somehow she understood.

Mark turned slightly away, hunched over his package.

She reached for the spade and raised it above her head and, gasping for air, brought it down against the back of his neck. The thud of metal against bone vibrated the length of the shaft and jarred her fingers. Mark moaned, turned in surprise, mouth open, and she brought the spade down a second time, striking him directly on the face, and he slumped back against the spine of the tree and the package fell out of his hands. She looked at the blood running from his forehead into his eyes. She hit him once more, smacking the head of the implement against his mouth, hearing air escape his open lips.

She wanted to strike him again, but she didn't. Her strength was gone. She stepped back, saw the slackness of his jaw, the pained glaze in his eyes, the way his hands had fallen to his side. She saw how the flashlight gleamed upon the package that had slipped from his fingers and watched as the wind, in its callous manner, flapped the oilskin and began to peel the papers one by one from the wrapper and suck them out into the impenetrable mystery that was the night. She watched them fly like crude kites, down and down toward the Sound.

She picked up the flashlight and then she turned and walked back in the direction of the house, the beam stretched in front of her. She didn't turn to look when she heard him call out to her in an enfeebled voice. She wasn't going to look back. Besides, his words were lost to her, scattered like his paper, his precious worthless paper.

She telephoned McClennan, told him to come to the house, *Come at once, don't wait*, then hung up and, in a daze, stood in the kitchen doorway and looked down toward the birch, which the wind played like a sad musical instrument. She trained the beam of the flashlight on the base of the tree.

There was no sign of Klein.

He might have dematerialized in the night. He might have been picked up and blown like a bag of leaves down toward the Sound where the surf screamed. He might have been no more than a phantom of her mind, except for a solitary item of evidence that lingered, a sheet of paper snagged in the branches of the tree where it flapped and flapped like some anaemic creature trying to escape.

She killed the flash and stepped back inside the kitchen and locked the door against the world and went from room to room drawing down blinds.

**39**

**LABOR** was hard and prolonged, a difficult parturition. Half-drugged, pushing a new life painfully out of her body, Sara had moments when she thought Mark was in the delivery room, masked and concerned, encouraging her, mopping her damp forehead. *It's going great*, he was saying. *It's coming along just fine. Hold my hand. Squeeze it as hard as you like.* Sometimes she heard the old woman whispering in her ear. *The screaming pink thing finally emerges, Sara.* These were the bad moments, clenching her teeth and hearing voices, the sensation of her womb tearing apart.

And then it was over, and she was empty and depleted and raw inside, and a nurse was holding the naked baby for her to see. *It's a girl, Sara. And she's perfect.*

A girl. The Russian's prediction.

Sara was wheeled to another room and slept for dreamless hours after, and when she woke the same nurse was standing at the bedside with the baby in her arms. She handed the child to Sara, who took it and held it carefully against her breasts.

"Come up with a name?" the nurse asked.

"I'll have to think hard about that." Sara looked down into the face of the child, tiny and vulnerable and unseeing and crumpled. The essence of innocence. She kissed her daughter's forehead. Her daughter, she thought.

"Just don't go choosing something like Wanda, which is what my folks inflicted on me. Always sounds like a woman with a real bad hairdo living in a trailer park." The nurse smiled and left.

A moment later John Stone entered the room and sat beside

the bed. He was dressed in what she recognized as his Sunday best, a tweed sports coat and pressed brown pants. He had a carnation in his lapel. He leaned over, gazed at the infant's face a long time.

"She's the most beautiful baby in the universe," he said. He touched the side of the baby's cheek with solemn tenderness, as if new life were a miracle that overawed him, an event irreducible to any mathematical formula.

Sara looked past him at the window. The first snow of the season had already fallen, and the trees outside were dead and white, delicate and skeletal. Fall had collapsed, and the sky was weighted with snows yet to come, and those whose business it was to predict weather were already saying winter was going to be long and harsh.

But that didn't matter to her. Long, dark, icy nights were of no concern.

"When do they release you from this place?"

"Tomorrow, I hope." She thought of the spare room she and her father had prepared in the old house in Port Jefferson. Freshly painted, a crib, mobiles tacked to the ceiling, colorful blinds, nursery characters stenciled on the walls. It was a temporary state of affairs until she could find what John Stone had called, with no trace of urgency, a more permanent situation.

The house overlooking the Sound was empty now, a For Sale sign posted outside. She'd auctioned off most of the furniture, and the rooms were a series of empty boxes that drew the curious and the creeps, more than it attracted genuine potential buyers. She pictured it a moment, snow piled against the porch, the birch tree bare—but she wasn't interested in these images. Past-life regression. Only the present concerned her. Only the baby.

"Call her Diana," her father said.

"Mother's name."

"Goddess of the moon."

The moon. She felt the baby's mouth around her nipple and she was flooded by a sense of this tiny child's dependency on her. It was a two-way street, one of mutual reliance. An impossibly small hand curled round her middle finger. The skin didn't even seem like skin, more like some silk membrane.

"Brown hair," her father said. "She'll have your coloring."

Something lay unsaid in her father's remark. *I don't want this kid to look anything like Mark Klein.*

"I'll come back tonight," John Stone said. He left the room on tiptoe, as if afraid of disturbing mother and baby. Sara shut her eyes and felt the quiet suction of the child's mouth against her breast.

Flowers arrived in the late afternoon, a bouquet wrapped in cellophane. The card attached contained a short message. CONGRATULATIONS, MOTHER! LOVE, TONY. She had a nurse place the roses in a vase on the nightstand.

Over the last couple of months Tony had called her two or three times a week, checking on her general well-being, asking if there was anything he could do, just name it, name it. He sometimes sounded like a doomed suitor. She was grateful for his concern, but she often thought he was like a guy pumping air into a puncture that was always going to leak. What it came down to was simple: she didn't want any connection with Rosenthal's or its former employees. She'd stashed all those reminders in a cargo hold of her brain, even if she sometimes felt she harbored stowaways—like Tony Vandervelt. She'd write him a note and thank him for the flowers and that would be that.

Next afternoon, she and the baby left the hospital in John Stone's car, which he'd washed and waxed and vacuumed, a fact that touched her. He drove in the hypercautious manner of a man who imagines the street is booby-trapped. He was going to be a guardian angel of a grandfather, watching over this child, fussing, probably reading books on infant development and nutrition and becoming along the way something of an expert. In his retirement, the logic of raising a baby would become the focus of his life.

He parked carefully in the driveway, ushered Sara and the baby down the drive, which he'd blown clean of snow. She wondered if she'd become accustomed to his solicitous *hovering.*

Indoors, she carried the child upstairs and set her down in her crib, then immediately picked her up again. "I think she can sleep with me, at least for the first few weeks."

She took the baby inside her own old room and placed her in the center of the bed. She sat watching the child and wondering about resemblances, while her father went downstairs to make tea. Then she rose and stood at the window and looked at how snow lay over everything in the front yard. The big tree, the ancient swing: white transformations. The whole street was white except for the occasional driveway and those places where cars had darkened the snow with exhaust. She listened to the knock and rattle of the heating system, water circulating through antique radiators, and she wrote the name Diana with a fingertip in the condensation on the windowpane and watched as the letters began to disintegrate and trickle down the glass.

She heard her father call out from the foot of the stairs. "Tea's ready."

She was about to turn from the window when she saw a car arrive at the bottom of the driveway. A familiar figure emerged, made his way up the drive. She listened to the sound his feet made on the porch, then he was ringing the doorbell. She went downstairs at once, hurried to the door, opened it.

McClennan said, "I understand congratulations are in order."

She looked at him, and what came back to her were the many hours she'd spent in his company during the past few months, the long questioning sessions. *Tell me about the Russian woman. Tell me again about Mark. Tell me about the shooting. What did Pacific say to you. Talk to me about Jennifer Gryce. Go through that last meeting with Sol. Talk about Borbokis*. The sessions were gentle, muted interrogations. McClennan soft-pedaled. There was no further talk of complicity. Some of Mark's negotiable bonds had been found scattered here and there in the landscape, blown by the wind, bleached.

"Can I come in?"

She opened the door. She was conscious of her father standing in the kitchen doorway behind her. McClennan rubbed his hands for warmth, and asked, "Everything went okay?"

She nodded. She went inside the living room and McClennan followed her, still working his hands together briskly. There were wet spots of melted snow on his grey overcoat.

"I'm glad," McClennan said.

"You've come all the way out here to tell me you're pleased," she said.

McClennan smiled. "Partly it's that."

"Let me guess the other part. You want to know if I've heard from Mark."

"Got it," he said.

She stared at the agent for a time. "The answer's no. Nothing. Not a word."

"You're sure?"

She didn't think this worth answering.

He said, "We keep getting reports. He's been seen in Louisiana, Arkansas, Oregon. You name it. There's never any substance to these sightings. It's easy to vanish if you really want to. Fake paper's simple to get. And it's a big country."

"And an even bigger world," she said.

McClennan stuffed his hands in his coat pockets. "I sometimes wonder what he's doing. What he's using for money." He stood beside the fire, warming his back. "I want him, Sara. I don't like to think of him out there, free as a bird."

"Maybe he's miserable. Maybe he's living in wretched circumstances. Who knows?"

"I hope he's cold and hungry," McClennan said, a vindictive bite in his words. He clearly couldn't bear the notion that Mark Klein had eluded him. Maybe he lay awake nights, wondering. Maybe he studied the reports of alleged sightings avidly and made lengthy long-distance phone calls.

She heard the very faint sound of the baby whimper. This was something new, an extra dimension to the boundaries of her hearing, a funny little shock of alarm. "I have to go," she said.

McClennan said, "We'll keep in touch."

She hurried upstairs, McClennan already dismissed from her mind. She heard the front door close. She went inside the bedroom and lifted the baby and bared her breast and the child's mouth found her nipple.

Her father appeared in the doorway. "I can't believe he's still badgering you."

"Hardly badgering, Dad. He's not interested in me anymore."

John Stone approached the bed, stared in a beatific way at mother and baby as if he had an image of madonna and child in his mind. "I want a photograph of this. I'm going to keep a complete record of Diana's development."

"You've named her already, I notice."

"You can't keep referring to a beautiful little girl as *It*," he said, and went off to fetch his camera.

Sara lay back, fed the baby. Her father returned and took his pictures. After, she set the child down and fell asleep.

When she woke the telephone on the bedside table was ringing and she fumbled for it in the dark and raised the cordless handset sleepily to her lips.

He said, "I called the hospital."

She didn't respond.

He said, "A girl. A healthy girl."

She closed her eyes. The baby made a small sighing sound. The air smelled of milk.

"Sara? You still there?"

"Yes," she said. She tried to picture Klein, where he was calling from. The connection was scratchy.

"You did good, kid," he said.

She thought: *I've been longing to hear his voice. Despite it all, despite everything, down through all the misery and deceit and murder, I've wanted to hear his voice.* She reached out, touched the baby's face.

"Is she gorgeous, Sara?"

"Yes, yes."

"I figured she would be," he said. "Go to the window."

"The window?"

She rose from the bed, parted the curtains, looked down into the street where a fresh snow was falling through lamps, falling and swirling. She saw an unlit car parked across the way and a man standing beside it with a mobile phone to his mouth. He looked up at her. She touched the windowpane, cold against her fingertips.

The man raised a hand to his lips and blew a kiss at her. She imagined she could feel the warmth of his breath.

She heard him say, "I love you, Sara."

She didn't speak. She just kept looking down into the street, watching Klein, seeing wind make wayward patterns with falling snow.

"A kid needs a father," he said.

He was gazing up at the window and, as he shifted his head

a little, she saw his features in the glow of a streetlamp.

"Come with me, Sara," he said. "I've got it arranged. Tickets. Passports. Everything."

"One big happy family," she said.

"That's the idea," he said.

He was dreaming. He was a dream figure in a world of dream arrangements. She understood: love was sometimes an addiction, a craving to be kicked, and there were withdrawal symptoms you had to get through in your own way and the effort was hard, but she'd do it, goddam, she'd do it.

"Talk to me, Sara," he said.

*Talk to me.* She was all out of talk. She had nothing to say. She walked to the bed and killed the connection, and switched off the phone. She lay down beside the baby and closed her eyes and after a while she heard the sound of a car roar, then fade in the distance, and she felt, if not regret, if not depression, then a small upsurge of sadness she knew would pass sooner or later.

She stroked the child's sleeping face.

Fall Victim to Pulse-Pounding Thrillers
by *The New York Times*
Bestselling Author

# JOY FIELDING

## SEE JANE RUN
### 71152-4/$6.50 US

Her world suddenly shrouded by amnesia, Jane Whittaker wanders dazedly through Boston, her clothes blood-soaked and her pocket stuffed with $10,000. Where did she get it? And can she trust the charming man claiming to be her husband to help her untangle this murderous mystery?

## TELL ME NO SECRETS
### 72122-8/$5.99 US

Following the puzzling disappearance of a brutalized rape victim, prosecutor Jess Koster is lined up as the next target of an unknown stalker with murder on his mind.

## DON'T CRY NOW
### 71153-2/$6.99 US

Happily married Bonnie Wheeler is living the ideal life—until her husband's ex-wife turns up horribly murdered. And it looks to Bonnie as if she—and her innocent, beautiful daughter—may be next on the killer's list.